MEET THE FORTUNES!

Fortune of the Month: Stacey Fortune Jones

Age: 24

Vital Statistics: Blond hair, green eyes, stretch marks (sigh)

Claim to Fame: Raising bubbly baby girl all on her own

Romantic Prospects: None, or so she thinks. Romance and diapers just don't mix.

"I'm sure you've heard all the rumors. Folks are saying that Colton is interested in me. Colton Foster? Don't be ridiculous! He's known me since I was born! He's seen me with skinned knees and braces and all sorts of teenage awkwardness. And I just gave birth six months ago. Sexy, huh?

"The only trouble is, I've started having these, uh, feelings for *him*. And I have no idea what to do about them. It's so inappropriate—not to mention embarrassing! And I have a sinking suspicion that—yikes!—Colton has *figured it all out*!"

* * *

The Fortunes of Texas:
Welcome to Horseback Hollow!

HAPPY NEW YEAR, BABY FORTUNE!

BY
LEANNE BANKS

MILLS & BOON

Published in Great Britain 2014
by Mills & Boon, an imprint of Harlequin (UK) Limited,
Eton House, 18-24 Paradise Road, Richmond, Surrey, TW9 1SR

© 2014 Harlequin Books S.A.

Special thanks and acknowledgement are given to Leanne Banks for
her contribution to THE FORTUNES OF TEXAS: WELCOME TO
HORSEBACK HOLLOW miniseries.

ISBN: 978 0 263 91250 0

23-0114

Leanne Banks is a *New York Times* and *USA TODAY* bestselling author who is surprised every time she realizes how many books she has written. Leanne loves chocolate, the beach and new adventures. To name a few, Leanne has ridden an elephant, stood on an ostrich egg (no, it didn't break), gone parasailing and indoor skydiving. Leanne loves writing romance, because she believes in the power and magic of love. She lives in Virginia with her family and a four-and-a-half-pound Pomeranian named Bijou. Visit her website, www.leannebanks.com.

This book is dedicated to my husband, Tony,
for takeout and tolerance, super editors Gail Chasan
and Susan Litman,
and genius plotter Marcia Book Adirim.

Chapter One

Stacey Fortune Jones was sure she had the cutest date at the New Year's Eve wedding reception for her cousin Sawyer Fortune and his bride, Laurel Redmond.

"Your baby is just gorgeous," Sherry James, one of her neighbors, said as she patted Stacey's six-month-old daughter's arm. "She has the best smile."

"Thank you," Stacey said. Clothed in a red velvet dress with a lace headband, white tights and red shoes, her little Piper was a true head turner. Stacey had enjoyed getting Piper ready for her first big night out, and it seemed her daughter was having fun. Her big green gaze took in all the sights and sounds of the celebration, and she smiled easily with everyone who approached. "She's a sweet baby now that she's gotten through her colic."

Sherry made a sympathetic clucking noise. "Colic can be hard on both the baby and the parents."

Stacey gave a vague nod. "So true," she said. In Stacey's case, there was no need for the plural. There was no dad to help. He'd abandoned Stacey before Piper had even been born. Thank goodness her parents had let her move back in with them.

"Well, you've obviously done a great job with her. She's the belle of the ball tonight," Sherry said.

"Thank you," Stacey said again.

"Oh, my husband's calling me," Sherry said. "You take care, now."

Jiggling her daughter Piper on her hip, Stacey headed for an empty seat at a table to give her feet a rest. Looking around, she couldn't believe that an airplane hangar could be transformed into such a beautiful reception site. Miles of tulle and lights decorated the space, and buffet tables groaned with delicious food. The sounds of a great band and happy voices echoed throughout the building. The guests, dressed in their finest, added to a celebratory mood. This wedding was the event of the season for the citizens of the small town of Horseback Hollow, Texas. People would be talking about it for years to come.

Although some might consider the choice of an airplane hangar a strange place to hold a wedding, it suited the groom and bride, since this was where the two were running a flight school together. No one had thought Sawyer or Laurel would ever settle down, let alone with each other. But the two stubborn yet free-spirited people had come to the conclusion that they were perfect for each other.

Stacey watched the newly married couple dance together and couldn't help thinking about the wedding she had been planning with her ex, Joe. Sometimes she wondered if she had ever really known Joe at all, or if she had been in love with an illusion of the man she'd wanted him to be. Now she didn't know if she'd ever find the love she saw on the faces of the bride and groom. Even though the hangar was filled with family and friends, and her little Piper was in her arms, Stacey suddenly felt alone.

"Hey," a male voice said. "How's it going?"

Stacey blinked to find her longtime neighbor, Colton Foster, sitting beside her. She gave herself a mental shake and tried to pull herself out of her blue moment. Colton's sister, Rachel, was Stacey's best friend; but Stacey had been overwhelmed with taking care of Piper, so she hadn't seen him except in passing since the baby had been born.

She'd known the Foster family forever. Colton had graduated several years earlier from the same high school she'd attended. He'd always been quiet and hardworking. He was the firstborn and only son of the Fosters and had taken his responsibilities seriously.

Tonight he wore a dark suit along with a Stetson, but he usually dressed his tall, athletic body in jeans and work boots. He had brown eyes that seemed to see beneath the surface, brown wavy hair and a strong jaw. Stacey knew of several women who'd had crushes on him, but to Stacey, he would always be Rachel's older brother.

"Great," she said. "I'm doing great. Piper doesn't have colic anymore, so I've actually gotten a few nights of sleep. My parents adore her. My brothers and sister adore her. She's healthy and happy. Life couldn't be better," she insisted, willing herself to believe it.

Stacey searched Colton's face. She couldn't help wondering if he'd heard anything from Joe since he and her ex had been good friends. Colton had even been asked to be one of the groomsmen for Stacey and Joe's wedding. The question was on the tip of her tongue, but she swallowed it without asking. Did she really want to know? It wasn't as if she wanted him back. Still, Piper deserved to know her father, she thought. Stacey's stomach twisted as she met the gaze of her quiet neighbor. Maybe Stacey just wanted to hear that Joe was miserable without her.

The silence between them stretched. "She's a cute baby," Colton finally said.

Stacey smiled at her daughter. "Yes, she is. Someone even called her the belle of the ball," she said. "How are things with you?"

"Same as always," he said with a shrug. "Working a lot of hours to keep the ranch going."

Stacey searched for something else to say. The

gap in conversation between her and Colton felt so awkward. She couldn't remember ever feeling this uncomfortable with him. "I haven't gotten out very much since Piper was born, so it's been a while since I've seen a lot of people or been to such a big party."

He nodded. "Yeah. Rachel tells me she drops by your house every now and then. She's been keeping us updated on how you're doing."

"Rachel has always been a good friend. I don't know what I would have done without her when—" Stacey broke off, determined not to mention Joe's name aloud. She cleared her throat and decided to change the direction of the conversation. "Well, I'm glad you're doing well," she said, almost wishing he would leave. Maybe then she wouldn't feel so awkward.

Another silence stretched between them, and Stacey almost decided to leave despite the fact that Piper was half-asleep in her arms.

"It's a new year," Colton finally said. "A new year is always a good time for a fresh start. Are you planning to go back to work soon?"

Stacey sighed. "I'm not sure what to do now. I loved my job. I was a nurse at the hospital in Lubbock, but the idea of leaving Piper just tears me up. Even though my mother would babysit for me, it wouldn't be fair. My mother is busy enough without taking on the full care of a baby. Plus, I hate the idea of being so far away if Piper should need me."

"Is there anywhere else closer you could work?" he asked.

"I've thought about that, but as you know, the employment opportunities here in Horseback Hollow aren't great. There's no hospital here. It's frustrating because I don't want to be dependent on my parents. At the same time, I'm Piper's one and only parent, and I'm determined that she gets all the love she needs and deserves."

Colton studied Stacey for a long moment and realized that something about his younger sister's friend had changed. She used to be so happy and carefree. Now it seemed as if there was a shadow clouding the sunny optimism she'd always exhibited. He couldn't help feeling a hard stab of guilt. He wondered if the conversation he'd had with Joe over a year ago had influenced the man to propose to Stacey. Maybe he shouldn't have warned Joe that he might lose Stacey to someone else if he didn't put a ring on her finger. If they hadn't gotten engaged, maybe she wouldn't have gotten pregnant and Joe wouldn't have left her. After Joe had left Stacey pregnant with his child, Colton's opinion of his friend had plummeted. Now he wondered if Joe had just felt possessive about Stacey. He obviously hadn't loved her the way she deserved to be loved. Colton had always known Joe's home life hadn't been the best when he was growing up, but in Colton's mind, that was no excuse for how Joe had treated Stacey.

More than Stacey's outlook had changed, Colton noticed. She just seemed more grown-up. His gaze dipped to her body, and he couldn't help noticing she was curvier than she used to be. She'd filled out in all the right places. He glanced at her face and saw that her eyes seemed to contain a newfound knowledge.

Stacey had become a woman, he concluded. She was no longer the young girl who'd giggled constantly with his younger sister Rachel. He watched her lift a glass to her lips and take a sip of champagne, then slide her tongue over her lips.

The motion made his gut clench in an odd way. He wondered how her lips would feel against his. He wondered how her body would feel....

Shocked at the direction his mind was headed, Colton reined in his thoughts. This was *Stacey,* for Pete's sake. Not some random girl at a bar. He cleared his throat.

Stacey glanced around the room. "There are a *lot* of Fortunes. I'm still trying to keep all the names straight."

"That's for sure. Do you know all of them?" he asked.

Stacey shot him a sideways glance. "I've been introduced to all of them. I'm trying my best to remember their names. Between my mother, her brother James and her sister, Josephine, they have thirteen children."

Colton gave a low whistle. "That's a lot."

"And that doesn't include the wives. Just about

all of James Fortune's children have gotten married within the last year," she said.

"I'm curious. What made all of you take on the Fortune name?"

She shrugged. "We did it for Mom. I know it sounds weird, but for Mama, finding her birth family has been a big deal. Even though her adoptive parents loved and adored her, there were things about her past that seemed a big mystery because she knew she was adopted. I think that meeting her brother James and her sister, Josephine, makes her feel more complete. For my mom, taking on the Fortune name is a symbolic way of declaring her connection to the Fortune family. Most of us have added the Fortune name out of respect to her. My brother Liam is holding out, though."

"How does your father feel about it?"

"That's a good question," she said. "My father is very stoic. He hasn't said anything aloud, and he has loved my mother pretty much since the dawn of time, but I have a feeling he may not like the name change. I'm not sure he would ever say it, because he's supportive of my mom. He would always have her back, but I wouldn't blame him if this pinched his ego a little bit."

"Speaking of your Mama Jeanne," Colton said. "She's coming this way."

Stacey smiled. "Betcha she wants to show off her grandbaby. Watch and see."

Stacey's mother wore her snowy white hair on

the back of her head, and she sported a nice but not fancy dress. Jeanne Marie Fortune Jones was one of the most welcoming women Colton had ever met. Everyone in Horseback Hollow loved the nurturing woman. Jeanne extended her arms as she got close to Stacey and the baby. "Give me that little peanut," Mrs. Jones said. "It's time for me to give you a little break."

"She's been fine," Stacey said, handing over the baby to her mother. "I think she is half-asleep."

"Already? At her first party?" Mrs. Jones adjusted Piper's headband. "I need to introduce her to a few people before she totally zonks out." Mrs. Jones glanced at Colton. "Good to see you and your family here tonight. We're glad you could make it," she said.

"Wouldn't miss it," he said. "It was nice of you to make sure we were invited."

"Well, of course you're invited. You're like family to us. What do you think of little Piper here?" she asked, beaming with pride.

"She's a pretty little thing," Colton said, although babies made him a little uneasy. Seemed as if they could start screaming like wild banshees with no cause or warning.

"That she is," Mrs. Jones said. "I just want to make sure James and Josephine get to see her. You take a little break, Stacey."

Stacey nodded and smiled as her mother left. "Told you she wanted to show her off."

Colton glanced at Stacey's mother as she joined her Fortune siblings at a table and bounced the baby on her knee. The other woman, Josephine, smiled at the baby and jiggled the baby's hand.

Stacey smiled as she looked at her mother and her aunt and uncle. They were still learning about each other, but they were growing in love for each other, too.

"So, how does it feel to be a Fortune?" Colton asked.

"I don't know," Stacey said. "It may take some time to figure it out."

"Well, it must be nice not to have to worry about money anymore," he said.

Stacey shook her head and gave a short chuckle. "You must not have heard. My mother gave back the Fortune money. She didn't feel right about accepting it."

"Whoa," Colton said.

Stacey nodded. "Her brother James wanted to give her a lot of money. But she felt that money rightfully should go to his children. Mama doesn't want her relationship with James and the rest of the Fortunes tainted by her taking money from him."

Colton shook his head. "Your mama is an amazing woman. That was an honorable thing to do."

"I think so, too, but not everyone agrees with her decision," Stacey said. "For Mama's sake, I hope everything will turn out okay."

At that moment, Jeanne Fortune Jones was in heaven. Sharing her grandbaby with her newly discovered brother and sister, with family all around, Jeanne felt complete. Jeanne had always known she was adopted. Her parents had loved her as if they'd given birth to her, perhaps more. Yet even with all that love and adoration, something had been missing. Now she knew what it was—her brother and sister. Joined together in the womb as triplets, separated for most of their lives, the three of them were back together again. To Jeanne, it all seemed a beautiful circle of life.

Her often-stern-faced brother James cleared his throat. "Jeanne, I still wish you would accept the money I tried to give you earlier. It feels wrong. Won't you reconsider?"

Jeanne immediately shook her head. Her conviction was clear as crystal on this matter. Jeanne knew that James's children had turned their backs on him because they'd misunderstood James's attempted generosity toward Jeanne. Now, after months of an angry, silent divide, James and his family were being reunited. "Absolutely not. I refuse to be the cause of a rift between you and your children. Besides, you earned that money. I didn't have anything to do with it."

James sighed. "But I feel guilty that I have so much and you have so little."

Jeanne shook her head and smiled as she looked down at her sweet granddaughter. "I've been around long enough to know that there are all kinds of riches. I have a wonderful husband, loving children and this beautiful grandchild. And now I have the two of you. My life couldn't be happier. I feel like I'm the lucky one."

"Do the rest of your family members feel that way?" James asked doubtfully.

Jeanne thought of her son Christopher and his resentment. Chris just had some growing up to do. He would realize what was truly important in due time. At least, she hoped he would. "Mostly," she said. "Look at how most of my kids have accepted the Fortune name. They know I would do anything for them, and they would do anything for me."

Jeanne noticed her sister seemed quieter than usual. "Are you okay, Josephine? Is this party too much for you?"

Josephine shook her head. "No. It's a grand party. You Texans know how to pull out all the stops," she said in her lovely British accent.

Jeanne Marie studied her refined sister in her luxury designer clothing. Who would have ever thought that she, Jeanne Jones, could be related to a woman who had married into the British royal family?

The thought made her laugh. She and James and Josephine had been joined in the womb. That was the ultimate equality. But more important than that, Jeanne knew herself, her heart and her family. She was beyond happy with her life. She sensed, however, that James and Josephine might not be so happy with theirs, but she hoped she was wrong....

"All of my children are single. I hope they will

find love someday," Josephine murmured under her breath.

"Of course they will," Jeanne said, patting her sister's hand. "It just takes some time."

Josephine looked at Jeanne with a soft gaze. "I'm so glad we found each other."

Jeanne squeezed her sister's hand. "I am, too."

From across the room, Stacey enjoyed watching her mother with her siblings, but then she caught sight of her brother Chris striding toward her. His face looked like a thundercloud. "Uh-oh."

"I need to talk to you for a moment," Chris said, and gave Colton a short nod. "Excuse us."

Stacey lifted her lips in a smile that she suspected resembled more of a wince. "Excuse me," she said, and followed Christopher to a semiquiet corner of the airplane hangar.

"Do you see how chummy Mama Jeanne is being with James and Josephine? It makes me sick to my stomach to see her being so nice to them," he said.

"Well, of course she's being nice to them. She's thrilled she finally found out that she has brothers and a sister. You know Mama has always wondered about her birth family."

"That's not the point," Christopher said. "I don't understand how she is all right with the fact that her brothers James and John grew up with boatloads of money. And her sister, Josephine, was married to British royalty, for Pete's sake. It's not fair that they're so wealthy and she's had to watch every dime."

Chris had always been ambitious, pretty much since birth. The status quo wasn't going to be enough for him. Stacey had long known he wanted more for himself and the whole family. Chris and their father, Deke, had rubbed each other wrong on this subject on more than one occasion.

Stacey hated to see her brother so upset when she knew her mother was thrilled with the recent discovery of her siblings. "Mama's life hasn't been so bad. She has all of us kids and a great husband. They both have good health and would support each other through thick and thin." She couldn't help thinking about how Joe had left her high and dry once he'd learned she was pregnant. Her father wouldn't dream of doing anything like that to her mother.

Chris's eye twitched, and Stacey could tell he wasn't the least bit appeased. "It's still not fair. Tell the truth. Wouldn't it be nice if we didn't have to worry about money? Think about Piper. Wouldn't you like to know she would have everything she needs?"

"Piper will have everything she needs. Her life may not be filled with luxury, but she will get what she needs," Stacey insisted, feeling defensive because she wasn't making any money right now.

"Yeah, but you gotta admit things could be easier," he said.

Stacey sighed. "They could be," she admitted,

but shook her head. "But I can't let myself go there. I'm going to have to make my own way. There's no fairy tale happening for me."

"I'm not asking for a fairy tale. I'm just thinking Mom should at least get a piece of the pie," he said. "Seems to me that Mom's new brother and sister are greedy and selfish."

"It's not James Fortune's fault that we aren't getting any Fortune money. James gave her money, and Mama *chose* to give the money back. James may be a little stiff, but he seems nice enough. He really didn't even have to offer the money to Mama in the first place, but he did. I bet if any of us really needed financial help that he would be glad to help."

Chris tilted his head to one side in a thoughtful way, and Stacey could practically see the wheels turning in his mind. "You may have a point. I think I'll have a word with *Uncle* James."

Stacey opened her mouth to tell him to think it over before he approached their new relative, but he was gone before she could say a word. Stacey twisted her fingers together. She wished Chris wouldn't get so worked up about this, but she feared her discussion with him hadn't helped one bit.

Sighing, she glanced away and caught sight of the bride and groom, Laurel and Sawyer, snuggling in a corner, feeding each other bites of wedding cake. The sight was so romantic. She could tell by the expressions on their faces that they clearly adored each other. Her heart twisted. She wondered if anyone would ever look at her that way.

Stacey gave herself a hard mental shake and reminded herself that her priority was Piper now. She surveyed the room, looking for her baby, and saw that her new aunt Josephine was holding Piper in her arms. Mama Jeanne was sitting right beside her. Stacey knew her mother would guard the baby like a bear with its cub. Stacey told herself she had a lot to be grateful for with such a supportive family.

Feeling thirsty, she navigated her way through the crowd toward the fountain of punch and got a cup. She took several sips and glanced up. Her gaze met Colton's. He was looking at her with a strange expression on his face. She felt a little dip in her stomach. What was that? she wondered. Why was he looking at her that way? And why did her stomach feel funny? Maybe she'd better get a bite to eat.

She wandered to one of the food tables and nibbled on a few appetizers.

"Everything okay with Chris?" Colton asked from behind her.

She turned around and was grateful her stomach didn't do any more dipping. "I'm not sure. Chris has some things he needs to work out. I wish I could help him, but he can have a one-track mind sometimes. Unfortunately, I think this may be one of those times."

"You want me to talk to him?" he asked.

"He might listen to you more than he does me,

but I think this is something he's going to have to work out on his own," she said and rolled her eyes. "Brothers."

He chuckled and looked at the dance floor. "I'm not the best dancer in the world, but I can probably spin you around a few times without stepping on your feet. Do you want to dance?"

She blinked in surprise. Stacey couldn't remember the last time she'd danced except with Piper. His invitation made her feel almost like a real human being, more than a mother. She smiled. "I'd like that very much."

Stacey stepped into Colton's arms, and they danced a Western-style waltz to the romantic tune. Of course she would never have romantic feelings for Colton, but she couldn't help noticing his broad shoulders and how strong he felt. It was nice to be held, even if it was just as friends. Taking a deep breath, she caught the scent of his cologne and leather. Looking into his brown eyes, she thought she'd always liked the steadfast honesty in his gaze. Colton was Mr. Steady, all male and no nonsense. Looking closer, she observed, for the first time, though, that he had long eyelashes. She'd never noticed before. Maybe because she'd never been this close to him?

"What are you thinking?" he asked.

She felt a twinge of self-consciousness. "Nothing important."

"Then why are you staring at me? Do I have some food on my face?"

Her lips twitched, and she told herself to get over her self-consciousness. After all, this was Colton. He might as well be one of her brothers. "If you must know, Mr. Nosy, I was thinking that you have the longest eyelashes I've ever seen on a man. A lot of women would give their eyeteeth for your eyelashes."

Surprise flashed through his eyes, and he laughed. It was a strong, masculine, happy sound that made her smile. "That's a first."

"No one else has ever told you that?" she asked and narrowed her eyes in disbelief. Although Colton wasn't one to talk about his romantic life, and he certainly was no womanizer, she knew he'd spent time with more than a woman or two. "Can you honestly tell me no woman has ever complimented you on your long eyelashes?"

"Not that I can remember," he said, which sounded as if he was hedging to Stacey. He shrugged. "The ladies usually give me other kinds of compliments," he said in a low voice that bordered on sensual.

Surprise and something else rushed through Stacey. She had never thought of Colton in those terms, and she wasn't now, she told herself. "What kinds of compliments?" she couldn't resist asking.

"Oh, this and that."

Another nonanswer, she thought, her curiosity piqued.

The song drew to a close, and the bandleader

tapped on his microphone. "Ladies and gentlemen, we have less than a minute left to this year. It's time for the countdown."

A server delivered horns and noisemakers and confetti pops. Stacey absently accepted a noisemaker and confetti pop and looked around for her baby. "I wonder if Piper is still with Mama Jeanne," she murmured, then caught sight of her mother holding a noisemaker for the baby.

"…five…four…three…two…one," the bandleader said. "Happy New Year!"

Stacey met Colton's gaze while many couples kissed to welcome the New Year, and she felt a twist of self-consciousness. Maybe a hug would do.

Colton gave a shrug. "May as well join the crowd," he said, and lowered his head and kissed her just beside her lips. Closer to her mouth than her cheek, the sensation of the kiss sent a ripple of electricity throughout her body.

What in the world? she thought, staring up at him as he met her gaze.

"Happy New Year, Stacey."

Chapter Two

Colton couldn't get Stacey Fortune Jones off his mind.

Even now as he was taking inventory in one of the feed sheds with his dad, he wasn't paying full attention. He told himself it was because beneath Stacey's sunny smile, he sensed a deep sadness. That bothered him, especially since he wondered if he could have prevented it. He remembered the day he'd told his friend Joe, Stacey's ex, that Stacey was a special girl. If Joe didn't want to lose her, then he'd better put a ring on it. The very next day Joe had proposed, and Stacey had gone full speed ahead with the wedding plans. The result had been a disaster and Colton still blamed himself. If only he'd kept his mouth shut. He'd known Stacey was crazy about

Joe. Colton had thought Joe had just needed a little nudge. How wrong he'd been.

His father turned to him. "Did you input that last number I gave you?"

Colton bit the inside of his jaw. "Sorry. You mind repeating it?"

"What's wrong with you?" his father asked. "You seem as if you're a million miles away. Did you catch that virus that's going around?"

Colton shook his head, thinking the only virus he had caught was the guilt virus. He'd been fighting that one for a while now, and it had only gotten worse when he'd seen Stacey at the wedding. "No. I was just thinking about that extension course I'm taking and if we're going to want to spend the money on the improvements to the ranch that I've been learning about during my last lesson."

"Well, we've already got these e-tablet gizmos. Part of me likes that you're keeping us up to speed, but these e-tablets weren't cheap."

"Yes, I know," Colton said, his lips twitching in amusement. "You sure like playing solitaire on yours when you're not using it for work, don't you?"

His father shot him a mock glare, then made a sound somewhere between a cough and a chuckle. "All right, you've made your point. Let's get back to work, so you can take a break. You're acting like you need it."

"I don't—"

"Then what's the last number I gave you?" his father countered.

Colton frowned. "Okay, give me the number again," he said, but he sure didn't want a break. He needed to keep busy so he wouldn't be thinking about how he had contributed to ruining Stacey's life.

Despite his father's encouragement to take a break after doing inventory, Colton drove his truck out to check some fences that had been questionable in the past. Although January wasn't the busiest time for the ranch since the foals wouldn't come until spring, there was still plenty to do. Keeping the mamas healthy, safe and fed meant he had to stay on top of the condition of the fences and the pastures.

Colton checked several stretches of fence and only found one weak area. He made a note of it and returned to the family ranch. He'd been born and raised in the sprawling ranch house. After he'd turned twenty-five, they'd added an extra wing so that he could have some privacy. The fact that his room was farther from the center of the house usually worked for him, but there were times he just wanted his own place. Someday soon he would broach the subject with his father. Colton had a lot of money in the bank and in investments, so he could easily fund the purchase of a new home, but building Colton's home seemed like a matter of pride for Colton's father, Frank. All too aware of ranch finances, Colton didn't want to provide any extra strain. His father was still strong and healthy, but his back wasn't the best. Colton wanted to ease his burdens, not make them worse.

As he climbed the steps to the porch, he thought of Stacey again and made a decision. He was going to try to find a way to help bring back her sunny disposition. There had to be a way. Passing by the den, he saw his sister Rachel watching a reality matchmaker show on television. Those kinds of shows drove him crazy. He couldn't understand why Rachel watched them. The couples never ended up staying together. Obviously he didn't understand the female psyche.

Colton shrugged. Maybe he should pick Rachel's brain. Not only was she female, but she was also Stacey's best friend. Perhaps she could give him a few ideas. He grabbed a glass of water from the kitchen, then returned to the den and sank onto a chair.

"How's it going?" he asked when Rachel couldn't seem to tear her attention from the television show.

"Pretty good," she said, glancing at him. "I'm taking a little break from making lesson plans for student teaching. How about you?"

"Good," he said. "It's quiet. No trouble. Have you heard anything about Dad's back?"

"Not lately," she said. "I wish he would go to the doctor. I don't see how he's going to get better if he doesn't try to do anything about it."

"I try to keep him from doing things that might hurt him, but I can't be by his side every minute," he said.

"True," she said. "He's lucky you're around as

much as you are." She shot him a playful smile. "Colton, the saint."

"Yeah, right," he said in a dark voice. "Listen, I wanted to ask you something."

"What's that?" she asked, glancing back at the television. "Mom told me to tell you there's a potpie in the fridge if you want to heat it up for dinner."

"I'm not asking about dinner. I want to know what women want," he said.

She swiveled her head around to gape at him. "Well, that's a loaded question."

He lifted his shoulders. "Seems pretty straight-on to me. What do women want?"

Rachel laughed. "There's no one perfect answer. It depends on the woman." She looked at him with curiosity in her eyes. "Who do you have in mind?"

Colton resisted the urge to squirm under her inquisitive gaze. He'd rather die than admit he had Stacey on his mind. "Forget I said anything," he said and started to rise.

"Now, wait just a minute. You asked me a question. The least you can do is give me a chance to try to give you some suggestions." She looked at him suspiciously. "Although I can't help wondering who you're trying to please. And I don't have to tell you that nothing stays secret in Horseback Hollow for long."

"I know," he said.

Rachel sighed in frustration. "Well, there are the die-hard regulars," she said. "Roses and flowers."

Colton shook his head. "Nothing that obvious."

"Hmm," Rachel said. "The truth is that what most women want is a man who listens."

Colton frowned and shook his head. "That can't be it."

Rachel stared at him for a long moment. "I have an idea," she said, picking up her cell phone and dialing.

"What are you doing?" he asked, but his sister wasn't paying any attention to him.

"Stacey," Rachel said, sliding Colton a sly glance. "My brother needs a consultation. Can you come over?"

Colton nearly croaked. "Stacey?" he echoed.

Rachel nodded. "Great," she said into the phone. "See you in a few minutes." She disconnected the call and smiled at Colton. "This is great. You'll have advice from two women instead of just one."

Oh, Lord, what had he gotten himself into? "I think I'll heat up some of that potpie," Colton said, hatching an escape plan.

"Don't go too far. Stacey will be here soon," Rachel said, then shot him a crafty glance. "And don't take off for your bedroom. I know where to find you."

Colton stifled a groan. This was why he needed his own place. He was too accessible. Colton heated the potpie and returned to the den, telling himself he would set a mental time limit of fifteen minutes for the insanity about to ensue. He scarfed down as much food as possible during the next few moments.

A knock sounded at the door, but Stacey didn't wait for anyone to answer. She'd been bursting through that door as long as he could remember. "Hey, Rachel, I'm here," she called as she made her way to the den. Dressed in a winter-white coat, she carried her baby on her hip with ease. Piper wore a red coat and cap, and her cheeks were flushed with good health. She stared curiously around the room with her big, green eyes.

"Give me that sweet baby," Rachel said, rushing to reach for Piper.

Piper allowed herself to be taken from Stacey, but the baby watched to make sure her mama was in sight. Rachel unfastened the baby's coat and took off her cap.

Stacey shrugged out of her own coat and glanced from Rachel to Colton. "What's this about a consultation? Why on earth would Colton need a consultation from us?"

Rachel's face lit with mischief. "Colton asked me what women really want. We need to brainstorm Colton's love life."

Stacey looked at Colton in confusion. "I always thought Colton got along as well as he wanted to in that department. I've heard from a few girls who—" She cleared her throat. "Well, they seemed to like him just fine."

"Thank you, Stacey. I have gotten along just fine

in that department, despite my sister's opinion," he said in a dry voice.

Rachel jiggled the baby on her hip. "Well, this one must be different if you're asking *me* what women want," Rachel said.

Colton checked his watch. Thirteen minutes to go. This was going to feel like an eternity.

"Who is this girl?" Stacey asked, curiously gazing at Colton.

"He won't tell," Rachel answered for him.

Colton figured his sister was good for something.

"Well, what kind of woman is she? Country or city?" Stacey asked.

"If she's here, she's only one kind," Rachel said. "Country. We have no city to speak of."

"Hmm," Stacey said, and Colton again resisted the urge to squirm. "You could take her to dinner."

"Out of town," Rachel added. "People are so nosy here."

"Flowers would be good," Stacey said.

"He said flowers are too obvious," Rachel said.

Stacey frowned. "Too obvious?" she echoed.

"What if I just wanted to cheer her up?" Colton asked. "What if I don't necessarily want to date her?"

Rachel scowled. "Oh, that's a totally different matter. You don't want to be with her?"

Colton ground his teeth. "That's not the priority."

"So, you may want to be with her in the future?" Rachel asked.

"Let's deal with the present," he said in a grumbly voice.

"In that case—" Rachel said.

"Just visit her," Stacey said firmly. "And let her talk, maybe about what's been going on with her. Try and keep the conversation light. Nothing heavy."

"Small talk," Rachel said cheerfully.

Colton frowned. "What the hell is small talk besides weather?"

Both Stacey and Rachel laughed. "Nothing too deep," Rachel said. "You can even talk about clothing."

Colton scowled. "Clothing?" he echoed.

Stacey and Rachel exchanged an amused glance. "Work on it," Rachel said. "Read the paper. There may be something there you can chit-chat about."

"You could take her to get ice cream," Stacey said.

"In the winter?" Colton asked.

"I love ice cream any time of year," she confessed.

"If you really want to cheer up a woman, you could take a DVD of a chick flick and watch it with her," Rachel added.

Colton made a face. "If you say so," he said.

"Well, you asked," Rachel said with a bit of a testy tone. "Is this girl sick or just depressed? I know you said flowers are too obvious, but you could just happen to have some extra chocolates in your truck. Chocolate makes just about everything better."

"Except labor pains," Stacey said. "Chocolate doesn't help with labor pains."

Colton cleared his throat. He didn't like the direction this conversation was headed in. "I think I'm done with my dinner now."

"I'll take your plate," Rachel said. "You take Piper."

Colton pulled back.

Stacey shot him a look of surprise. "Oh, for goodness' sakes. You're not afraid of a baby, are you?"

"Of course I'm not afraid," he said, lying through his teeth. She was cute, but she was so *little*.

"Then, you can hold her," Rachel said, pushing Piper into his arms. "She's not radioactive."

Colton held the baby away from his body, staring into her face. She squirmed in his hands.

"You need to hold her closer," Stacey said. "She feels insecure in that position."

"I'm not gonna drop her," he said.

"I know that, but she doesn't," Stacey said.

He sat and gingerly set her on his lap, and she stopped wiggling.

Piper cooed at him, lifting her finger toward his face. She seemed to stare at his every feature. What amazing concentration she had. He inhaled and caught a whiff of sweet baby smell. Colton felt a strange sensation inside him, as if the baby was trying to communicate with him. She was a cute thing. He felt an odd protective feeling for the child even though Piper wasn't his. It was as if he was suddenly driven to keep her safe. At the same time, he was terrified she was going to start screaming any minute.

"You look so nervous, Colton. I can take her," Stacey said, lifting the baby from his arms.

Colton felt a huge sense of relief. At the same time, he wouldn't mind breathing in Piper's sweet scent again.

"So, did our advice help?" Stacey asked as she shifted Piper onto her hip.

Colton couldn't stop his gaze from flowing down her curvy body, then up again. A flash of what her nude body might look like slid through his brain. Colton gulped. Stacey—his sister's friend, the literal girl next door—was unbelievably sexy. Colton wondered if he was going insane.

"Isn't she sweet?" Stacey asked.

Colton lifted his head in a round nod. "Sweet," he said. *But frightening,* he thought, although he would never admit it in a million years. Colton was no baby expert, and he had no idea what to do with a tot like Piper. For that matter, he wasn't sure what to do with all the forbidden thoughts he was having about Stacey.

Later that night when Stacey had finally put Piper to sleep, she headed for her own bed after she'd washed her face and brushed her teeth. She couldn't shake the image of Colton holding Piper. The baby had taken to Colton almost immediately. He didn't know it, but Stacey did. Colton had looked wary about Piper, but the baby had clearly found him fascinating. She'd stared into his face as if she'd wanted to memorize every feature.

Stacey had found herself watching him more than she ever had in the past. Crazy, she told herself and closed her eyes and took several deep breaths. She counted backward from two hundred and finally fell asleep and into a vivid dream. Piper was crawling down the aisle of a chapel wearing her christening gown. Her sweet baby finally reached the altar, and Joe stood, with his back to Stacey.

"I do," Joe said.

Her heart pounding, Stacey tried to scream, but no sound came from her mouth. She felt utterly helpless.

"Joe," she whispered. "Joe…"

Stacey rushed toward the altar. "Joe," she called.

Stacey watched Joe bend over to pick up Piper. Her heart melted. Joe was going to love Piper. Her baby was finally going to have a daddy. It seemed to take hours, but Stacey finally reached her groom and touched his shoulder.

He turned, but her groom wasn't Joe.

It was Colton.

Alarm rushed through her.

Stacey awakened in a sweat. *Joe? Colton?* This couldn't be. "Colton," she whispered aloud and sat up in her bed. Why was she dreaming of Colton? Why was she even thinking of him? He was her neighbor, her best friend's brother. Ridiculous, she told herself. Beyond ridiculous. She shook her head and tried to push away the image of the tall, sexy cowboy.

Stacey forced herself to relax. She'd learned to seek sleep when her baby slept. Taking several deep breaths, she told herself not to think about Colton. She shouldn't think about his wide shoulders and his insanely curly, dark eyelashes. She shouldn't think about his strong jaw and great muscles and dependability. He was the kind of man who would always stand beside a friend and support him or her.

Colton was also a man who was clearly interested in another woman at the moment. Why else would he have sought Rachel's help about what women really want?

The reality of that made Stacey feel a little cranky, although, for the life of her, she couldn't say why.

"Go to sleep," she told herself. She would be so busy tomorrow with Piper that she would truly regret one minute of sleep she'd lose thinking about Colton.

The next day, just after Stacey put Piper down for her afternoon nap, she heard a knock at the front door. She knew that her mother had gone to a sewing circle meeting and her father was outside working, so she wanted to catch whoever was at the door before they awakened Piper. Heaven knew, Stacey cherished nap time.

She raced toward the front door and whisked it open. Colton stood on the front porch holding a pie. Surprise and pleasure rushed through her. "Well, hello to you. Come on inside."

"I can't stay long. My mother fixed a batch of

apple pies, and she thought your family might enjoy one," he said, following her.

"We certainly will. This will go great with the dinner I'm fixing tonight. Please, tell her I said thank you. Would you like some coffee?" she asked.

"No need," he said. "I really can't stay long. You're fixing dinner, you say? Do I smell pot roast?"

"You do," she said, and took the pie to the kitchen and quickly returned. "Since I'm not bringing home the bacon right now, I try to help around the house as much as possible. I fix dinner and clean while Piper naps. It's the least I can do. I'm also thinking about doing some after-school tutoring in math and science. I can have kids come here and Piper's not walking yet. I hear once the babies start walking, it's a whole different ballgame."

"I'm sure it is," he said.

Stacey looked up at Colton and noticed his eyelashes again. When had he become sexy-looking? she wondered. Although she'd certainly always known Colton was male, she just hadn't thought of him as a man. And she shouldn't be thinking that way now either.

The silence stretched between them, and Stacey felt heat rush to her face. "Are you sure I can't get you a cup of coffee? It's the least I can do with you bringing over a pie."

"Trust me. I didn't bake that pie," he said in a dry tone. "But I'll take a cup if you're insisting. I'll be working outside, and it won't hurt to get warmed up before I face the cold."

"Just a moment," she said, and returned to the kitchen to pour Colton's coffee. As she reentered the den, she gave him the cup. "Any problems or just the regular endless chores?"

He nodded. "I need to do a little work on some fences. My dad's back isn't what it used to be, so I try to tackle anything that may cause him pain."

"That's nice of you," she said. "He refuses to go to the doctor, doesn't he?"

Colton nodded again. "He doesn't believe in it. Says it's a waste of time and money. The last time he went to the doctor, he nearly died from a burst appendix. And we almost had to beat him into going."

"I remember when that happened," Stacey said. "It was a long time ago. I'm sure someone has told him that there have been huge advances made in medical science."

"All of us have told him that, but he'd rather eat nails than admit he's hurting."

"Maybe you can persuade him to go to the doctor if you take him out for lunch in Vicker's Corners sometime," she suggested.

"Possible," he said. "Rachel might have better luck with him than I would. He has always let her get away with murder."

Stacey laughed. "She would disagree and give you half a dozen examples of when she has gotten in trouble. But even I know he has been harder on you."

"Yeah," he said. "But I always felt as if I had good parents. I'm sure you feel the same way, too."

"True," she said. "My father can be a little remote sometimes, but he's as solid as they come. After I had Piper, both my parents insisted I come back here to live with them." A slice of guilt cut through her. "I just wish I could give Piper what I had growing up." She felt the surprising threat of moisture in her eyes and blinked furiously. "It just wasn't meant to be."

Colton squeezed her arm. "Don't be so hard on yourself. From where I sit, it looks as if you're doing a dang good job. That baby is surrounded by people who love her. That's more than a lot of kids can say."

The tight feeling in her chest eased just a little from his words of encouragement. "Thanks. I have my share of doubts."

"Well, stop your doubting. You've got a healthy baby, and she's doing great," he said. "Besides that, you've got a slice of Olive Foster's famous apple pie in your future tonight."

"The only way I'll get a slice is if I hide it until after the meal," she said.

"Well, that's a no-brainer," he said, and leaned toward her in a way that seemed much sexier than it should. "Hide the pie. Indulge yourself."

Stacey's heart raced at Colton's instruction. A naughty image of how she could indulge herself with Colton raced through her mind, but she immediately slammed the door on her thoughts. After all, the last time she'd indulged herself she'd gotten pregnant.

Chapter Three

"I'm sorry I can't go with you," Rachel said to Stacey on her cell phone. "My friend Abby called me at the last minute to babysit, and it's her anniversary."

"I understand. You and I can catch up later," Stacey said, even though she dreaded attending Ella Mae Jergen's baby shower. Ella Mae was married to a hotshot surgeon, and the couple owned houses in both Lubbock and in the next town past Horseback Hollow. Ella Mae was pregnant with her first baby. The shower was a big deal for Horseback Hollow because Ella Mae had been born and raised there and her parents still lived in town. The shower was being held in the Jergen's mansion in the next town. Stacey couldn't help feeling intimidated.

Ella Mae, however, had been supportive of Stacey and had attended the shower for Piper, so Stacey was determined to return the favor.

"What's wrong?" her mother asked as Stacey put a pot of beans on for dinner while she held Piper on her hip.

"Nothing," Stacey said.

"Doesn't sound like nothing to me," Jeanne said, and put a lid on the beans. "Let me hold my grand-baby."

All Stacey had to do was lean toward her mother, and Piper extended her chubby little arms to her Gabby. Stacey checked the chicken and vegetables. "Looking good," she murmured.

"You don't have to cook every night," her mother said as she clucked over Piper.

"I'm not contributing to the household with green stuff, so I want to contribute in other ways," Stacey said.

"I don't want you overdoing it," her mother said.

"I'm not. I'm young and healthy," she said.

"That sounds like something I said when I was younger," her mother said. "You still didn't answer my question about your conversation with Rachel."

Stacey sighed. "Ella Mae's baby shower is to-night."

A brief silence followed.

"Oh," her mother said, because she knew that the Jergens were wealthy and anything they did had to be, oh, so perfect. "Do you want me to go with you?"

Her mother's offer was so sweet that it brought

tears to her eyes. Stacey put down her spoon and went to her mother to hug her. "You're the best mother in the world. You know that, don't you?"

Jeanne gave Stacey a big squeeze, then pulled back with a soft chuckle. "What makes you say that?"

"Because you always do the right thing. I wonder if I can do half as many right things as you have," Stacey said, looking into her mother's eyes and wishing that just by looking, she could receive all of her mother's wisdom.

Her mother slid her hand around Stacey's shoulders and gave her another squeeze. "You're already doing the right thing. Look at this gorgeous, healthy baby. You're a wonderful mother."

"Thanks, Mom," Stacey said, feeling as if she'd just received the highest praise possible.

"You don't have to go to Ella Mae's baby shower. Just drop off a gift," her mother said.

"No," Stacey said with a firm shake of her head. "She came to my shower. I should go to hers."

Jeanne pressed her lips together. "If you're sure…"

"I am," Stacey said. "And you already said you don't mind watching Piper. Right?"

"Not at all," her mother said. "You don't ask me often enough. I love my little Piper girl."

Stacey's heart swelled with emotion. "I'm so blessed," she said.

"Yes, you are," her mother said. "Now go get ready for Ella Mae's shower. You hold your head high. Don't forget it. You've done the right thing, and you're a good mother. Just make sure you're the second one out the door."

Stacey looked at her mother in confusion. "Second one out the door?"

"I never told you this before, but if you ever go to a party that you don't want to attend, then you can be the second one to leave. You don't want to be the first, but being the second is fine," her mother said.

Another word of wisdom Stacey swore to remember. "I'll be watching for who leaves first."

"And if anyone starts making insinuating comments about Joe, then pull out Piper's baby pictures. That should shut them up right away."

Stacey smiled at her mother. "Thanks, Mom."

Stacey raced to her room to pull on a black dress and boots. She put on some lip gloss and concealer, then threw on a colorful scarf and her peacoat.

"See you later, Mom," she called, then headed for her Toyota. Thank goodness snow and sleet had stayed away from Horseback Hollow during the past week. She started her car and got to the end of the driveway before she realized she had forgotten the gift for Ella Mae's baby.

Stacey backtracked and collected the gift, then returned to her trusty car. She headed out of Horseback Hollow toward the next town, then took several turns down several back roads until she reached the gated driveway for Ella Mae's house. The gate lifted to allow her entrance, and Stacey rode down the paved drive to the front of the Jergen mansion.

The windows of the house were lit, and the front door was open. Stacey knew what she would find inside. A crystal chandelier and exquisite high-profile designer furniture and decor.

Stacey was accustomed to homemade decorations and freshly painted rooms. Mama Jeanne decorated her home with family photos and mementos. The Joneses' home was warm and welcoming, but furniture had been chosen for durability, not how pretty it was.

A man approached Stacey as she paused in the driveway. "May I park your car, ma'am?"

Stacey blinked. "Excuse me?"

"Yes, ma'am. I'm the valet for the evening," he said.

Stacey blinked again. Heaven help her. *Valet? Don't fight it,* she told herself. *Let him park the car.* She would have to park her own all the nights thereafter, and that was okay.

Stacey accepted a nonalcoholic basil-something cocktail. She would have preferred a beer. She joined in with the socializing and the games and predicted that Ella Mae would have a boy. Stacey suspected that Ella Mae's husband would want a boy right off the bat, so she hoped Ella would be able to seal the deal with a male child.

When it came time for the big reveal of the baby's sex, it was done via cake. Blue. Stacey had been correct. Everyone cheered.

Ella Mae circled the room with her posse and stopped to visit with Stacey.

"I'm so glad you could come," Ella Mae said. "I know you've been busy with your baby."

"So true," Stacey said. "You'll learn soon enough."

"Well, I'll have help," Ella Mae said. "I'll have a husband and a nanny."

Stacey lost her breath. She felt as if she'd been slapped. She took a careful breath and remembered what her mother had said. She pulled out her cell phone. "Have you seen my Piper? She's just gorgeous, don't you think?" she asked as she flipped through the photos.

"What a darling," one of Ella Mae's friends said. "She's beautiful."

Stacey nodded. "And good as gold."

A couple moments later Ella Mae and her pack moved on. Stacey watched the door and saw two guests leave. It was time for her to go. On the drive home she decided to stop at the Superette to pick up some bananas for Piper. Piper loved bananas. Luckily, the Superette had quite a few. Then she headed to the only bar in town, the Two Moon Saloon, with the intention of drinking half a beer. She would be fine driving after drinking a whole beer, but Stacey wouldn't risk anything. Since she'd become a mother, everything had changed. She couldn't take any chances.

She went to the bar and ordered a beer. The first time in nearly a year and a half. She took a sip and felt so guilty she asked for a glass of water. Sensing the gazes of several men on her, she sipped at her water and wondered if coming here had been a good idea after all.

The bartender put another beer in front of her. "The guy at the end of the bar bought this for you."

Stacey glanced down the bar but didn't recognize the man. "Oh, I can't accept it. I don't know him."

"I can't take it back," the bartender said.

Feeling extremely uncomfortable, Stacey took another sip of water and eyed the door.

"Fancy meeting you here," a familiar male voice said.

"Oh, thank goodness," she said, and stretched both of her hands toward Colton.

"Problem?" he asked, glancing down at her hands clutching his arm.

"I just went to Ella Mae Jergen's baby shower. She made a snarky comment about my missing baby daddy. I came here for a beer, but I couldn't make myself drink it. And some guy bought me another beer. Save me," she said.

Colton chuckled and gently extracted her fingers from his arm. "Hey, Phil, buy Stacey's admirer a beer on me."

"Thank you," she said. "I was just going to drink half a beer, but I felt guilty after the first sip. Do you know how long it's been since I had a drink at a bar?"

"Apparently too long," Colton said.

"Maybe," she said.

"You don't have to give up living just because you had a baby," he said.

She nodded, but she didn't really agree.

Colton lifted her chin with his finger. "Your life is not over. You can still have fun," he said.

"I have fun," she said, unable to resist the urge to squirm. "I have lots of fun with Piper."

Colton shot her a doubtful glance. "You need to start getting out more. And I don't mean baby showers."

Stacey lifted her eyebrows at Colton's suggestion. "You don't mean dating, do you?"

"You don't have to date. You just need to get out. You're acting—" He broke off.

Stacey frowned. "I'm acting how?"

Colton scrubbed his jaw. "I don't know how to say this."

"Well, spit it out," she said. "I want to know."

Colton sighed. "You're acting…old."

Stacey stared at him in disbelief. *"Old?"* she repeated. "I'm acting *old?*" She couldn't remember when she'd felt so insulted. "I'm only twenty-four. How can I be old?"

"I didn't say you *are* old," Colton said in a low voice. "I said you're *acting* old."

"Well, I have a baby now. I need to be responsible," she said.

"I agree, but you don't have to stop living your life," he said.

Stacey paused, thinking about what Colton had

told her. "You're Mr. Responsibility. I can't believe you're telling me to cut loose and be a wild woman."

"I didn't say you should be a wild woman. I just said you need to get out more," he said.

"Hmm," Stacey said. "I'm going to have to think about this." She paused. "I wonder who I could call if I decide to get out. If I decide I want to have half a beer."

"You can call me," Colton offered. "Remember, I'm Mr. Responsibility."

In her experience, Stacey knew that Colton *was* Mr. Responsibility. He always had been and she valued that quality in him now more than ever. But lately, when she looked at Colton, she couldn't seem to forget what it had felt like to dance in his arms on New Year's Eve. And that almost kiss they'd shared. Almost, but not quite. She wondered what a real kiss from him would feel like. Stacey almost wished he'd kiss her and she would be disappointed, so she could stop thinking about him so much.

The next day, Colton showed up unexpectedly at the Joneses' house. Stacey was happy to see him even though he seemed intent on asking her father's thoughts about some issue with the cattle. She brought Colton and her father some coffee. Colton tossed her a smile but kept talking with her father.

Stacey couldn't help feeling a little jealous of the time he was spending with her father. She knew Piper would awaken any moment, and her time would then be divided. *Hurry up, Dad.* But she knew the mental urging was useless. Her father was usually stone quiet, but when it came to talking about the ranch, once he got going, he didn't stop.

She checked her watch and felt her stomach clench as she waited for Piper to call out for her. Finally, her father took a potty break. *Hallelujah.*

"Better today?" Colton asked her as he headed for the door, where Stacey waited on the porch.

She nodded. "I guess so. Sorry if I freaked out on you last night."

"You didn't," he said. "It's like I said. You just need to get out more. I know your mama would be more than happy to watch Piper for you every now and then."

"I don't want to burden her," Stacey said as she stepped out of the front porch with him. "They've taken Piper and me in. I don't want to take advantage of them."

"You wouldn't ever do that," he said. "Listen, how about if I take you to the bar and grill in town? What's a good day for you?"

Surprise rippled through her. "Are you sure? I don't want to intrude on your, uh, relationship with your new girlfriend."

He hesitated a half beat. "She won't mind," he said. "When do you want to go?"

"I think Thursday may work. I'll have to ask Mama first. Can I get back to you?"

"Sure," he said, and squeezed her arm just like one of her brothers would. "Remember to smile."

She stared after him as he started to walk away. "Wait," she said, and he turned around. "Do I frown that much?"

He paused. "You used to seem a lot happier," Colton said. "I hate to see you so sad and burdened."

"My life is different now," she said.

"But is it sad?" he asked.

She took a deep breath and thought about his question. "Not really." She smiled. "I'll call you about dinner at the grill followed by a beer. I appreciate the pity date."

"It's no pity date," he said. "We've known each other a long time. We should be able to cheer each other up. You may have to do it for me sometime," he said.

"That's hard for me to imagine," she said.

"You never know," he said, and her father returned to the den, ready to talk ranching.

Stacey gazed at Colton. There was more to him than she'd ever thought. Stacey wondered what it would be like to go on a real date with Colton. She wondered how it would feel to be the object of his affection. Rolling her eyes at herself, she shook her head and went to the laundry room to wash another load of baby clothes.

The next day, Stacey played with Piper, after cleaning the house and fixing dinner. She couldn't help thinking about Colton's offer for an evening out.

It wouldn't be fancy, but it would be a relief. She debated calling him ten times over, then finally gave in. He didn't pick up, so she hung up. Five minutes later, she called again. He still didn't answer, but this time she left an answer.

A half hour later, he returned her call. "Hello?" she said as she stirred soup for dinner and held Piper on her hip.

"Need an escape?" Colton asked.

She gave a short laugh. "How did you know?"

"Saw the hang-up, then heard the desperation in your voice mail," he said.

"I'm not that desperate," she said, even though she really needed an evening out.

"I know. Everyone needs an escape hatch every now and then," he said.

"What's yours?" she asked.

"If I really want to get away, I can go into town or even Vicker's Corners," he said.

"But you don't have a baby," she said.

He chuckled. "That I don't," he said. "It won't be fancy. Tomorrow night okay? What time do you want me to pick you up?"

"Five-thirty," she said.

"Early night?"

She laughed. "These days I only do early nights," she said. "You have a problem with that?"

"None at all, I'll see you tomorrow at five-thirty." He chuckled. "Call me if you need to escape earlier."

Stacey couldn't help smiling. "I'll pace myself. Bye for now."

The following day, Stacey's afternoon fell apart. Piper woke up early from her nap, and Stacey feared she'd burned the baked spaghetti casserole. She was having a bad hair day, and Piper was so cranky, Stacey wasn't sure she should ask her mother to babysit for the evening.

"Are you teething, sweetie?" she asked Piper.

Piper's sweet face crumpled in pain. Stacey sighed. "Mama, she's so fussy. I'm not sure I should leave her with you."

Her mother extended her arms to Piper, but Piper turned away. "Oh, come on, you sugar," Jeanne said to Piper. "I'll take care of you. Rub your sore gums with something that will make you feel better."

"No rum," Stacey said.

"I wasn't thinking of rum," Mama Jeanne said with an innocent expression on her face.

"No whiskey," Stacey added.

"I would never numb a baby's gums with whiskey," her mother said. "But bourbon…"

Stacey sighed. "Let me find the Orajel. I should have given it to her earlier."

"You know what your doctors say. You need to stay on top of the pain. You've told me that too many times to count when my hip was hurting."

"You're right, Mama. I should have done better for Piper," she said, feeling guilty.

"Well, don't leap off a ledge. She's not suffering

that much," her mother said, snatching Piper from her arms. "Go put on some lipstick and blush. You look worn out."

Piper fussed and squabbled, but didn't quite cry. "You're sure you'll be okay?"

"I've had a lot more babies than you have, sweetheart," Jeanne said.

"I'm working hard to meet a high standard," Stacey muttered.

"Hold on there," her mother said, putting her hand on Stacey's arm. "You're a great mother. Don't let anyone tell you otherwise. I didn't have to take care of my babies by myself. I had your father to help me, and trust me, he walked the floor many times at night to comfort all of you."

"I just feel bad that Piper won't have the kind of mother and father I had," Stacey said.

"Piper's getting plenty of loving. Her mama needs to stop trying for sainthood. Enjoy your evening out. It will be good for you and your baby."

"If you say so," Stacey said.

"I do. Now, go put on some lipstick," she said.

"Colton won't care. He's just taking me out to be nice," Stacey said, halfway hoping her mother would deny it.

"Maybe so, but it will make you feel better. That's the important thing," her mother said.

"Right," Stacey said, and headed to her room to remake herself for a trip to the grill where she would eat a burger and fries. This was how her life had evolved. Her big exciting night within a month was a trip to the grill.

Pathetic, she thought, but couldn't deny she was just glad to get away from the ranch. She put on lipstick, a little blush and some mascara. At the last moment, she sprayed her wrists with perfume.

"Stacey," her mother called from down the hall. "Colton's here."

A rush of excitement raced through her, and she rushed down the hall. Colton stood there dressed in jeans, a coat and his Stetson. "Hi," he said. "You look nice."

"Colton is afraid of Piper," her mother announced.

"I'm not afraid of her," he corrected. "She just looks so happy in your arms that I don't want to disrupt her."

Stacey chuckled under her breath. "You can go after a bear on your ranch, but a baby brings you to your knees."

Colton scowled at her. "I can shoot a bear."

Both Stacey and her mother erupted with laughter. "We should give him a break," her mother said. "Y'all enjoy yourselves." She lowered her voice. "Drink a beer for me."

"Mama," Stacey said, shocked.

"Oh, stop. Even a mother of seven likes to kick up her heels every now and then. See you later," she said, and returned to the kitchen.

Stacey met Colton's gaze. "I never expected that."

"Me either," Colton said, then lifted his lips in a crafty grin. "But I liked it."

Colton helped her into his truck and drove into town. "So, have you figured out what you want on your burger? Cheese, onions, mustard…"

"Cheese, mustard, grilled onions and steak sauce," she said. "I don't need the whole burger. I want the bun and fixin's."

"And French fries?" he asked.

"Yes, indeed," she said.

"We can take the burger into the bar if you want your beer with your meal," he said.

"The bar is loud," she said. "I can have a soda or water with my burger. It will be nice to hear myself think."

"Does your baby scream that much?" he asked.

Stacey shook her head. "Piper's much better now that she's done with her colic. But now she's teething. I need to remember to soothe her gums. I forgot today."

"Must be hard. All that crying," he said.

"She sleeps well at night and usually takes a good long nap. I'm lucky she's not crawling right now. She's really a good baby, Colton. I could have it much harder," she said, wanting Colton to like Piper.

"Yeah," he said, but he didn't sound convinced.

"Is my Mama right? Are you afraid of Piper?" she asked in a singsong voice.

"I'm not afraid of a baby," he said, his tone cranky. "I just haven't been around babies very much."

Stacey backed off. She wanted the evening to be pleasant. "How do you like your burger?"

"As big as I can get it. Mustard, mayonnaise, onion, pickle, lettuce and tomato," he said.

"You can have half of mine," she offered.

"We'll see. Maybe your appetite will improve now that you're out of the pen," he said.

She laughed, but his teasing made her feel good. "You are so bad."

"And you are so glad," he said.

"Yeah," she said. She couldn't disagree.

Colton pulled into the parking lot of The Horseback Hollow Grill, and he helped her out of his truck. His gentlemanly manners made her feel younger and more desirable. They walked into the grill and had to wait a few minutes for a table. Maybe more than one person needed an escape tonight, Stacey thought.

They sat, ordered, and the server delivered their sodas. Stacey took a long, cool sip of her drink and closed her eyes. "Good," she said.

"Simple pleasures are the best," Colton said.

Stacey looked at Colton for a long moment and shrugged her shoulders. "So, talk to me about grown-up stuff."

His eyes rounded. "Grown-up stuff?" he echoed.

"Yes," she said. "Movies, politics, current events."

"Well, politicians are as crooked as ever. There are blizzards and tsunamis. Wait till summer and there will be hurricanes, mudslides and fires." He grimaced. "I hate to admit it, but I haven't seen a movie lately. Rachel is watching the reality shows. I watch a lot of the History Channel," he said.

"What about movies?" she asked. "Do you like James Bond?"

He nodded. "I did see the most recent one. Lots of action."

"And lots of violence," she said.

"Yeah, but the good guy wins."

"That's most important," she said, and the server delivered their meals.

"That was fast," she said.

"Burgers are what they are known for," Colton said, and took a big bite out of his.

Stacey took a bite of her own and closed her eyes to savor a burger someone else had cooked for her. "Perfect amount of mustard and steak sauce," she said. "But all I need is half."

"You sure about that?" Colton teased, taking another big bite.

"I'm sure," she said, and enjoyed several more bites of her burger. She ate a little more than half and stopped. "Oh, no. Now I'm full. How can I eat the fries? Let alone drink a beer?"

"You need to learn to pace yourself," Colton said as he stared at his fries.

Stacey liked the wicked glint in his eyes that belied his practical advice. "Maybe I should fix some fences. Maybe that would help my appetite," she said, unable to force herself to eat even one French fry.

"Relax. We can hit the bar in a few minutes. There's no rush. Rest your belly," he said.

Not the most romantic advice, but Stacey stretched and took a few deep breaths. "I may have to take lessons from you on pacing myself."

"I'm available for hamburger-eating pacing lessons," he said with a mischievous grin that made her stomach take an unexpected dip.

A few minutes later, Stacey gave up on her fries, and she and Colton walked to the connecting bar. Colton ordered a couple of beers, and Stacey took a sip. Country music was playing in the background. If she closed her eyes, she could almost time travel back to over a year ago when she and Joe had just gotten engaged. She'd been unbelievably happy. Her future had been so bright. She'd clearly been a big fool.

Stacey hiccupped. "Oh, my," she said and hiccupped again.

"Drink too fast?" he asked.

"I didn't think so," she said, but hiccupped again. "It's just been so long since I sat down and drank even half a beer."

"Maybe you need one of those sweet mixed drinks," he said. "I'm not sure the bartender here can do that for you."

"It depends on whether he has vodka or not. I'm pretty sure he doesn't keep cranberry juice on tap."

Colton laughed. "You're right about the cranberry juice. I see Greg Townsend over there. He's the president of the local ranchers' association. Do you mind if I have a word with him?"

"Please, go ahead," she said. "Let me catch my breath."

"I'll just be a minute," he said.

Stacey closed her eyes, took a breath and held it. She counted to ten. Memories of how foolish she'd been with Joe warred with her enjoyment of her evening with Colton.

"Can I buy you another beer?" an unfamiliar male voice asked.

Stacey opened her eyes to meet the gaze of a man she didn't know. "Excuse me?" she said. He was tall and wore a Stetson. He also had a beard. She wasn't a big fan of beards.

"Can I buy you another beer?" he repeated, extending his hand. "I'm Tom Garrison. I haven't seen you around here before. I work at the Jergen's ranch."

"Oh, I know the Jergens," she said and briefly shook his hand. "Well, I know Ella Mae."

"And you are?" he asked.

"Stacey," she said, suddenly noticing her hiccups had disappeared. "Stacey Jones. Stacey Fortune Jones," she added, because the Fortune part was still very new to her.

"A pleasure to meet you, Stacey Fortune Jones," he said. "I'm kinda new in town and a little lonely since it's winter. Maybe you could show me around."

"Oh," she said, shaking her head and feeling uncomfortable. "I'm super busy. I have a little baby."

She figured that would put him off. Most men were afraid of babies who weren't their own.

"I like babies," he said. "I'm good with them."

Stacey began to feel just a teensy bit nervous. She searched the room for Colton. "Good for you, but, like I said, I'm super busy."

"I don't see a ring on your finger. That must mean you're not taken," he said, moving closer.

"Well," she said, trying to shrink against her bar stool. She wished Colton would return. He would know how to take care of this pushy man. "Like I said, I'm extremely busy..."

"I could give you a good time," he said. "Make you laugh. Maybe more..."

"Or not," Colton said, suddenly appearing next to the pushy cowboy. "She's with me."

Stacey breathed a sigh of relief.

"She was sitting here all by herself when I saw her," Tom said.

"For all of two and a half minutes. Go stalk someone else," Colton said. "Trust me, she's not your type."

"She's everybody's type," Tom grumbled, but walked away.

"Hmm," Colton said. "Can't leave you alone for even two minutes. There you go, seducing the new locals."

"I didn't seduce anyone," she protested. "I was just trying to get rid of my hiccups." She frowned. "I think my beer is flat."

"You want another one?"

"No. I just want to go home," she said and stood. "I'm glad you came back when you did. This was good enough for me. I won't be wondering how the other half lives. I'd rather eat a meal I've prepared and watch a good TV show." She met his gaze with a lopsided smile. "I'm getting old, aren't I? An old mama."

Colton shook his head. "Nah. You're just growing up. And you're the hot kind of mama, so keep up your guard."

Chapter Four

Colton wasn't sure his evening out with Stacey had been all that successful. She'd been quiet on the way home. He was bummed that he hadn't been able to cheer her up more. He wondered if he'd made things worse. He focused on his work at the ranch during the next couple of days and avoided the inquiring glances from the rest of his family.

As he drove home after a long day outdoors, his cell phone rang. It was Stacey. He immediately picked up. "Hey. What's up?"

"I'm trying to find Rachel," Stacey said. "I need her help."

"I'm just pulling into the drive. Let me see if I can find her and I'll call you back," he said.

Colton strode into the house and called for his sister. "Rachel," he called. "Rachel."

No answer. His parents didn't even respond.

He looked through the house and called a few more times. Sighing, he stabbed out Stacey's cell number. "Hey," he said. "No sign of Rachel or my parents."

"Darn," Stacey said. "My parents have gone to a town meeting."

"Oh, mine must have gone to the same meeting. This place is like a ghost house," he said and chuckled. "I think my voice may be echoing off the walls."

"Oh, bummer," Stacey said.

He heard the despair in her voice. "What's wrong?"

"Rachel was my last hope since my parents are out, and my sister Delaney isn't feeling well."

"Last hope for what?" he asked, pacing the hallway in his house.

"Well, you know my brother Toby took in three foster kids," she said. "He called me tonight and said the youngest is feeling bad. He has no experience with sick kids, so he asked me to come over and I said I would. But I don't want to expose Piper to anything. I don't want her to get sick."

"Yeah," Colton said. "That's rough."

She sighed. "I hate to leave Toby hanging. Would you mind watching her for a little while so I could help him out?"

Colton froze. The idea of taking care of a baby

terrified him. He could do a lot of things, but he had no experience with babies. But he couldn't leave Stacey in such a bind, could he? Well, darn. He inhaled. "Okay, I'll do it, but you need to give me lots of instructions. This isn't like roping a calf."

"She'll be easy. I promise. I'll write down lots of instructions and put them in the diaper bag," Stacey said. "I can't tell you how much I appreciate this."

"Yeah," Colton said, and headed back to his car. It occurred to him that he would rather get stomped by a bull than take care of a baby.

He drove his truck the short distance to the Joneses' ranch and pulled in front of the house. His family had celebrated with the Jones family many times. Their home was as familiar to him as his own.

But a baby wasn't familiar to him at all.

Colton ground his teeth, then forced himself to present a better attitude. He could handle this. He'd handled far more difficult situations. Piper was just a six-month-old baby. How hard could it be, he asked himself, but he was sweating despite the freezing temperature outside.

He stomped up the porch steps and lifted his hand to knock on the door, but it swung open before his knuckles hit wood. Stacey looked up at him with a hopeful expression on her face as she held her baby on her hip. "She should go to sleep soon," Stacey said. "She's just a little worked up tonight."

"Worked up," he repeated, feeling more uneasy.

Stacey fluttered her hands. "Oh, it won't last

long," she said. "She'll get tired. Let me grab my coat, and I'll be back before you know it."

She thrust Piper into his hands. He stared at the baby, and she stared back at him. Mistrust brewed from his side, and he saw the same mistrust in the baby's eyes. "What am I supposed to do with her?" he asked.

"Rock her, walk her. Feed her only if you're desperate because she's already been fed." Stacey buttoned a peacoat and handed him a diaper bag. "This is my complete bag of tricks," she said. "This will be a breeze. You're going to surprise yourself. Trust me. Thank you so much," she said, and rushed out the door.

Colton resisted the urge to renege. Barely. After Stacey was gone, he looked at Piper. She let out a little wail. Colton dived into the diaper bag, skipped everything and went straight for the bottle.

Piper sucked it down, then stared at him and gave a loud, powerful burp.

"Whoa," Colton said, backing away from the sound. "How'd you do that?"

Piper squirmed and fussed.

Colton bobbed up and down. "Hey. Your tummy's full. You should be better."

Piper whined in response.

Colton grimaced. He had been hoping food would be the quick fix. It usually was for him. He patted her back and continued to walk. Piper whined and occasionally wailed. Colton had no idea how to please the baby.

Oh, wait. Maybe she had a messy diaper.

Eewww, he thought. He didn't want to change a diaper. That was just too gross. But maybe that would turn the trick and the baby would stop fussing.

Groaning to himself, Colton went to the magic diaper bag and pulled out a diaper, a packet of wipes and a changing pad. "Okay. Okay," he said to Piper as he set her down on the pad. "Give me a break. This is my first time."

Piper stuck her fingers in her mouth and gazed up at him with inquisitive green eyes.

At least she wasn't crying, he thought and lifted her gown. "Okey, doke. We can do this," he said because some part of him remembered that he'd seen a few people talk to babies. It wasn't as if they understood. Maybe they just liked the sound of a human voice.

Who knew?

He looked at the diaper, and for the life of him, he couldn't figure out which was the front and the back.

Piper began to squirm and make noises. They weren't fussy, but they were getting close.

"I'm getting there," he promised. "Just give me a little extra time."

He pulled open the dry diaper, then carefully unfastened the baby's dirty diaper. Colton glimpsed a hideous combination of green, yellow and brown.

"Oh, Piper. How could you?"

The baby squirmed and almost seemed to smile. Heaven help him.

Colton pulled out a half dozen wipes and began rubbing her front and backside. Six wipes weren't enough, so he pulled out some more and cleaned her a little more. Afterward, he tossed some baby powder on her and put on the disposable diaper.

Sweat was dripping from his forehead. "There. We did it."

Piper began to fuss.

"Well, thanks for nothing," he said, picking up her and the dirty diaper. He wondered if there was a special hazardous-waste disposal container in the house for the baby's diapers. He didn't see one, so he tossed it in the kitchen trash and felt sorry for the poor fool who lifted the lid to take out the garbage.

He jiggled Piper, but she was still fussy. He wondered if he shouldn't have fed her. He cruised the hallways of the house. Piper never broke into a full cry, but he could tell she was right on the edge.

Desperate, he tried to sing. "Mamas, don't let your babies—"

Piper wailed.

"Not a good choice," he muttered and jiggled her even more. He walked and talked, since talking worked better than singing did. She calmed slightly, but he could tell she still wasn't happy. This female was definitely difficult to please.

After thirty minutes, she was still fussy and Colton was growing desperate. He headed for the magic diaper bag and sat down to dig through it. Piper sobbed loudly in his ear as he searched the bag.

"Give me a break," he said. "I'm trying." He dug his way all the way to the bottom and grabbed hold of a bottle. Pulling it out, he stared at a bottle labeled, "Last resort".

Colton was pretty sure he was at his last resort. He opened the bottle and found a wand. "Well, damn," he said, and began to blow bubbles.

Piper immediately quieted and stared at the bubbles.

Colton continued to blow, and Piper began to laugh. It was the most magical sound he'd ever heard. He blew the bubbles, and she giggled. Her reaction was addictive.

"Well, who would have known?" he muttered under his breath. Maybe everyone should come armed with a bottle of bubbles. He blew bubbles past the time he was tired from it, and Piper finally rested her head on his shoulder. Colton wasn't taking any chances, though, and he kept up his bubble blowing.

Finally, he glanced down and saw that Piper's eyes were closed—half moons with dark eyelashes fanned against her creamy skin. She was one beautiful kid, he thought. The spitting image of Stacey. He gently strolled through the hallways again.

Weariness rolled through him. He'd been up before dawn and trying to work through a mile-long list of chores his father shouldn't do. The sofa in the den beckoned him. He wondered if he could possibly sit down without waking Piper.

Colton decided to give it a shot. He slowly eased down onto the sofa. Piper squirmed, and he froze. *Don't wake up,* he prayed. He waited, then leaned back, inch by inch. "We're okay," he whispered. "We're both okay."

Colton relaxed against the side of the sofa and slinked down. He rested his head backward and moved the baby onto his chest. "Don't wake up." He rubbed her back until he fell asleep.

"Stick out your tongue, Kylie," Stacey said to her brother's youngest foster child.

Redheaded Kylie reluctantly stuck out her tongue. Stacey saw no signs of strep. "I'm sorry you feel bad, sweetie," she said.

"I can stick out my tongue," Kylie's older brother, Justin, said and fully extended his tongue from his mouth. The boy's expression had a disturbing resemblance to a rock singer.

"Not necessary, but thanks, sweetie," she said.

Stacey turned to her brother Toby. "Her temperature is normal, and her lymph nodes feel fine. I would give her some extra liquids and try to help her get some extra rest." She rubbed Kylie's arm. "Do you feel achy?" she asked.

Kylie shook her head. "No, but my head hurts."

"I'm so sorry," Stacey said. "I bet a cool washcloth would feel good. If she can't sleep, she can take some children's Tylenol. In the meantime, Kylie needs some rest, comfort and cuddling."

"Does that mean I get to use the remote for the TV?" Kylie asked.

Stacey laughed. "I think you are definitely due the remote."

"But I wanna see SpongeBob," Justin said.

"You can see SpongeBob anytime," Toby said, rubbing Justin's head. "Let's just pile on the couch and watch what Kylie wants to watch."

Her brothers sighed but scrambled onto the couch. "I hope it's not a princess movie," Brian, the eleven-year-old, said.

"I want *Monsters,*" Kylie said.

"Again?" Brian said in disgust.

"Kylie gets to choose tonight. If you don't like her choice, you can get ahead on your homework or read a book," Toby said.

Stacey did a double take. She still couldn't quite get used to seeing her bachelor brother turn into an instant dad by agreeing to take on these three kids. Then again, Toby had always had a generous heart, so she really shouldn't be surprised. Stacey knew he'd met the kids when he'd volunteered at the Y. When he'd learned their mother had died at an early age and that their father wasn't around, he'd tried to give them some extra encouragement. When their situation had gone from bad to worse and the aunt who'd been caring for them was forced into rehab,

Toby had stepped forward to take them into his house by becoming a foster dad.

"Well, I'd better head back to the house. I couldn't find anyone except Colton to take care of the baby while I was gone," she said, packing up her little medical bag.

"Colton?" Toby echoed, giving a startled laugh. "You asked Colton Foster to take care of Piper?"

Stacey lifted her hands. "He was my only choice. Everyone else was busy, and I didn't want to leave you in the lurch."

Toby sighed. "Well, tell him I said thank you. I'll feel better about Kylie now that you've checked her."

"You still need to keep an eye on her. You should check her temperature and symptoms in the morning. It's a shame the kids' regular doctor is out of town," she said. "I wish we had a clinic in Horseback Hollow. Maybe I could get a job there," she said. "That's wishful thinking," she murmured, then looked up at her brother and squeezed his arm. "Are you okay?"

"Yeah," Toby said, but raked his hand through his hair. "This situation definitely has its ups and down. It all goes along smoothly for a few days, then it seems like we hit a big bump in the road."

Stacey pulled on her coat and walked to the door. "Regrets?" she asked in a low voice.

Toby shook his head firmly. "I did the right thing, and they're good kids. They make me laugh every day."

"Well, I admire you, Toby. Not many men would

do what you've done," she said. Three kids, all red-heads with tons of energy.

"I think I'm getting a lot more out of this than I expected," he said.

She gave her brother a big hug. "Call me anytime, and bring the kids over to visit Piper. When they're well," she quickly added.

"I'll do that," he said and opened the door. "Drive safely," he instructed, protective as ever.

"Good night. Get that cool washcloth for Kylie. See if it helps," she called over her shoulder and got into her car.

Stacey drove toward her house, growing more nervous with each increasing mile she covered. It wasn't that Piper was a bad baby, but at times she could be demanding and very vocal. Stacey hoped the baby had calmed down enough to fall asleep. She supposed that if Colton had really needed anything, he would have called her. As she pulled in front of the house, the lights from inside welcomed her. She got out of the car, climbed the stairs and opened the door.

She paused for a long moment, listening for the sound of Piper. All she heard was quiet. Stacey breathed a sigh of relief. Piper must have fallen asleep. She was surprised the television wasn't on. She would have expected Colton to turn on a ball-game once he'd put Piper in her crib.

Stepping into the den, she caught sight of Colton napping on the sofa with Piper asleep on his chest. Her heart swelled with emotion. If that wasn't the sweetest sight she'd ever seen, she thought. Seeing her daughter being held by a good strong man reminded Stacey of everything Piper was missing on an everyday basis. Tears filled her eyes, and she blinked furiously to keep them at bay.

First things first, she thought. Get the baby to bed. She gingerly extracted Piper from Colton's chest, praying the baby wouldn't awaken. Then she tiptoed to the small nursery in the room next to hers and put Piper down in her crib. Piper gave a few wiggly moves, and Stacey held her breath. Then the baby sighed and went back to sleep.

Stacey returned to the den and touched Colton's shoulder. He didn't awaken. She gave him a gentle shake, then another. The man was dead to the world. He must be worn out, she thought. He'd probably put in a full day at the ranch, yet he'd still agreed to watch Piper for her.

A rush of sympathy flooded through her. Stacey had lived on a ranch long enough to know it involved hard backbreaking work and long hours. It wouldn't hurt him to rest a little longer, she thought, and pulled the blanket from the back of the sofa and put it over him.

Backing away, she pulled off her coat and hung it in the closet, then returned to the den. Sinking onto the chair across from the sofa, Stacey allowed herself the luxury of looking at Colton while he was unaware. She wondered why she'd never noticed how attractive he was before. Sure, she'd known him her entire life, but she wasn't blind.

He was as strong as they came. Broad shoulders and she'd bet he might even have a six-pack. She blushed at the direction her mind was headed. He had a bit of stubble on his chin. His hard masculinity was at such odds with those eyelashes, she thought.

She wondered what it would be like to sleep with him and wake up with him. Would he be grouchy or sweet in the morning? She wondered what kind of lover he would be. She'd only had one, Joe. Their lovemaking sessions had often felt rushed to her, and although it wasn't something she discussed, she'd never felt completely, well, satisfied after sex with Joe.

Stacey wondered if Colton was the kind of man to take his time with a woman. Although she hadn't paid much attention, she'd heard of more than one woman he'd left more than happy after a night together. Lately, she was becoming much more curious about Colton. She kept reminding herself that he was interested in someone else, but that didn't seem to take the edge off her...curiosity.

At that moment, she heard the front door open and her father talking to her mother. "That meeting went on forever," he grumbled.

"Everyone has a right to speak their mind," Jeanne said.

"Well, they could speak a little faster," he said, and closed the door firmly behind him.

Stacey saw Colton jolt awake at the sound. He glanced around. "What the—" He broke off and shook his head.

"Hi," she said.

"Hey," he said, rising quickly.

"Listen, thank you for taking care of Piper," she said, also getting to her feet.

"No problem," he said, rubbing his face. "I guess I'll head home—"

Her mother and father entered the den. "Well, hello there, Colton. It's good to see you."

"Colton agreed to watch Piper while I checked out Kylie for Toby. He said she wasn't feeling well and their doctor is out of town, so he wanted me to come over and make sure she was okay. She just had a headache. I think Toby may be a little nervous fostering those three kids. Can't say I blame him."

"I'm glad Kylie is okay. It sure was nice of you to come over here and look after Piper," Jeanne said.

"That, it was. She can run you ragged at bedtime," her father said sympathetically.

"Daddy," Stacey said in an accusing tone.

"But she's a cute one and we love her," her father added.

"Of course we do," her mother said. "Why don't you join us for some hot chocolate before you leave? I can have it ready in no time."

"You don't need to do that," Colton said, appearing a bit embarrassed.

"I want to," Jeanne said. "Now sit down and relax,

and I'll have that hot chocolate for you before you know it."

Colton sighed and sat down on the edge of the sofa. "Is there anyone who can say no to your mother?"

"Not for long," Stacey said, laughing. "How was Piper?"

Colton nodded. "She did fine," he said in a non-committal tone.

Stacey read between the lines. "She was a beast, wasn't she? I was afraid of that. Even though I'd fed her, she seemed unsettled." Stacey sighed. "I'm sorry."

"I wouldn't call her a beast," Colton said. "Now," he added and chuckled, "amazing how something so small can get you so twisted trying to get her to calm down."

"How did you get her calm?" she asked, curious.

"You mean after I gave her the bottle in your magic bag and changed the toxic dump of her diaper?" he asked.

"Oh," she said, cringing.

"Yeah, I might need to take the kitchen trash out tonight before I leave," he said.

Her mother entered the room with cups of hot chocolate filled with mini-marshmallows. "This will help you sleep better once you get home, Colton," she said.

"I think Piper may have worn him out, so he may not need any help falling asleep," Stacey said.

"Oh, dear," her mother said, wincing. "She's gotten so much better during the last month. Did she have a rough night?"

"I wonder if she sensed that I was in a tizzy about getting over to Toby's house," Stacey said.

"Well, I speak from experience. Babies can sense our moods. Especially their mom's moods. At the same time, she may have just had a little tummy ache. Can I get you something to eat, Colton?"

"No, I'm fine, Mrs. Jones. Mrs. Fortune Jones," he corrected.

Her mother smiled. "That was sweet," she said. "But you've known me long enough to call me Jeanne." Her mother looked at Stacey. "Now, what on earth made you think to call Colton to take care of Piper?"

"I was trying to reach Rachel and she didn't pick up. I was hoping Colton could reach her," Stacey said.

"Oh," her mother said with a glance that combined intuition and suspicion. "Colton was definitely the man of the hour tonight, wasn't he?"

Uncomfortable with her mother's almost knowing expression, Stacey cleared her throat. "Yes, he was."

Chapter Five

A couple days later, Colton went into town to get some special feed and pick up a few things from the Superette for his mom. He would almost swear his mother could sense when he was headed into town because she always seemed to have a list of items for him to pick up from the small grocery—well, the only grocery—in town.

Using the term town might have been an exaggeration. Colton may have lived his entire life in Horseback Hollow, but he'd traveled enough to know his birthplace was more about wide open spaces than tall buildings and city conveniences. The *town* was just two streets long.

Colton glanced at the list his mother had given him and picked up apples, bananas, onions, tomato sauce and pasta. He hoped that meant spaghetti was in his near future. He added a can of green beans to his basket.

"Hey. What are you doing here?" a familiar voice spoke up from behind him. He turned and saw Stacey standing in the aisle.

"Just picking up a few things," he said. "What about you?"

"Formula and baby food for Piper," she said. "I just took something to the post office for Mom."

She glanced at his food items. "Spaghetti," she said more than asked. "Are you cooking for someone special?"

Confused, he cocked his head to one side. "Someone special?"

"Don't be shy," she said with a coy smile. "Cooking for your lady friend. I have a great recipe for spaghetti sauce, but you need sausage and cheese," she said.

He shrugged. "I haven't ever fixed spaghetti before unless it was from a can."

"Well, you've got to do better than that for a woman. If you're cooking for two, you could add some delicious bread and salad and call it good," she said. "And something chocolate. Women love chocolate."

Colton opened his mouth to protest, but she didn't let him fit a word in edgewise.

"I could help you," she offered. "Why don't I give you a cooking lesson? If you're anything like my brothers, you've relied on your mother your entire life for your meals, so you never bothered to learn."

That was a little insulting, he thought. But true.

"You sure you won't tell me who you're cooking for?" she asked.

"My lips are sealed," he said. It was easy to keep that secret since his so-called lady love didn't exist.

She gave a little huffy sigh. "Okay, well, I can still give you a few tips on your cooking. Is tonight okay?"

"I guess," he said, trying to recall his parents' busy schedule. He thought they were playing bridge tonight.

"Okay, I'll see you around six, and I'll help you fix a spaghetti dinner that will wrap your lady friend around your little finger. Make sure you pick up some sausage and fresh Parmesan cheese. I'm assuming you already have beef," she said.

"Yeah," he said. He lived on a cattle ranch. He darned well should have beef.

"Okay. See you later," she said and strode away.

Colton stared after her, distracted by the wiggle in her walk and her cute backside. He gave himself a shake. Why had he agreed to a cooking lesson? Especially for the sake of his imaginary girlfriend? He swore under his breath. This was getting worse and worse.

Stacey paid at checkout and walked to her car with her purchases. She felt a little cranky and wasn't sure why. Climbing into her car, she started the engine and headed for her house. She turned on the radio to listen to a few tunes to cheer herself up. It didn't quite work, though. Seeing Colton at the Superette purchasing food to feed the woman he clearly had a crush on made her grind her teeth. It must be nice to have a man work that hard to please you, she thought. She wouldn't know because no man had ever tried that hard to make her happy.

Frowning, she tried to push aside her feelings. It wasn't as if she wanted Colton to be cooking for her. Even though she'd looked at him with a little lust the other night, she'd decided that was an aberration. She couldn't really believe that she wanted Colton. Stacey told herself she was just lonely for some attention. That had to be it.

She returned home and unloaded her car while Piper napped.

"Are you sure you're okay?" her mother asked. "You're awfully quiet."

"I'm fine. Do you mind watching Piper for a little while tonight?"

"Of course not. Do you have plans?"

"I, uh, offered to give Colton a cooking lesson. He said he's trying to cheer up an unnamed female," she confessed.

Her mother lifted her eyebrows. "Oh, my," she said. "How generous of you. You know Colton keeps such a low profile. It's easy to underestimate him as, well, a romantic possibility."

"Not really," Stacey said. "I've heard some rumors about girls that liked him just fine."

"Oh, really," her mother said and paused. "Well, I think you're very sweet to help him prepare a dinner for another woman."

"I'm not doing that," Stacey snapped, then deliberately took a breath. "I'm just giving him a cooking lesson. He's like all my brothers except Toby. He can't cook worth a darn because his mother has cooked for him his entire life."

Her mother tilted her head. "Are you criticizing me for cooking for my family?"

Stacey closed her eyes and smiled, shaking her head. She went to her mother and gave her a big hug. "Of course not. You're the best mother any of us could have. But you have to admit those boys like having their meals put in front of them."

"You're right about that," she said ruefully and returned Stacey's embrace.

Stacey's cell phone rang, and she pulled it out of her purse. She didn't recognize the number. "Stacey Fortune Jones," she answered.

"Stacey, this is Sawyer. We have a situation here at the flight school. We need your help."

Stacey's pulse picked up. "What's wrong?"

"There's been an accident. My pilot Orlando has been hurt. The paramedics are on the way, but it will take a while, and the doctor's not in town."

"Oh, that's right," she said, remembering the same doctor who took care of Toby's foster children covered the whole town. "I'll be right there," she said, and turned to her mother. "I have to go. There's been an emergency at the flight school."

"Oh, no," her mother said. "Is it serious?"

"I think so," Stacey said grimly as she ran to her room to grab her medical bag.

Pulling into the flight school, she stopped her car and ran toward the figures beside the burning plane. Stacey went into nurse mode when she assessed Orlando Mendoza. She checked his blood pressure and pulse and noted that the pilot kept going in and out of consciousness. He'd likely suffered a concussion, and she could see he'd sustained a compound fracture of his left leg and another fracture of his left arm, so she made a temporary brace for each to prevent unnecessary movement and loss of blood. Although she was able to stabilize him until the paramedics arrived, she couldn't be certain that he hadn't suffered internal injuries, as well.

Stacey watched the ambulance drive away from the airport, then returned home and took a quick shower. The entire time, she kept thinking about Orlando Mendoza. She'd wished she could do more for him, but it was a miracle he'd survived the crash. She checked in on Piper and her mother and answered Mama Jeanne's twenty questions about the accident. Unfortunately, Stacey wasn't sure how everything would turn out for Orlando. This was one more reason Stacey wished there was an emergency facility closer to Horseback Hollow. Her hair still wet, she put it on top of her head and headed out the door to go to the Fosters' house.

After driving the few minutes to the Fosters, Stacey raced to the porch and knocked on the front door. "I'm sorry I'm late," she said when Colton answered the door. "Did you hear about the accident at the flight school?"

He shook his head. "I just got in from the field. What happened?"

"One of the planes from the flight school went down and the pilot was injured. Orlando Mendoza. The paramedics were taking a while to get there, so Sawyer asked me to come and do what I could to stabilize him."

"Oh, man," Colton said. "You think he'll make it?"

"I don't know. He was unconscious most of the time and he had a badly broken arm and leg," she said, her mind flashing back to a visual of the man.

"Hmm," Colton said. "Listen, you look pretty upset. We don't have to do this cooking lesson."

She shook her head. "I can't do anything now for him except pray. I could really use a distraction."

Colton gave a slow nod. "Okay," he said with a lopsided grin. "If teaching me how to fix Stacey's spaghetti will distract you, then that's what we'll do."

"Fine," she said and headed for the kitchen. "Let's start with chopping that onion. Some key things you need to know about making spaghetti are that you shouldn't overcook the noodles and you should break up the meat before you put it in the pan. But don't overwork it," she instructed.

"I'm taking mental notes," he said.

"You won't just be taking mental notes," she said. "You'll be doing the work. You remember what you do more than you remember what someone says."

"That sounds like something my father would say," he said.

"It's actually something my father once said," she said, and met his gaze. "It must be a conspiracy."

He chuckled. "You must be right."

"Wash your hands," she said.

"Yes, Mama," he said.

She shot him a disapproving look.

"Whoa," he said, lifting his hand in mock self-protection. "You've got lasers shooting from your eyes."

"One of my superpowers. Let's get to work," she said. She noticed that Colton possessed a much better sense of humor than Joe had. Not that she was comparing.

Stacey felt overly aware of Colton's physical presence in the kitchen as they prepared the meal. His shoulders grazed hers. Her hip slid against his. She put her hand over his to show him how to chop the onion. She couldn't help noticing his hands. They were large, but there was nothing awkward about the way he used them. For an instant, she couldn't help thinking about how his hands would feel on her body. The image heated her from the inside out.

Stacey tried to ignore her feelings. She helped Colton drain the pasta, and he was just way too close. Way too strong. And she was way too curious. She looked directly into his brown eyes and glimpsed a spark that mirrored hers.

She could have, should have looked away, but she didn't.

His nostrils flared slightly, and she couldn't tell if he was having the same problem with curiosity and self-restraint that she was. "This looks good," he said.

"It should be," she said, and turned away to stir the sauce. "It's best to cook this a longer time, but thirty minutes will do if you're in a rush." She lifted a spoonful of sauce and blew on it for a few seconds. She took a tiny taste. "Yum."

She offered him a sample from the same spoon. Colton covered her hand with his to steady the spoon and took a taste. He nodded. "That's good. Hard to believe I fixed it," he said with a half grin.

"Yes, it is," she said, and threw back her head in a laugh. "I'm surprised at how well you do in the kitchen."

"You never knew a lot of things about me," he said.

Her stomach took a dip to her knees, and her sense of humor suddenly vanished. "That's very true. Maybe you could say the same about what you know about me."

"Maybe I could," he admitted and stepped closer to her.

In theory, Stacey could have turned away. In reality, she probably should have. But she was just too curious and too, well, warm. She wanted to feel Colton Foster's chest against hers. She wanted to feel his arms around her. She wanted to feel his lips on hers.

Stacey gave in to all her bad urges and flung herself into Colton's arms. His hard chest against her breasts felt so much better than she'd expected. His arms around her gave her a melting sensation. And his kiss made her want so much more. How could his mouth be both firm and sensual? How could such a little taste of him send her into a frenzy?

She opened her mouth, and he took her with a kiss that sent her upside down. She couldn't resist the urge to wiggle against him. Colton gave a low groan that made her burn. She felt his hand travel to the small of her back to pull her even closer. She was breathtakingly aware of his hard body from his chest all the way down to his thighs.

Oh, yes, she thought. *More, give me more.*

The force of her need bowled her over. Panic raced through her. This was Colton, and she was getting ready to make a fool of herself.

Stacey pulled back, knowing her face was flaming red. She was embarrassed all the way down to her toes. "Oops. I should go. I really should go," she managed and refused to meet Colton's gaze. She wondered how she would survive this, but couldn't focus on that. She grabbed her coat and ran out the door.

Stacey drove home with her window down so she could cool off. Despite that, when she walked in the door she still felt as if she were on fire. Fanning her face, she pulled off her coat and threw it on a hanger.

She gnawed the inside of her lip as she walked toward the kitchen. She needed a very, very cold glass of water. She just wasn't sure if she was going to drink it or pour it over her head.

"Stacey?" her mother called from the den. "Is that you?"

She took a deep breath and tried to compose herself. She walked to the doorway of the den. "It's me. How was Piper?"

"No trouble at all," her mother said. Her father was sitting next to her, dozing on the sofa. "She fell asleep like that," her mother said, snapping her fingers and smiling.

"I'm glad to hear that. Thank you again for looking after her," Stacey said.

"You know I will look after her anytime," her mother said.

"Yes, but I don't want to take advantage of you," Stacey said.

"It's not taking advantage," her mother insisted. "It's my pleasure. Besides, I know you would never take advantage of me. Enough about that." She waved her hand. "So, how did the cooking lesson with Colton go?"

Stacey forced a smile. "Great. I think he's ready to fix my super spaghetti recipe all by himself."

"Good for him," her mother said. "You're a sweet girl to help him do that for another woman. Colton's a good man. I might not be as generous as you are."

Stacey managed to laugh. "I've known Colton forever. He's just like a brother."

"But he's not really a brother," her mother said, then shrugged. "Doesn't matter. Can I fix you some hot chocolate?"

"No, thanks, Mama. I think water will do. I'm off to bed," Stacey said, and went to the kitchen to get that tall glass of ice water. Maybe she should get two.

The next day, Stacey prepared enough food for a month of meals. Thank goodness, the Jones family had a big roomy freezer.

Her brother Jude dropped by before dinner. "Wow," he said, when he looked at all the casserole dishes on top of the counter. "Are we feeding the entire town of Horseback Hollow?" he asked.

Stacey shot him a quelling glance. "This would feed far more than the township of Horseback Hollow. Technically, we don't even live in the township of Horseback Hollow."

Jude shrugged his shoulders. "True, so why did you cook so much?"

Stacey considered keeping her feelings to herself,

but if anyone should understand, it would be Jude. Everyone knew he fell in love or like at the drop of a hat. She'd always thought of him as a Romeo. "I'm cooking to distract myself from something that's bothering me. I have a crush on Colton Foster," she whispered.

Silence followed. "Colton Foster? When did this happen?"

"Recently," she said. "I didn't plan it. And I think he has feelings for another woman."

"Who?" Jude asked.

She shook her head. "I don't know. He's been cagey about it."

"You've talked to him about another woman and you still have a crush on him?" he asked in disbelief.

"It didn't happen exactly like that. Don't fuss at me," she said. "I thought you would understand."

"Hell, no," Jude said. "Don't jump into a new romance. It's not in your best interest."

She gave a double take at his advice. "Says the guy who falls in love or like at least once a month."

"I don't want you to get hurt. Colton's a good guy, but if he's involved with another girl…"

"I didn't say he was involved," she said. "He just said he wanted to make her happy."

Jude winced. "That's a big deal, Stacey. Guys don't talk about making a woman happy if they aren't already pretty committed."

"Thanks for the encouragement," she murmured as she bundled up another casserole for the freezer.

Jude squeezed her shoulder. "I'm just looking out for you."

She took a deep breath. "I know. It just seems ironic for you to be warning me away from my feelings for Colton."

"Maybe I'm changing in my old age," he said. "Or maybe I just don't want you to get hurt again."

Stacey thought about Joe and frowned. "I know it may sound crazy, but I feel as if my engagement to Joe was a lifetime ago."

"I still wouldn't mind kicking him into next week," he said. "He shouldn't have abandoned you."

"He couldn't handle the commitment," she said, and only felt a twinge of sadness over the situation. She had begun to realize that Joe's abandonment was his issue more than hers. "It's taken a while for me to realize this, but I wouldn't want him if he stayed with Piper and me out of obligation. At the same time, I feel terrible that Piper doesn't have the daddy she deserves. But the truth is, I'm not sure Joe deserves her."

Jude studied her for a long moment. "Dang, girl. You've grown up."

She smiled at her brother. "You think?"

"Yeah," he said, and waggled his finger at her. "Just don't go falling for the local cowboys. I don't want you to get hurt." His gaze slid to the pot on the stove. "Can you share any of that soup? The smell is killing me."

"That bad, huh?" she asked, smiling at his description.

"Have a little pity," he said.

"Tell the truth," she said. "When was the last time you prepared a full meal for yourself or anyone else?"

"Grilled cheese and canned soup count?"

She shook her head.

He sighed. "A long time."

"That's what I thought," she said. "Maybe you're due for a cooking lesson."

"I'll tell you a secret, Stacey. It's my goal to never need to cook for myself. That is the goal of most bachelors," he said.

"Well, at least you're honest," she said, and planted a kiss on his cheek. She fixed a large container of soup for him to take home. She spent the next hour storing meals. Piper awakened, and Stacey gave her a half bottle of baby food and her bottle. Afterward, it was time for baby calisthenics. Stacey set Piper on her belly and watched her do dry swimming. Piper grunted and groaned as she exercised.

When Piper's groans turned to cries, Stacey whisked her up in her arms and walked to the kitchen with her. Stacey finished wrapping up her meals for storage and put a few portions in the refrigerator. Her father was always grateful when she packed a lunch he could take outdoors.

Tucking Piper into a baby pack, Stacey began to clean the public areas of the house. She took care of the den, foyer and kitchen and began to feel tired. Pulling Piper from the sack, Stacey sank onto a chair in the den and told herself not to think about Colton.

Even her Romeo brother, Jude, had warned her away from her feelings. But Stacey couldn't keep her mind off of Colton. She wanted to be close to him. Very close.

She concentrated on rocking Piper, then burping her. Stacey knew she needed to focus on Piper. Her baby needed her love and devotion.

Unfortunately, Stacey was all too aware of her own needs. How was she supposed to make those needs disappear?

The next afternoon while her mother made some calls to her circle group, Stacey folded laundry in the den. Piper took a nap. Stacey did the hated job of folding sheets. Was there any good way of folding fitted sheets? With the television on a news show, she folded several linens.

A knock sounded at the door, and she rushed to keep whoever was on her porch from knocking again. She didn't want Piper waking from the noise. It was amazing how precious her child's sleep had become to her, she thought. She wondered if she should start putting a note on the front door when Piper was napping. Or would that be a bit too cranky?

Stacey opened the door and saw Colton on the porch. Her heart took a huge dip.

Colton removed his Stetson. "We need to talk."

Chapter Six

"I'm sorry. I shouldn't have taken advantage of you," Colton said.

Stacey felt her face heat with embarrassment and cringed. "Oh, no, I'm sorry. I shouldn't have interfered. I was supposed to be helping you with your girlfriend and ended up kissing you. I knew you had plans with her, but you and I got close and I stopped thinking about your girlfriend. I was just thinking about you and—"

"Stop," he said, and took her mouth in a kiss, then pulled back. "There is no girlfriend."

She stared at him in confusion. "No girlfriend?"

"No girlfriend," he repeated. "There is no one else I can think about right now. You're the only woman on my mind," he said.

Floored, Stacey could only gape at him. "I don't know what to say."

"You don't have to say anything. Just know that I didn't want to take advantage of you," he said and walked away.

Stacey gawked after him, wishing she could produce some magic words, but her tongue wouldn't even form basic syllables. "Colton," she finally managed, but he was already in his truck.

She was at a pure loss. He'd given her no chance to respond. How could she tell him how she really felt? How could she let him think their kiss was totally his fault? She raced to the back of the house and found her mother in between phone calls.

"Piper's asleep. Do you mind watching her for a while?" she asked.

"Not at all," her mother said. "Is there a problem?"

"I just need to go somewhere," she said, and didn't want to hang around long enough for her mother to question her further. Her mother was extremely intuitive. Stacey grabbed her purse, pulled on her coat and headed for her car. As she drove toward the Foster house, she tried to find the words to explain her feelings for Colton. She kept rehearsing several verbal scenarios, but none seemed adequate.

With no great plan in mind, she stomped up the steps to the Foster house and rapped on the door. A few seconds passed, and she knocked again.

The door whipped open and Colton looked at her. "What are you doing here?" he asked. "Listen, we don't have to talk about what happened again. I know you don't think of me that way," he said. "In a romantic way."

"Stop telling me what I think," Stacey said. She didn't know any other way to express her feelings for Colton except for kissing him, so that's what she did. She pulled him against her and kissed him as if her life depended on it.

Colton couldn't help but respond. He wrapped his arms around her and drew her to him. He clearly couldn't resist her. "You feel so good," he muttered. "Taste so good," he said, sliding his tongue past her lips.

Stacey felt herself heating up way too quickly. She wriggled against him, wanting to feel every bit of him. She wanted his skin against hers. She slid her hands up to the top of his head and continued to exchange open mouth kisses with him.

"I want you so much," she whispered.

"What do you want, Stacey?" he muttered.

"All of you. I want all of you," she said, her need escalating with each passing moment.

Colton's hands traveled to forbidden places. Her breasts and her read end. Beneath his touch, she felt herself swell like a sensual flower.

"Are you sure about this?" Colton asked, teasing her nipples to taut expectation.

"Yes, yes," she said, clawing at his chest. "I want you so much."

"Then you're gonna get me," he muttered and

pulled her up into his arms and carried her down the hallway. He took her into his bedroom and set her down on his bed.

"You're sure?" he asked a second time.

"More than sure," she said, and whipped off her shirt and bra. "Are you?" she asked, daring him.

One, two, three heartbeats vibrated through her, and Colton began to devour her with his hands and mouth. She had never felt such passion in her life. He made every inch of her body burn with desire and need for him. Stacey hadn't felt this alive in months...or ever.

She kissed his chest and belly...and lower. He groaned and took her with the same hunger.

"You taste so good," he said.

"So do you," she said, and pressed her mouth against his in a fully sexual kiss.

"I want to be inside you," he said, his tone desperate.

"I want you the same way," she said.

He pulled some protection from his bedside table, and finally, he pushed her legs apart and thrust inside her.

Stacey gasped.

"What?" he asked.

"You're just—" she said and broke off.

"I'm just what?" he asked, poised over her.

She took a deep breath and laughed breathlessly. "Big. You're big."

He shot her a sexy smile. "I'll try to make that work for you," he said, and began to move inside her.

They moved in a primitive rhythm that sent her twisting and climbing toward some new high she'd never experienced. She continued to slide against him, staring into his dark, sexy eyes.

When had Colton become so desirable to her? What did it matter? she asked herself and threw herself into making love to him. Stacey clung to his strong shoulders, and with every thrust, he took her higher and higher.

"You feel so good," he muttered. "So good."

Stacey felt herself clench and tremble. A climax wracked through her. She could hardly breathe from the strength of it.

Seconds later, she felt him follow after her, thrusting and stretching in a peak that clearly took him over the edge. He clutched her to him and gasped for breath.

Stacey clung to him with all her might. "Two words," she whispered. "Oh, wow."

He rolled over and pulled her on top of him. "When did you turn into the sexiest woman alive?"

Stacey laughed. "Me?"

"Yeah, you," he said, and kissed her again.

She sifted her fingers through his hair, enjoying every sensation that rippled through her. She loved the feeling of his skin against hers, his hard muscles. She slid her legs between his and savored his hard thighs. His lips were unbelievably sensual.

"I'm not sure how this happened," she said.

"Neither am I," he said. "But I'm glad it did."

They made love again until they were breathless. She wrapped her arms around him, shocked by how he'd made her feel. Stacey was in perfect bliss.

After that second time, Colton looked down at Stacey, all warm, sexy and satisfied in his bed, and felt a triple shot of terror. What the hell had he done? He hadn't just kissed his sister's best friend. He'd made love to her. Twice.

He held her tightly against him but was horrified by what he had done. "You're an amazing woman."

"You're a flatterer, but I'll take it," she said, cuddling against him.

"This is great, but I don't want us to have to make excuses to my family," he said.

A sliver of self-consciousness slid through her eyes. "Oh, good point," she said and bit her lip. She moved off of him, and he immediately regretted the absence of her body and sweetness.

Stacey quickly pulled on her clothes. "I should leave."

"Let me walk you to your car," he said, still full of questions and regrets. He pulled on his jeans and shirt.

Stacey grabbed her coat that had been left on the foyer floor. "I'm glad your mother didn't discover that," she said.

"We're talking about building a separate house, soon," he said.

"I understand the need for privacy," she said. "I don't have it. But I'm lucky to be able to live with my parents."

"I feel as if I should drive you home," he said, still upset with himself and overwhelmed by his feelings.

"I'm okay," she said, but she looked uncertain. The mood between them suddenly seemed awkward.

"Are you sure?" he asked.

She pressed her lips together in a closed-mouth smile. "Yes, I am," she said and shrugged. "I guess I'll see you around."

"Right." He nodded, thinking they had moved way too fast. Stacey had big responsibilities, and he might not be the right man to help her with them. He hadn't considered his previous experience with Piper a rousing success. "We'll talk later," he said, and helped her into her car.

"Yeah," she said, but didn't meet his gaze. She started her car and tore out of his driveway faster than a race car. He wondered if she regretted going to bed with him. He couldn't blame her. His parents' ranch wasn't exactly the most romantic environment.

Colton struggled with his own emotions over what they'd just done. They were friends, weren't they? If that was true, why had he wanted her so much? Why did he still want her? Whatever was happening between him and Stacey was complicated as hell.

* * *

Stacey forced herself not to look in her rearview mirror as she pulled away from the Foster ranch. She had clearly lost her mind, rushing back to tell Colton that she wanted him, too. Even though he'd said she'd been on his mind, it wasn't as if he'd said he wanted her in a forever way. She'd better not forget that. She'd been through a similar situation with Joe, although he'd given her an engagement ring. With Colton, he'd made no promises. He'd just taken what she'd eagerly offered, but afterward the expression on his face had been one of discomfort.

Buyer's remorse, she thought. He'd taken the goods, but now he wasn't sure he wanted them.

Pain twisted through her. She felt like a fool. Why had she believed Colton was different? She was all too familiar with this scenario. She'd been through it and lived to regret it during the past year of her life. When would she learn? she castigated herself. When would she stop throwing herself at men only to learn they only wanted her for a little while? Not forever. She wondered if she and Colton had just made a big mistake.

How could they go back to being friends now? Was that what he wanted? Humiliation flamed so hot it was as if a hole burned in her stomach. She pulled to a stop in front of her parents' home and shook her head at herself.

Glancing in the mirror, she saw that her hair was a mess, her lipstick smudged halfway across her face.

If her mother caught sight of her, she would know that Stacey hadn't just been running errands. Jeanne Fortune Jones was one of the most intuitive women on the earth, especially when it came to her children.

Stacey searched through her purse and found an elastic band but no brush. She raked her fingers through her hair and pulled it into the low messy bun she frequently wore. She pulled out a tissue and wiped the gloss off her face, then reapplied just a little to her lips. She checked the buttons on her coat, making sure they were properly fastened.

Holding her breath, she decided to make a dash through the foyer. "Well, there you are," her mother said from the kitchen. "I was starting to wonder where you'd gone so long."

"Sorry, Mom," Stacey said, pulling at the buttons on her coat. "I've got to use the bathroom or I'm going to burst. I'll be out in just a few," she said, and ran down the hall. She took her time, then hid out in her bedroom a little longer.

"Stacey, dinner's ready," her mother called.

Stacey cringed, then stiffened her spine. She could and should focus on Piper. As she stepped into the kitchen, she was relieved to see her brothers Liam and Jude sitting down to the table along with her father and mother. Her father and her brothers were too busy talking about the ranch to notice her. Her mother had put Piper in her high chair. As soon as Piper spotted Stacey, she lifted her hands and smiled in joy.

Even though the baby wasn't speaking yet, her nonverbal language soothed Stacey's heart, and she immediately picked up her baby. "Well, hello to you, Sweet Pea," she said, and sat down with Piper in her lap.

"She's never going to learn to be happy in her high chair if you don't leave her in there," Jeanne said.

"I'll put her in her seat in a couple minutes. How could I resist that smile?" Stacey asked.

"Your food will get cold," her mother warned.

Stacey shrugged. "I'm not that hungry."

Her brother Liam glanced at her. "In that case, I'll take Stacey's share."

Her mother shook her head. "You will not," she said. "Besides, there's plenty to go around. Stacey made this meat loaf yesterday, so she deserves a few bites."

"I hope you didn't mind putting it in the oven," Stacey said, rising to get some dry cereal for Piper.

"Not at all. You were just gone longer than I expected, so I started getting a little worried," she said, and Stacey felt the unasked question in her mother's voice.

She sighed, knowing she would have to fib, and heaven knew she wasn't any good at deception. "I ordered something for Piper, and I wanted to see if it had been delivered to the P.O. box yet. No luck, and there was a long line at the post office," she said. Part of her tale was true. She *had* ordered something for Piper, but it wasn't due for days. "Then I stopped by to visit Rachel, but she wasn't there. She had saved a recipe for homemade baby food I thought I might try. I guess the whole trip was a washout. Was Piper okay while I was gone?" Stacey sprinkled some cereal on the top of Piper's high chair, then set her child in the seat.

"An angel. She took a long nap and woke up in a quiet mood," her mother said, and finally took a bite of her own food. Her mother was usually the last to eat. "You need to sit down and eat," she told Stacey.

"I am," Stacey said and took her seat. She forced herself to take a bite.

"Did you happen to see Colton when you stopped by the Fosters'?" her mother asked as she took a sip of coffee.

Stacey's bite of meat loaf hung in her throat, and she coughed repeatedly.

"What's wrong with you? Are you choking?" her brother Jude asked, then thumped her on her back.

"Water," her mother said, standing up and leaning over the table to pick up Stacey's glass of water and press it into Stacey's hand.

Stacey took a few sips. Everyone looked at her expectantly. "Sorry," she said sheepishly. "I think I tried to breathe the meat loaf instead of eat it."

Liam chuckled. "Make sure you teach that little one over there a different technique."

"I will, smarty-pants," she said, and was determined to take the focus off herself. "The Winter Festival is right around the corner. I can't decide whether to bake apple/blueberry pies, chocolate pies or red velvet cupcakes."

"Apple/blueberry," her father said.

"Chocolate," Liam said.

"All three," Jude said.

Her mother laughed. "Aren't you glad you asked their opinions? Any of those sound good to me, but make sure you bake an extra one of whatever you end up making for us, or there's going to be a lot of complaining," Jeanne said, tilting her head toward her husband and sons.

Stacey smiled in relief. She would escape an inquisition this time.

The next few days, Stacey developed a plan for her tutoring service. She knew her strengths were math and science, so she decided to focus on those subjects as she contacted the local schools. She also sent an email to Rachel since she knew her friend was doing her student teaching this semester.

Her mother caught her reviewing a flyer at the kitchen table and gave a sound of surprise. "When did you decide to start tutoring?"

"I've been thinking about it for a while. Piper is older, but still manageable. I'm hoping to schedule the sessions during after-school hours. She takes a long afternoon nap, so I'd like to take advantage of that time and bring in a little bit of money."

Her mother frowned. "If you needed money, you

should have asked for it. Your father and I are happy to help you," she said, squeezing Stacey's shoulder.

Stacey's heart swelled at her mother's support. "You and Dad are already letting me stay here without paying rent. I don't like feeling as if I'm not contributing." She sighed. "I don't like feeling like a deadbeat."

Her mother sat down beside her. "Oh, sweetheart, you're no deadbeat. You fix the meals and do the laundry and cleaning here. For goodness' sakes, I barely have to lift a finger with all you do."

"Thanks, but—"

"No buts," Jeanne said. "We know that Joe hasn't offered any financial support, and he should have. At some point, you may have to confront him about that."

Stacey shook her head. "I hate the thought of it. He rejected both of us so thoroughly. I hate the thought of asking him for anything."

"But he *is* your baby's father," her mother said. "He has some responsibilities."

"I wish he wasn't Piper's father. I wish her father was someone more responsible, mature. Someone who adored her." A lump of emotion caught in her throat. "I wish—" she said, her voice breaking. She took a deep breath. "It doesn't matter what I wish. I'm probably never going to find anyone that loves me and Piper, and I need to stop whining about it. Piper and I are so blessed that my family loves us and supports us."

"Well, of course we love you," her mother said.

"But you're young, and you have a long life ahead of you. You'll find someone—"

"I don't think so," Stacey interrupted. "I can't count on that. I can't hope for it. I've just got to focus on doing the right thing for Piper, and I think tutoring is the right thing."

"If you're sure," her mother said. "And you know I'm happy to babysit for Piper anytime you need."

"Thank you, but I'm hoping I can do this while she's napping," Stacey said.

Her mother studied her for a long moment. "I worry that you don't get out with people your age very much. You and Rachel see each other now and then, but not that often. I wondered if you and Colton might be getting friendly."

"Oh, no. He was just trying to be nice and brotherly," she said, although her teeth ground together when she said it.

"If you say so," her mother said. "There's no reason you two can't enjoy each other as friends."

"Hmm. We'll see," Stacey said in a noncommittal voice. "At the moment, I need to make some copies of these posters and call in some favors from my teacher friends."

"All right. You sound like a busy girl. Are you still going to make desserts for the Winter Festival?" her mother asked.

"That's next week and I've already got it on my calendar," Stacey said. "I've got it under control."

Stacey did her best to stay busy during the next

days. She didn't want to think about Colton. She couldn't help feeling dumped. Thank goodness, no one except she and Colton knew what had happened between them. The longer the time passed, the more she knew, for certain, that now that he'd indulged his passion for her, he was done with her. She would have felt a bit more used if she didn't recall how much pleasure she'd experienced with him. Every once in a while, a stray image crossed her mind of the way he'd felt in her arms, the way he'd kissed and caressed her. Every time she had one of those thoughts she wanted to stomp it from her mind the same way she would stomp a spider. This was not the time for her to be thinking about her sexual needs.

Darn Colton Foster. Ever since Joe had abandoned her, Stacey had buried all her interest in sex. It hadn't been that difficult. But being around Colton had brought those emotions back to life, and these feelings were not convenient.

Not at all.

"Colton, I need you to take my pies to Dessert Booth number three-B at the Winter Festival tomorrow," Olive Foster said when he walked into the kitchen late Thursday evening.

Colton shook his head. "I've got a mile-long list of chores I have to do tomorrow. Maybe Rachel can do it."

"Rachel is student teaching. She can't do both,"

his mother said. "You'll only have to be there three hours."

"Three hours," he echoed, incredulous. "Why can't I just drop them off?"

"Because they need people to help work the booth," she said. "And I'm volunteering to help the handicapped at the festival."

"You may need to help Dad if he decides to do any of the chores I have planned for tomorrow," Colton grumbled.

His mother shot him a sharp look. "That's a terrible thing to say about your father."

"You know he has a problem with his back, even though he won't admit it," he said.

She sighed. "I'll guilt him into coming with me. That should keep him out of trouble."

"Kinda like you're guilting me into working a bake sale?" he returned.

"Colton, you are bordering on being disrespectful. What's wrong with you lately, anyway? You've been as grumbly as a bear with a sore paw. Are you having girl trouble?"

"Oh, for Pete's sake." Colton lifted his hand. This was not a conversation he wanted to have with his *mother*. "Just stop, Mom. I'll do the darn bake sale." Hell, he would do ten bake sales as long as he never had to discuss this subject with his mother again.

After lunch, the following day, Colton loaded up his truck with his mother's apple pies and drove to the Winter Festival. There was already a mile-long

line of people waiting to get inside, but since he was
a so-called vendor, he walked right in. It took him
a while, but he finally found his assigned booth. He
set the pies on the card table and turned around to
get the second batch.

He was in such a hurry he nearly walked straight
into someone just outside the booth.

"Don't," she said, and *she* sounded remarkably
like Stacey. He should know since he'd been hearing
her voice in his dreams every night. "Don't knock
over the cupcakes," she said.

Colton grabbed two of the boxes that threatened
to fall off the tower of desserts she carried and noticed Stacey was hauling Piper on her back at the
same time she carried the desserts. "For Pete's sake,
what are you doing?"

"I brought cupcakes and pies. I couldn't decide
which to bake, so I made both," she said, striding
toward the same booth where he just set down his
mother's apple pies. Stacey frowned, then looked up
at Colton. "What are you doing here?"

"My mother guilted me into bringing her pies and
working this booth," he said.

"Well, that's just great," Stacey said, clearly disgusted. "Just great."

"Hey, my mother pushed me into this," he said.
"Don't blame me."

"I'm not blaming you for bringing your mother's
pies," she said, but he could hear she hadn't finished
her sentence. There was more to it.

"You're blaming me for something," he said. "I can hear it in your voice."

"I'm blaming you for not calling me, Colton Foster. That was pretty rotten, unless you just wanted me for a quick roll in the hay," she said, and turned away from him.

Chapter Seven

Colton thought about responding to Stacey, but he couldn't find the right words. So he returned to his truck, swearing all the way as he hauled in the second load of pies. How could he explain himself? He wanted her, but he wanted to be sensible. With her history, he thought they should take their time. Plus, there was a baby involved. He didn't want to mess things up.

"Hey, Colton, you sure you don't want to share one of those pies with us while we wait out here in the cold?" a neighbor called from the crowd.

Colton paused only a half beat. "I don't have a fork handy for you," he said in return.

"I don't need a fork. I'll just eat with my hands. I love your mama's pies," the neighbor called back.

Colton chuckled despite his black mood and shook his head, walking to the dessert booth he would share with Stacey. His chuckle faded as he reentered the booth and set down the second haul of pies.

"You might want to put those on the table against the wall," she said as she arranged the desserts on the front table. "We don't want them to know we have a lot of them. They'll buy faster if they're afraid we'll run out."

"True," he said, and moved half the pies to the back table. "Are the cupcakes okay?"

"The frosting on two of them got smashed, but the rest are okay," she said.

"I can eat the damaged ones," he offered.

She shot him a disapproving glance. "We may have someone desperate enough to buy them," she said. "We're trying to make money for the mobile library, not stuff our faces."

"I wasn't suggesting we stuff *our* faces," Colton said. "I just wanted to stuff *mine*."

Stacey rolled her eyes and turned away, but Piper craned her head around to look at him. He couldn't deny she was cute. She batted her big eyes at him. Colton hid his face in a game of silent peekaboo.

After a few times of peekaboo, Piper let out a gurgling laugh. It was, Colton thought, one of the best sounds in the world. He played peekaboo again, and Piper let out a joyous shriek.

Stacey whipped around and glared at him. "What are you doing?"

"Nothing," he said. "Nothing."

"Hmm," she said in a short, disbelieving tone. "The attendees should be coming through soon." She turned her back to him again.

Piper looked at Colton, and he wiggled his fingers and smiled at her. She smiled coyly, then giggled.

Stacey glanced over her shoulder at Colton.

"What?" he asked.

She made a huffing sound and turned away to arrange a display of cupcakes. Colton couldn't help noticing Stacey's backside. He couldn't help remembering squeezing her curvy hips as he slid inside....

Colton felt his body instantly respond to the memory and visual. He shifted his stance and cleared his throat. "How have you been doing?"

Stacey immediately whipped around and stared at him with a wide-eyed gaze. "Since when?"

Colton shrugged. "Since last week."

"Oh, you mean since the day we had sex twice in your bed and you rushed me out the door because you didn't want your family asking questions and then chose not to call me. Even once."

Colton's gut twisted. Just in case he'd wondered, he now knew that Stacey had wanted him to call. He'd been unsure about how she'd felt since he'd taken her in his bed. Before, during and afterward, he'd wished that he could take her somewhere more private, but he'd been so hungry for her, and she'd seemed to feel the same way about him. Someone had to get control in this situation, although he was pretty sure he was nowhere near control. He didn't know if he could trust Stacey's feelings for him. To be honest, he wasn't sure if he was a rebound man for her.

"I wasn't sure you wanted me to call," he admitted.

She screwed up her face in a confused expression. "Why would you think that?"

"Well, you left pretty fast," he said.

"After you pushed me along," she said.

"I was trying to protect you," he said. "Did you really want to have to explain to anyone in my family why you were walking out of my bedroom with your hair all messed up and your coat on the floor in the hallway?"

Her hostility lowered a couple of notches. "I guess not," she said and paused. "But that still doesn't explain why you haven't called," she practically spat at him and turned around as the first attendees began to wander toward their booth.

After that, everything turned into a blur. It seemed that everyone who stopped at the booth wanted a pie or cupcake. The cupcakes went first because they were pretty and inexpensive. Every time Colton sold one of those cupcakes, he had to resist the urge to eat it. Red velvet with cream cheese frosting. His mouth watered. He kept hoping he could persuade Stacey to give him one of the defective cupcakes, but they were moving so quickly that he was losing hope. The booth was so tight she brushed against him every time she moved from the front to the back. He didn't know which was worse, the temptation of Stacey's body or of her red velvet cupcakes. Another brush of her sexy hips against his and his question was answered. He wanted Stacey a lot more than he wanted cupcakes.

"I need to ask a favor of you," she said, pulling at the straps of her baby carrier.

He shrugged. "What do you need?"

"To go to the bathroom. I'd prefer to go without Piper. Can you take her for a bit?" she asked.

"Sure," he said, feeling lame for not offering sooner. "Can I have one of those cupcakes in exchange? Half?" he added when he saw her frown. He needed some sort of consolation for how much he wanted her and couldn't have her, although he suspected a cupcake wasn't going to do the job.

"Half," she said, and eased the carrier from her shoulders. "You want to put her on your back?" she asked.

"That sounds good," he said, and turned around so she could help strap the carrier on him.

"I'll put her so she's facing away from you. That way she'll keep her fingers out of your hair. I'll be back soon," she said.

"We'll be here," he said.

Piper made an indistinguishable noise, but she didn't cry, so he figured he was good. He continued to sell pies and cupcakes, although the cupcakes were growing scarcer. "I need to put this cupcake in a protective place," he murmured and hid the treat behind his cup of coffee at the back table.

He smelled a peculiar odor, but was too busy to focus on it when a rush of attendees bought pies. Thank goodness, the pies were popular. Colton couldn't deny, however, that he was ready for this to be over. He'd rather be driving posts in dry ground than this.

Stacey returned, appearing breathless. "Sorry. The restroom was on the other side, and there was a line."

"There is always a line for the ladies room," he muttered and turned his back so Stacey could help disengage him from Piper.

"Oh, no," she said. "Oh, no."

"What's wrong?" he asked. "Is she okay? She's been quiet for a while."

"That's because she fell asleep," Stacey said.

"And that's bad because?" he asked.

"That's not the bad part," Stacey said. "Piper pooped all over your back."

"Oh, great," he muttered. Now he understood the source of the strange odor. "I'm glad someone feels better."

Colton and Stacey shut down the booth until the next volunteers were scheduled to appear. They were mostly sold out, anyway. Stacey helped Colton out of the baby holster, and she took Piper to the restroom while Colton headed home. This was one of the rare instances that Colton didn't have a fresh shirt in his car, so he drove with his windows open due to Piper's stink bomb.

He headed straight for the shower, stuffed the shirt in the washer on rinse, then fixed himself a bowl of soup from the Crock-Pot on the kitchen counter. Colton parked himself in a chair in the den to watch an action movie. He wanted to think about anything except Stacey and Piper, and it wasn't just because Piper had cut loose on him. He had been trying to dodge his feelings for Stacey since they'd been together, and seeing her today had felt like a slap in the face. Even though he saw his orderly life veering out of control when he was with her, he'd missed her terribly, and now he didn't know what to do.

A knock sounded, and Colton rose from his chair and opened the door. Stacey stood on the front porch holding a small covered plate. "I'm really sorry about what happened with Piper. It doesn't happen that often, but, well, babies can be messy. I kept back a couple of the cupcakes for you. I hope you'll accept them along with my apology."

His chest tightened at the kind gesture. "That was nice of you," he said. "Would you like to come in?"

She bit her lip. "I have Piper in the car."

He hesitated. "Bring her in. There's chicken noodle soup in the Crock-Pot. I'm just watching a movie."

"Are you sure?" she asked, her gaze searching his.

"Yeah, I'm sure," he said.

Stacey returned to the car and pulled Piper from

her car seat, along with a diaper bag. Colton rushed to take the bag for her. He wouldn't admit it aloud, but he was still a little gun-shy with the baby.

Stacey pulled a blanket from the diaper bag and spread it on the floor in the den while Colton ladled soup into a bowl for her and poured a glass of water. Colton returned to find the baby propped against some kind of pillow thing that kept her from falling over.

"Does she like that?" he asked.

"She can actually sit by herself, but she eventually topples. She didn't get much of a nap today, so I thought she could use a break," she said, and placed a couple of toys next to the tot. "I'm hoping for an early night."

"I'll say," he said, and set Stacey's soup on a tray on the end table.

"Thanks," she said, taking a seat on the sofa. She took a spoonful of soup. "This is good. It's nice eating someone else's food for a change."

"Yes, it is. That's probably why my mother does most of the cooking. She's good at it, so we just let her do it," he said.

"My brothers don't cook either. I got more interested in cooking when I went to nursing school," she said. "Then, after I got engaged, I wanted to take my mother's recipes with me when I got married. But that didn't work out," she said, and took another spoonful of soup.

An uncomfortable silence stretched between them.

"I'm sorry I didn't call," he finally admitted. "I wanted to." How could he tell Stacey that he feared he was a rebound man for her?

She looked up at him in surprise. "You did?"

"Of course I did," he said. "I didn't exactly hide how I felt with you when you were in my bed."

She looked away. "Well, I have a previous experience with someone who wanted to go to bed with me, but then left."

His gut clenched. "I don't want you to feel that way, but it just seemed as if everything was moving fast. It was out of control."

She nodded. "I wanted you, but I didn't want to want you."

"Exactly. I wasn't ready for what I was feeling," he said.

She gave another slow nod and took another sip of her soup. "Does that mean you want to forget what we did and go back to being friends?"

"That might be like trying to put the toothpaste back in the tube," he said. "I always want to be your friend, but I'd be lying if I said I don't want to be more."

Stacey met his gaze. "Then what do you want to do about it?"

The sexy challenge in her green eyes felt like a velvet punch in his gut. "Maybe we could spend some more time together. Go to Vicker's Corners, see a movie, take some walks when it's not freezing. Go for hot chocolate," he said, and wondered if she would find his suggestions lame.

She gave a slow smile. "That sounds nice, but people are gonna talk. I'm used to gossip, but you're not."

"I can handle it," he said defensively, although Colton had never liked people getting in his business. "I'm just probably not as nice about it as you are," he said and chuckled.

At that moment, he heard his parents walk through the front door. "Yoo-hoo," his mother called. "We're home."

Piper, who had been surprisingly quiet, looked up from playing with her toy.

Colton's mother and father came to a dead stop as they glanced into the den. "Hello, Mr. and Mrs. Foster," she said, rising from the sofa. Colton also rose. "I stopped by with a few of my red velvet cupcakes, and Colton offered me some of your delicious soup."

"Good for both of you. I'm glad Colton showed you some hospitality. Frank and I heard there was a mishap with the baby at the winter festival today, but couldn't get the details."

Stacey chuckled. "I'll let Colton fill you in on that. I should be getting Piper home."

"I'll just say I'll wash the shirt I wore today twice," he said.

His father gave a nod. "Been there, done that. It's good to see you and the baby, Stacey. I hope you don't mind if I get some of that soup."

"Not at all," Stacey said.

"Oops. Sounds as if there might have been a little mess," Colton's mother said. "Don't rush off," she said as Stacey put away Piper's baby paraphernalia. "Let me see that sweet little munchkin. She's growing like a weed."

Mrs. Foster extended her arms to the baby and smiled when Stacey handed Piper to her. "What a friendly little sweetheart. Your mother says she's sleeping through the night most of the time."

"That's right. We had a rough time the first few months, and she still has her moments. But don't we all?" Stacey said.

"I can tell you're a good mother. I always knew you would be. You just seem to roll with whatever comes your way. I know Rachel is going to be upset that she didn't get to see you and the baby," Mrs. Foster said. "Are you sure you can't stay?"

"I really should go," Stacey said. "I'm hoping for an early night. It's good to see you."

"Same here," his mother said, then plopped the baby in Colton's arms. "Here. You carry Piper out to the car. Stacey could probably use a little break from hauling around this little chunk of love after today."

Colton automatically stiffened but soldiered up. He couldn't disagree with his mother. After his limited experience with Piper, he was surprised Stacey wasn't exhausted all the time. From what he could tell, branding an entire herd of cattle would be easier than watching over a baby.

He carried Piper to the car and let Stacey fasten her into her safety seat. Piper fussed a little at the confinement. "You just better get used to this," Stacey said in a kind but matter-of-fact voice. "You'll be sitting in a safety seat every time you get in the car." She shook a toy connected to the front of the seat to distract the baby, and Piper quieted down.

"You're good with her. I'll say that much. She can be a handful," he said, shaking his head.

"She's curious and sweet, but you're right. She has her moments," Stacey said.

"That's when those bubbles come in handy," he said.

Stacey stared at him and smiled. "So you *did* use the bubbles that night you kept her for me?"

"Hey, I had to hit the ground running. That diaper bag is like a bag of tricks," he said.

"You almost sound as if you're still afraid of her," Stacey said. "My little Piper couldn't terrify a big, strong man like you, could she?"

"Of course not," he lied because the baby did have the ability to scare him more than a fright movie. "I'm just no baby expert like you are."

"Maybe she'll grow on you," Stacey said softly.

"Maybe," he said. Piper's mother was growing on him. He leaned toward Stacey and took her mouth in a lingering, sweet kiss that made something inside him fill up and want more at the same time. "I'm glad you came over. I'll call you."

"I'm going to be really upset if you don't," she warned.

He liked hearing that bit of testiness in her voice. It made him think she wanted him, too. "No problem," he said and kissed her again. He pulled back. "You're habit-forming."

"That's good to hear," she said. "I think your mother is watching from behind the curtains in the front room. She may ask questions. That's what mothers do."

"That's okay. I have the perfect answer," he said, putting his index finger under her chin.

"What's that?"

"Nunya. Nunya business," he said, and her laughter made it worth the inquisition he knew he would face when he went inside the house.

That night, Stacey slept better than she had in months, partly because Piper slept long and hard, and partly because being with Colton just made her feel better about life. He didn't have to do much. Just his presence made her feel calmer and more optimistic. She didn't want to overthink his effect on her. Stacey just wanted to enjoy it.

He called her on her cell the next morning, and she could tell he was outside and the wind was blowing. "Good mornin'," he said.

"Good morning to you. How long have you been out and about?" she asked as she toted Piper around the kitchen.

"Since a couple hours ago. You know the routine. I have to get up early in order the get the heavy chores done so my father doesn't hurt his back," he said.

"I wish you could talk him into seeing the doctor," she said. "It's as if he's in complete denial of this health problem."

"You're exactly right. He's in denial until he ends up in bed for a few days. Then he takes it slow. A few weeks after that, he thinks it'll never happen again. But enough of my crankiness. How would you like to go into town and get a burger at the grill? Early dinner?"

"That sounds like fun, but my parents are going to be at the winter festival all day, so I would have to bring Piper," she said. When he didn't immediately respond, she filled the gap of silence. "We can go another time. We don't have to go today."

"No," he said. "Let's take her with us. What time will work?"

"I'd like to get her back on schedule with her afternoon nap. Is four-thirty okay?"

"Sure. I'll pick you two ladies up at four-thirty. See you then," he said and disconnected the call.

Stacey felt a spurt of excitement and danced around the room with Piper. "We have a date."

She spent the morning entertaining Piper, then ran laundry and cooked a big pot of chili in the afternoon. She changed her clothes three times and might have changed them once more if Piper hadn't awakened. Her brother Jude must have smelled the chili from miles away because he stomped into the house an hour after she'd put it on the stove. Her brothers were at the family dinner table more often than not, despite the fact that they had their own places to live.

"Thank goodness there's food," he said. "I'm starving." He looked at Stacey and Piper and gave a double take. "You two look as if you're headed someplace special," he said.

Stacey resisted the urge to squirm. "Just going to the grill with a friend," she said.

"Rachel?" he asked as he grabbed a bowl from the cabinet.

She shook her head. "Nope. Do you mind setting that Crock-Pot on low and putting the lid on it if you leave before Mom and Dad get home? I think they should be here within a half hour," she said.

"Sure," he said and grabbed a spoon. "Any crackers or bread?"

"Crackers are in the cupboard." A knock sounded at the door, and her heart leaped with silly excitement. "Gotta go."

"Hey, you never said who is going with you to the grill," he said.

"That's right," she said, unable to stifle a little giggle. "I didn't. See you later," she said, and ran to the door and threw it open.

"Hi," she said, thinking it was ridiculous to be so excited about going to the grill in town. This proved the point that she really needed to get out more often.

"Hi to you and Miss Piper," he said. "You're both looking beautiful. You ready to go?"

"Thank you, and we are," she said.

"I'll carry Piper to the truck. I see you have the magic tricks bag," he said, gingerly taking the baby in his arms.

"It goes wherever Piper goes," she said. "Listen, do you mind if we take my car? I've already got the safety seat, and it'll be easier to keep it in there than switch it from my car to yours again."

"Good plan," he said. "It didn't occur to me."

"Probably because you haven't spent a lot of time with babies," she said.

"My mistake," Colton said. "The education of Colton Foster continues. I'll let you fasten her into that contraption," he said after he carefully set Piper into the seat.

As usual, Piper complained about the confinement, and Stacey distracted her. Within a couple moments the baby calmed.

"Have you ever tried to take her on a road trip?" he asked.

"Not unless you call the hour drive to Lubbock a road trip," she said. "She's really not a bad rider, but I wonder if she might get fed up with it after several hours. I have visions of throwing everything but the kitchen sink into the backseat to keep her amused."

"I think my parents must have done that when we took a trip to Dallas one time, although my Dad wouldn't put up with any foolishness when we got older."

"My father is the same way, maybe even more so," she said. "Deke Jones is a stand-up guy, but I have to admit that he didn't join me for any tea parties when I was a little girl. He was too busy for that."

"It's funny the things we remember. My mother showed up for most of my basketball games, but my father only came to a few each season. I always knew they both loved me, and that's what's important," he said.

"Very true," she said. "Now that I've had Piper, though, I find myself wishing she had everything I had growing up and more."

"Like what?" he asked.

"She has some of it," Stacey said. "A safe, warm home and family who love her, but—" She broke off, feeling self-conscious.

"But what?"

"Nothing," she said, feeling her face grow warm with embarrassment. "You'll think I'm crazy."

"No. I won't. Tell me."

Stacey smiled and shook her head. "I'm hoping I can talk one of her uncles into having a couple tea parties with her," she said. "I think it's good for little girls to have good men who are involved in their lives."

"I'm sure you're right about that," he said. "What do little girls eat at tea parties, anyway? I can't believe they like tea."

"Juice and cookies," she said.

"That's not all that bad," he said.

"No. It's the little chairs and pretending that makes it tough for a grown man," she said.

"Which of your brothers have you targeted for this?" he asked.

"I have a year or two before the parties will begin," Stacey said. "But I'm thinking Toby would be a natural. He's already a foster father. If not him, I may be able to con Jude into the job, especially if Piper serves something I've made."

"Sounds as if you're planning ahead," he said.

"Once I had Piper, I couldn't just think about the moment anymore. I had to think about the future, too."

"Is that why you seem sad sometimes?" he asked.

Stacey looked at him in surprise. "You think I seem sad?"

"Well, different. You used to seem happier," he said.

She thought about that for a moment. "I worry more," she confessed as he pulled into the small parking lot for The Horseback Hollow Grill.

He cut the engine and turned to her. "No worrying for the next couple of hours," he told her. "After all, you're about to eat a gourmet meal with the handsomest guy in Horseback Hollow," he joked.

Stacey smiled. The gourmet meal was a stretch,

but she was beginning to think that Colton was the best man in Horseback Hollow. She wondered why she'd never noticed until now.

Chapter Eight

"Oooh, what a cute baby," the server at The Grill said, then glanced at Stacey and Colton. "What a good-looking family. I bet you hear that all the time. I'm Maureen, and I'm new here in Horseback Hollow." Her gaze returned to Piper. "Look at that chin," she said, tickling it. "Just like Daddy's. Now, what can I get for you today?"

"Burger loaded and hot chocolate," Colton said. "What about you?" he asked Stacey.

"Grilled cheese and hot chocolate. Extra marshmallows please," she added.

"Will do," Maureen said and turned away.

"Sorry about that," Stacey said.

"Sorry about what?" he asked.

"That the waitress said Piper looked like you," she

said, feeling extremely awkward. She didn't want Colton to feel pushed into a relationship with either herself or Piper.

"She said we have the same chin," he said, rubbing his own chin and glancing at Piper. "I just didn't know I already had two."

Relief raced through her, and she swatted at him. "Stop that. She clearly only has one chin, but there's no denying those chipmunk cheeks. She looks as if she's packing a load of acorns." Stacey rubbed her daughter's cheek. "But you're gorgeous, anyway," she said.

"She is. She looks like you. Minus the chipmunk cheeks," he said.

"I'll take that as a compliment," Stacey said, and Maureen returned with their hot chocolate.

"Anything else I can get you?" she asked.

Colton glanced at Stacey. "We're good," she said.

Their food was served just moments later, and Stacey relished her grilled cheese sandwich. Although Piper was well-fortified with cereal on her high-chair tray, she watched every bite that Stacey took.

"She's getting more interested in food," Stacey said. "Especially whatever I'm eating."

"Can't blame her. What does she get? Dry cereal? She looks as if she wants to reach right over and grab the rest of your sandwich. You're clearly starving her."

"Right," Stacey said, shooting him a mock chastising look. "This is probably more than you want to know, but she's allowed to have strained and pureed fruits, vegetables and meats."

Colton made a face. "I didn't hear hamburger on that list."

"She doesn't have any teeth. She'd have to gum it," Stacey said.

A woman stopped by their table. "Why, Stacey Jones. I haven't seen you in ages."

Stacey recognized the woman as a member of her church. Stacey had missed quite a few Sundays since Piper had been born. Truth be told, she'd missed more than she'd attended since she'd gotten pregnant. "Mrs. Gordon, it's good to see you. How is your family?" Stacey asked as she stood and gave the woman a hug.

"We're hanging in there. My husband has had a terrible time with gout, but we keep plugging. Look at your baby. She's just gorgeous," Mrs. Gordon said, and glanced at Colton in confusion. "Colton Foster, right? For some reason, I thought your fiancé's name was Joe."

Stacey's stomach knotted. "He was. Joe moved to Dallas. But Piper is thriving, as you can see."

"Yes, she is. And how nice for both of you to have big, strong Colton around," Mrs. Gordon said in a coy voice.

"Hmm," Stacey said, so ready for the woman to move along. "Thank you for stopping by," she said. "And please give your husband my best."

She sank back onto her seat. "Why does everyone have to know everything about everyone around here?" she muttered and took a sip of her hot chocolate. She wondered how long she would be answering questions about Joe and why they weren't together. At this point, it looked like forever.

After they finished their meal, Colton drove Stacey and Piper back to Stacey's house. "You're awfully quiet," he said.

"I know I said that we have to expect people to talk here in Horseback Hollow because that's what they do, but I hate having to talk about Joe. People always look at me with pity. Poor Stacey. She couldn't keep her man," she said.

"Joe's leaving wasn't your fault. He couldn't handle the responsibility of a baby. He's the loser in this situation, not you," he said. "If you need another way of looking at it, aren't you glad that you and Piper aren't stuck with a man who doesn't love you? You deserve better than that."

"When he first left, I was in shock. I couldn't believe he would abandon his own child and me. It made me wonder if I ever really knew him," she said.

"Do you wish he would come back and the two of you could get back together?" Colton asked.

"I did for a while," she confessed. "It sounded like the perfect ending to a fairy tale that had gotten off track. But I don't know that I would ever be able to trust him again. I do know that I'm not the same woman who fell for him years ago. I just wish he wouldn't have rejected Piper. That's the worst part," she said.

Colton pulled the car to a stop in the Joneses' driveway. He leaned toward her. "I'm not sure this little outing cheered you up all that much."

She blinked at him. "I didn't know that was the purpose," she said. "I thought we just wanted to spend some time together. We did that with no melt-downs from Piper, and I had terrific hot chocolate and company."

"You're some kind of woman, Stacey, and don't you forget it," he said as he lowered his mouth to take hers in a delicious kiss.

Stacey felt her heart race. Her body immediately responded. His kiss triggered all sorts of forbidden emotions and sensations. She slid her hands beneath his jacket to pull him closer. He responded by nearly hauling her onto his lap.

"Damn this console," he muttered and kissed her again. He slid one of his hands from her waist up-ward to her breast.

Her nipples turned hard, and she felt her need for him pool in all her secret places. "Oh, Colton," she whispered and scrubbed at his chest, wishing she could feel his naked skin.

His kiss turned hot with want and need, and she strained toward him, her body and mind recalling how good he'd felt inside her. She wanted him that way again. Now.

The sound of Piper gurgling and talking her baby

language penetrated past the mist of arousal crowding her mind. Colton froze. Stacey did the same.

Frustration nicked through her. "This is hard," she said.

"In more ways than one," Colton said, his voice taut with forced denial. "Between you living with your parents and me living at the ranch, I feel like a randy teenager," he said and pulled back.

Stacey felt the same sense of dissatisfaction she heard in his voice. "What do you usually do? How do you usually handle things when you and a woman—" She broke off, wondering if she really wanted to know about Colton's previous partners.

"That's part of the reason I want a place of my own," Colton said. "Privacy. But I've felt as if I needed to keep an eye on my father, and I haven't wanted to tell my parents I want to build. The time is coming sooner than later, though. In the past, the women had their own places or we spent the night in Vicker's Corners."

"A whole night?" she echoed. "I'm trying to imagine spending the whole night away from home without a lot of questions." She sighed. "I wish this were easier."

He kissed her lightly on the mouth as if he didn't want to get anything started between them again. "Most good things don't come easy. Let me walk you and Piper to the door."

Stacey said good-night to Colton and walked

through the door. No sooner had she closed the door behind her than her brother Jude appeared.

"So, you went out with Colton again? Are you sure that's a good idea?"

Taken aback by his confrontational manner, she tilted her head at him. "I enjoyed Colton's company, a grilled cheese sandwich and hot chocolate. Is there anything wrong with that?"

"Well, not really," Jude said.

"We had a chaperone. Nothing naughty happened. Trust me, nothing naughty *can* happen," she grumbled.

"I just want you to be careful. I don't want to see you get hurt like you did with Joe," he said.

"Colton is nothing like Joe. Nothing," she said, and took Piper to the nursery. It was true that Colton was nothing like Joe, but Colton had never asked her to marry him. Stacey felt a stab of concern that Colton wasn't interested in being anybody's baby daddy, which also meant he wouldn't want to be Piper's daddy.

That night when she went to bed, it took her a long time to fall asleep.

Colton did a last check around the north pasture, then returned to the house. Grabbing a cup of decaf, he sank onto one of the recliners in the den. He halfway watched a basketball game through his drooping eyes. Feeling himself drift for a few moments, he awakened when his father walked into the room and got into the other recliner.

"Hey," Colton said.

His father nodded.

"You worn out from the second day of the winter festival?" Colton asked.

His father gave a heavy sigh. "Your mother insists on staying for the whole thing, and she wants me to stay with her."

"Your back okay?" Colton asked.

"A little sore. Nothing unusual," his dad said.

"Any time you want to go for lunch in Vicker's Corners, I'm glad to take you. There's a chiropractor there," he said.

"Chiropractor?" his father said. "Don't they crack your bones and put you in traction? Sounds as if that would make you worse."

"They make adjustments," Colton said. "They help get your back in alignment."

"Hmmph," his father said in disbelief. "Well, that's not why I came in here. Your mother wants me to talk to you."

"About what?" Colton asked, feeling curious and studying his father.

His father sighed. "It's about Stacey and her baby."

Colton frowned. "What about them?"

"Well, it's not really any of our business," his father began, and Colton immediately knew this wasn't a discussion he wanted to have with his father.

His father cleared his throat, obviously uncomfortable. "You need to be careful with Stacey," he said. "After what Joe did, she doesn't need anyone taking advantage of her."

Indignation rolled through him, and he pushed the recliner into the upright position. "I wouldn't take advantage of Stacey. What makes you think I would?"

"Well, you look as if you're getting, uh, friendly with her," he said. "I mean you look as if you want to be more than friends," he said, then rubbed his face with his hand. "Oh, for Pete's sake. Just treat her right. That's all I'm gonna say."

Colton met his father's gaze. "I'll treat her right. You and Mom don't need to worry."

"Good," his father said. "I'm glad that's over. Who's playing tonight, anyway?"

"The Bulls and Lakers," he said.

His father nodded. "Looks like a close game."

Colton didn't respond. His mind was too busy with his father's remarks. He resented the interference. He was a grown man. Colton stood. "I'm gonna hit the sack," he said. "Good night."

Colton headed down the hall and was intercepted by his sister, Rachel. In no mood for anyone else's comments, he lifted his hand. "Don't say a word," he said.

She frowned at him. "About what?"

"About Stacey and me," he said.

Her eyes widened in surprise. "Stacey and you?" she echoed. "What's going on? I've been crazy busy and haven't had a chance to talk with her for several days."

"Never mind," he said, and headed for his wing of the ranch.

Rachel bobbed along behind him. "Are you two seeing each other? That would be so cool," she said. "As long as you don't hurt her. You have to swear you won't hurt her, but I love the idea. I'll call her right now."

"She's got a little baby," Colton said. "She might be in bed trying to get some sleep."

Rachel's face fell. "True. Well, give me the scoop. When did this happen?"

"Rachel," he said as gently as he could, "it's none of your business."

The next morning, Stacey awakened with a different sense about herself and her life. She realized that in many ways she'd been hiding from the world, ashamed of how her relationship with Joe had ended, embarrassed that she and Piper had been dumped by him. The whole situation had made her feel like that mathematical expression *less than*.

She was ready to start reclaiming her life. Taking a quick shower and getting dressed, she fed Piper and dressed her in a cute outfit with stockings. She met her parents just as they were headed out the door to church.

Her mother looked at her in surprise. "Where are

you two going looking so spiffy? Is there a mother/ baby beauty contest I haven't heard about?"

Stacey laughed in pleasure at the sweet way her mother had voiced her curiosity. "Piper and I are going to church this morning."

"Oh, my." Her mother covered her mouth and sniffed. "I've been waiting for this day."

"I hadn't turned into a total heathen," Stacey said.

"Oh, no. Not that," her mother said. "I'm just so proud of you and Piper. I want everyone to see what a good job you're doing with her. I think you will be an inspiration to many people."

"I don't know how inspiring I'll be if she starts screaming in church," Stacey muttered. "But I think it's time."

"Yes, it's time," her father said impatiently and pointed at his watch. "If we don't get moving we'll be late."

"You can sit with us," her mother said as they were hustled out of the house. "I'll be happy to take Piper out if she gets fussy."

"I'll take her out," her father said. "Especially if she starts fussing before the offertory."

"Deke," her mother said in disapproval. "Shame on you."

"What? I'm just being a nice granddaddy," he said and chuckled. He helped Jeanne into his truck, and Stacey tucked Piper into the car seat in her Toyota, then followed her parents to church.

She felt a twinge of nostalgia as she walked into

the small chapel her family had attended since before she was born. She'd celebrated so many holidays and Sundays in this place. As soon as she walked inside with Piper in her arms, she saw several familiar faces. She waved at each of her neighbors, then took her seat with her parents.

Piper did well until the minister began to speak. She got a little squirmy, but Stacey couldn't blame her. There'd been plenty of times she had gotten fidgety when a minister spoke. Despite her squirminess, Piper didn't let out a peep until the congregation sang a benediction.

"Good job," she said, praising the baby, and left the pew. Several people greeted her and made a fuss over Piper. There was no mention of Joe, but Stacey was prepared in case someone did. She made her way to the back of the church and found Rachel waiting for her with open arms.

"I decided to come to church at the last minute today. I'm so glad I did. Look at you and Miss Piper," she said, squeezing the baby's hand. "All dressed up for church. She must have done well during the service. I didn't hear her."

"She, ahem, *sang* during the benediction," Stacey said.

Rachel giggled. "Good for her. She'll be in the choir before you know it. Listen, I'm sorry I haven't been in touch with you. Changing careers to education and doing my student teaching has made me crazy. I had no idea how much time the lesson plans and parent meetings would take."

"No worries," Stacey said. "I know you've been busy."

"Not so busy that I should be the last to know that you are dating my brother," Rachel said.

Stacey groaned. "Oh, no. Not you, too. It seems as if everyone has an opinion about us seeing each other. And it's not as if either of us has any privacy where we live."

Rachel raised her eyebrows. "Privacy?" she echoed. "You want privacy with my brother?"

Stacey shook her head and waved her hand. "Forget I said anything."

"You sound like Colton," Rachel said. "He didn't want to talk about it either."

"Well, who wants to talk about a relationship when it's first starting? Who knows where this will go? Colton has a lot on his mind with your father's back problem. He keeps trying to talk your dad into seeing a doctor, but your father won't go. Colton says he's got to stay one step ahead of your dad to keep him from hurting himself."

Rachel nodded. "My father avoids doctors at nearly all cost."

"I think Colton wonders if you might be more successful with your father than he has been," Stacey said, hoping she'd managed to distract Rachel from her questions. "I need to get Piper home to change and feed her, so I need to head out to my car."

Rachel tagged along. "Well, just so you know, I'm all for this. Colton is a great guy, and you're the best friend I could ever have. He would be lucky to get you, and in a way, maybe you would be lucky to get him, too. Especially after Joe," she said.

"I don't want my relationship with Colton to have anything to do with Joe," Stacey said as she buckled the baby into her car seat. "I want to leave that behind."

"Kinda hard to do when Joe is Piper's father," Rachel said.

"He's been invisible for over a year. I need to move on," she said.

Rachel met her gaze and nodded. "Good for you. But when it comes to my brother, you need to know something," she said and lowered her voice. "He's slow at making the moves, so you may have to help him along."

Stacey bit her lip to keep from laughing at Rachel's warning. She couldn't help thinking of the scorching lovemaking she'd experienced with Colton. "I'll keep that in mind," she managed.

"Good," Rachel said. "I'll call you soon. Maybe I could babysit for you sometime."

"You may have a hard time squeezing me in with your student teaching," Stacey said.

"Maybe," Rachel conceded and gave Stacey a hug. "But I have three reasons to try to make that happen."

"Three?" Stacey said, hugging her in return.

"My brother, you and me. Wouldn't it be cool if you were both my best friend and sister-in-law?"

The possibility gave Stacey a jolt. "Oh, Rachel, don't go there. These are very early days."

"Well, it's not as if you haven't known each other forever."

"Yes, but I haven't always had a baby. I'm not at all sure Colton is ready to be a father to a child that isn't really his."

"He might need a little persuading, but I think it could be done." Rachel shivered. "It's too cold for me out here. I'll call you."

Stacey watched Rachel race to her car and tried to unhear the words she'd just heard, but it was like trying to unring a bell. What if she and Colton got married? Was it even a possibility? Her heart squeezed tight with a myriad of emotions. She closed her eyes and shook her head. She shouldn't even think about it.

The next day, Colton went into town to get some equipment to repair some fences and overheard a couple of workers talking about something happening at the bar.

"So, what's going on?" he asked.

"*Live* music at the Two Moon Saloon on Tuesday," the worker said.

"Really? I can't remember the last time there was live music at the bar," Colton mused.

"And I hear there might be dancing," the worker said. "I'm taking my girlfriend."

"Hmm," Colton said. He wondered if Stacey would be able to go on such short notice. On the way home, he called and left a message about the live music and continued on with his chores.

Stacey must have returned his call while he was out fixing a fence. Her mom would keep Piper. She sounded excited. He hoped that whoever was performing didn't bomb. The smile he heard in Stacey's voice did strange things to his gut. He felt a little lighter, a little less burdened as he pulled into the driveway to his house. His conversation with his father had kept him awake for an extra hour last night, but Colton knew he wanted to spend time with Stacey and she felt the same way about him. He knew his mother and father shouldn't be involved in this decision, and if they intervened again, he would have to speak his piece.

Colton stomped up the steps to the house with the winter wind whistling through his coat. He was dog-tired and all he wanted was a home-cooked meal. If that wasn't available, he would heat some canned soup and make a sandwich.

"Hiya," Rachel called as he passed the den. She appeared to be doing lesson plans or grading papers.

"How's it going?" he asked.

"I wish I'd earned my first degree in education. This is so time-consuming," she said.

"I'm not sure it changes much, sis," he said. "I

never hear teachers talking about how much extra time they have."

"True, I guess," she said. "But I like it, so maybe I won't notice the time."

He nodded. "I'm gonna get whatever is available in the kitchen."

"Wait," she said, scrambling to her feet. "I talked to Stacey at church yesterday," she said.

"Great," he said and moved toward the kitchen.

"I also talked to her today. Amazing what I can learn about my brother from his girlfriend," she said, following him.

He shot her a quelling glance.

"What I mean is I didn't realize how bad Dad's back is. Stacey said you've offered to take him to Vicker's Corners to see a doctor, but he won't do it," she said.

"That's right," he said, opening the fridge and hoping to find something wonderful. He spotted a small bowl of leftover beef stew and snatched it up.

"She also said that you thought Dad would be more likely to go with me to Vicker's Corners to see a doctor."

"Right again," he said. He put the stew in the microwave, then pulled some sliced ham, cheese and bread out of the fridge and went to the counter. "The trouble is you'd have to trick him."

Rachel frowned. "What do you mean?"

"You would need to make an appointment with him and find some other reason for him to go. You'd take him to lunch, then take him to a doctor's appointment and beg for forgiveness afterward. He would forgive you within twenty-four hours, less if he got some relief from his back pain."

Rachel's frown deepened. "That sounds like a lot of trickery," she said.

"As if you haven't done the same ten times over for less honorable reasons," he returned as he slapped the meat and cheese on the bread and slathered it with Dijon mustard.

"I wish Dad would be more reasonable about medical treatment," she muttered, crossing her arms over her chest.

"You and me both," he said, when the microwave beeped. He grabbed his bowl of stew and sandwich. He would worry about water later.

Rachel poured a glass of ice water and sat down at the kitchen table. She put the glass at the place opposite from her. "Well, sit down," she said, waving her hand. "We have to figure out exactly when and how I'll do this trickery."

"Dad is a sucker for his little girl. Just invite him to go to lunch with you, then take him to a doctor afterward," Colton said.

"Stacey and I didn't just talk about Dad," Rachel said.

A bite of sandwich lodged in Colton's throat. He coughed repeatedly and washed it down with a gulp of water. "Oh, really," he said in a deliberately non-committal tone.

"Yes," Rachel said. "Stacey said the two of you could use some privacy. What do you say about that?"

"Privacy begins at home," Colton said.

Rachel made a face at him. "I'm trying to help."

"Then stay out of it," he said. "There's a baby involved. I don't want to be responsible for messing up that child's life. I'm taking it slow or not at all."

Chapter Nine

Colton sat across from Stacey in the Two Moon Saloon while a trio played. They might not win any awards, but folks got up to dance every now and then.

"This is fun," she said as she took a sip of her mixed drink.

Colton had smuggled in some cranberry juice for her to mix with vodka and ice. He'd known the bar wouldn't keep much juice on hand. If they did, their supply would quickly deplete on a busy night like tonight, with more women asking for mixed drinks instead of beer or straight liquor. It appeared many Horseback Hollow men had viewed the live music at the bar as a good date-night opportunity, so more women took part in drinks with their men.

"I'm glad you like it," he said, taking a long swallow from his beer.

"You don't like the group?" she asked.

"I like them fine," he said. "It's nice to hear some live music here for a change."

"I agree," she said, and the trio began to play a slow song. "Any chance you would dance with me?"

"Sure," he said, his body tightening at the sexy expression in her eyes.

Colton led her onto the tiny dance floor and pulled her against him. "You feel good," he whispered into her ear.

"You feel good, too," she said, and stretched her body so that it molded against his.

Colton couldn't help wishing they were both naked. Stacey was so sweet and inviting. He couldn't resist her. With every beat of the song, he felt the gentle friction of her feminine body against his. He grew harder with each touch.

She lifted her head, and it was the most natural thing in the world for him to take her mouth. She slid her sweet, silky tongue in his mouth, and his internal temperature turned hotter and hotter. He couldn't help but return her kiss.

His heart slamming against his chest, he squeezed her against him, and she stroked his jaw. The music ended, but he didn't want to release her.

She breathed against his throat, and it was all he could do not to lead her out of the bar and take her in his truck. He took a deep breath to pull himself under control. "I guess we should sit down now," he said in a low voice.

"I guess we should," she said, looking up at him with wanting for him in her eyes. "But that's not what I want."

"Me neither," he said. "It stinks."

She gave a slow smile that sizzled with sexuality. "Yes, it does," she said and pulled back.

Colton prayed that his arousal would calm down. He still wanted her, but his mind knew this wasn't the place or the time. They returned to the table and he took a drink of his beer while she took a sip of her cocktail.

She met his gaze with an alluring smile. "This makes me feel young again. Lately, I've been feeling kinda old and tired."

"You need to give yourself a break. Piper's got that kick of Fortune Jones in her. She's going to let you know when she wants something, and she'll try to make you race to get it for her."

Stacey lifted her eyebrows in surprise and took a sip of water. "What makes you say that? Are you implying that she's spoiled?"

"Not at all," Colton said. "I'm just saying she's— assertive. Isn't that what everyone is supposed to be these days?"

Stacey pressed her lips together, then let out a big laugh that filled him all the way up inside. "That sounds mighty close to calling my baby a brat."

"She's not a brat," Colton said. "Not yet."

Her eyebrows flew up to her hairline. "Not yet?" she echoed.

"Right," he said. "She's not even walking. She won't turn bratty until she's three."

Stacey gave a slow nod. "Good to know."

"Do you really disagree?" he asked.

"I just hope I do this parenting thing right. I don't want to be too harsh or too permissive. It's not as easy as it looks," she said.

"You're doing great," he said, and put his hand over hers.

"Thanks," she said, and her smile made his gut do strange things.

"Well, well," a male voice said. "A new couple. What would Joe say?"

Colton glanced up to see Billy Hall, Joe's best friend, sneering at Stacey and him.

"Hey, Billy. How are you doing?" Colton asked as politely as he could manage.

"I'm doing great. I just wonder what Joe would think if he found out one of his groomsmen was kissing his ex," Billy said.

"Joe is history," Stacey said. "He hasn't been around for over a year."

Billy pursed his lips. "Oooh, that's harsh. He might not like that."

"How would you know?" Colton asked.

"We talk every now and then," Billy said.

"You ever tell him what a useless piece he was to leave Stacey and his child?"

Billy gave an awkward shrug. "Well, no. He's my friend. I couldn't call him names." Billy paused. "But I could tell him his ex was taking revenge on him by getting involved with one of his best friends. How you like those leftovers?"

Without a pause, Colton rose and shook Billy hard.

Stunned, Billy stumbled backward. "What the—"

"Don't insult Stacey again," Colton said, clenching and unclenching his fist. "Ever."

"Hey, I was just taking up for Joe," Billy said.

"He doesn't need you to take up for him. He's doing fine," Colton said. "He isn't getting up in the middle of the night to take care of a baby. He's not giving Stacey one dime of support."

Billy's eyes widened, and he lifted his hands. "Okay, okay. I get your message." He turned toward Stacey. "Sorry," he said and walked away, wiggling his shoulders as if he were trying to straighten out his spine.

His heart still slamming against his rib cage, he sat down and took another long sip of beer. "Sorry about that," he said.

She pulled his hands into hers. "That was very nice of you. Not necessary, but—"

"Very necessary," he said. "You don't deserve that. Joe's not here. He hasn't done anything to redeem himself in this situation."

She lifted his hand to her lips and kissed it. "I'm not thinking about Joe anymore."

Colton felt a dozen emotions slamming through him, but the way she kissed his fist made his heart turn over like a tumbleweed. "You deserve better."

"I'm getting better," she told him.

They finished their drinks, and Colton drove Stacey home. What he wanted was to bring her to his bed and make love to her, but that wasn't going to happen tonight. He stopped the car and she immediately unfastened her seat belt and pulled his face toward hers. She took his mouth in a kiss that blasted through him like a ball of fire. Sweet Stacey had somehow turned into a sexy tigress, and he was reaping the benefit.

She slid her hands over his chest down to his abdomen and lower. Colton was torn between telling her to stop and begging her to continue. At the same time, his hands moved of their own volition to her breasts. With her coat open, he tugged at her sweater and slid his hands upward.

She continued kissing him, devouring him with her delicious mouth. She reached to unbuckle his belt at the same time the floodlights spilled over the front yard of her parents' home.

"Whoa," he said, stilling her hands even though he was dying for her to continue. He could just imagine her mother or father coming out for a friendly chat.

"What? Why?" she asked, looking at him with such a sensual, needy gaze that he could hardly stand it.

"Lights came on," he said gently and pulled her into an embrace.

Stacey gave a low growl of frustration. "This is ridiculous. We're adults, not teenagers."

His heart slamming into his chest at what felt like a hundred miles an hour, he took a deep breath. "I'll figure something out."

She sighed, then leaned her forehead against his chest. "Pretty crazy. Who would have thought I would be taking a cold shower because my best friend's brother is making me too hot?"

"You were hot before I came around," he said.

"You didn't notice before," she reminded him.

"I wasn't supposed to notice," he told her, rubbing her soft cheek with his hand. "You belonged to somebody else," he said, thinking of Joe. Joe, who hadn't stood by her when he should have.

After her date with Colton, Stacey felt as if she had a little more bounce in her step. Although she was still juggling her household commitments and taking care of Piper, she was thrilled to book her first tutoring session on Thursday afternoon. A mom with an elementary-school-age boy named Frasier brought her son to the ranch for Stacey to work some magic on him by helping him with math.

Stacey injected as much enthusiasm into the session as possible, but Frasier seemed quite listless. At one point he even laid his head down on the kitchen table. Concerned that he might be sick, Stacey mentioned the boy's condition to his mother. She felt a little guilty accepting the money from Frasier's parent, but made a mental note to perhaps give him an extended or free session in the future.

As soon as the boy left, Piper awakened from her nap. Stacey changed the baby, then carried her into the kitchen. "What a good girl to sleep all the way through my tutoring session. You're the best, aren't you?" she said to Piper as she gave her daughter a bottle. Piper sucked down her bottle in no time, and Stacey patted her back to help counter air bubbles.

"There my girls are," her mother said as she entered the house with bags of groceries. "Let me help you with those," Stacey said and pulled out a quilt for Piper. "Looks like you bought out the store."

Her mother laughed. "This was my big trip. I went to Vicker's Corners. Of course, if you add in gas, it may be a wash. But the grocery store there has a much better selection, and the prices are a little better."

Stacey rushed to her mother's sedan to help bring in the rest of the bags of groceries. "I see that you picked up some baby formula and baby food. I can reimburse you for that since I had my first tutoring session," Stacey said proudly.

Her mother smiled at her. "I forgot about that. How did it go?"

"Okay, except I hope that little boy wasn't sick. He sure didn't act like he felt well. I hope it will go better next time," she said.

"Oh, dear," her mother said. "I've heard there are a couple things going around. One is a quick but nasty stomach virus. Make sure you wash your hands."

"Good point. And I'll wipe down the table," she said. Stacey cleaned her hands and the table and helped put the groceries away as quickly as possible. She knew Piper would be wanting some food. Sure enough, just as Stacey unloaded the last bag, Piper let out a squawk.

"You go ahead and get her. I can take care of the rest," Mama Jeanne said.

Stacey put the baby in her high chair and pulled out a jar of pureed green beans. "Yum, yum," Stacey said. "Green vegetables."

Not Piper's favorite, but she must have been hungry because she eagerly consumed the first few bites. "She looks like a little bird when she eats from the spoon."

"She'll be reaching for that spoon any time now, and every mealtime will turn into a mess. Mark my words," her mother said.

"No problem. I'll just need a washcloth or paper towel. Oh, I meant to tell you that Piper and I will be riding with Colton to the Rothwell wedding on Saturday. The Rothwells are lucky that the Jergens offered them the use of their heated barn for their reception. I'm sure that's why they were able to invite so many people."

"Seems as if you and Colton are spending more and more time together," her mother said.

Stacey hesitated, then glanced at her mother. "You may as well offer your opinion on it, since everyone else has."

"Well, I wouldn't dream of interfering," her mother said. "Colton is a fine, fine young man. I just hope you two won't rush into, well, the physical aspect of a relationship. After all, you have a young baby."

Stacey gaped at her mother. "Mama, do you really think I would turn around and get pregnant again?"

"We're a very fertile family," her mother said. "Colton is likely quite the virile male and—"

Stacey covered her ears. "I don't want to discuss this anymore," she said. "It's not like Colton and I have lots of opportunities, between him living at his parents' house and me living at mine. Add in a baby and, oh, my gosh—"

"It's not that I don't approve of Colton because I very much do," her mother continued as if Stacey hadn't spoken. "I just don't want you to get into a situation where—"

"Stop," Stacey said. "Stop, stop, stop. Please."

Her mother pressed her lips together. "I like Colton," her mother said. "I like him better than I ever liked Joe. Your father does, too."

"Did you run into anyone interesting at the store?" Stacey asked because she had to change the subject, and it seemed that her mother knew everyone within a thirty-mile radius.

"As a matter of fact I did," her mother said. "Laurel Fortune was buying avocados in the produce department when I was there. She's such a sweet girl. Gave me a hug right away. I asked her how married life was, and she said the married part was great, but that she and Sawyer are very upset about the recent accident at their flight school."

"Oh, that's right. Did she say how Orlando is doing?" Stacey asked.

"He's still in the hospital, but they think he will recover. It may take a long time. She said how thankful she and Sawyer were that you were able to come and help stabilize Orlando until the paramedics arrived."

"I was glad I could help, but I was very concerned when I left," Stacey said.

"Don't dare tell anyone, but Laurel confided in me that the investigation has just started, but she and Sawyer are worried that it may not have been an accident."

Stacey gasped. "Oh, no. That would have been horrible. She thinks someone may have deliberately done something to cause the crash?"

"They don't know, but they're suspicious. Not everyone is happy about Fortunes coming to Horseback Hollow," her mother said, a worried expression on her face.

"Oh, that's ridiculous. It's not as if the Fortunes

are trying to take over the whole town. And why would they? They're all about making money, and there's not that much money to be made in Horse-back Hollow."

"The Fortunes aren't all about money," her mother corrected her. "They've made the best from their op-portunities and profited from them. Don't forget they are very active in charitable causes." Her mother took a breath. "And there's the fact that my brother James tried to give me a huge sum of money, although I probably shouldn't bring that up because the whole subject can get some people worked up."

Stacey couldn't help thinking of her brother Chris, who was still upset that her mother hadn't accepted the Fortune money; but she didn't say it aloud be-cause she didn't want to add to her mother's misery.

"Stacey, are you angry that I turned down that money?" her mother asked in a quiet voice.

Surprised that her mother would ask her, Stacey shook her head. "You did what you thought was right. Do I wish I had the financial assurance to make sure that Piper will always have what she needs? Sure, but I know I can take care of that. Maybe not right now, but I'll make it happen. In the meantime, Piper and I both have something much more important than money. We have your love and support, and that's worth far more than money."

Her mother sniffed and walked across the room to hug her daughter. Stacey closed her eyes at the sensation of her mother's loving arms around her.

This, more than anything, was what she wanted to be able to give Piper the rest of her life.

"It makes me so proud to know what a good heart and soul you have. It makes me feel as if your father and I did something right," Jeanne said.

"Mama, I can assure you that I'll make plenty of mistakes, but you gave me a good heart and a strong sense of right and wrong. I also appreciate the value of hard work. Piper and I will be fine," she said, thrilled because she was finally starting to believe it.

Colton put on his tie and jacket and took one last glance in the mirror. This would be his first planned, semiformal evening with Stacey and Piper. He wanted it to go as well as possible. He hoped Piper was in a good mood because that could make a big difference.

He strode toward the front door.

"Woo-hoo, you look great," his mother called.

Colton smiled and turned to meet her gaze. "Thanks, Mom. You look great yourself."

"Well, thank you, sweetheart," she said, and moved toward him to give him a kiss on his cheek. "You going to pick up Stacey and her baby?"

"I am," he said. "I'll see you at the wedding and reception."

"You look good," his mother said. "She's a lucky girl."

"Thanks," he said. *I'm a lucky guy.*

He drove to the Joneses' ranch and knocked on

the door. He waited a couple moments, and Stacey finally answered the door.

"Sorry," she said. "I haven't been feeling great, and it took extra time to get Piper ready. The great news is she seems to be in a good mood."

"I'm all for Piper being in a good mood," he said, and studied Stacey for a moment. "You look a little pale. Are you sure you want to go?"

"I'm sure," she said. "This will pass. I probably haven't had enough water. I've been busy all day long."

"If you're sure," he said.

"I'm sure," she said and smiled. "Let's go."

Colton helped Stacey and Piper into Stacey's car, then got behind the wheel. He drove down the driveway of the Joneses' ranch and turned onto the main road. Stacey's silence bothered him. He drove a few miles down the road.

"I need you to stop," Stacey said. "I feel sick."

Colton immediately pulled to the side of the road. Stacey stumbled out of the car and got sick on the side of the road. He wasn't sure if he should comfort her or leave her alone. After a few moments, she got back in the car.

"I'm sorry, but I don't think I should go to the wedding. I think I caught a stomach virus from the little boy I was tutoring. Please take me back home," she said, and leaned her head against the headrest.

"Right away," he said, and made a gentle U-turn in the middle of the road. He took a quick glance at her and saw that she was taking deep breaths. He pushed the button to lower the passenger window.

"Thank you," she said.

Colton pulled into the driveway and stopped in front of the house. Stacey flew out of the car. "I'm sorry. I'll get Piper in a couple minutes," she said, and raced through the front door of the house.

Colton sat in the car, staring after her. Piper squirmed and cooed. It wasn't an unhappy sound, just an acknowledgment that the car had stopped. He took a deep breath but didn't glance back at the baby. He suspected that if he looked at her, she might start squawking.

He waited two more minutes, but there was no sign of Stacey. Well, darn, he was going to have to take Princess Piper inside. Stepping out of the driver's seat, he turned to the backseat and searched for the release of the safety seat. Piper squirmed, but she didn't yell at him. He finally found it and pulled her into his arms. Slamming the door behind him, he trudged up the steps to the house and walked inside to complete silence in the house.

Hearing the flush of a commode from the back of the house, he walked farther inside. "Stacey?" he called, once, twice, but there was no answer.

Colton sighed and looked at Piper. "Looks like it's me and you kid," he said. He suddenly realized he'd left the magic bag in the car and returned to retrieve it. The second time Colton entered the house, he decided not to call out to Stacey. She was clearly ill. That left him with one task, taking care of Piper.

"So, how's your diaper? Can you give me a little warning if you're going to do a complete blowout?" he said. "I'll need a whole box of those wipe things."

Piper looked at him and lifted her finger to his mouth.

"Is that your way of saying shut up? I thought women wanted men to talk more," he said.

Piper made garbled baby language, but it wasn't fussy, so Colton had hope. "You know, this isn't that much different than talking with most women. Most of the time I don't understand what they're saying."

Piper continued with her baby talk.

"I wonder if you know what you're saying," he said. "I should probably check your diaper, even though I don't want to."

Colton gave a peek and a touch. "Just wet," he said, excited in a way that he could never explain to a bunch of guys at the bar. "No poo. I can do this," he said, and put her down on the sofa and changed her diaper.

"Time for a bottle?" he asked and pulled one out of the magic bag.

Piper reached for it. He sank down on the couch while she sucked down the formula. When she was finished, she looked as if she were in a stupor. He propped her up on his leg. She let out a belch that would rival that of a trucker's.

"Whoa, that was impressive," he said and patted her on the back.

Piper let out another loud, extremely unfeminine belch.

"Way to go," he said.

Piper looked up at him and gave him a milky smile. That smile melted his heart. She was a sweetheart. In some dark part of his mind, he couldn't help wondering how Joe could have left her. How could he give up the opportunity to be a father to this sweet little girl?

Chapter Ten

Piper spit up a little on his suit's pant leg. Colton bit his lip, remembering the blowout at the festival. *Could be worse,* he thought, and removed his coat and tie. If Piper ruined his shirt, he could wash it. The tie and coat were more problematic. He lifted her in his arms and walked around the kitchen.

Colton wanted to check on Stacey, but he also wanted to give her some privacy. He'd had a couple stomach viruses in his life, and all he'd wanted to do was lie on the bathroom floor and pray for relief.

Piper began to babble again. Colton was just thanking his lucky stars that the sounds she was making were happy ones. "So, who do you like better? Spurs or Mavericks?"

Colton carried Piper around for a half an hour. It

seemed the easiest way to keep her happy. She grew drowsy in his arms, though, and he didn't know if he should put her down for the night. Plus, he was worried about Stacey. He meandered down the hallway to Stacey's room.

"Hey, Stacey," he said and tapped at the door. "Are you okay?"

"No," she called. "My stomach has been inhabited by an alien, and it has turned itself inside out."

He swallowed a grin. It must be a good sign that she could joke. "Can I do anything for you?"

"Just make sure Piper is taken care of if I croak," she said.

His heart squeezed tight. "Don't joke about that," he said.

Silence stretched between them. "I'm not gonna croak," she said. "I'm just gonna wish I could croak."

"Are you sure I can't get anything for you? Water? Soda?" he asked.

"Maybe some soda," she said. "Clear soda," she clarified.

"Done," he said and went to the kitchen. Juggling Piper from one arm to the other, he searched the refrigerator and found a can of seltzer. He poured it into a glass with ice and took it back to her bedroom.

"Got the soda," he said, knocking at the door.

A moment later, the door opened, and Stacey looked up at him as she propped herself against the doorjamb. He could honestly say she looked like death warmed over. She was pale, and her eyes were red-rimmed. "I can only take a sip," she said, and reached out to take a tiny drink.

"Are you sure you don't need to go to the hospital in Lubbock?" he asked. "You look pretty bad."

"I'm in the worst part of the virus," she said. "I just need to stay hydrated. One sip at a time." She closed her eyes. "I need to lie down. Can you watch Piper a little longer?"

"Yes, I just need to know—"

"Thanks," she said and shut the door.

Colton looked at the door for a long moment, then looked at Piper. Her eyes moved in a slow blink. "You look very sleepy," he said. "But I don't want you to wake up in the middle of the night. Maybe a late-night snack?"

He returned to the den and pulled out the magic bag. Rifling through it, he found a jar of peaches. "Sound good?" he said to her.

She drooped against his shoulder. Colton opened the jar and fed her while she rested in his arms. It required far more coordination than it took to wrestle a calf and brand it.

Piper scarfed down the pureed peaches and let out a hearty burp. Colton figured a poop was coming any moment. He felt a sudden surge of warmth on his legs. "Wait, wait, wait," he said, and lifted her up before she ruined his suit pants.

He laid her down on a blanket and grabbed the whole container of wipes. "I can do this," he said to himself. "I've done it before." Colton opened Piper's diaper and winced. Quickly, he cleaned her up and fastened her new diaper only to have her refill it.

"Oh, Lord, help me," he muttered and started cleaning her up again. Sprinkling powder on her, he fastened yet another diaper on her. Taking the little girl in his arms, Colton tossed the two dirty diapers into the kitchen can and walked toward the nursery.

Rummaging around the room, he found a gown. With some trouble, Colton removed Piper's shoes, tights and dress, then pulled on the gown. She whined at him several times.

"Cut me some slack. I haven't done this before," he said. He caught sight of some booties and pulled them on her feet. "Comfy?" he asked.

She wiggled and stared up at him. He stared back at her for a long moment and felt as if he was seeing the beginning and ending of the earth in her eyes. He couldn't look away.

Piper wiggled again, and he shook his head. He must have imagined that strange feeling, he thought. He picked her up and paced around the room. After a few moments, he decided to try out the rocking chair. He rocked her for several moments, then set her down in her crib on her back.

Bracing himself for her cry, he held his breath and waited. Colton counted to one hundred. No sound from Piper. He almost couldn't believe it.

Leaving the room and carefully closing the door behind him, he glanced back at Stacey's room. He wondered if he should check on her. Lost in a quandary, he stared at her door.

"Is there a problem?" Stacey's mother asked.

Colton nearly jumped out of his skin. He'd been so focused on Stacey and Piper he hadn't heard Stacey's parents enter the house. "Stacey got sick on the way to the wedding," he whispered, not wanting to awaken Piper. "We came back, but she was too sick to take care of the baby. I looked after Piper, and she's fallen asleep."

"If there's one thing I know, it's not to wake a sleeping baby," Jeanne said.

Colton smiled. "I'm with you on that, but I'm a little worried about Stacey. Would you mind checking on her?"

Jeanne disappeared into Stacey's room for a moment, then returned to the hallway. "She's falling asleep as we speak. I think the worst of the virus is past. I feel bad that this was her first experience tutoring."

"Knowing her, she won't quit," Colton said.

"Very true," Jeanne said to him and squeezed his arm. "Thank you for looking out for Stacey and Piper tonight."

"Piper was a breeze," Colton said. "I just wish I could have helped Stacey a little more."

"You helped her by taking care of Piper." Jeanne gave him a considering glance. "Looks like Piper may be getting used to you."

"I think I just got lucky with her tonight," Colton

said. "I always feel as if I'm spinning the roulette wheel with that little one."

"Don't underestimate yourself," Jeanne said.

"If you say so," he said. "You sure you don't want me to hang around a little longer in case you need an extra set of hands?" he asked, feeling oddly reluctant to leave Stacey and Piper.

"I'll be fine," she said and chuckled. "I had to juggle babies when they were sick many times when my children were young."

"I guess so," he said, and felt a little foolish. Of course Jeanne Fortune Jones knew what she was doing. The woman had seven children, after all. "I'll head on home, then. Tell Stacey to give me a call when she's feeling better."

"I'll do that," her mother said. "Thank you again for looking after both of them."

He nodded and collected his tie, jacket and hat. "Good night," he said, and headed toward his truck. Colton had an odd, empty, gnawing sensation in his gut as he drove home. He should have been relieved to hand over the reins of Piper and Stacey's care to Jeanne, but he wasn't. Taking care of a temperamental baby while Stacey was sick? It should have been one of the most miserable evenings of his life. He should have run screaming the second Stacey's mom came home. Instead, he'd taken to the task quickly—and more easily than he'd imagined possible. And walking away from Piper—and her beautiful mother—was getting tougher by the day.

Something was wrong, very wrong. He needed to rethink all this.

Over the next couple of days, Colton brooded over his relationship with Stacey. With everyone else voicing an opinion about it, he needed to figure out his own thoughts. In a different situation, in a different—bigger, more crowded—town, he and Stacey could allow their relationship to develop naturally with little intervention. Since, however, both of them lived at home with their families, it seemed they were overwhelmed by prying eyes. Colton had feelings for Stacey and Piper, stronger feelings than he wanted to have at the moment, but he wasn't sure what he should do about those feelings—or what he wanted to do about them. Colton wanted to take things slow. He wanted to be careful. There was a baby involved, for Pete's sake. At the same time, he wanted so badly to be with Stacey and Piper. And yet he couldn't stop thinking about Joe. Why had he abandoned Stacey and Piper? How could he have? Colton had known that Joe's father hadn't been around much, but surely that wouldn't have prevented Joe from being the husband and father Stacey and Piper needed.

The quandary frustrated him so much that he worked outside until it turned dark. Maybe if he wore himself out, he would fall asleep without thinking about Stacey and Piper. He walked into the house with two goals in mind, a meal followed by a shower, but he caught sight of his sister Rachel grading papers in the den.

"Oh, there you are," she called out to him, jumping up from the sofa. "I thought you might have fallen in a hole."

"No, but I've been digging a few," he said, and continued to the kitchen. He foraged through the refrigerator and found some leftover baked chicken and rice. "How's life as a student teacher?"

"Busy, busy. But not so busy that I can't offer to babysit so you and Stacey can have an evening out by yourselves," she said, and shot him a cheeky grin.

"That's nice of you," he said and heated his leftovers in the microwave. "I'll have to check with Stacey when she's feeling better."

"Oh, she's feeling better," Rachel said. "I talked to her today. She hasn't called you yet because she's embarrassed that she got sick and you had to take care of Piper."

"I didn't mind taking care of Piper. I was glad to do what I could to help Stacey when she felt so bad," he said impatiently.

"What's wrong with you?" Rachel asked. "You seem grumpy."

"I'm just tired," he said, pulling a mug from the cabinet. "I've been up since the crack of dawn, working outside in this wind."

"Hmm," she said, crossing her arms over her

chest. "Are you sure it isn't anything about Stacey? You're not leading her on, are you?"

Frustration ripped through him, and he slammed the cabinet door. Swearing under his breath, he shook his head. "That's part of the problem," he said. "Everyone is watching every move Stacey and I make. Everyone feels the need to offer an opinion. Did you ever think we don't need your opinion? Did you ever think we don't want to hear what you think?" he challenged his sister.

Rachel drew back, her eyes widened in surprise. "Why are you so touchy? I just said you shouldn't lead her on. You know that, too."

"Then why did you feel the need to tell me?" he asked. The microwave dinged, signaling his food was ready. He poured himself a cup of decaf and took his dinner to the table.

"I just thought I should make sure," she said. "Stacey has been through a hard time. You know what happened with Joe."

"I do," he said. "You think I should stop seeing her?"

Rachel blinked. "Well, no. Why would you say that?"

"Because it's starting to look as if everyone either wants me to make a lifetime commitment right off the bat or pull back. Those are two extreme choices, considering we just started seeing each other. I've never dated a woman with a child before. I don't know if I'm ready to be an instant father. I don't know that much about kids, let alone babies."

Rachel sank onto the kitchen chair across from him and sighed. "This kinda stinks for you," she said. "Everyone is so excited for Stacey to get involved with a man who would be both a good husband and father that they're jumping to conclusions. Do you wish you hadn't started seeing her?"

"No. I *do* wish everyone would stay out of our business, but I don't see how that's going to happen. I have feelings for Stacey, and for Piper, too, but I have to figure out how to slow this down and get it more under control," he said.

Rachel nodded. "I know control has always been important to you, but good luck with it. I hear it doesn't always work in the romance department. My offer to babysit Piper sometime still stands. Otherwise, I'll let you figure this out on your own."

After eating his dinner and taking a hot shower, Colton went to bed, but he still didn't sleep well. He tossed and turned, trying to figure out what he should do about Stacey.

It was so cold that by afternoon the next day, he decided not to torture himself by staying outside any longer and chose to work in one of the barns close to the house. Hearing the barn door swing open, he turned to see Stacey standing in the doorway holding Piper in one hand and a basket in the other.

His gut took an involuntary dip at the sight of them. Both pairs of eyes were trained on him expectantly. "Hey there," Stacey said, and lifted her lips in a hesitant smile. "Have you recovered from taking care of us on Saturday night?"

"I think the more important question is whether you've recovered. How are *you* feeling?" he asked.

"Much better. It was a twenty-four hour virus. I've been holding my breath because I was afraid either you or Piper might catch it. You haven't felt sick, have you?"

"No, but I'm lucky that way. I don't get sick very often," he said, thinking he might not have gotten the stomach virus, but he still felt as if he'd caught some sort of emotional virus that was keeping him bothered and interrupting his sleep.

"I'm glad to hear that," she said. "I wanted to thank you. Seems like I'm doing that a lot lately," she said and smiled again. "I made some chocolate-chip cupcakes for you. You seemed to like the other ones."

She lifted the basket toward him, and he moved forward to take it. "You didn't have to do that, but thank you."

"My pleasure," she said, and the silence stretched between them. He felt her searching his face, but he couldn't offer her any answers if he didn't have any answers for himself.

She cleared her throat. "Well, I guess I'll go now. Thank you again for taking care of us on Saturday."

"I'm glad I could help," he said, and watched her walk out the barn door. Part of him screamed that he should go after her. But Colton had no clue what he would say.

* * *

Stacey walked away from the Fosters' barn with a lump in her throat. She couldn't bear to return to her house right away, so she drove into town and wandered around the Superette with Piper perched on her hip. Stacey knew she'd gotten her hopes up about Colton, and she clearly shouldn't have.

She picked up a couple bananas for Piper and seriously checked out the chocolate bars.

"Oh, no," a female voice said from behind her. "I'm counting on the hope that I won't crave chocolate once I deliver this baby. You're scaring me, Stacey."

Stacey turned around to find Ella Mae Jergens looking at the candy-bar display. She smiled at the pregnant woman. "I've always loved chocolate," she said. "Pregnancy didn't make it any worse, so don't base your fear on me."

"You're so sweet," Ella Mae said. "I really have to watch my weight. I'm married to an important man, and there will always be women chasing after him."

Stacey felt sorry for Ella Mae if she thought her husband would stray due to a little pregnancy weight. "I'm sure he adores you and sees you as truly beautiful."

Ella Mae smiled. "You've always been a nice girl. I was glad to hear you've been spending time with Colton Foster. Other people have been saying the only reason you got involved with Colton was to get back at Joe, but I didn't believe them. You ignore those rumors and hold your head high, Stacey. You deserve a good man."

Stacey's heart tightened with distress. "What other people have been saying that?" she asked. The only time she'd heard the horrible rumor was from Billy, Joe's friend.

"Oh, I don't know," Ella Mae said. "I heard it from my mother, who heard it from someone else. You know how this town is. Any kind of gossip, true or false, spreads like wildfire. Don't pay any attention to it. It will pass. But I will get just one candy bar," she said, and grabbed one from the display. "Here comes my mother. I'm spending the day with her. Take care, now," Ella Mae said, and headed for the checkout.

Sick from Ella Mae's comments, Stacey put the bananas back and fled the store. Could the day get any worse?

After Stacey returned home, she couldn't muster much conversation. Her mother tried to make small talk as the two baked side by side in the kitchen, but Stacey just wasn't in the mood. She wondered if having to take care of Piper on Saturday night had pushed Colton over the edge. Even though he'd always been sweet to the baby, he wasn't her birth father. He may have looked at his experience Saturday night and feared for his future.

Or had he heard more about the nasty rumor that Ella Mae had repeated to Stacey? Stacey knew that people in Horseback Hollow liked to gossip, but she was sick over the latest outright lie that was spreading like fire.

"You're very quiet, Stacey," her mother said as Stacey washed some pots and pans. "Are you feeling ill again?"

"No, no. I'm fine," she said, and dried the lid to a pot.

"Is something bothering you? I talked with your father last night about your financial concerns and he doesn't want you worrying," she said. "If you need more money—"

"I don't," Stacey said. "I got another student lined up for tutoring this week, but I know I'm not going to be making a lot of money right now. I'll figure that out later."

Her mother nodded and spread out a dish towel on the counter to dry. "Okay. Is there anything else on your mind? You know you can talk to me."

Stacey inhaled and sighed. "I'm not sure this thing with Colton is going to work out," she confessed and fought the urge to cry. She wiped the already clean counter for the third time.

"Why not?" her mother asked. "Did you decide you don't have feelings for him?"

"Oh, no," Stacey said, and swallowed her deep disappointment. "I have feelings for him, but I just don't think Colton is ready to be a daddy."

"Well, you could have fooled me. You should have seen how he hovered over Piper on Saturday night," her mother said with a firm nod of her head.

"That was just one night, Mama," she said. "He may be thinking he's not ready to take us on a full-time basis," Stacey said. "I can't really blame him. A lot of men wouldn't want to father someone else's child."

"You can't possibly believe that," her mother said. "Colton Foster is a good man. He would always do what's right."

"But how is it right for him to take on the responsibility for a child that isn't his?" Stacey countered. "How is it fair?"

Her mother frowned. "I think you may be jumping the gun. You need to give Colton a little time."

"I'm trying not to pressure him, but everyone we run into seems to want to make a comment or give advice about us seeing each other. I don't know," she said, shrugging even though she was miserable. "Plus, I haven't told you, but there's a terrible rumor going around about us. Some people seem to think that the only reason I've started spending time with Colton is to get back at Joe."

"Well, that's a complete fabrication. How would Joe even know that you're seeing Colton since he hasn't bothered to check on you or his baby?" her mother asked, indignantly. "If I were a lesser person, I could wish some bad things on that boy. Leaving you in the lurch like that. With a note, no less. Thinking about it still makes my blood boil."

Stacey knotted her fingers together, then pulled

them apart and knotted them again. "This is turning into a big mess. I think I'd better give Colton some space."

Jeanne Marie Fortune Jones stepped in line at the tiny Horseback Hollow post office. Her mind hopped and skipped to different issues weighing on her—Stacey's romantic predicament and her troubled son Christopher—as she patiently waited her turn.

"Hello, Jeanne. Good to see you," Olive Foster said as she got in line behind her neighbor. "How are you?"

"Good, thank you. I see you have packages," Jeanne said. "Christmas gifts you need to return?"

Olive nodded. "I overdid it this year, and my husband, Frank, can be so hard to please," she said with a heavy sigh. "What about you?"

"I'm sending a letter to my—" She broke off and smiled. "My sister in England, and another to my brother James. I know everyone uses email these days, but I thought both of them might enjoy a letter."

"That's nice of you. Are you still getting used to being a Fortune?" Olive asked.

Jeanne nodded and stepped forward. "It's still hard to believe, but it's wonderful having brothers and a sister and all these new nieces and nephews."

"I think it's so sweet that your children added the Fortune name," Olive said. "It shows a lot of family unity."

"Not all of them have," Jeanne said, thinking of Liam. "But they're all adults and it would be wrong for me to push them. They should make this decision on their own. It's not a perfect situation, but I'm glad most of them are interested in getting to know their new family." Jeanne thought, too, of her son Chris and the resentment he held against the Fortunes and their wealth. She wished he could let go of his ill feelings, because she knew he would be much happier if he did.

"How is Stacey doing? I heard she got sick the other night," Olive said.

"Yes, she did, but she's much better now. Colton took care of the baby during the worst part of it. You've raised a fine young man."

Olive beamed with pride. "Thank you. We're very blessed with both our children," she said.

Jeanne hesitated, wondering if she should say anything else. "I know that Stacey has enjoyed spending time with him lately."

"Yes, we are pleased about that. Stacey's a wonderful young lady."

Silence stretched for a long moment between them. "Of course, I understand if things don't work out. They've just started seeing each other, and we don't know what will happen in the long run."

Olive looked pensive and stepped closer to Jeanne. "It's none of my business, but is something wrong between them?" she asked in a lowered voice. "Colton hasn't said a word about her the past few days, and he seems a bit withdrawn."

"Well, I have to confess I've been concerned lately, too. Even though I love Colton, I told Stacey to be careful about getting involved again. She didn't seem to appreciate me giving my opinion," Jeanne said. "It's hard to hold your tongue when you worry about your children."

"I know what you're saying. I hate to admit it, but I asked my husband to speak to Colton about spending time with Stacey. I wanted it made clear that he shouldn't take advantage of her." Olive winced. "I wonder if I should have kept my thoughts to myself."

"They're adults and very responsible," Jeanne said. "I'd hate to think I helped to mess up anything by sticking my nose in their business."

"Me, too," Olive said miserably. "I suppose it wouldn't help to bring it up to Colton in casual conversation."

"Probably not," Jeanne said.

Olive sighed. "I guess we'll just have to do what we should have done from the beginning. Be quiet and hope for the best."

Jeanne nodded in agreement, but she worried about her daughter. Stacey had already been hurt enough. "Please don't tell anyone, but someone has started a terrible rumor," she confided to Olive.

"About Stacey and Colton?" Olive asked in surprise.

"Yes. Someone, and we don't know who, has been

saying that the only reason Stacey has been spending time with Colton was to get back at Joe because he left her. The reason I'm telling you is because I want you to know that is absolutely not true. I think Stacey has fallen for your son, but she feels as if she needs to back off and give him some breathing room."

Olive frowned and shook her head. "Why is it that people find it necessary to gossip about people who are just trying to do their best? If someone is stupid enough to repeat that rumor to me, I'll set them straight. You can count on it."

Jeanne felt a surge of gratitude inside her at Olive's protectiveness of Stacey. "You've always been the best neighbors we could have. I would love it if we could be in-laws," Jeanne said. "I'll be saying my prayers and crossing my fingers that our children will work this out."

Chapter Eleven

Piper had lost her favorite binky. Or, *someone* had lost Piper's favorite pacifier. Perhaps her father's hunting dog had eaten it. The who didn't matter. The fact was that Stacey needed to get a replica of the favorite binky immediately. As Stacey headed out the door on a cold, rainy winter night, Jude called out, "Hey, do you mind picking up a burger for me from The Grill?"

"You just ate chicken potpie," she retorted, pulling up her hood.

"I'm still hungry," he said mournfully as he walked into the den with Piper in his arms.

Stacey couldn't turn him down. He was doing her a favor by pacing with Piper, who had been crying without stop for nearly an hour. With the windshield wipers whipping from side to side, Stacey drove to the Superette, praying that she would find the treasured binky. The rain spit in her face as she rushed through the door. She studied the poor selection of binkies and chose two—just in case—then checked out.

Next stop, The Grill. She went inside and placed the take-out order. Pacing the front of the restaurant, she heard the jukebox playing one of her favorite songs in the bar and peeked inside at what the other half were doing tonight.

She caught a quick glimpse of Colton nursing a beer and froze. He must have sensed her looking at him because he glanced up, and his gaze locked with hers. Wanting to avoid him, she pulled back inside and prayed Jude's burger would be ready soon. She haunted the cash register. *"Hurry, hurry,"* she whispered under her breath.

"Hey, what are you doing out on a wicked night like tonight?" Colton asked from behind her.

Stacey took a deep breath and turned around. "I could ask the same of you."

Colton shrugged. "Cabin fever. I just needed to get away from the house. What are you doing here?"

"Piper lost her favorite binky, and I had to try to find one like it. Jude asked me to pick up a burger for him. He's pacing with Piper, so it's the least I can do, even though he's already had dinner."

"You want to come in here while you wait?"

She shook her head. "No, thanks." She glanced

at the checkout, but there was no sign of her take-out order. "Listen, I just want you to know the rumors aren't true."

He frowned at her. "What rumors?" he asked.

"About me." She swallowed over the sudden lump that formed in her throat. She thought she'd gotten control of herself during the past few days. Why had that control evaporated so quickly? "There was a rumor that the only reason I got involved with you was to get back at Joe. I just need you to know that isn't true."

He stared at her in disbelief. "Who said that?"

"Well, I heard from someone who heard from someone from someone, so I don't know. It's just important to me that you know it's not—"

She broke off as an attractive brunette approached Colton from behind and looped her arms around him. "Hey, baby, where'd you go?"

Colton glanced at the woman in surprise. "I thought you were busy with someone else."

She shook her head and nuzzled him seductively. "I was just trying to get your attention."

Colton cleared his throat and looked at Stacey. "Uh, this is Mary," he said.

"Malia," the woman corrected with an indulgent grin. "He's so cute, isn't he?"

"Uh-huh," Stacey said.

"Maria is new in town," he said, still messing up the woman's name. "I just met her tonight."

Stacey couldn't believe her eyes. "Nice to meet

you, Malia. How did you end up in Horseback Hollow?"

"I needed to get off the grid. Violent ex," she said. "This seemed like a good choice."

"I hope it will work out for you," Stacey said, and finally Jude's order was delivered to the register. She was so relieved she nearly shouted. "Oh, there's my takeout. Have a nice evening. I need to get back home." She paid her bill and ran out the door to her car.

Just as she slid onto her seat, Colton caught the door before she could close it. "Hey, that wasn't what you think it was," he said, rain pouring down over his head and jacket.

"It's okay," she forced herself to say. "There are no strings between us. You can do what you want. Malia probably doesn't have any little kids."

"That's not what's important," he said.

"I'm not so sure about that, and I can't say I blame you. If I were a man, I might not want to take on the baggage of a baby that wasn't mine. I understand, Colton. I really do," she said, although she wished things could be different.

Colton shook his head, but she couldn't handle this discussion any longer. Her sadness overwhelmed her. "I need to go," she said, and pulled her car door shut.

Colton called himself ten times a fool during the next twelve hours. He could barely sleep when he thought of the injured expression on Stacey's face. He should have stopped her. He shouldn't have let her go. He should have told her how much he'd missed her and that he wanted to work things out with her. Instead, he'd stood in the rain trying to come to grips with the ridiculous rumor she'd relayed to him.

Colton spent the day working in the barn. The sound of silence, however, echoed inside his mind. Unable to bear the scrutiny of his family, he decided to go into town again and get a burger from The Grill. He didn't know where else to go. This was yet another time when he needed his own place.

After placing his order, Colton carried his burger and fries from the grill to the bar and ordered a beer, hoping he didn't run into Mary or whatever her name was. He stared up at the basketball game playing on the television while he ate his meal.

"Long time, Colton," a voice from his past said.

Colton glanced over his shoulder to see Joe Hitchens. He blinked. "Hey, Joe, what you doing here?"

"I decided to pay a visit from Dallas," Joe said. Colton noticed Joe was a little chubbier than when he'd left Horseback Hollow all those months ago.

"You left town kinda fast," Colton said.

Joe shrugged. "It was a rough time for me."

"For you," Colton said, beginning to seethe. "What about Stacey?"

"She was early enough along that she could have taken care of the pregnancy," Joe said.

"Taken care of the pregnancy?" Colton echoed.

"That's what she did. She delivered that baby and has taken care of her with no help from you."

"I meant," Joe said, lowering his voice, "she could have gotten rid of the pregnancy."

Colton gaped at the man in disbelief. "You mean get rid of Piper?"

"Is that what she named the baby? I heard it was a girl," Joe said.

"But you never bothered to call her or offer any kind of support," Colton said. He pushed aside his food. He had lost his appetite.

"She knew I didn't want a kid. She shouldn't have gotten pregnant," Joe said.

"As if you had nothing to do with it," Colton said, growing angrier with each passing second. "You bastard," he said, standing and punching Joe in the face.

Colton's knuckles throbbed, and Joe covered his face.

"What the—" Joe said. "You know what kind of father I had. I didn't ever want to be a father after the kind of example my dad set. He was gone more than he was with my mom and me."

"That's no excuse. You're the lowest of the low," Colton said in disgust. "I don't know how you can call yourself a man. We've been friends since high school, but I don't recognize you anymore. When did you turn yourself into the kind of person you've become?"

"You must have gotten pretty close to Stacey to be so defensive," Joe said. "Did you go to bed with her?"

It was all Colton could do to keep from hitting Joe again. "Go back to Dallas," he said. "You don't belong here."

"Who do you think you are? Dating my ex? Bros don't cheat on bros. You know the guy code," Joe said.

"What guy code? You haven't been here for over a year. What rights do you have?" Colton asked.

"That baby is mine. That woman was mine," Joe said.

"*Was* is the operative term. What do you know about Piper?" Colton demanded.

Joe narrowed his eyes, then shifted from one foot to the other. "Not much."

"Why are you even here now?" Colton asked. "You haven't been here for months, not even when your baby was born."

Silence stretched between them. "Someone told me you and Stacey had gotten involved," Joe confessed.

"You would come back into town for that, to stake your claim on a woman you ran out on, but not when the baby was born?" Colton asked, shaking his head. "Are you crazy?"

"I should have known you wouldn't understand." Joe rubbed at his cheek where Colton had punched him. "So, is the baby okay?" Joe asked reluctantly.

"She's as close to perfect as a baby can get. She's gorgeous. Big green eyes and blond hair just like Stacey. She's got a kick to her personality. If she doesn't like what you're doing, she'll let you know. But she's the sweetest thing in the world when she falls asleep on your shoulder. Makes you feel as if everything in the world is the way it should be."

Joe stared at Colton. "You love her. You love *my* daughter," he accused.

Colton met Joe's astonished gaze and nodded. "Yeah. I guess I do. I really do."

Joe raked his hand through his hair and shook his head. "I don't know what to say."

"I do," Colton said. "You need to man up or shut up. If you want Stacey and your daughter back, then you need to go tell her. I think Stacey deserves better than you, but there's more involved in this situation. There's Piper," Colton said. "I'll give you twenty-four hours."

Joe stared at him, clearly affronted. "Who are you to tell me I've got twenty-four hours?"

"I'm the man who has changed your baby's diaper, rocked her to sleep and had her poop down my back," Colton said. "Have you done any of that?"

Joe looked at him in hostile silence.

"That's right. You haven't. You've got twenty-four hours. Don't mess with me, Joe. I'm disgusted with you," Colton said, and tossed some cash on the counter and walked away.

The next twenty-four hours passed by in minute-by-minute increments. Colton thought about Stacey and Piper when he drove home, when he took his evening shower, when he brushed his teeth and when he tried to go to sleep. His attempt to sleep was completely futile.

When he got up in the morning, he didn't know how he was going to get through the day, so he did it the only way he knew how. Working. He worked clear through until six that evening. As he walked toward the house, he told himself that he only had an hour and a half to go.

"Hey, sweetheart," his mom said as he walked through the door. "You want some dinner?"

"I'm not that hungry," he muttered.

"Well, you should take in a little nourishment after spending all day outside," she said. "I fixed a pot roast. I think you'll like it."

Colton didn't protest as his mother fussed over him and urged him to take a seat at the kitchen table. In this situation, it was easier to acquiesce than fight her. His mother was clearly in supernurture mode. Colton took a few bites of pot roast and potatoes.

"You must be sick," his mother said. "You're not eating."

"The pot roast is great, but I have some things on my mind, Mom," he told her.

"What?" his mother said. "What's on your mind?"

"I don't want to talk about it," he said and rose from his chair.

"Is it Stacey Fortune Jones?" she asked.

The question stopped him in his tracks. "And what if it is?"

His mother sighed. "Give her the benefit of the doubt. Her mother says she has fallen for you. But don't tell her that I told you," his mother said.

His heart swelled at the possibility that Stacey could have *fallen* for him. He wondered when that had happened. He wondered *if* it had happened. "How do you know?"

"I met up with Jeanne the other day at the post office and we got to talking." His mother broke off and pressed her lips together. "But I'm not going to say anything else. I shouldn't interfere. This is between you and Stacey."

Colton stared at his mother in disbelief. "You give advice and opinions about everything, but now you're clamming up?"

His mother lifted her finger. "Colton, don't you bait me. I'm determined to do the right thing. You and Stacey need to figure out what's best for you," she said and turned away.

Colton, watching the clock every other minute, sighed and put his plate in the fridge to eat later. "Sorry, Mom. I'm just not hungry right now. I'll eat it for lunch tomorrow." Colton grabbed his coat and headed for his truck. Eighteen minutes to go.

He drove around for ten minutes.

Colton spotted a deer crossing the road in front of him and slowed down. The driver of a semi must have panicked, though. Colton tried to swerve out of the incoming path of the truck. But he was too late. The impact jolted him. He heard the sound of glass shattering. Pain seared through him, and everything went black.

Stacey put Piper down with ease and tossed a load of laundry into the washer for lack of anything else to do. She still couldn't get over seeing that other woman pawing Colton. He had appeared surprised, but perhaps that was because he hadn't expected the woman to follow him out of the grill. Stacey suspected Malia was everything Stacey wasn't. Employed, with no baby and no stretch marks. Malia had looked like a girl ready to have a good time, and now that Stacey was a mom, she had to think twice about throwing caution to the wind for the sake of a good time. She had to think about her little Piper.

Still, the image of Colton with Malia made her so edgy she felt as if her nerve endings were being rubbed raw with a wire brush. There wasn't anything she could do about it, she told herself. The fact that Colton hadn't tried to call her in nearly two days spoke volumes.

Stacey turned the television in her bedroom on low volume in hopes of distracting herself, but the reality show just irritated her even more. She brushed her teeth and dressed for bed, praying that she would get some relief with sleep. Just as she pulled back her covers and reached to turn out her lamp, her cell phone vibrated with an incoming call.

Spotting Rachel's number on the ID, Stacey debated letting it go to voice mail. She didn't want to discuss her feelings about Colton right now, especially with his sister. Sighing, she picked up, ready to say she didn't want to talk about Colton.

"Hey, Rachel," Stacey said. "What's up?"

"Oh, Stacey, it's terrible," Rachel said, nearly sobbing. "Colton has been in a bad accident. His truck was hit by a semi. The ambulance is taking him to the Lubbock General E.R."

Stacey's heart turned cold. She tried to make sense of what Rachel had told her. The only thing she knew for certain was that Colton had been hurt. "Do you know anything about his condition? Did they tell you anything?"

"All we know is that he's unconscious, and there may be internal injuries. Mom and Dad are driving to Lubbock in their car, and I'm going in mine. Stacey, I'm scared. I'm afraid I'm going to lose my brother."

For a moment, Stacey couldn't breathe. *She* was afraid of losing Colton, too. Even if they went back to being friends, Stacey didn't want to lose Colton. Just knowing he was alive on the earth gave her a good feeling inside her. He was a wonderful man, and the thought of not being able just to see him again made her feel like crying. Anxiety coursed through her. But some part of her professional training as a nurse kicked in.

"Don't give up yet," she said. "I'm sure he's getting good care."

"Oh, Stacey, I wish you could be here," Rachel said.

"I'm on my way," Stacey promised, even if she

had to drag Piper out of bed. She wanted to be there for Colton. She wanted to be there for his family.

Stacey changed into jeans and a sweater, then awakened her mother and told her the horrible news.

"Oh, no," Jeanne said. "That's terrible. Do you have any idea if they think he'll recover? Poor Olive and Frank must be beside themselves."

"I'd like to go to Lubbock to be with them. I'll take Piper with me, but—"

Her mother shook her head. "No. Absolutely not. I'll watch over her. You go ahead, but please be careful. And call us with any news."

Stacey gave her mother a hug and grabbed a bottle of water before she pulled on her coat and left the house. Driving through the night, she thought about all the times she'd spent with Colton. An image of him playing ball as a child flashed through her head. She remembered playing tag with Rachel, him and her brothers. Later on, when they'd become teenagers and she'd passed him in the hall, he'd never been too cool to wave to her as a younger student.

Now that she knew him as a man, her feelings were even stronger. Yes, he'd become the most sexy man in existence to her, but it was partly due to his tenderness and encouragement. It was partly due to the way that he tried so hard with Piper. How could she possibly resist Colton after all that?

She made the drive in record time and pulled into the parking lot at the hospital. She rushed inside to the E.R. but didn't see any Fosters. Her stomach dipped. She prayed that the worst hadn't happened. Stacey asked the registration desk about Colton, and a few moments later, she was ushered back to a waiting room.

Rachel rose and soared into Stacey's arms. "I'm so glad you're here."

Stacey couldn't help seeing Mr. and Mrs. Foster standing beside a row of chairs. Mrs. Foster's eyes were bloodshot from tears, and Mr. Foster looked dazed and shocked. Stacey's heart went out to them.

"Any news?" she asked.

"He's being examined. They said he's still unconscious," Rachel said, sniffing.

"They're looking after him," Stacey said, but she was so scared. She just couldn't show it. She turned toward Colton's parents and embraced Mrs. Foster.

"Oh, Stacey, I just want him to be okay," Mrs. Foster said.

Stacey squeezed Colton's mother tight. She wanted Colton to be all right, too. More than anything. She took a deep breath, knowing that waiting could be the worst. "Can I get coffee for any of you?"

Rachel and her parents shook their heads, all murmuring *no*.

The vigil began.

The minutes crept by slowly, feeling like days instead of hours. Stacey tried to make small talk but gave up after a half hour had passed. All of them were worried sick. Why hadn't a doctor or nurse entered the waiting room to speak to them?

Stacey was just about to prod someone at the emergency-room desk for details when a doctor walked in, still wearing his surgical scrubs. "Mr. and Mrs. Foster?" he said. "I'm Dr. McMillan. Your son took a hard hit. He has a concussion and some bad bruises. I have to say it's a miracle that your son didn't sustain more serious injuries. We'll keep him under observation until we're sure he's out of the woods from that concussion."

"Oh, stars," Mrs. Foster said, sinking onto a chair.

Stacey's heart was hammering in her head. "How much blood has he lost? Has he been conscious at all? Is there any lung damage? What about—"

"Whoa," the doctor said. "One at a time."

Stacey forced herself to pace her questions, and the doctor answered each one.

"When can the family see him?" she asked.

He glanced at his watch. "Let's give it another few moments," he warned.

The doctor left the room, and Rachel, wiping away the tears in her eyes, grabbed Stacey. "It sounds as if he's going to be okay," she said.

Stacey wanted to see Colton and touch him, check his stats to be sure, but she nodded. "It sounds very good."

Moments later, the Fosters were led back to see Colton in recovery. Stacey paced the waiting room, praying and wishing for Colton. Ten minutes later, a nurse appeared in the doorway. "Stacey, I understand you're Colton Foster's girlfriend. The rest of the family requested your presence."

Stacey nodded and followed the nurse to the recovery room. Colton was receiving fluids and oxygen. Her heart squeezed tight in fear. At the same time, she knew these measures were medically necessary.

"Why does he have all these tubes?" Mr. Foster asked, his face filled with fear.

Rachel reached for Stacey's hand.

"All these things are helping support Colton to recover from his injuries and the accident," Stacey said. "Soon enough, he won't be needing the line for fluids. Later, they'll only give him oxygen as needed. This is the worst, except for any bruising and swelling he may have. It looks like they're taking good care of him. That's what's important."

"Stacey, I'm so glad you're here," Rachel said.

"Me, too," Olive said and grabbed Stacey's hand.

Mr. Foster took a deep breath and looked at his son.

The three of them stood in the recovery area for several moments. "Even though Colton is unconscious, he can hear your voices, so talking is good for him."

Rachel immediately went to Colton's side and started chatting. Her voice suddenly broke. "I love you, big brother. Wake up soon," she said, and kissed him gently on his forehead.

His mother took a turn next. "I'm sorry I didn't

answer your questions tonight," she said and sniffed. "I love you. Everybody loves you."

His father stepped closer. "You're a good man. A good, strong man. Get better, son. We're here for you."

Stacey's throat tightened in a knot of emotion. She hated how much all of them were hurting. She didn't want to think about her own feelings. The three of them looked at her expectantly, as if they wanted her to speak to Colton, too.

Stacey slowly walked to Colton's side and gently touched his shoulder. "Hey, you. What are you doing playing chicken with semis?" She bit her lip. "We want you to get better, but don't work too hard at it. Let the medicine help you," she said.

Colton's eyelids fluttered. He opened his mouth and coughed. "Stacey? Stacey?"

Stunned that he would call her name, she leaned closer. "I'm here. I'm here. What do you need?"

"Joe?" he said.

She frowned. "Joe?"

"Did he come see you?"

Stacey figured Colton must be talking out of his head. "No. I haven't seen Joe," she said, but Colton had fallen asleep.

Chapter Twelve

Stacey sat by Colton's side for the next several hours. She urged Mr. and Mrs. Foster to return home, but Rachel insisted on staying. Colton awakened for short periods. Sometimes he blinked his eyes. He often asked questions as to why he was in the hospital. He asked again about Joe but fell back asleep.

"Why do you think he keeps asking about Joe?" Rachel asked.

"I have no idea," Stacey said. "Joe hasn't been in town for ages."

"Maybe he has amnesia. Maybe this is part of his concussion," Rachel suggested.

"I don't know," Stacey said. "If it keeps happening, maybe we should ask the doctor about it."

Colton's parents returned and shooed both Rachel and Stacey away to take a break. Gritty-eyed and tired, but mostly confident that Colton was on the road to recovery, Stacey returned home and fell into bed. When she awakened, it was early evening, and she checked on Colton via his parents. He'd been moved to a room and was doing much better.

Stacey sighed with relief and spent the rest of the afternoon taking care of Piper. Her daughter seemed thrilled to see her, which eased some of the upset and trauma she'd experienced during the past week. Rocking Piper to sleep was the purest form of therapy for Stacey. She kissed her sweet baby's head and put her to bed. Afterward Stacey updated her mother about Colton and his injuries. Thank goodness, her mother didn't ask any probing questions about Stacey's feelings about Colton. She went to bed, planning to visit Colton the next morning.

The next morning, Stacey dressed Piper in a cute pink outfit and made the hour-long trip to Lubbock. Piper snoozed on and off, and was so quiet Stacey had to check every now and then to make sure the baby was breathing. When they arrived at the hospital, Stacey changed Piper's diaper in the backseat of the car in the parking lot. The cold winter wind whipped around her. Piper's eyes widened like saucers from the chill.

"Wheee, that's breezy, isn't it?" she said, quickly

refastening Piper's pink outfit and pulling her baby up against her.

Stacey tucked Piper under her coat as she made her way to Colton's room, where his parents sat next to him.

"Hi," she said. "I thought you might enjoy some visitors."

Colton looked up, and, seeing Piper, he gave a groggy smile. "Hey, how's the little one doing?"

"Great. She barely made a peep on the way. An hour's drive. There's hope that she will be a good traveler."

"Joe didn't come to see you, did he?" Colton asked.

Stacey slid a questioning glance toward Colton's parents, but his mother just shook her head and rose. "Come on, Frank. Let's get some coffee."

"I just had coffee," Frank said.

"Well, I want some more," Olive said firmly.

Frank sighed and rose to his feet. "Thanks for coming," he said to Stacey and gave a little wave to Piper.

"You've mentioned Joe several times," Stacey said. "I thought it was a result of your concussion. Why do you keep talking about him? Did you have a hallucination?"

Colton gave a short laugh, then grabbed his bruised ribs. "No hallucination. He showed up at the bar the other day."

Shocked and confused, Stacey stared at Colton. "Joe? In Horseback Hollow? Are you sure?"

"Yeah, I punched him in the face," Colton said.

Stacey covered her mouth with her free hand. "Oh, my goodness. How did that happen?"

"Easy," Colton said. "He opened his mouth and started talking. I gave him twenty-four hours to go see you. Then, I told him I was taking my turn."

Stacey sank onto a chair, pulling Piper onto her lap. She shook her head but felt no sadness. "He never showed."

Colton took a deep breath and winced. "The night of the wreck, I was counting down the minutes to come see you."

Stacey's heart squeezed tight. "Oh, Colton, no." She rubbed her forehead. "That means you would have never had that accident if you had decided to stay home and wait until morning."

"I couldn't wait," Colton said. He closed his eyes. "I have a confession to make. Back before Joe proposed to you, I told him he needed to put a ring on your finger. You're a special girl, and someone was going to steal you away. He proposed to you the next day." Colton sighed, opening his eyes, his gaze full of regret. "I always felt guilty—that maybe you wouldn't have gotten pregnant if I hadn't given Joe that push."

Stacey blinked at the revelation. She felt a rush of emotions. All those months ago, Colton had been protective of her. What Colton told her just confirmed what she already knew. Joe had never truly loved her. He might not have wanted to lose her, but he hadn't loved her. "I hate that he had to be pushed along, and that I believed in him. I hate that he abandoned both Piper and me. But I could never regret having Piper. She's the light of my life."

"Yeah, but that doesn't change the fact that you've been through a terrible time because of Joe."

"Why did you give him twenty-four hours?" Stacey asked.

Colton shrugged his shoulders and winced slightly. He looked away, then back at her. "I'm in love with you. I don't know exactly when it happened or how. It just did. I fell in love with you. And Piper. Maybe I shouldn't have threatened Joe—"

"Stop," she said breathlessly and nearly fell out of the chair. "Did you just say you love me?"

He narrowed his eyes. "Yeah, I did."

"And Piper. You love her, too?"

"I do," he said, almost defiantly.

Stacey jumped from her chair and planted a kiss on his mouth. "I love you, too, Colton Foster. So very, very much."

He met her gaze. "Are you sure?"

"Very, very sure. I feel like the luckiest woman in the world. Say it again, please. Say you love me again so I can be sure. I feel like I dreamed it."

"I love you, Stacey Fortune Jones. I want you to be Stacey Fortune Jones Foster," he said.

Her heart stopped in her chest. "I feel as if I'm walking in a dream."

"I want to make your dreams come true as much as I possibly can," he said. "Even if that means sitting in tiny chairs I'm afraid of breaking for the sake of having a tea party with Piper."

Stacey's eyes filled with tears. "Oh, Colton."

Piper made a chirpy sound, and he turned to her. "I wanted to take this slow and be sensible, but life is too short. Stacey and Piper, will you marry me?"

"Yes, yes and yes," Stacey said and kissed Colton again.

His parents walked into the room. "Everything okay?" Mrs. Foster asked.

"Everything's great," Colton said. "Stacey, Piper and I are getting married."

"Well, thank goodness," his mother said, her voice full of relief and emotion. "We couldn't be happier."

"I guess we're going to have to build a house on the ranch for you three," Mr. Foster said. "We'll get started as soon as possible."

"Dad, I'd really like you to see a doctor about your back. I don't want you working on a house for me when you might hurt yourself."

His father frowned and shrugged. "Your sister's taking me for an appointment to see a doctor next week. I didn't want to do it, but she told me I owed it to you. I'm gonna hire a full-time hand and a few part-time guys, too. It's time. I've got more money in the bank than anyone knows, but don't spread that around. We'll get through. I just want you to get well."

Stacey squeezed one of Colton's hands. "This means you can concentrate on getting better," she said. "That's what we all want."

The next day, Colton arrived home from the hospital and was recovering by leaps and bounds. His doctor called him superhuman because he was healing so quickly. Stacey constantly chided him to take his time and rest, but she could see he found it hard not to forge into his regular routine. She visited him every day, and every day, it seemed as if their love for each other grew stronger.

A few days after that, Colton stood with her in the den of her parents' home. The room was usually a warm, welcoming place for family and visitors, but not today.

Today, the visitor was the biological father of her child. Stacey had fought the meeting with Joe, but Colton had insisted that she and Piper deserved some support from Joe. Stacey couldn't be less interested in seeing Joe. In many ways, she didn't want Piper exposed to such a man. She could only hope that someday he would grow up.

A knock sounded at the door, and she looked at

Colton. "You'll be okay," he said. "I'm here with you. You're just looking out for Piper. Remember that."

Stacey took a deep breath and answered the door to her former fiancé and Piper's biological father. He didn't look nearly as handsome as she remembered. She wondered how that had happened. "Hi, Joe. Come on inside," she said.

Joe entered with a slightly ill expression on his face. "Yeah, uh. I know I need to give you child support," he said. "I should have done it before, but I just couldn't face the idea that I had a child. I'll catch up," he promised.

"That's good," Stacey said. She wouldn't thank him. This was long overdue. "Do you want to see her?"

Joe took a deep breath. "Yeah. Yeah. I want to see her," he said as if he were facing the guillotine.

"I'll go get her," Stacey said, and collected Piper from her mother who was staying in the kitchen. Jeanne was still too angry with Joe to face him, and Stacey had made sure her father was working away from the house that day. She picked up her precious baby girl and carried her to the front foyer.

Joe stared at Piper for a long moment. "She's beautiful."

"Yes, she is and always has been," Stacey said. "I can't thank you for how you left us, but I can thank you for giving her to me."

Joe pursed his lips together in sadness. "I'd like to try to see her every now and then."

"I think she deserves that," Stacey said. "I think she deserves the best you can give her."

Joe gave a slow nod. "I don't know how to be a good father. I never had one. I'm gonna need some hints and nudges. My father was never there for me when I needed him. I was afraid I couldn't be a good father when you told me you were pregnant. That's why I told you that you should—" He cleared his throat. "I was wrong," he said in a gruff voice.

"You can put your meetings with Piper on your schedule on your smartphone calendar. You put your other appointments on there, don't you?" Colton asked.

"Yeah. I never thought of that," Joe said.

"You can start now, then," Colton said. "Input a date three weeks from today to call Stacey about when you can see Piper."

Joe pulled his cell phone from his pocket and tapped the information into his calendar. "Done. I'm sorry for the pain I've caused you, Stacey. But I'm going to try and—" Joe glanced at Colton. "It looks like you're in good hands now."

Stacey smiled. "Best hands ever," she said.

Ten days later, Rachel insisted on taking care of Piper for a full twenty-four-hour time period. Colton had completely recovered from the accident. He picked up Stacey and drove his new truck to Vicker's Corners so they could take a stroll downtown and spend the night at a bed-and-breakfast after dinner.

"It's perfect, but freezing," Stacey said, snuggling her gloved hands in his.

"It's the dead of winter," he said and looked down at her. "But I'm glad you think it's perfect."

"If I'm with you, it's perfect," she said. "And if you're recovering—"

"Mostly there," he said.

"But don't push it," she urged. "If you're recovering, that's perfect, too. Things could have been terribly different." Her heart caught at the thought of losing Colton, and her smile fell.

Colton caught her chin with his thumb. "Hey, no sad faces tonight. We're together and happy, right?"

Stacey nodded. "Yes, yes, yes."

"I like the sound of that word," he said with a sly, sexy look. "Let's have dinner," he said, and they stepped inside the restaurant.

The host led them to a table in front of a fireplace. "Oh, this is fabulous. I feel as if I'm in heaven."

"It gets better," he promised.

They ordered dinner and were served a delicious meal. Stacey savored every bite. She patted her belly toward the end of the dinner. "I don't think I can eat any more, but I would love some of that chocolate dessert."

"I'll get it to go," he said.

After he paid the check, they walked to their charming suite at the bed-and-breakfast. Stacey couldn't remember a more wonderful evening. With Piper in Rachel's care, and the full support of her family and Colton's, she couldn't feel happier to have such a special evening with Colton. A bottle of champagne welcomed them as they walked into the room. A gas fire flickered in the fireplace.

"Like it?" he asked.

"Oh, it's amazing," she said. "I love a gas fireplace. No work and all the pleasure."

"Does that mean you'd like that in my house plans?" he asked.

"I don't need a gas fireplace to be happy with you," she insisted.

"I've got a lot packed into my savings account, Stacey. Speak up about what you want," he said, putting his arm around her back.

"Okay," she whispered. "Gas fireplace and hot tub big enough for you and me."

Colton's eyes darkened with sensuality. "Sold. I like the way you think," he said, and took her mouth in a kiss.

With Colton holding her in his arms, she almost forgot about her surroundings. It was so good to hold him and kiss him. It was so good to be alone with him and to know he was healed from the accident.

Colton pulled back. "Let's have a glass of champagne," he said.

Stacey would rather have had a bucketful of Colton, but she went along with him. He pulled the champagne bottle from the ice and popped the cork. Grabbing a glass, he spilled the bubbly liquid into the flute and offered it to her. He poured a second flute for himself.

"To you," he said. "The woman I love. I've asked you once, but I want to do it the right way this time."

Colton knelt on one knee, and Stacey's breath hung in her throat. The past few weeks had caused such a roller coaster of emotions. She felt as if she were taking another heart-pounding turn on the ride. "What are you doing?"

He pulled a jeweler's box from his pants pocket and flipped it open to reveal a beautiful diamond ring. "Will you marry me?"

Stacey's heart squeezed so tight she could hardly speak. "Oh, yes, Colton. I can't believe how lucky I am."

Colton rose to his feet and kissed her again. "I feel the same way, Stacey Fortune Jones. I can't wait for you, Piper and me to start our lives together."

Stacey couldn't believe how her life had turned out. She was in love with the best man ever, and her daughter would have a daddy to show her the stuff of which a real man was made.

Stacey had never believed much in chance, but

she'd just received the best fortune ever in Colton Foster. Love forever. She'd come from a long line of lovers, and now she was getting her chance at the love of a lifetime.

* * * * *

'Can we get this as well? I think Tyler'd love it.'

'You mean, *you* love it.'

Emmy seemed to like simple, childlike things. And Dylan hadn't quite worked out yet whether he found that more endearing or annoying. He certainly didn't loathe her as much as he once had. She was good with the baby, too.

Her eyes crinkled at the corners. 'OK, then, let's ask him.' She picked up the cot toy, crouched down beside the pram, switched it on and let Tyler see the lights and hear the lullaby.

Tyler's eyes went wide, then he laughed and held his hands out towards it.

Emmy looked up at Dylan and smiled. 'I think that's a yes.'

Again a surge of attraction hit him. Was he crazy? This was Emmy Jacobs, who sparred with him and sniped at him and was his co-guardian. She was the last person he wanted to get involved with. But at the same time he had to acknowledge that there was something about her that really got under his skin. Something that made him want to know more about her. Get closer.

BOUND BY A BABY

BY
KATE HARDY

© Kate Hardy 2013

Published in Great Britain 2014
by Mills & Boon, an imprint of Harlequin (UK) Limited,
Eton House, 18-24 Paradise Road, Richmond, Surrey, TW9 1SR

© 2013 Pamela Brooks

ISBN: 978 0 263 91250 0

23-0114

Harlequin (UK) Limited's policy is to use papers that are natural, renewable and recyclable products and made from wood grown in sustainable forests. The logging and manufacturing processes conform to the legal environmental regulations of the country of origin.

Printed and bound in Spain
by Blackprint CPI, Barcelona

Kate Hardy lives in Norwich, in the east of England, with her husband, two young children, one bouncy spaniel, and too many books to count! When she's not busy writing romance or researching local history she helps out at her children's schools. She also loves cooking—spot the recipes sneaked into her books! (They're also on her website, along with extracts and stories behind the books.) Writing for Mills & Boon has been a dream come true for Kate—something she wanted to do ever since she was twelve. She has been writing for Medical Romance™ for over ten years now, as well as for other Mills & Boon® lines. She says it's the best of both worlds, because she gets to learn lots of new things when she's researching the background to a book: add a touch of passion, drama and danger, a new gorgeous hero every time, and it's the perfect job!

Kate's always delighted to hear from readers, so do drop in to her website at www.katehardy.com.

For Gerard, Chris and Chloe—
the best research team ever—with all my love.

CHAPTER ONE

'I ASSUME YOU know why you're both here,' the solicitor said, looking at Emmy and then at Dylan.

Of course Emmy knew. Ally and Pete had asked her to be their son Tyler's guardian, if the unthinkable should ever happen.

If. She swallowed hard. That was the whole point of her being here. Because the unthinkable *had* happened. And Emmy still couldn't quite believe that she'd never see her best friend again.

She lifted her chin. Obviously today was about making things all official legally. And as for Dylan Harper—the only man she'd ever met who could make wearing a T-shirt and jeans feel as if they were a formal business suit—he was obviously here because he was Pete's best friend and Pete and Ally had asked him to be the executor of their will. 'Yes,' she said.

'Yes,' Dylan echoed.

'Good.' The solicitor tapped his pen against his blotter. 'So, Miss Jacobs, Mr Harper, can you confirm that you're both prepared to be Tyler's guardians?'

Emmy froze for a moment. *Both?* What was the man talking about? No way would Ally and Pete have asked them both to be Tyler's guardian. There had to be some mistake.

She glanced at Dylan, to find him looking straight back at her. And his expression was just as stunned as her own must be.

Or maybe they'd misheard. Misunderstood. 'Both of us, Tyler's guardians?' she asked.

For the first time, the solicitor's face showed an expression other than smooth neutrality. 'Did you not know they'd named you as Tyler's guardian in the will, Ms Jacobs?'

Emmy blew out a breath. 'Well, yes. Ally asked me before she and Pete revised their wills.' And she'd assumed that Ally had meant *just* her.

'Pete asked me,' Dylan said.

Which almost made Emmy wonder if Ally and Pete hadn't spoken to each other about it. Though obviously they must've done. They'd both signed the will, so they'd clearly known that both of their best friends had agreed to be there for Tyler. They just hadn't shared that particular piece of information with either Dylan or herself, by the looks of things.

'Is there a problem?' the solicitor asked.

Apart from the fact that she and Dylan disliked each other intensely and usually avoided each other? Or the fact that Dylan was married—and Emmy was pretty sure that his wife couldn't be too pleased that her husband had been named co-guardian with another woman, one who was single? 'No,' she said quickly, and looked at Dylan. This was his cue to explain that no, he couldn't do it.

'No problem,' Dylan confirmed, to her shock.

'Good.'

Good? No, it just made everything much more complicated, Emmy thought. Or maybe it meant he intended to fight her for custody of the baby: family man versus single mum, so it was obvious who'd win. But she didn't have a chance to protest because the solicitor went on with the reading of the will. 'Now, obviously Ally and Pete left financial provisions for Tyler. I have all the details here.'

'I'll deal with it,' Dylan said.

Immediately assuming that a flaky, air-headed jewellery designer wouldn't have a clue what to do? Emmy knew that was how Dylan saw her—she'd overheard him say it to Pete, on more than one occasion—and it rankled. She'd been her own boss for ten years. She was perfectly capable of dealing with things. Whereas he was so uptight and stuffy, she couldn't even begin to imagine him looking after a baby or a toddler. Given that Ally had always been diplomatic about Dylan's wife, merely saying that she worked with Pete, Emmy was pretty sure that Nadine Harper was from the same mould as Dylan. A cold workaholic who wouldn't know what fun was if it jumped out in front of him and yelled, 'Boo!' And not the sort that Ally would've wanted caring for her son.

But the solicitor was off again, going through the details of the arrangements made in the will. Emmy had to ignore her feelings and listen to what the man was telling her before she got completely lost. This was *important*.

And then at last it was all over.

Leaving her and Dylan to pick up the pieces. Together. Unthinkably.

She gave the solicitor a polite smile, shook his hand, and walked out of the office. On the doorstep of the building, she came to a halt and faced Dylan.

'I think,' she said, 'we need to talk. Like *now*.'

He nodded. 'And I could do with some coffee.'

There were shadows under his cornflower-blue eyes, and lines at the corners betraying that he hadn't slept properly since the crash; for the first time ever, Dylan actually looked vulnerable—and as if he hurt as much as she did, right now. It stopped her from uttering the kind of snippy remarks they usually made to each other.

'Make that two of us,' she said. On the sleep front, as well as the need for coffee. Vulnerability, no way would she admit to. Especially not to Dylan Harper. No way was she giving him an excuse to take Tyler from her. He and Nadine were *not* taking her place.

'Where's Tyler?' Dylan asked.

'With my mum. She'll ring me if there's a problem.' She lifted one shoulder, daring him to criticise her. 'I didn't think the solicitor's office would be the best place for him.'

'It isn't.'

Another first: he was actually agreeing with her. Maybe, she thought, they might be able to work something out between them? Maybe he'd be reasonable? A baby wouldn't fit into his busy, workaholic lifestyle. It'd be tough for Emmy, too, but at least she'd spent time with her godson and would have some clue about looking after him.

'Shall we?' she asked, indicating the café across the road.

'Fine.'

At the counter in the café, Emmy ordered a latte. 'What would you like?'

'I'll get these,' Dylan said immediately.

She gave a small but determined shake of her head. No way was she going to let him take charge. 'I offered first.'

'Then thank you—an espresso would be great.'

'Do you want anything to eat?'

He grimaced. 'Thank you for the offer, but right now I really can't face anything.'

She, too, hadn't been able to choke much down since she'd heard the news. It seemed that the situation had shaken him as much as it had shaken her. In a way, that was a good thing. Maybe they could find some common ground.

'If you go and find us a table, I'll bring our coffee over,' she said.

And she was glad of that small space between them. Just so she could marshal her thoughts. Right now, she didn't want to fight with Dylan. She just wanted her best friend back. For everything to be the same as it had been, three days ago. For Pete to have taken Ally on a surprise anniversary trip to Venice, for them to be happy and for Ally to be texting her to let her know they were on their way back and couldn't wait to see their little boy and tell her all about the trip. For them to be *alive*.

Emmy paid for the coffees, and carried them over to the quiet table Dylan had found for them in the corner.

'So you had no idea Pete had asked me to be Tyler's guardian?' Dylan asked.

Typical Dylan: straight in there. No pussyfooting around. Though, for once, she agreed with him. They needed to cut to the chase. 'No. And you had no idea that Ally had asked me?'

'No.' He spread his hands. 'Of course I said yes when he asked me—just as you obviously did when Ally asked you.' He sighed. 'I know you shouldn't speak ill of the dead—and Pete was my best friend, the closest I had to a brother—but what the *hell* were they thinking when they decided this?'

'They're both—*were* both,' she corrected herself, wincing, 'only children. Pete's dad is nearly eighty and Ally's mum isn't well. How could Pete and Ally's parents be expected to cope with looking after a baby full-time? And it isn't going to get any easier for them over the next twenty years. Of course Pete and Ally would ask someone nearer their own age to be Tyler's guardian.'

Dylan gave a pained sigh. 'I didn't mean *that*. It's obvious. I mean, why *us*?'

Why ask two people who really didn't get on to take care of the most precious thing in their lives? Good question. Though that wasn't the one uppermost in her mind. 'Why you and me instead of you and your wife?' she asked pointedly.

He blew out a breath. 'That isn't an issue.'

'If I was married and my husband's best friend asked him to be the baby's guardian if the worst happened, I'd be pretty upset if another woman was named as the co-guardian instead of me,' Emmy said.

'It isn't an issue,' Dylan repeated.

Patronising, pompous idiot. Emmy kept a rein on her temper. Just. 'Don't you think this discussion ought to include her?'

'You're the one who said we needed to talk.'

'We do.' She switched into superpolite mode, the one she used for difficult clients, before she was tempted to strangle him. 'Could you perhaps phone her and see when's a good time for her to join us?'

'No,' he said tightly.

Superpolite mode off. 'Either she really, *really* trusts you,' Emmy said, 'or you're even more of a control freak than I thought.'

'It isn't an issue,' Dylan said, 'because we're separated.' He glared at her. 'Happy, now?'

What? Since when had Dylan split up with his wife? And why? But Emmy damped the questions down. It wasn't any of her business. Whereas Tyler's welfare—that was most definitely her business.

'I guess it makes this issue a bit less complicated,' she said. Especially given what the social worker had suggested to her yesterday—something Emmy had baulked at, but which might turn out to be a sensible solution now.

She took a sip of coffee. 'Maybe,' she said slowly, 'Pete and Ally thought that between us we could give Tyler what he needs.'

He narrowed his eyes at her. 'How do you mean?'

'We have different strengths.' And different weaknesses, but she wasn't going to point that out. They were going to need to work together on this, and now wasn't the time for a fight. 'We can bring different things to his life.'

He folded his arms. 'So I do the serious stuff and you do all the fun and glitter?'

Emmy had been prepared to compromise, but this was too much. And this was exactly why she'd disliked Dylan from practically the moment they'd met. Because he was judgemental, arrogant, and had the social skills of a rhino. Either he genuinely didn't realise what he'd just said or he really didn't care—and she wasn't sure which. She lifted her chin. 'You mean, because I work with pretty, shiny things, they distract my poor little female brain from being able to focus on anything real?' she asked, her voice like cut glass.

His wince told her that he hadn't actually meant to insult her. 'Put that way, it sounds bad.'

'It *is* bad, Dylan. Look, you know I have my own business. If I was an airhead, unable to do a basic set of yearly accounts and work out my profit margins, then I'd be starving and in debt up to my eyeballs. Just to clarify the situation for you, that's not the case. My bank account's in the black and my business is doing just fine, thank you. Or will you be requiring a letter from my bank manager to prove that?'

He held her gaze. 'OK. I apologise. I shouldn't have said that.'

'Good. Apology accepted.' And maybe she should cut him some slack. He'd said that Pete was as close to him as a brother, so right now he was obviously hurting as much as she was. Especially as he was having to deal with a relationship break-up as well. And Dylan Harper was the most formal, uptight man Emmy had ever met, which meant he probably wasn't so good at emotional stuff. No doubt lashing out and making snippy remarks was his way of dealing with things. Letting it go—this time—didn't mean that she was going to let him walk all over her in the future.

'OK, so we don't get on; but this isn't actually about us. It's about a little boy who has nobody, and giving him a stable home where he can grow up knowing he's loved and valued.' And this wasn't the first time she and Dylan had had to put their differences aside. They'd managed it for Pete and Ally's wedding. When, come to think of it, Dylan's wife had been away on business and hadn't been able to attend, despite the fact that she worked with the groom and was married to the best man.

Emmy and Dylan had put their differences aside again two months ago, in the same ancient little church where Ally and Pete had got married, when they'd stood by the font and made their promises as godparents. Dylan's wife had been absent then, too. So maybe the marriage had been in trouble for a while, and Pete knew what was going on in Dylan's life. Which would make a bit more sense of the decision to ask both Dylan and Emmy to be Tyler's guardian.

She looked Dylan straight in the eye. 'I meant every word I said in church on my godson's christening day. I intend to be there for him.'

Was Emmy implying that he wasn't? Dylan felt himself bristling. 'I meant every word I said, too.'

'Right.'

But he couldn't discern an edge in her voice—at least, not like the one that had been there when he'd as good as called her an airhead. And that mollified him slightly. Maybe they could work together on this. Maybe she'd put the baby first instead of being the overemotional, needy mess she'd been when he'd first met her. Emmy wasn't serious and focused, like Nadine. She was unstructured and flaky. Something Dylan refused to put up with; he'd already had to deal with enough of that kind of behaviour in his life. No more.

'Look, Ally and Pete wanted us to take care of their baby, if anything happened to them.' She swallowed hard. 'And the worst *has* happened.'

Dylan could see the sheen of tears in her grey eyes, and her lower lip actually started to wobble. Oh, no. Please don't let her cry. He wasn't good with tears. And he'd seen enough of them in those last few weeks with Nadine to last him a lifetime. If Emmy started crying, he'd have to walk out of the café. Because right now he couldn't cope with any more emotional pressure. As it was, he felt as if the world had slipped and he were slowly sliding backwards, unable to stop himself and with nothing to hang on to.

She dragged in a breath. 'We're going to have to work together on this and put our personal feelings aside.'

'Fair point.' They didn't have a lot of choice in the matter. And at least she was managing to hold the tears back. That was something. 'We'll work together.' Dylan was still slightly surprised at how businesslike she was being. This wasn't Emmy-like behaviour. She'd been late the first three times they'd met, and given the most feeble of excuses. And he'd lost count of the times he'd been over at Ally and Pete's and Ally had had to rush off to pick up the pieces when yet another of Emmy's disastrous relationships had ended. It was way, way too close to the way his mother behaved, and Dylan had no patience for that kind of selfishness.

And his comment about the glitter hadn't been totally unfounded. He was pretty sure she'd choose to do the fun things with Tyler and leave him to do all the serious stuff. Emmy was all about fun. Which wasn't enough: sometimes you had to put the fun aside and do what needed to be done rather than what you wanted to do. 'So you've been looking after Tyler?'

'Since they left.' She shrugged. 'Babysitting.'

Except now it wasn't babysitting anymore. There wasn't anyone to hand Tyler back to.

She blew out a breath. 'The social worker came to see me last night. She said that Tyler needs familiarity and a routine. So I guess the first thing we need to do is to set up a routine, something as near as possible to what he's used to.'

Considering the chaos that usually surrounded Emmy Jacobs, Dylan couldn't imagine her setting up any kind of routine. But he bit his tongue. He'd already annoyed her today. Right now he needed to be conciliatory. For his godson's sake. 'Right.'

'And, as the solicitor said, we're sharing custody.'

'Meaning that one week you have him, the next week I do?' Dylan suggested. 'Fine. That works for me.'

'It doesn't work at all.'

He frowned at her, not understanding. 'Why not?'

'Just as Tyler gets settled in with me, I have to bring him to you; and just as he gets settled with you, you have to bring him to me?' She shook her head. 'That's not fair on him.'

'So what are you suggesting?'

'The social worker,' she said, not meeting his gaze,

'suggested that Tyler stays in his own home. She says that whoever cares for him needs to, um, live there, too.'

He blinked. 'You're planning to move into Ally and Pete's house?'

She coughed. 'Not just me.'

What she was saying finally sank in. 'You're suggesting *we live together*?' The idea was so shocking, he almost dropped his coffee.

'No.' She lifted her chin, looking affronted. 'The social worker suggests that we share a house and share Tyler's care. Believe you me, it's not what I want to do—but it's the most sensible solution for Tyler. It saves us having to traipse a tired and hungry baby all over London at times that don't suit him. We'll be fitting round him, not the other way round.'

'Share a house. That sounds like living together, to me.' Something Dylan knew he wasn't good at. Hadn't he failed spectacularly with Nadine? His marriage had broken up because he hadn't wanted a family and the wife he'd loved had given him an ultimatum. A choice he couldn't accept. And now Emmy Jacobs—a woman who embodied everything he didn't like—seriously expected him to make a family with *her*?

'It isn't living together. It's just sharing a house.' Her mouth tightened, and she gave him a look as if to say that he was the last person on earth she'd choose to live with.

He needed to be upfront about this. 'I don't want to share a house with you,' he said.

'It's not my idea of fun, either, but what else—?' She paused. 'Actually, no, there *is* an easy solution to this. You can agree to me having full-time care of Tyler.'

'That isn't what Pete and Ally wanted.' And he didn't think Emmy was stable enough to look after Tyler, not permanently. Then again, Dylan couldn't imagine himself taking care of Tyler, either. He knew practically nothing about babies. He'd never even babysat his godson. Pete and Ally had never asked him, knowing that his personal life was in chaos and his head wasn't in the right place. And Dylan was guiltily aware that he'd jumped at the excuse rather than face up to the fact that he wasn't a very good godfather.

He'd agreed to be Tyler's guardian. Of course he had. For the same reason that Emmy had agreed, probably, wanting to support his best friend. But he'd never thought it would actually happen. He'd considered himself to be a safety net that would never need to be used.

And now...

Lack of sleep. That was why his head was all over the place. There was a black hole where his best friend had once been. And now there were all these new demands on him and he wasn't sure he could meet them. He'd promised to be there for Tyler, and he hated himself for the fact that, now he actually had to make good on that promise, he didn't want to do it. He resented the way that a baby could wreak such havoc on his life and turn everything upside down; and then he felt guilty all over again for resenting someone so tiny and defenceless, because it wasn't the baby's fault and—well, he was being *selfish*.

Emmy was offering him a get-out. It would be, oh, so easy to take it. And yet Dylan knew that he'd never respect himself again if he took it—if he did what his mother had done, and dumped all his responsibilities on someone else. If he ignored a child who needed him.

'I know it isn't what Pete and Ally wanted,' Emmy said, clearly oblivious to the turmoil in Dylan's head. 'But it's not fair to keep uprooting Tyler, just to suit ourselves.'

'He's a baby. He's not even going to notice his surroundings,' Dylan said.

'Actually, he is. And if we did alternate weeks he'd have to get used to two different sets of rules, two different atmospheres. That's too much to expect.'

'And you're an expert on childcare?' he asked, knowing how nasty it sounded but unable to stop himself, because it was easier to fight with her than to admit how mixed up and miserable he felt right now.

'No. But I've read up on it. I've spent time with him. And I know how Ally wanted him brought up.'

'Fair point,' he muttered, feeling even more guilty. He hadn't done any of those things.

'You don't want to live with him, but you don't want to let me have full-time care of him, either.' She sighed. 'So what *do* you want, Dylan?'

'Pete and Ally back. Life as it was supposed to be.' The words came out before he could stop them.

'Well, unless you can turn into a superhero and spin the world round the other way to reverse time, and then stop the accident happening…' She looked away. 'Life isn't like the movies. I wish it could be. That I could wave a magic wand and everything would be OK again. But I can't. I'm a normal godmother, not a fairy godmother. And we have to do what's right for Tyler. To make his world as good as it can be, now his parents are gone and he has only us.'

She was right. Which made Dylan feel even more guilty. He was acting like a spoiled brat, crying for the moon and stars. And it was *wrong*. 'So what do you suggest?'

'The way I see it, we have two choices. Either we do what Pete and Ally wanted, and we find some way to be civil to each other while we bring up their child, or you let me bring him up on my own.'

'Or I could bring him up on my own,' Dylan suggested, nettled that she hadn't listed it as a third option.

She scoffed. 'So, what? You get a live-in nanny and

dump his care on her, and see him for two seconds when
you get home from work?'

'That's unfair.'

'Is it?' she asked pointedly.

He'd rather have all his teeth pulled out without anaes-
thetic than admit it to her, but it was probably accurate. 'I
don't want to live with you.' He didn't want to live with
anyone.

'Newsflash. I don't want to live with you, either. But I'm
prepared to put Tyler's needs before mine. Just as I know
Ally would've done for me, if our positions were reversed.'

And just as Pete would've done for him. Disgust at
himself flared through Dylan's body. At heart, he really
was a chip off the old block, as selfish as his mother. And
that didn't sit well with him. He didn't want to be like her.
'Caring for a baby on your own is a hell of a commitment.'

'I know. But I'm prepared to do it.'

'Pete and Ally knew it was too much to ask one person
to do. It's why they asked us both.'

'And you've had second thoughts.' She shrugged. 'Look,
it's fine. I'll manage. I can always ask my mum for help.'

Which was a lot more than Dylan could do. And how
pathetic was he to resent that?

'I need some time to think about this,' he said. Time
where he could work things out, without anyone crowding his head. Where he could do what he always did when
he made a business decision: work out all the scenarios,
decide which one had the most benefits and least risks.
Plan things without any emotions getting in the way and
messing things up. 'How long is it until you need to get
back to Tyler?'

'Mum said she could babysit for as long as I needed. I
had no idea how long things would take at the solicitor's.'

He made a snap decision. 'OK. We'll meet again in an hour. When we've both had time to get our heads round it.'

'I don't need t—' she began, then shut up. 'You're right. I've had time to think about what the social worker said. You haven't. And it's a big deal. Of course you need time to think about it. Is an hour enough?'

He'd make sure it was. 'An hour's fine. I'll see you back here then.'

CHAPTER TWO

FRESH AIR. THAT would help, for starters. Dylan found the nearest park and walked, ignoring the noise from tourists and families.

Pros and cons. He didn't want to live with anyone. He was still licking his wounds from the end of his marriage—ironic, considering that he'd been the one to end it. And even more ironic that, if Nadine had waited six more months before issuing that ultimatum, she would've had her dream.

But it was too late, now. He couldn't go back. He didn't love her anymore, and he knew she was seeing someone else. Someone who was prepared to give her what he wouldn't. What hurt most now was that he'd failed at being a husband.

That left him with a slightly less complicated situation; though it didn't make his decision any easier. If he did have to live with someone else, an emotional, flaky woman and a tiny baby would be right at the bottom of his list. He had a business to run—something that took up as much of his energy as he could give. He didn't have *time* for a baby.

But...

If he backed out, if he let Emmy shoulder all the responsibilities and look after the baby, he'd only be able to block out the guilt for a short time. It would eat away at him, to the point where it would affect his business decisions and therefore the livelihoods of everyone who worked for him. Besides, how could he live with himself if he abandoned the child his best friend had loved so dearly?

Given how often he'd been dumped as a child, how could he do the same thing to this baby?

He couldn't let Tyler down. Couldn't break a promise he'd made.

Which meant he had to find a way of coexisting with Emmy.

She'd said earlier that they wouldn't be living together, just sharing a house. They could lead completely separate lives. All they'd need to do was to set up a rota for childcare and then brief each other at a handover. He could do that. OK, so he'd have to delegate more at work, to carve out that extra time, but it was doable. His flat was on a short-term lease, so that wasn't a problem. And he had no intention of getting involved with anyone romantically, so that wouldn't be a problem in the future, either.

So the decision was easy, after all.

He walked back to the café, and was slightly surprised to find that Emmy was already there. Or maybe she'd never left. Whatever.

'Coffee?' he asked. 'You paid last time, so this one's on me.'

'Thank you.'

He ordered coffee then joined her at the table. 'If we're going to share a house and Tyler's care, then we need to sort out some ground rules. Set up a rota.'

She rolled her eyes. 'Obviously. Childcare and housework.'

'Not housework. We'll get a housekeeper.'

She shook her head. 'I can't afford to pay a housekeeper.'

'I can. So that's settled.'

'No. This is shared equally. Time and bills.'

Did she have to be so stubborn about this? It was a practical decision. The idea was to look at how they could make this work, with the least pain to both of them. Why do something he didn't have time for and didn't enjoy, when he could pay someone to do it? 'Look, I'm going to have a hard enough time fitting a baby into my work schedule, without adding in extra stuff. And I'm sure it's the same for you. It makes sense to pay someone to clean the house and take some of the pressure off us.'

'I can probably stretch to paying someone to clean for a couple of hours a week,' she said, 'but that's as far as it goes.'

'So you're saying we both have to cook?'

'Well, obviously. It's a bit stupid, both of us cooking separately. It makes sense to share.' She stared at him. 'Are you telling me you can't cook?'

He shrugged. 'I shared a house with Pete at university.' And Emmy must know how hopeless Pete was—had been, Dylan corrected himself with a jolt—in the kitchen. 'So it was starve, eat nothing but junk, or learn to cook.'

'And what did you opt for?'

Did she *really* have to ask? He narrowed his eyes at her, just to make the point that she was being overpicky. 'I learned to cook. I only do basic stuff—don't expect Michelin-star standard—but it'll be edible and you won't get food poisoning.' He paused as a nasty thought struck him. 'Does that mean *you* don't cook?'

'I can do the basics,' she said. 'I shared a house with Ally at university.'

And Ally was an excellent cook. Dylan had never turned down the offer of a meal at his best friend's; he was pretty sure it must've been the same for Emmy. 'And she did all the cooking?' he asked.

'Our deal was that she cooked and I cleaned.' Emmy shrugged. 'Though I picked up a few tips from her along the way.'

But she wasn't claiming to be a superchef. Which made two of them. Basic food it would have to be. Which wasn't much change from the way he'd been living, the last six months. 'Right. So we'll pay a cleaner, and have a rota for childcare and cooking.'

He took a sip of his coffee, though it didn't do much to clear his head. Three days ago, he'd been just an ordinary workaholic. No commitments—well, *almost* no commitments, he amended mentally. No commitments once his divorce papers came through and he signed them.

Today, it was a different world. His best friend had died; and it looked as if he'd be sharing the care of his godson with a woman who'd always managed to rub him up the wrong way. Not the life he'd planned or wanted. But he was just going to have to make the best of it.

'So who looks after Tyler when we're at work?' he asked.

'We take turns.'

'I'm not with you.'

'Ally wasn't planning to go back to work until after his second birthday. She wanted to be a stay-at-home mum and look after her own baby.' Emmy looked awkward. 'I don't think she would've wanted us to put him in day care or get a nanny.'

'We're not Ally and Pete, so we're going to have to make a decision that works for both of us,' Dylan pointed out. 'We both have a business to run. Taking time off work isn't going to happen. Not if we want to keep our businesses running.'

'Unless,' Emmy suggested, 'we work flexible hours. Delegate, if we have to.'

'Delegate?' He frowned. 'I thought you were a sole trader?'

'I am, but you're not.'

He almost asked her if she was using the royal 'we', and stopped himself just in time. That wasn't fair. She was trying. And he bit back the snippy comment that she was trying in more than one sense of the word.

'Are you a morning or an evening person?' she asked.

He usually worked both. That had been another of Nadine's complaints: Dylan was a workaholic who was always in the office or in his study. 'Either.'

'I prefer working in the evenings. So, if you're not bothered, how about you go in early and I'll take care of Tyler; and then you take over from me at, say, half-three, so I can get on with my work?'

'And what if I need to have a late meeting?'

'We can be flexible,' she said. 'But if you're late back one day, then you'll have to be home much earlier, the next day, to give me that time back.' She shrugged. 'There might be times when I have meetings and need you to take over from me. So I guess we're going to have to be flexible, work as a team, and cover for each other when we need to.'

Work as a team with a woman he'd always disliked. A woman who reminded him of the worst aspects of his mother—the sort who'd dump her responsibilities on someone else with no notice so she could drift off somewhere to 'find herself'.

Dylan pinched himself, just to check that this wasn't some peculiar nightmare. But it hurt. So there was no waking up from this situation.

'OK. We'll sort out a rota between us.' He paused. 'I still don't want to live with you, but I guess the only option is to share the house.' It didn't mean they had to share any time together outside the handover slots.

'So when do we move in to Pete and Ally's?' she asked

'I have to sort out the lease on my flat,' he said.

'And I'll need to talk to the bank about subletting my flat, to make sure it doesn't affect the mortgage.'

Dylan was surprised. He hadn't thought Emmy would be together enough to buy her own place.

'And they might be able to put me in touch with a good letting agency,' she finished.

She'd obviously thought this through. Then again, she'd had time to think about it. The social worker had talked to her about it already.

'So we could move in tomorrow.'

He'd rather not move in at all, but he had no choice. Not if he was going to carry out his duty. 'Tomorrow.' He paused. 'Look—we really need to put Tyler first. We don't like each other, but we've agreed to make an effort for his sake. What happens if we really can't get on?'

'I don't know.'

'In a business, if you hire someone in a senior role, you'd have a trial period to make sure you suited each other. Then you'd review it and decide on the best way forward.'

'This isn't a job, Dylan.'

'I know, but I think a trial period might be the fairest way for all of us. Give it three months. See if we can make it work.'

She nodded. 'And, if we can't, then you'll agree that I'll have sole care of Tyler?'

He wasn't ready to agree to that. 'We'll review it,' he said. 'See what the viable options are.'

'OK. Three months.' She paused. 'But if anything big

comes up, we discuss it before the situation gets out of hand.'

That worked for him. 'Agreed.'

'So that's settled.' She lifted her chin. 'Before we go any further, I need to know something. Is there anyone who'd be upset about us sharing a house?'

He frowned. 'I've already told you, I'm separated from Nadine. It won't be a problem.'

'What about the woman you had an affair with?'

He stared at her in disbelief. 'What woman?'

'Oh, come on. It's the main reason why marriages break down. Someone has an affair. Usually the man.'

Was she really that cynical?

Had that happened to her?

He couldn't remember Pete or Ally ever talking about going to Emmy's wedding, but at the end of the day a marriage certificate was just a piece of paper. Maybe Emmy had been living with someone who'd let her down in that way. 'Not that it's any of your business why my marriage broke up, but for the record neither of us had an affair,' he said tightly.

Colour stained her cheeks, 'I apologise.'

Which was something, he supposed. 'There's nobody who would be affected by us sharing a house,' he said quietly.

Or was there another reason why she'd asked? A way to introduce the subject, maybe, because there was someone in her life who'd be upset? 'If it's a problem for you, I'm happy to—'

'There's nobody,' she cut in.

Was it his imagination, or did she suddenly look tired and miserable and lonely?

No. He was just reflecting how he felt on her. Tired and miserable, because he'd barely slept since the news of the crash; and lonely, because the one person Dylan could've talked to about this—well, he'd been *in* that crash and he wasn't here anymore.

'Though I could do without a string of dates being paraded through the house,' she added.

He raised an eyebrow. 'I'm not quite divorced yet. Do you really think I'm dating?' Despite the fact that he knew his almost-ex wife was, he wasn't.

She grimaced. 'Sorry. I take that back. It's not your fault I have a rubbish taste in men. I shouldn't tar you with the same brush as them.'

He'd been right, then. Someone had let her down. More than one, he'd guess.

Dylan had never noticed before, probably because he'd been more preoccupied with being annoyed by her, but Emmy Jacobs was actually pretty. Slender, with a fine bone structure highlighted by her gamine haircut. Her hair was defiantly plum: not a natural shade, but it suited her, bringing out the depths in her huge grey eyes.

Though what on earth was he doing, thinking about Emmy in those sorts of terms?

Better put it down to the shock of bereavement. He and Emmy might be about to share a house and the care of a baby, but that was as far as it would go. They'd be lucky to keep things civil between them. And he definitely wasn't in the market for any kind of relationship. Been there, done that, and failed spectacularly. It had taught him to steer clear, in future. He was better off on his own. It meant there was nobody to disappoint. Nobody to walk away, the way his mother had and Nadine had.

'I assume you have a set of keys to Pete and Ally's house?' he asked.

She nodded. 'You, too?'

'So I could keep an eye on the place while they're not

there. For emergencies. Which I always thought would be a burst pipe or something like that. Not…' His throat closed, and he couldn't get the words out. For the first time in years, he was totally speechless.

To his surprise, Emmy reached across the table to take his hand and squeezed it briefly. With sympathy, not pity. 'Me, too. I keep thinking I'm going to wake up and discover that this is all just some incredibly realistic nightmare and everything's just fine. Except I've woken up too many times already and found out that it's not.'

Whatever her faults—and Dylan knew there were a lot of them—Emmy's feelings for Ally and Pete were in no doubt. Surprising himself further, he returned the squeeze. 'And we've still got the funeral to go through.'

She sighed and withdrew her hand. 'I guess their parents will want to arrange it.'

'You said yourself, Pete's dad is elderly and Ally's mum isn't well. They'll need support. I was going to offer to sort it out for them. If they tell me what they want, I can arrange it.'

'That's good of you to take the burden off their shoulders.' She took a deep breath. 'Count me in on the support front. Anything you need me to do, tell me and I'll do it.'

She wasn't being polite, Dylan knew. The tears were shimmering in her eyes again. And he wanted to get out of here as fast as he could, before she actually started crying. 'Thanks. I guess we'd better exchange phone numbers. Home, work, whatever.'

She nodded, and took her mobile phone from her handbag. It was a matter of seconds to give each other the details. 'And we'll meet at the house after work tomorrow to sort out the rota.'

'OK. I'll call you when I'm on my way.'

'Thanks.' She drained her cup. 'I'd better get back to Tyler. See you later.'

He watched her walk out of the café. The woman who annoyed him more than anyone he'd ever met. The woman he was going to move in with tomorrow.

Yeah, life was really throwing him a curveball. And he was just going to have to deal with it. Somehow.

The next morning, Emmy unlocked the door to Pete and Ally's three-storey Georgian house in Islington, pressed in the code for the alarm, and put her small suitcase down in the hallway.

'It's just you and me for now, Ty,' she said softly to the baby, who was securely strapped into his sling and cradled against her heart. 'We're home. Except—' her breath caught '—it's going to be with me and Dylan looking after you, from now on, instead of your mum and dad.'

It still felt wrong. But over the course of the day she managed to make a list of the rest of the things she needed to bring from her flat, feed Tyler, give him a bath and put him to bed in his cot, and make a basic spaghetti sauce for dinner so that all she'd have to do was heat it through and cook some pasta when Dylan turned up after he'd finished work.

Home.

Would she ever come to think of this place as home? Emmy thought with longing of her own flat in Camden. It was small, but full of light; and it was *hers*. From next week, a stranger would be living there and enjoying the views over the local park. And she would be living here in a much more spacious house—the sort she would never have been able to afford on her own—with Dylan and Tyler.

Almost like a family.

Just what she'd always wanted.

Well, she didn't want *Dylan*, she amended. But Emmy had envied part of her best friend's life: having a husband who loved her and a gorgeous baby. Something Emmy had wanted, herself. A real family.

'But I didn't want to have it *this* way, Ally,' she said softly. 'I wanted someone of my own. Someone who wouldn't let me down.' Someone that maybe somebody else should've picked for her, given how bad her own choices of life partner had been in the past.

And that family she was fantasising about was just that: a fantasy. The baby wasn't really hers, and neither was the house. And she was sharing the house with Dylan Harper, as a co-guardian. She couldn't think of anyone less likely to be the love of her life, just as she knew that she was the exact opposite of the kind of women Dylan liked. Chalk and cheese wasn't the half of it.

But then again, Tyler might not be her flesh and blood, but he was her responsibility now. Her godson. A baby she'd known for every single day of his little life. A baby she'd cradled in her arms when he was only a few hours old, sitting on the side of her best friend's hospital bed and feeling the same surge of love she'd felt for the woman who'd been as close as a sister to her.

She drew her knees up to her chin and wrapped her arms round her legs, blinking away the tears. 'I promise you I'll love Tyler as if he was my own, Ally,' she said softly into the empty room. 'I'll do my best by him.'

She just hoped that her best would be good enough. Though this was one thing she really couldn't afford to fail at. There wasn't a plan B.

The lights on the baby listener glowed steadily, and Emmy couldn't hear a thing; Tyler was obviously sound asleep. She glanced at her watch. Hopefully Dylan wouldn't be too much longer. In the meantime, she had a job to do.

She uncurled and headed back to the kitchen, where she took a large piece of card and marked it out into a two-week rota for childcare and chores. She worked steadily, putting in different coloured sticky notes to show which were her slots and which were Dylan's.

All the way through, she kept glancing at her watch. There was still no sign of Dylan, and it was getting on to half-past seven.

This was ridiculous. Had he forgotten that he was meant to be here, sorting things out with her? Or was he just in denial?

And to think he'd pegged himself as the sensible, organised one.

Yeah, right.

Irritated, she picked up her mobile phone and rang him.

He answered within two rings. 'Dylan Harper.' Though he sounded absent, as if his attention was elsewhere.

'It's Emmy,' she said crisply. 'Emmy Jacobs.' Just in case he was trying to block that out, too.

There was a pause. 'Oh.'

'Are you not supposed to be somewhere right now?' She made her voice supersaccharine.

'You suggested we meefairt at the house today after work.'

'Mmm-hmm. Which is where I am now. So are you expecting me to stay up until midnight or whenever you can be bothered to turn up and sort things through?'

He sighed. 'Don't nag.'

Nag? If he'd been fair about this, she wouldn't have to nag. 'This is meant to be about teamwork, Dylan. There's no "I" in team,' she reminded him.

'Oh, spare me the clichés, Emmy,' he drawled.

Her patience finally gave out. 'Just get your backside over here so we can sort things out,' she said, and hung up.

CHAPTER THREE

IT WAS ANOTHER hour before Emmy heard the front door open, and by that point she was ready to climb the walls with frustration.

Be conciliatory, she reminded herself. Do this for Pete and Ally. And Tyler. Even though you want to smack the man over the head with a wok, you have to be nice. At least for now. Make things work. It's only for three months, and then he'll realise that it'd be best if you looked after Tyler on your own. Come on, Emmy. You can do this. *Smile.*

'Good evening. Is pasta OK with you for dinner?' she asked when he walked into the kitchen.

He looked surprised. 'You cooked dinner for me?'

'As I was here, yes. By the way, that means it's your turn to cook for us tomorrow.'

'Uh-huh.' He looked wary.

'One thing you need to know. If I get hungry, I get grumpy.' She gave him a level stare. 'Don't make me wait in future. You *really* won't like me then.' Which was a bit ironic. He didn't like her now, and he hadn't even seen her on a really bad day.

'You could've eaten without me,' he said. 'I wouldn't have minded just reheating something in the microwave.'

'I had no idea how long you were going to be, and I would've felt bad if you'd turned up while I was halfway through eating my dinner.' She paused. 'Do you really work an hour's commute away from here?'

'No. I work in Docklands. About half an hour away.' At least he had the grace to look embarrassed. 'I had to finish something, first.'

She blew out a breath. 'OK. Take the lecture as read. We're sharing Tyler's care so, in future, you're either going to have to learn to delegate, or you'll have to work from home when the baby's napping.'

Hearing his godson's name seemed to galvanise Dylan. 'Where is he?'

'Asleep in his cot.' She gestured to the kitchen table. 'Sit down. I've made a start on the rota, given what we discussed yesterday morning. Perhaps you can review it while I finish cooking dinner, and move any of the sticky notes if you need to.'

'Sticky notes?' He looked puzzled.

'Because it's a provisional rota. Sticky notes mean it's easy to move things around without the rota getting messy. Once we've agreed our slots, I'll write it in properly. I'll get it laminated. And then we can use sticky notes day by day to make any changes to the rota—that way it'll be an obvious change so we'll both remember it.'

'OK.' He looked at her. 'Sorry.'

Dylan Harper had apologised to her? That was a first. Actually, no, it was the second time he'd said sorry to her in as many days. And, even though Emmy thought that he more than owed her that apology just now, she decided to be gracious about it. Be the bigger person. 'It's a bit of a radical lifestyle change for both of us. I think it'll take us a while to get used to it.'

He nodded. 'True.'

She concentrated on cooking the pasta and heating the sauce, then served up their meal at the kitchen table.

He put the card to one side. 'The rota looks fine to me. I notice it's a two-week one.'

'I thought that would be fair, giving each other alternate weekends off.'

'Yes, that's fair,' he agreed. He ate a mouthful of the pasta. 'And this is good. Thank you. I wasn't expecting dinner. I was going to make myself a sandwich or something.'

She knew exactly where he was coming from. 'I do that too often. It doesn't feel worth cooking for one, does it?'

'Especially if cooking isn't your thing.' He blew out a breath. 'I never expected to be living with—well, *you*.'

He'd made that perfectly clear. He really didn't have to harp on about it. 'We'll just have to make the best of it, for Tyler's sake,' she said dryly.

'Agreed. How did you get on with the mortgage and the letting agency?' he asked.

'It's all sorted. I'm letting my flat in Camden from Monday. You?'

'It's a short-term lease. Nadine has the house.'

His wife. 'Have you told her about this?'

His expression said very clearly, *that's none of your business*, and she shut up. No, it wasn't her business. And he'd already said that nobody would be upset by him sharing a house and Tyler's care with her.

'I'll go back to my place tonight to pick up the basics, and move the rest in over the next few days.' He looked at her. 'I assume you've done the same?'

'Yes to the basics today, but I haven't chosen a room yet. I was waiting for you.' She grimaced. 'I'm really glad Ally and Pete have two spare bedrooms as well as the nursery. I don't think I could face using their room.'

'Me, neither.' He shrugged. 'Which of the spare rooms I have doesn't bother me. Pick whichever one you like.'

'Thanks.' Though it wasn't the bedroom that concerned her most. 'Can I use Pete's study? I work from home,' she explained, 'and I need somewhere to set up my equipment. And that means a room with decent lighting.'

She was glad she'd been conciliatory when he said, 'That's fine by me. I can work anywhere with a laptop and a briefcase. So you have, what, some kind of workbench?'

It was the first time he'd ever shown any interest in her work, and it unnerved her slightly. She wasn't used to Dylan being anything other than abrupt to her. 'Yes, and I have a desk where I sketch the pieces before I make them. And before Tyler gets mobile I'll need to get a baby gate fixed on the doorway. I don't want him anywhere near my tools because they're sharp and dangerous.' She looked at him. 'Are you any good at DIY?'

'No. I'd rather pay someone to do it,' he said.

That was refreshing. The men she'd dated in the past had all taken the attitude that having a Y chromosome meant that they'd automatically be good at DIY, and they weren't prepared to admit when they were hopeless and couldn't even put a shelf on straight. Then again, she wasn't actually dating Dylan. He might be easy on the eye—she had to admit that he was good-looking—but he was the last man she'd ever want to date. He was way too uptight. 'OK. I know the number of a good handyman. I'll get it sorted.'

He looked at their empty plates. 'I haven't organised a cleaner yet.'

'And I wouldn't expect a cleaner to do dirty dishes,' Emmy said crisply. 'Especially as Ally and Pete have a dishwasher.'

'Point taken. I'll stack the dishwasher, then go and pick up my stuff.'

She chose her room while he was out, opting for the room she'd stayed in several times as a guest. It was strange to think that—unless things changed dramatically during their three-month trial—she'd be living here until Tyler had grown up. And even stranger to think she'd be sharing the house with Dylan Harper. Even if it might only be for a short time.

Still, she'd made a promise to Ally. She wouldn't back out.

She unpacked the small case she'd brought with her, then checked on Tyler. He was still sound asleep. Unable to resist, she reached down to touch his cheek. Such soft, soft skin. And he was so vulnerable. She and Dylan really couldn't let him down, whatever their doubts about each other. 'Sleep tight, baby,' she whispered, and went downstairs to the kitchen to wait for Dylan. She'd left the baby listener on; she glanced at it to make sure the lights were working, then put a cello concerto on low and began to sketch some ideas for the commission she'd been working on before the whole world had turned upside down.

When Dylan came back to the house, he was surprised to discover that Emmy was still up. He hadn't expected her to wait up for him. Or was she checking up on him or trying to score some weird kind of point?

'Is Tyler OK?' he asked.

She nodded. 'He's fast asleep.'

'Whose turn is it on the rota for night duty?' Then he grimaced. 'Forget I asked that. You've been looking after him since Ally and Pete went to Venice, so I'll go tonight if he wakes. Do I need to sleep on the floor in his room?'

'No. There's a portable baby listener.' She indicated the device with lights that was plugged in next to the kettle. 'Plug it in near your bed, and you'll hear him if he wakes. The lights change when there's a noise—the louder the noise, the more lights come on. So that might wake you, too.'

'Is he, um, likely to wake?' He didn't have a clue about how long babies slept or what their routines were. Pete had never talked about it, and Dylan hadn't really had much to do with babies in the past. His mother was an only child, so there had been no babies in his family while he'd been growing up; and Pete was the first of his friends to have a child. Babies just hadn't featured in his life.

Although he'd accused Emmy of leaving him to do the serious stuff, he was guiltily aware that he'd never babysat his godson or anything like that, and she clearly had. She'd been a better godparent than he had, by far—much more hands-on. He'd just been selfish and avoided it.

'He'd just started to sleep through, a couple of weeks back; but I guess he's picked up on the tension over the last few days because he's woken every night since the accident.' Emmy sighed. 'He might need a nappy change or some milk, or he might just want a cuddle.'

'How do you know what he needs?' Babies were too little to tell you. They just screamed.

'The nappy, you'll definitely know,' she said dryly. 'Just sniff him.'

'*Sniff* him?' Had she really said that?

She smiled. 'Trust me, you'll know if he has a dirty nappy. If he's hungry, he'll keep bumping his face against you and nuzzling for milk. And if he just wants a cuddle, hold him close and he'll settle and go to sleep. Eventually.'

'Poor little mite.' Dylan felt a muscle clench in his cheek. 'I hate that Pete's never going to get to know his son. He's not going to see him grow up. He's not going to teach him to ride a bike or swim. He's not going to…' He blew out a breath. 'I just hate all this.'

'Me, too,' she said softly. 'I hate that Ally's going to miss all the firsts. The first tooth, the first word, the first

steps. All the things she was so looking forward to. She
was keeping a baby book with every single detail.'

'I never thought I'd ever be a dad. It wasn't in my life
plan.' Dylan grimaced. 'And I haven't exactly been a
hands-on godparent, so far. Not the way you've been. I'm
ashamed to say it, but I don't have a clue where I should
even start right now.'

'Most men aren't that interested in babies until they
have their own,' she said. 'Don't beat yourself up about
it too much.'

'I've never even changed a nappy before,' he confessed.
There really hadn't been the need or the opportunity.

'Are you trying to get out of doing night duty?'

Was she teasing him or was she going to throw a hissy
fit? He really wasn't sure. He couldn't read her at all.
Emmy was almost a stranger, and now she was going to
be a huge part of his life, at least for the next three months.
Unwanted, unlooked for. A woman who'd always managed
to rub him up the wrong way. And he was going to have
to be nice to her, to keep the peace for Tyler's sake. 'No,'
he said, 'I'm not trying to get out of it. But you know what
you're doing—you've looked after Tyler for the last few
days on your own. And I was just thinking, it might be an
idea if you teach me what I need to do.'

She blinked at him. 'You want *me* to teach *you*?' She
tested the words as if she didn't believe he'd just said them.

'If I don't have a business skill I need, I take a course
to learn it. This is the same sort of thing. It might save
us both a lot of hassle,' he said dryly. 'And I think it'd be
better if you show me in daylight rather than tell me now.
You know the old stuff about teaching someone—I hear
and I forget, I see and remember, I do and I understand.'

She nodded. 'Fair enough. I'll keep the baby listener

with me tonight. But, tomorrow, please make sure you're back early so I can teach you the basics—how to change a nappy, make up a bottle of formula, and do a bath. By early, I mean before five o'clock.'

When was the last time he'd left the office before seven? He couldn't remember. Tough. Tomorrow, he'd just have to make the effort. 'Deal,' he said.

'OK. See you tomorrow.'

He realised that she'd been working when she closed a folder and picked up a handful of pencils. But then again, hadn't she said something about preferring to work in the evening? So he squashed the growing feeling of guilt. She was self-employed. A sole trader who didn't need to keep to traditional business hours. She obviously worked the hours that suited her.

'See you tomorrow,' he said. 'Which room did you pick?'

'The one opposite Tyler's.'

Which left the one next to Pete and Ally's room for him. 'OK. Thanks.' And then he realised he hadn't brought any bedding with him.

'The bed's already made up,' she said. 'I used linen from Ally and Pete's airing cupboard. I don't think they'd mind and it'd be a waste not to use it.'

He pushed a hand through his hair. 'Sorry. I didn't realise I'd said that aloud.'

'It's a lot to take in. A lot of change.' She shrugged. 'We'll muddle through.'

'Yeah. Sleep well.' Which was a stupid thing to say; of course she wouldn't, because Tyler would wake up.

But she didn't look annoyed. Her eyes actually crinkled at the corners. Again, Dylan was struck by the fact that Emmy Jacobs was pretty. And again it tipped him off balance. He couldn't even begin to think about Emmy in that way; it would make things far too complicated.

'Sleep well, Dylan,' she said, and strolled out of the kitchen.

Given how late Dylan had been the previous night, and the fact that Emmy had asked him to be back before five, he thought he'd better take the afternoon off to deal with the baby-care issues. He walked in to the house to find Emmy playing with the baby and singing to him, while the baby gurgled and smiled at her.

This felt distinctly weird. He'd never been that interested in babies and he'd never wanted a family of his own—which was most of the reason why he'd married Nadine, because she'd been just as dedicated to her career as he was and didn't pose any kind of emotional risk. Or so he'd thought. He hadn't expected her to change her mind and give him an ultimatum: give me a baby or give me a divorce. He didn't want a baby, so the choice was obvious.

And now he was here. Instead of being in his minimalist Docklands bachelor flat, he was living in a family home. Sharing the care of a tiny, defenceless baby. And he didn't have the least idea about what he was doing.

Emmy looked up at him. 'Hey, Ty, look, it's Uncle Dylan.' She smiled. 'You're back early.'

It was the first time Dylan could ever remember Emmy smiling spontaneously at him, as if she were genuinely pleased to see him, and he was shocked that it made him feel warm inside.

Was he going crazy, reacting like this to her?

No, of course not. It was just because he'd been knocked off balance by Pete and Ally's death. Grief made him want to hold someone, that was all; to feel connected to the world, still. He was *not* becoming attracted to Emmy Jacobs. Even though he was beginning to think that maybe she wasn't quite who he'd always thought she was.

'We agreed you were going to teach me about nappies and baths,' he said. 'And you asked me to come back early. Here I am.' He spread his hands. 'So let's get it sorted.'

She blew a raspberry on Tyler's tummy, making the baby giggle. 'He's clean at the moment, so we might as well hold off on that side until he really needs a nappy change. But he's wide awake, so you can play with him.'

'Play with him?' Dylan repeated. He knew it was ridiculous—he was the head of a very successful computer consultancy and could sort out tricky business problems quickly and effectively. But he didn't have a clue about how to play with a baby. He'd never done it. Never needed to do it.

She rolled her eyes. 'Dylan, you can't just sit and work on your laptop when you're in charge and Ty's awake. You need to play with him. Read to him. Talk to him.'

Dylan frowned. 'Isn't he a bit young for books?'

'No. Pete used to read to him,' she said softly. 'Ally read up about it and she wanted Tyler to have a good male role model. So Pete always did the bedtime story.'

OK. Reading to a baby couldn't be that hard. Talking, too. But playing…where did you start? He didn't know any baby games. Any nursery rhymes.

As if the panic showed on his face, she smiled at him. 'Come and give him a cuddle.'

And this was where Dylan got nervous. Where things could go terribly wrong. Because he didn't have a clue what he was doing. And he hated the fact that he had to take advice from someone as flaky as Emmy, because she clearly knew more about babies than he did. 'Do I have to hold his head or something?'

'No. He's four months old, not a newborn, so he can

support his head just fine. He can't sit up on his own yet, but that'll happen in a few weeks.' She looked at him. 'OK. You might want to change.'

'Why?'

'Unless you don't mind your suit getting creased and needing to go to the cleaner's more often.'

The question must've been written all over his face, because she added, 'You're going to be on the floor with him a lot.'

She had a point. 'I'll be down in a minute.' Dylan took the stairs two at a time to his room, then changed into jeans and T-shirt.

When he came downstairs, she gave him an approving look. 'Righty. He's all yours.'

Panic seeped through Dylan. What was he meant to do now?

She kissed the baby. 'See you later, sweetie. Have fun with Uncle Dylan.' And then she went to hand the baby to him.

He could muddle through this.

But it was important to get it *right*.

'Uh—Emmy.' He really hated this, but what choice did he have? It was ask, or mess it up. 'I don't know what to do.'

She rolled her eyes. 'We've already discussed this. Play with him. It's not rocket science.'

She wasn't going to make this easy for him, was she? 'I haven't had anything to do with babies before.'

She scoffed. 'He's four months old and he's your godson. Of course you've spent time with him.'

'He's always been asleep or Ally was feeding him. Pete and I didn't do baby stuff together, not like you and Ally.'

She looked at him and nodded. 'It must really stick in your craw to have to ask *me* for help. And if I was a different kind of woman, I'd just walk away and let you get on with it. But Tyler's needs come first, so I'll help you.'

'For his sake, not mine. I get it. But thank you anyway.'

'So how come you're so clueless? Pete always said you were the brightest person he knew—Ally, too. And you're the same age as the rest of us. I don't understand how, at thirty-five years old, you can know absolutely nothing about babies.'

Although he knew there was a compliment in there, of sorts, at the same time her words were damning. And he was surprised to find himself explaining. 'I'm an only child. No cousins, no close family.' At least, not since his grandmother died. His mother had never been close to him. 'Pete and Ally were the first of my friends to have children, and I…' He sighed. 'I guess I've been a bit preoccupied, the last few months.'

'Relationship break-ups tend to do that to you.' She looked rueful. 'And yes, I know that from way too much experience. OK. I never thought I'd need to show you any of this, but these are the kinds of things he likes to do with me.' She sat on the floor and balanced Tyler on her knees. 'Humpty Dumpty sat on the wall. Humpty Dumpty had a great…' She paused, and the baby clearly knew what was coming because he was beaming his head off. 'Fall,' she said, lowering her knees as she straightened her legs, and managing to keep the baby upright at the same time.

Her reward was a rich chuckle from the baby.

Something else that made him feel odd. 'And you always do the pause?' he asked, to take his focus off his feelings. This was about learning to care for a baby, not how he felt.

'I do. He's learned to anticipate it. He loved doing this with Ally. She used to string it out for ages.' She blew a raspberry on the baby's tummy, making him laugh, and handed him to Dylan. 'Your turn.'

'Humpty Dumpty sat on the wall,' Dylan intoned, feeling absolutely ridiculous and wishing he were a hundred miles away. Or, better still, back at his desk—where at least he knew what he was doing. 'Humpty Dumpty had a great...' He glanced at Emmy, who nodded. 'Fall,' he finished, and straightened his legs, letting the baby whoosh downwards but supporting him so he didn't fall.

Tyler laughed.

And something around Dylan's heart felt as if it had cracked.

There was a look of sheer wonder on Dylan's face as Tyler laughed up at him. He really hadn't been exaggerating about being a hands-off godfather, and this was obviously the first time he'd actually sat down with the baby and played with him. Emmy had the feeling that Dylan Harper, the stuffiest man in the world, kept everyone at arm's length. Well, you couldn't do that when you lived with a baby. So this was really going to change Dylan. It might make him human, instead of being a judgemental, formal machine.

When he did the Humpty Dumpty game for the third time, and laughed at the same time as the baby, she knew he was *definitely* changing. Tyler was about to turn Dylan Harper's life upside down again—but this time, in a good way.

'OK for me to go to work?' she asked.

'Sure. And, um, thanks for the lesson.' He still looked awkward and embarrassed, but at least they'd managed to be civil to each other.

Hopefully they could keep it up.

'No problem,' she said. 'I'll be in Pete's study if you get stuck with anything.'

CHAPTER FOUR

DYLAN WAS SURPRISED to discover how much he enjoyed playing with the baby. How good it was to hear that rich chuckle and know that he'd given Tyler a moment of pure happiness. If anyone had told him three weeks ago that he'd be having fun waving a toy duck around and quacking loudly, he would've dismissed it as utter insanity. But, this afternoon, it was a revelation.

He was actually disappointed when Tyler fell asleep.

Though it wasn't for long. The baby woke again and started crying, and Dylan picked him up almost on instinct. Then he wrinkled his nose. Revolting. It looked as if he needed another lesson from Emmy. He went to find her in Pete's study.

'Problem?' she asked.

'He needs a nappy change. Can you show me how to do it?'

'Ah, no. You're the one who said, "I do and I understand" is the best. I'll talk you through it.'

When they went upstairs to the nursery, Emmy did at least help Dylan get the baby out of his little all-in-one suit, for which he was grateful. But then she stood back and talked him through the actual process of nappy-changing.

How could someone so small produce something so—so *stinky*? he wondered.

He used wipe after wipe to clean the baby.

And it was only when he realised Emmy was grinning that he thought there might've been another way of doing it—one that maybe didn't use half a box of wipes at a time. 'So you're perfect at this, are you?' he asked, slightly put out.

'No—it usually takes me three or four wipes. Though Ally used to be able to do it in one.' Her smile faded, and she helped him put Tyler back in his Babygro.

'I'm going to do some work,' she said. 'Call me when Tyler needs a bath. His routine's on the board in the kitchen, so you'll know when he's due for a feed. If he's grizzly before then, try him with a drink. There's some cooled boiled water in sterilised bottles in the fridge.'

Again, Dylan was surprised by Emmy's efficiency. Maybe he'd misjudged her really badly, or he'd just seen her on bad days in the past—a *lot* of bad days—and taken her the wrong way.

'Oh, and you need to wind him after a feed,' she added. 'Hold him upright against your shoulder, rub his back, and he'll burp for you.'

'Got it.'

'Are you sure you can do this?'

No. He wasn't sure at all. But he didn't want Emmy to think that he was bailing out already. 'Sure,' he lied.

He carried Tyler downstairs and checked the routine board in the kitchen—which Emmy had somehow managed to get written up properly and laminated while he'd been at work. Apparently the baby needed a nap for about an hour; then he'd need a bath and then finally a feed.

And it was also his turn to make dinner.

He hadn't even thought about buying food. He'd only focused on the fact that he'd needed to get everything done and leave the office ridiculously early. He opened the fridge door, and was relieved to discover that there were ingredients for a stir-fry. And there were noodles and soy sauce in the cupboard. OK. He could work with that.

Now, how did you get a baby to sleep?

He sat down, settling Tyler against his arm. Sure, he'd given his godson a brief cuddle before, but Ally had understood that he wasn't used to babies and wasn't much good at this, so she hadn't given him a hard time about it. But it also meant she hadn't talked to him about baby stuff. And Emmy had just left him to it.

'I have no idea what to do now,' he said to the baby.

Tyler just gave him a gummy smile.

'Emmy seems to know what to do with you. But I don't.' OK, so he'd enjoyed playing with the baby, but was that all you were supposed to do?

'She's abandoned us,' he said, and then grimaced. 'And that's not very fair of me. If she'd stayed, I would've assumed she didn't trust me to do a good enough job with you and was being a control freak. So she can't win, whatever she does.'

Maybe he needed a new approach to Emmy. And she had given up some of her work time to show him how to care for Tyler. As she'd pointed out, she could've left him to muddle through and fall flat on his face, then gloated when he'd made a mess of things. But she hadn't. She'd played nice.

Maybe she was nice. Maybe he hadn't really given her a chance, before.

'I don't know any nursery rhymes,' he told the baby. Except for "Humpty Dumpty". He made a mental note to buy a book and learn some. 'I could tell you about computer programming.'

Another gummy smile.

'Binary code. Fibonacci sequence. Debugging.' He could talk for hours about that. 'Algorhythms.'

Well, the baby wasn't crying. That was a good thing, right? Dylan carried on talking softly to Tyler, until eventually the baby's eyes closed.

Now what? Did he just sit here until the baby woke up again? Or did he put the baby to sleep in his cot? He wished he'd thought to ask Emmy earlier. It wouldn't be fair to disturb her now. She needed time to get on with her work. And he could really do with checking his emails. OK. He'd put the baby down.

Gingerly, he managed to move out of the chair and placed the baby on his playmat. The mat was nice and soft, and Tyler would be safe there. Did he need a blanket? But his little hands felt warm. Maybe not, then.

While Tyler slept, Dylan caught up with some work on his laptop.

Not that it was easy to concentrate. He kept glancing over at the baby to check that everything was all right.

Eventually Tyler woke, and Dylan saved the file before closing the laptop and picking the baby up. 'Bath time. We need to go and find Emmy.'

He carried the baby through to Pete's study. The door was open, and soft classical music was playing. Another surprise; he'd pegged Emmy as someone who would listen to very girly pop music, the kind of stuff that was in the charts and that he loathed. Although he'd gone into the office earlier, he hadn't really taken any notice. He'd never seen her in a professional environment before, and there was a different air about her. Total focus and concentration as she worked on something that looked very intricate.

If he interrupted her now, would it make her jump and wreck what she was doing?

He waited, jiggling the baby as he'd seen her do, until

her hands moved away, and then he knocked on the open door. 'You said to come and get you when Tyler woke up and it was bath time.'

She looked up from her workbench, smiled, and put her tools down. 'Sure.'

He caught a glimpse of the work on her bench; it looked like delicate silver filigree. Again, it wasn't what he'd expected from her; he'd thought that she'd make in-your-face ethnic-style jewellery, or lots of clinking bangles.

'All righty. We need a bottle of boiled cooled water from the fridge.' She collected it on the way up to the bathroom.

'What's that for?' he asked.

'Washing his face—it's how Ally did it. She has what she calls a "top and tail" bowl.'

'A what?'

'To give him a quick wash instead of a bath. But you still use it for his face when you give him a bath.'

'Right.'

In the bathroom, she put the baby bath into the main bath. 'It's easier to use this than to put him in a big bath, because he can't sit up all on his own yet.'

'When will he do that?'

'When he's about six months old.'

Dylan looked at her, not sure whether to be impressed at her knowledge or annoyed by the one-upmanship. 'How come you know so much about babies?' Had she wanted a child of her own? he wondered. Were all women like Nadine, and just woke up one morning desperate for a baby?

'My bedtime reading,' she said lightly. 'I'll lend you the book, if you like—you'll probably find it useful.'

She undressed the baby, though Dylan noticed that she left Tyler's nappy on, and wrapped him in a towel. 'This is just to keep him warm while we're filling the bath. It needs to be lukewarm, and you need to put the cold water in first—it's better for it to be too cool, and for you to add a bit more warm water, than the other way round.' She demonstrated.

'How do you know when it's the right temperature?'

'You check the temperature of the water with your elbow.' She dipped her elbow into the water. 'If it feels too warm, it'll be too hot for the baby.'

'Why don't you use that thermometer thing?' He gestured to the gadget on the side of the bath.

She laughed. 'That was one of Pete's ideas. You know how he loves gadgets.' Her smile faded. 'Loved,' she corrected herself softly.

Awkwardly, Dylan patted her shoulder. 'Yeah.'

She shook herself. 'OK—now you pour the cooled water into the bowl, dip a cotton wool pad into it and squeeze it out, so it's damp enough not to drag his skin but not so wet that water's going to run into his eyes, then wipe his eyes. You need to use a separate one for each eye; apparently that's to avoid infection.'

'Right.' He followed her instructions—which were surprisingly clear and focused—and then worried that he was being too clumsy, but the baby didn't seem to mind.

'Now you wash his face and the creases round his neck with a different cotton wool pad.'

When he'd finished doing that, she said, 'And finally it's bath time.' She eyed his clothes. 'Sorry, I should've told you. Tyler likes to splash his hands in the bath, so you might get a bit wet.'

Dylan shrugged. 'It doesn't matter. This stuff will wash.'

She gave him an approving smile. It should've annoyed him that she was taking a position of superiority, but instead it made him feel warm inside. Which was weird. Emmy shouldn't make him feel warm inside. At all. He stuffed that into the box marked 'do not open' in his head, and concentrated on the task in hand.

'What about his hair?' he asked, looking at Tyler's soft fluffy curls.

'Do that before you put him in the bath,' she said. 'Keep him in the towel so he's warm, support his head with your hand and support him with your forearm—then you can scoop a little bit of water onto his hair and do the baby shampoo.'

Dylan felt really nervous, holding the baby—what if he dropped Tyler?—but Emmy seemed to have confidence in him and encouraged him as he gave Tyler a hair-wash for the very first time.

'Now you pat his hair dry. Be gentle and careful over the fontanelles.'

'Fontanelles?' he asked.

'Soft spots. The bones in his skull haven't completely fused, yet.'

That made Dylan feel even more nervous. Could he inadvertently hurt the baby? He knew he was making a bit of a mess of it, but she didn't comment.

'OK, now check the bath water again with your elbow.'

He dipped his elbow in. 'It feels fine.'

'Good. Now the nappy comes off, and he goes into the bath—support him like you did with the Humpty Dumpty thing.'

So far, so easy. Tyler seemed to enjoy the bath; as Emmy had warned him, there was a bit of splashing and chuckling.

Emmy stayed while he got the baby out of the bath and wrapped him in a towel with a hood to keep his head warm, then waited while Tyler did the nappy and dressed Dylan in a clean vest and Babygro.

She smiled at him. 'See, you're an expert now.'

Dylan didn't feel like it; but he was starting to feel a lot more comfortable around Tyler, thanks to her. 'I'm trying, anyway.'

'I know you are—and that's all Tyler would ask for,' she said softly.

Dylan remembered how he'd thought she was trying in more than one sense; yet she wasn't judging him that way. He felt a bit guilty. 'I looked in the fridge. Is chicken stir-fry all right for dinner?'

'That'd be lovely, thanks.'

'Good. I'll call you when it's ready.'

'Are you OK about feeding him?' she asked. The doubts must have shown on his face, because she added, 'Just put the bottle of milk in a jug of hot water for a couple of minutes to warm up, then test it on the inside of your wrist to make sure it's warm but not hot.'

'How do you mean, test it on the inside of my wrist?'

'Just hold the bottle upside down and shake it over your wrist. A couple of drops will come out. If it feels hot then the milk's too hot.' She looked slightly anxious. 'Don't take this the wrong way—I'm not meaning to be patronising—but when you feed him you need to make sure the teat's full of milk, or he'll just suck in air.'

'Right.'

'And when you put him in his cot at bedtime, his feet need to be at the bottom of the cot so he doesn't end up wriggling totally under the covers and getting too hot.'

'OK,' he said, hoping he sounded more confident than he felt.

'Call me if you get stuck,' she said.

Which would be a cop-out. He could do this. It wasn't that hard to feed a baby, surely?

He managed to warm the milk, then sat down and settled the baby in the crook of his arm. Remembering what she'd said about the air, he made sure he tilted the bottle. The baby was very focused on drinking his milk, and Dylan couldn't help smiling at him. There was something really satisfying about feeding a baby, and he wished he'd been more involved earlier in the baby's life instead of backing off, fearing the extra intimacy.

This was what Nadine had wanted from him. What he hadn't been able to give, although now he was doing it for his best friend's child because he simply had no other choice. Except to walk away, which he couldn't bring himself to do.

He couldn't imagine Nadine doing this, even though he knew she'd wanted a baby of her own. She wouldn't have been comfortable exchanging her sharp business suits and designer dresses for jeans and a T-shirt. Dylan simply couldn't see her on the floor playing with a baby, or singing songs.

Unlike Emmy. Emmy, who'd been all soft and warm and cute…

He shook himself. He hadn't wanted children with Nadine. So her ultimatum of baby or divorce had given him an obvious choice. And he didn't want to think about his relationship with Emmy. Because, strictly speaking, it wasn't actually a relationship; it was a co-guardianship. They were here for Tyler, not for each other.

'Emotions and relationships,' he said softly to the baby, 'are very much overrated.'

When the baby had finished feeding, Dylan burped him in accordance with Emmy's instructions, then carried him up to the nursery and put him in his cot. There was a stack of books by the cot; Dylan found one in rhyme and read it through, keeping his voice soft and low. Tyler's eyelids seemed to be growing heavy; encouraged, Dylan read the next two books. And then finally Tyler's eyes closed.

Asleep.

Good. He'd managed it.

He touched the baby's soft little cheek. 'Sleep well,' he whispered.

Then he headed for the study and knocked on the open door.

Emmy looked up. 'How did you get on?'

'Fine. He's asleep. Dinner in ten minutes?'

'That'll be great. I'll just finish up here.'

She joined him in the kitchen just as he was serving up.

'OK if we eat in here, tonight?' Dylan asked.

'That's fine.' She took her first mouthful. 'This is very nice, thank you.'

He flapped a dismissive hand. 'It wasn't exactly hard—just stir-fry chicken, noodles, vegetables and soy sauce.'

'But it's edible and, more importantly, I didn't have to cook it. It's appreciated.'

There was an awkward silence for a few moments.

Work, Dylan thought. Work was always a safe topic. 'I saw that necklace you were making. I had no idea you made delicate stuff like that.'

'You mean you thought I just stuck some chunky beads on a string and that was it?' she asked.

He felt his face colour with embarrassment. 'Well, yes.'

She shrugged. 'There's nothing wrong with a string of chunky beads.'

He thought of his mother, and wanted to disagree.

'But no, I do mainly silverwork—and I also work with jet. I carve animals.'

'Like those ones on the shelf in Tyler's room?'

She nodded. 'Ally wanted a Noah's ark sort of thing, so I'd planned to do her one a month.'

'They're very good.'

'Thank you.' Emmy inclined her head at his compliment

but he noticed that she accepted it easily. She clearly knew she was good at what she did. Just as he was good at what he did. Something they had in common, then.

'Why jet?' he asked.

'We always used to go to my great-aunt Syb's in the school summer holidays, up in Whitby.'

'Dracula country,' he said.

She smiled. 'Well, it's known for that nowadays, but it's also the Jurassic coastline, full of fossils—that's why there's lots of jet and amber in the cliffs there.'

'Amber being fossilised tree resin, right?'

She nodded. 'And jet's fossilised monkey puzzle tree. They used to use it a lot in Victorian times for mourning jewellery, but it's been used as jewellery for much longer than that. There are some Roman jewellery workshop remains in York, and archaeologists have found gorgeous jet pendants carved as Medusa's head.'

Dylan noticed how her eyes glittered; this was clearly something she felt really passionate about. For a second, it made him wonder what her face would look like in the throes of passion, but he pushed the thought away. It was way too inappropriate. He needed to keep his focus on work, not on how lush Emmy Jacobs' mouth was. 'And that's when you got interested in making jewellery, at your great-aunt's?'

She nodded. 'We used to go beachcombing for jet and amber because Great-Aunt Syb's best friend Jamie was a jeweller and worked with it. I was fascinated at how these dull-looking, lightweight pebbles could suddenly become these amazingly shiny beads and flowers. Jamie taught me how to work with jet. It's a bit specialised.' She grimaced. 'I'd better warn you, it does tend to make quite a bit of dust, the really thick and heavy sort, but I always clean up after I've worked.'

If she'd said that a week ago, he would've scoffed; from what he'd seen, Emmy Jacobs was as chaotic as his mother. But now, having shared a house with her for a day and discovered that she ruled her life with lists and charts, he could believe it. She might appear chaotic, but she knew exactly what she was doing. 'How do you sell your jewellery? Do you have a shop?' He hadn't thought to ask before.

'No. I sell mainly through galleries—I pay them a commission when they sell a piece. Plus there's my website.'

'So what's the plan—to have a shop of your own?'

She shook her head. 'If I had a shop, I'd need to increase production to cover all the extra expenses—rent, utilities and taxes, not to mention staffing costs. And I'd have to spend a lot of time serving customers instead of doing the bit of my job that I like doing most, creating jewellery. And then there's the worry about who'd cover the shop when an assistant was on holiday or off sick…' She grimaced. 'No, I'd rather keep it this way.'

She'd clearly thought it all through, taking a professional view of the situation, Dylan thought. He would never have expected that from her. And it shook him to realise how badly he'd misjudged her. He'd always thought himself such a good judge of character. How wrong he'd been.

'So what actually do you do?' she asked. 'I mean, Pete said you're a computer guru, but I assume you don't actually build computers or websites?'

He smiled. 'I can, and sometimes that's part of a project, but what I do is software development—bespoke stuff for businesses. So I talk to them about their requirements, draw up a specification, then do the architecture.'

'Architecture?' She looked puzzled.

'I write the code,' he said, 'so the computer program does what they want it to do. Once the code's written, you set up the system, test it, debug it, and agree a maintenance programme with the client.'

'So businesses can't just buy a software package—say like you do with word-processing, spreadsheets and accounting programs?'

'Obviously those ones they can, but what my clients tend to want is database management, something very specific to their business. So if they had a chain of shops, for example, they need to have the tills linked with the stock system, so every time they sell something it updates and they can see their stock levels. Once they get down to a certain stock level, it triggers a reorder report, based on how long it takes to get the stock from the supplier,' Dylan explained. 'It's also helpful if the till staff take the customer's details, because then they can build up a profile for the customer based on past purchases, and can use that knowledge to target their marketing more specifically.'

'Very impressive,' she said.

He shrugged. 'It's basic data management—and it's only as good as the data you feed in. That's why the requirements and spec side is important. What the client thinks they want might not be what they actually want, so you have to grill them.'

'I can see you'd be good at that,' she said, then winced. 'Sorry, that was rude. I'm not trying hard enough.'

He should've been annoyed and wanting to snipe back; but he liked the fact that she was being honest. Plus he was beginning to suspect that she had quite a sharp wit, something he appreciated. 'It's OK. We've never really got on before, so we're not exactly going to be best friends, are we?'

'No, but we don't have to be rude to each other, either.'

'I guess not.' He paused. 'So do you use a computer system?'

'Sort of. I do my accounts on a spreadsheet because I'm a sole trader and don't need anything more complicated, but I did have my website designed so I could showcase my work and people could buy what they wanted online from me direct. It shows whether the piece they want is in stock or if they need to order it and how long it'll take—but, yes, I have to update that manually.'

Dylan made a mental note to look up her website. Maybe there was something he could add to it to make her life easier. Which didn't mean he was going soft; making things run smoothly for her meant that he wouldn't have to prop up their roster for more than his fair share of effort.

'So what's your big plan?' she asked. 'Expansion?'

'Pretty much keep doing what I do now,' he said. 'I have a good team. They're reliable and they're prepared to put in the hours to get the projects in on time.'

'And you like your job?'

'It's like breathing, for me,' he said honestly. Something that Nadine had never really quite understood. His job was who he was.

'Same here,' she said, surprising him. It was something else they had in common.

When they'd finished the meal, she said, 'It's my turn to do the dishes, and I'm not weaselling out of it—but there's something I need to share with you. Back in a tick.'

She returned with a book and handed it to him.

He read the title. '*The Baby Bible*. What's this?'

'You asked me how come I know so much about babies. It's because of this. I bought it when Ty was born, so I'd know what to do when Ally asked me to babysit. It tells you everything you need to know—how to do things, what all the milestones are.' She spread her hands. 'And if that doesn't work then I'll bring in my other secret weapon.'

'Which is?'

She looked slightly shame-faced. 'Ring my mum and ask her advice.'

He thought about what would happen if he rang his mother and asked for help with a baby. No, it wasn't going to happen. He was pretty sure his mother hadn't been able to cope with having a baby or a child, which was why she'd dumped him on her parents so many times. The only person he could've asked about babies was his grandmother, but she'd died a year ago now. After he'd married Nadine, but before the final split. And, although she'd never judged, never actually said anything about it, Dylan knew his grandmother had thought the wedding was a huge mistake.

How right she'd been.

What would she think about this set-up?

What would she have thought about Emmy?

He shook himself. 'Do you need it back soon?'

'I've read it through cover-to-cover once. But if you could leave it in Tyler's room or the kitchen when it's my shift, so I can refer to it if I need to, that'd be really helpful.' She glanced at her watch. 'Do you mind if I go back to work now and do the washing up later?'

'Sure—and I'm on nights tonight.'

'I would say sleep well, but...' She shrugged. 'That's entirely up to Tyler.'

'Yes.' And Dylan wasn't so sure he'd sleep well anyway. He still had to get his head round a lot of things. New responsibilities, having to share his space with someone else when he'd just got used to his bachelor lifestyle, and having a totally new routine for starters. Not to mention that getting to know Emmy was unsettling, because all his preconceptions about her were starting to look wrong. 'Sleep well,' he said, and went to settle down with his new reading material.

CHAPTER FIVE

THE BABY WOKE at half past three, and the wails coming through the baby listener seemed incredibly loud.

Dylan surfaced from some weird dream, switched off the baby listener and staggered out into Tyler's nursery.

According to what Emmy had told him—and what he'd read last night—screaming meant the baby was dirty, hungry, tired or wanted a cuddle. He picked the baby up and sniffed him. Nothing like yesterday's appalling whiff, so Tyler didn't need a nappy change. It was the middle of the night, so he could be tired—but then again, he wouldn't have woken if he was tired. So was he hungry, or did he just want a cuddle?

He probably wanted his mum. Though, Tyler was way too little to understand that Ally couldn't be there for him anymore. Not like Dylan's mother, who hadn't been there because she hadn't wanted to; Tyler had been very much loved by both his parents. And it was wrong, wrong, *wrong* that they'd died so young.

The baby nuzzled him.

Hadn't Emmy said that was a sign of hunger?

'OK, Ty, food it is,' he whispered. He took the baby down to the kitchen, managed to switch on the kettle and get the milk out of the fridge, and walked up and down with the baby, stroking his back to sooth him and jiggling him.

Dear God, why had nobody told him that babies were so *loud*? If Tyler carried on much longer, Emmy was bound to wake. And that wasn't fair because this was his shift, not hers, and he should be able to deal with this.

It seemed to take forever to heat the milk, and Tyler's wails grew louder and louder. Eventually Dylan managed it and tested the milk against his wrist. It wasn't as warm as yesterday, but hopefully it would be warm enough to keep the baby happy.

He sat in the dark while the baby guzzled his milk.

'Better now?' he asked softly. Not that he was going to get an answer.

Then he remembered about the burping thing. The last thing he wanted was for the baby to wake again, crying because his tummy hurt. Dylan felt like a zombie as it was. He held Tyler on his shoulder and rubbed the baby's back, then nearly dropped the baby when he heard a loud burp and felt an immediate gush of liquid over his bare shoulder. What? Why hadn't Emmy warned him about this? It hadn't happened last time. Had he done something wrong?

The baby began to cry again. Oh, hell—the burped-up milk had probably soaked his clothes, too, and he'd be cold. He needed a change of clothes; Dylan couldn't possibly put him back into his cot in this state.

Luckily the overhead light in the nursery was on a dimmer switch. Dylan kept it as low as possible, and hunted for clean clothes. Tyler seemed to have grown four extra arms and six extra legs, all of which were invisible, but eventually Dylan managed to get him out of the Babygro.

The nappy felt heavy; clearly that needed changing, too, before Dylan put clean clothes on the baby. But when he settled Tyler on the changing unit and opened the nappy, the baby promptly peed over him. Dylan jumped back in shock, then dashed forward in horror. This was his first night in charge and he was making a total mess of it. The baby could've rolled over and fallen off the changing station and been badly hurt.

His heart was hammering. Please, no. He'd already lost Pete and Ally; he couldn't bear the idea of anything happening to Tyler. Even though the baby had disrupted his life, even though it panicked him that he didn't know what he was doing, he was beginning to feel other emotions than just resentment towards Tyler.

He tried to make light of it, even though he was in a cold sweat. 'Help me out here, Ty,' he muttered. 'I'm new at all this.'

But finally the baby had a clean nappy and clean clothes. Dylan put him in the cot and made sure the covers were tucked in properly; within seconds Tyler had fallen back to sleep in his usual position with his arms up over his head, looking like a little frog.

Dylan went back to his room feeling almost hung-over. It was way too late to have a shower; the noise from the water tank would wake Emmy. So he simply sponged off the worst of the milk at the sink in his en-suite, and fell into bed. How did parents of newborns cope with even less sleep than this? he wondered as he sank back into sleep. How had Pete not been a total zombie?

The next morning, his alarm shrilled at the usual time. Normally Dylan woke before his alarm, whereas today he felt groggy from lack of sleep. He staggered out of bed and showered; he didn't feel much better afterwards, though at least he didn't smell of burped-up milk anymore.

He went to the nursery to look in on Tyler. The baby was asleep in his cot, looking angelic. 'It's all right for some,' Dylan said wryly. 'I could do with a nap. So have an extra one for me.'

He dragged himself downstairs. Was it his imagination, or could he smell coffee?

Emmy was in the kitchen, sitting at the table with a mug of coffee. She raised an eyebrow when she saw him. 'Rough night?' she asked.

'Apart from Ty throwing up half the milk over me and then peeing over me...'

She burst out laughing and he glared at her. 'It's not funny.'

'Yes, it is.'

'You could've *warned* me he'd do that.'

She spread her hands. 'To be fair, he hasn't actually done that to me. But Ally told me he once did it to Pete.'

'Just don't tell me it's a male bonding thing,' he grumbled.

'And I thought you were supposed to be a morning person.' She laughed, and poured him a mug of coffee. 'Here. This might help.'

'Thanks. I think.' He took a sip. 'I was useless last night. I nearly let him fall off the changing station.'

She flapped a dismissive hand. 'I'm sure you didn't.'

'I jumped back from him when he peed on me.'

'Which is a natural reaction, and you would've been there to stop him if he'd started to roll.'

It still made him go cold, how close it had been. '*Can* he roll over?'

'Yes.' She rolled her eyes. 'Stop panicking, Dylan. You know what to expect now. You won't let him fall.'

How could she have so much confidence in him, when he had absolutely none in himself? And what had happened to her, anyway? The Emmy Jacobs he knew would've sniped about him not being good enough. This Emmy was surprisingly supportive. Which made him feel even more adrift. He was used to being in charge and knowing exactly what he was doing. Right now, he was winging it, and he hated feeling so useless.

He covered up his feelings by saying, 'I could do with some toast. Do we have bread?'

'Not much. But it's my turn for the supermarket run today, so I'll get some.'

'Right.'

'Any food allergies, or anything you hate eating?'

'No to the first, offal to the second.'

She smiled. 'That makes two of us. I'll pick up dinner while I'm out.'

He thought about it. Really, this was much like sharing a student house. Except it wasn't with his friends, it was with a near stranger. And he had the added responsibility of a baby. 'We need to sort out a kitty.'

'Sure. We can do that later.'

'And we need a rota for doing the shopping. Or maybe we could get the shopping delivered.' He frowned. 'Do you have a car?'

'Yes. And I know how to fit Ty's baby seat in it.' She paused. 'What about you?'

'Yes to having a car. I don't have a clue about a baby seat.'

'We only have one baby seat between us. I think we're going to need one for your car as well as mine.'

He frowned. 'So I need to take another afternoon off?'

She shrugged. 'Or we could go at the weekend.'

Her weekend on, his weekend off—and he was going to have to spend it doing baby stuff instead of catching up with work. Great. Yet more disruption. And then the guilt surged through him again. It wasn't Tyler's fault that he needed to be looked after—or that Dylan had agreed to do it. 'OK. We'll go at the weekend,' he said.

Saturday morning saw them in the nursery department of a department store in the city.

'Your baby's gorgeous,' the assistant said, cooing over Tyler.

Dylan was about to correct her when Emmy said, 'Yes, we think so.' She shot him a look, daring him to contradict her.

He thought about it. Strictly speaking, Tyler *was* their baby. Just not a baby they'd actually made together.

Then he wished he hadn't thought about making babies with Emmy. How soft her skin would be against his. How she smelled of some spicy, floral scent he couldn't quite place. How it made him want to touch her, taste her…

Oh, hell. He really couldn't have the hots for *Emmy*. He hadn't even looked at another woman since he'd split up with Nadine. Abstinence: that had to be what was wrong with him. That, or the fact that he'd done the night shift, the previous night, and Tyler had woken three times, so lack of sleep had fried his brain.

He shut up and let Emmy do the talking.

And then Emmy spied a cot toy, something that apparently beamed pictures of stars and a moon on the ceiling and played a soft tinkling lullaby.

'Can we get this as well? I think he'd love it.'

'You mean, *you* love it.' Emmy seemed to like simple, childlike things. And Dylan hadn't quite worked out yet whether he found that more endearing or annoying. He certainly didn't loathe her as much as he once had. She was good with the baby, too.

Her eyes crinkled at the corners. 'OK, then, let's ask him.' She picked up the cot toy, crouched down beside the pram, switched it on and let Tyler see the lights and hear the lullaby.

Tyler's eyes went wide, then he laughed and held his hands out towards it.

Emmy looked up at him and smiled. 'I think that's a yes.'

Again a surge of attraction hit him. Was he crazy? This was Emmy Jacobs, who sparred with him and sniped at him and was his co-guardian. She the last person he wanted to get involved with. But at the same time he had to acknowledge that there was something about her that really got under his skin. Something that made him want to know more about her. Get closer.

And that in itself was weird. He didn't do close. Never had. He didn't trust anyone to let them near enough—even, if he was honest with himself, Nadine.

The rest of the weekend turned out to be Dylan's first weekend of being a dad. Although it was officially Emmy's weekend on duty, he somehow ended up going to the park with her to take Tyler out for some fresh air. He noticed that she talked to Tyler all the time, even though there was no way a baby could possibly understand everything she said. She pointed out flowers and named the colours for him; she pointed out dogs and birds and squirrels.

She was clearly taking her duties as godmother and guardian really seriously, and Dylan was beginning to wonder just why he'd ever disliked her so much. Then again, this new Emmy didn't have a smart-aleck mouth. She didn't snipe, and she wasn't cynical and hard-bitten like the Emmy Jacobs he was used to.

Which one was the real Emmy? he wondered. Was she letting her guard down and letting him see the real her? Or was this just some kind of mirage and Spiky Emmy would return to drive him crazy?

They stopped at the café in the park, and Emmy asked for a jug of hot water to heat Tyler's milk. While she found them a table, he bought the coffees. He'd seen her looking longingly at the cinnamon pastries, so he bought her one of those as well.

'That's really kind of you,' she said when he brought the tray over to their table.

But her eyes were full of anguish. What was going on here? 'What's wrong?' he asked.

She sighed. 'I struggle with my weight. And no, that isn't your cue to tell me that I'm fine as I am. My job's pretty sedentary, so I only manage to keep my weight under control because I go to an exercise class three times a week. But things have changed, now, and I'm not going to have time for classes anymore. I haven't been since the week before Ally and Pete went to Venice.'

'You miss your classes?'

She shrugged. 'I'll manage.'

'That's not what I asked. You miss them?'

'Yes,' she admitted. 'It's ridiculously soon. But yes, I miss them. I spend too much time sitting at my desk—I really lose track of time when I'm working—and the classes used to help me get the knots out and stretch my muscles.'

'When are they?'

'Mornings. Straight after the school run.' She shrugged. 'So when Ty's at school, in four years' time or so, I can go back to them.'

'Maybe,' he said, 'we can change our rota. I'll go in to the office a bit later, on the mornings when you have a class—though obviously that means I'll be back later on those days to make up the time.'

'You'd do that for me?' She looked startled, almost shocked; and then she gave him a heart-stopping smile. It was his turn to be shocked then, by how much her smile affected him. How it made him feel as if the room had just lit up. 'Thank you, Dylan. What about you—do you do anything you've had to give up and miss already?'

'The gym,' he admitted. 'It's my thinking time. And I kind of like the endorphin hit at the end.'

'Let me know when your sessions are, and we'll switch the rota round.' She looked at the pastry, then at him, and gave him another smile. 'Thank you, Dylan. That's so nice.'

'Pleasure,' he responded automatically. And he stifled the thought that actually, it was a pleasure, seeing her made happy by such a little thing.

He'd surprised himself, offering to change the rota so she could do her weekly classes. And she'd surprised him by immediately offering to do the same for him. Why had he ever thought her selfish, when she so obviously believed in fairness? Had he just read her wrong in the past, and it had snowballed to the point where it was easier to dislike her than to wonder if he'd got it wrong? Not wanting to think about his burgeoning feelings, he said, 'I've been talking to Pete's parents about the funeral. They'd like it to be in the same church where Pete and Ally got married.'

She nodded. 'Ally's parents said the same.'

'Good. It makes it easier that they agree.' He paused. 'But Pete's parents also said they want the wake at the house rather than in a hall somewhere.'

'So we'll have to cater it, you mean?'

He nodded.

She blew out a breath. 'Then I vote we get the local deli to do as much of it as possible, so all we have to do is lay stuff out on serving platters on the dining room table. And I'll rope my mum in to help. Between us we can manage the drinks.'

There was no point in asking his mother to help. Dylan

couldn't remember whether she was in India or Bali, but he knew she was on retreat somewhere, and he also knew from experience that she wouldn't allow anything to interrupt that. Even if her only child really needed her help. He'd learned that one at a pretty early age. 'Right,' he said shortly.

She narrowed her eyes. 'Is everything OK, Dylan?'

'Yes.' He raked a hand through his hair. 'Just this whole thing…I still can't quite get my head around it. I still keep thinking Pete's going to walk through the door and ask us if we missed him.'

'Me, too,' she said. 'Ally's the first person really close to me I've lost. I guess it's a normal reaction, but I wonder when I'm going to stop missing her.'

'You don't stop missing her. You just get better at dealing with it.'

She said nothing, just looked at him. Those wide grey eyes were full of empathy rather than pity, so he found himself unexpectedly telling her the rest. 'My grandmother. She died last year. It's little things that catch you—a bit of music that reminds me of her, or walking past someone who's wearing the same perfume. Or seeing something in the shop that I know she'd love, and suddenly remembering that she's not going to be here for her birthday or Christmas so there's no point in buying it.'

She reached over and squeezed his hand. Just long enough to let him know that she understood and sympathised, but not long enough to be cloying. Weird. He hadn't expected to actually start *liking* Emmy.

He gave her the smallest, smallest smile. 'I'll talk to the vicar and sort that side of it out. The funeral directors just want a decision on the casket. Can I ask you to sort the food and drink?'

'Sure. Does anything else need doing?'

'I'm doing a eulogy for Pete. Do you want to do one for Ally?'

She shook her head. 'I don't think I could stand up there and do it. I would...' She paused, clearly swallowing back a sob. 'Well, I don't want to let her down by crying through it. She deserves more than that.'

He'd done enough presentations in his time to be able to get through it. 'I'll do it for you, if you like. Just tell me what you want to say and I'll read it out.'

She swallowed hard. 'Thank you.'

'No problem.'

'I could do a wall, though,' she said. 'I could scan in some of the photographs from when they were small, as well as the digital ones I've got from more recent years. We could talk to their parents and get their favourite memories as well.'

'That's a good idea. I'll talk to Pete's again while you talk to Ally's?'

'That works for me.'

'I think they'd like to stay at the house, that night,' Dylan said. 'I was thinking, it wouldn't be fair for either couple to stay in Pete and Ally's room.'

'You're right,' she agreed. 'It's my night on call, so I can use a sleeping bag in Tyler's room.'

'And I'll take the sofa,' he said.

Funny how their minds were in tune on this one.

Would they be in tune in other ways, too? The thought crept insidiously into his head and lodged there, and even though he tried to block it out he couldn't help being aware of just how attractive Emmy actually was.

She leaned down to touch the sleeping baby's cheek. 'You'll definitely know your mum and dad, Ty. Dylan and I, we have photographs and memories, all sorts of things we can share with you when you're older. Your mum did a "This Is Your Life" book for me when I was thirty, and I can do something like that for you of her.'

'I'll chip in with stuff about your dad,' he said, touching Tyler's other cheek.

They shared a glance and Dylan wondered—did it have to take the death of our best friends for us to get along? It was odd how easily they'd fallen into teamwork—since they'd moved into the house, he hadn't sniped once and neither had she—and he was shocked to realise that he actually liked her. A lot. Emmy was funny, clever, good company. How had he never noticed that before?

Emmy just about managed to get through the funeral, though she couldn't help bawling her eyes out during 'Abide With Me'. The bit about where was Death's sting always got to her. 'Amazing Grace' put a lump in her throat as well, and when the church echoed to Eva Cassidy singing 'Somewhere Over the Rainbow' there wasn't a dry eye anywhere.

Though she was glad that everyone was wearing bright colours rather than black, to celebrate Ally and Pete's life and the precious memories. It was important to share the good stuff as well as mourn them. To give them a decent send-off.

Tyler was an angel.

And Dylan was amazing.

He was sitting in the front row, next to her; when he stood up to do the eulogies from the pulpit, she couldn't take her eyes off him. Even though the tears were spilling down her cheeks as he spoke the words she'd written about her best friend.

She hugged him when he returned to his seat. 'You did a fantastic job,' she whispered. 'Just perfect.'

* * *

Dylan returned the hug, even though bits of him worried that he quite liked the feel of Emmy in his arms. He dismissed it simply as grief coming out. He *wasn't* attracted to Emmy Jacobs.

Ha—who was he trying to kid? Of course he was.

But he couldn't act on that attraction, for Tyler's sake. Getting involved with Emmy would make everything way too complicated. It would be better to keep his distance, the way he always did.

Friends neither he nor Emmy had seen since university days had come to the funeral. Back at the house, everyone was talking about the room divider Emmy had made with the photographs, sharing memories and the house echoed with as much laughter as tears.

The food was working out, too. Emmy was bustling around, sorting out the drinks and topping up the empty plates. Her mum had helped out and done way, way more than his own mother would've done if she'd been there. Between the three of them, they'd managed to handle this.

Finally everyone went and the clearing up started.

'You look really tired,' Emmy said gently to Ally's and Pete's parents. 'Why don't you go and lie down for a bit? Dylan and I can sort all this out.'

'We can't leave you to do all this, love,' Ally's dad said.

'Yes, you can. It's been a really tough day for us all, and I can't even begin to imagine how hard it's been for you. You need some rest. I'll bring you up a cup of tea in a minute.'

'Thank you, love,' Pete's mum said.

Again, Dylan found himself marvelling. Pete and Ally's parents clearly knew Emmy well and liked her. He was beginning to think that he was the one who was totally out of step. She'd been brilliant today. He made a mental note to cut her more slack in future.

Emmy's mum stayed to help, then kissed Emmy good-bye and, to Dylan's surprise, gave him a hug. 'Take care of yourself and call me if you need me, OK? That goes for both of you. Any time.'

He found himself envying Emmy's closeness to her mum. If only his own mother had been like that, maybe things would've been different. Maybe he would've known how to really love someone and not made such a mess of his marriage. Though he appreciated the way Emmy's mother had included him. How would Emmy have got on with his family? He had a feeling that Emmy would've liked his gran, and his gran would've liked Emmy.

And this was dangerous territory. He couldn't let himself think about this.

Emmy put Tyler to bed while he finished moving all the furniture back. Then she took a tray up to Pete and Ally's parents with tea and sandwiches.

When she came back down, Dylan noticed that she looked upset.

'Are you OK?' he asked.

She nodded. 'They're not coming down again today. I think it's exhausted all of them.' She bit her lip. 'It's so wrong, having to bury your child. It isn't the natural order of things. I really feel for them. Today they all seemed to age ten years in a matter of seconds. Did you see Ally's dad walking into church? He had to hold on to the side of the pew until he composed himself. It's not that long ago he was walking down that aisle with Ally on his arm in that gorgeous fishtail dress, and you and Pete were waiting at the altar.'

'Yeah, I remember,' Dylan said softly. 'And you're right. Burying a parent must be hard, but it's more the natural order. Burying your child must be the worst feeling in the world.'

'And there's nothing we can do to make it better.' Her voice cracked and she looked anguished.

'I know, but I think we did Pete and Ally proud,' he said. 'Everyone was here celebrating them.'

She nodded. 'You're right. I think it's what they would've wanted.'

He wandered over to look at the photos on the divider, and saw the one of Emmy and Ally together as students.

'Your hair looks absolutely terrible. Whatever made you dye it blue?'

She came to join him and shrugged. 'I was a design student. We all did that sort of thing back then.'

'It looks nice now. Obviously it's not your natural colour but it suits you. It brings out your eyes.' He reached out to brush a lock of hair from her face.

'Careful, Dylan. Anyone might think we were on the way to being friends, with you paying me compliments like that.'

He raised an eyebrow. 'Maybe we are.'

She dragged in a breath. 'I wish it hadn't taken Ally and Pete to die before we started to see—well, what *they* saw in us.'

'Me, too.' He gave her a crooked smile. 'We can't change the past. But, for what it's worth, I'm sorry I misjudged you. You're not the needy, flaky mess I thought you were.'

Her eyes filled with tears. 'I'm sorry I misjudged you, too. You're still a bit judgemental, and you open your mouth before you think about what's going to come out of it. You might have the social skills of a rhino, but you do have a heart.'

Did he? Sometimes he wasn't so sure. He'd built so many walls around it that it was lost.

She rubbed her eyes with the back of her hand. 'Now I'm being wet. Ignore me.'

'It's OK. I'm not that far off crying, myself,' he admitted. He looked at her. 'Do you want a glass of wine?

She nodded.

'Me, too. Come on.'

He poured them each a glass of wine and then put some soft piano music on before curling up on the opposite end of the sofa to her. Her toes touched his ankle, but it didn't make him want to pull away. Weirdly, he felt more comfortable with her now, on one of the saddest days of his life, than he ever had before.

'I like this. What is it?' she asked.

'Einaudi. You work to classical music, don't you?'

'Vivaldi—not "the Four Seasons", because that's been overplayed to the point where I find it almost impossible to listen to it, but I like his cello concerti. They're calming and regular, good to work to.'

'I was looking at your website,' he said. 'You're very talented.'

She looked surprised, but inclined her head in acknowledgement of the compliment. 'Thank you.'

'But you could really do with a proper stock management program. I've written one and tested it for you. Let me know your admin password, and I'll install it for you.'

Her eyes widened. 'You've written me a program?'

'It's only a simple one.' He flapped a dismissive hand. 'It's pretty intuitive, so it won't take you five minutes to get to grips with it.'

'You've actually written me a program.' Tears glittered in her eyes.

He shrugged, feeling awkward. 'It's no big deal, Emmy. It wasn't that time-consuming.'

'But you still made the time to do it. Which is amazing, especially as we've both got all these new responsibilities and we're adjusting to all the changes in our lives.' She dragged in a breath. 'Thank you, Dylan.'

'It was entirely selfish of me,' he said. 'If it makes your life easier, then our rota will run more smoothly.'

She gave him a look that told him she didn't believe a word of it. That she knew he'd done it partly because he'd wanted to do something nice for her, even though there was no way he'd ever admit that out loud. 'Even so. Thank you.' She bit her lip. 'I just wish it hadn't taken—well, *this*, to get us in any kind of accord.'

'Me, too. But we've cracked the first week and a half. We're both there for Tyler. We'll make this work,' he said. And he meant every single word.

CHAPTER SIX

OVER THE NEXT few weeks, Emmy and Dylan settled in to their new routine. They shared Tyler's care during the week; Emmy had found a Pilates class nearby, which was scheduled at a similar time to her old class, and Dylan had found a gym nearby, too. And Emmy was surprised at how quickly she'd got used to the routine of working and family life.

'You know, Ty, I never thought it would end up being like this,' she said, jiggling the baby on her lap. 'I thought he'd be a nightmare to share a house with. Fussy and demanding and annoying. But he's actually OK, when you get to know him. He still has the social skills of a rhino, but I think that's because nobody taught him, not because he's too arrogant to care.'

Tyler cooed at her.

She laughed. 'He's better with you, too. I've heard him reading to you. Funny, he said he never wanted to be a dad, but he's managing just fine with you.' Her smile faded. 'I can't quite work him out. Why was he so adamant that he didn't want kids? And why did his marriage break up?'

She jiggled Tyler still further. 'Before we became your guardians, I would've said that Dylan was the problem. Nobody could put up with someone who's that formal and stuffy.' She frowned. 'Except that's not what he's really like. Now we've managed to reach a truce, I think I actually like him. He's got a dry sense of humour, and that smile…'

No. She wasn't going to allow herself to think about his smile and how it made her feel. She needed to keep her head where Dylan Harper was concerned, and keep this strictly—well, not business, exactly, but co-guardianship meant being professional and letting her head rule her heart. Total common sense.

She couldn't ask Dylan why he didn't want kids or why his marriage had fallen apart, because she knew it would annoy him. Dylan didn't like emotional stuff. Even if she did manage to push past that particular boundary, he was intensely private and she knew he'd give little away.

'I guess I'm going to have to learn not to ask,' she said, and Tyler gave her a solemn look as if he agreed.

The baby had started sleeping through the night again; clearly he was beginning to settle after the huge upheaval in his life. But when he began to wake two or three times in the night again, Emmy was at her wits' end.

'Lavender oil?' Dylan asked when she suggested it as a solution.

'A couple of drops on a hankie in his room. Apparently it's relaxing.'

'That's so flaky,' Dylan said. 'There's no scientific proof that it works.'

'I don't care. It's worth a try.' When he continued to look sceptical, she said, 'We have to do *something*, Dylan. I mean, I know we're taking alternate nights to go in to him—but when he wakes up, he's yelling loudly enough to wake whoever's not on duty.'

'I guess so.'

'I don't know about you, but I feel like a zombie.' She couldn't help yawning.

'Me, too,' he admitted. 'OK. Try the lavender oil.'

But it didn't work.

The next day, Emmy made an appointment with the health visitor. 'We might have a solution,' she told Dylan when he came home. 'Ally's health visitor says either he's starting to cut teeth, or he's ready to start solid food.'

'So what do we do now? Buy jars of stuff?' Dylan asked.

Emmy shook her head. 'We start with baby rice and mix it with his milk—so then the taste is quite near what he's used to.' She produced a packet of organic baby rice she'd bought at the supermarket on the way home from seeing the health visitor. 'So let's do this.'

Dylan read out the instructions from the back of the packet, and Emmy followed them.

'It doesn't look much,' Dylan said doubtfully. 'Are you sure you measured out the right amount?'

'I did what you read out,' she said, and sat down with Tyler. She put a tiny amount of the rice on the end of the spoon. 'Come on, sweetie, just one little mouthful,' she coaxed, and put the spoon into Tyler's open mouth.

The result was baby rice spattered all over her.

Dylan smothered a laugh. 'Sorry. But...'

'I look ridiculous. I know.'

'Let me see if I can persuade him to try it,' Dylan suggested.

But he got nowhere, either.

He looked at Emmy. 'So, Ally didn't do any of this with him?'

Emmy thought about it. 'She did talk about weaning him. She said she was planning to start—' she gulped '—when she got back from Venice.'

But that moment was never to happen.

Dylan patted her shoulder briefly in sympathy, then

grabbed a paper towel, wetted it under the tap, and wiped the spattered baby rice from her face.

She gave him a wry smile. 'I'm glad you used water on that paper towel before you wiped my face.'

'A dry towel wouldn't have got it off.'

'That's not what I meant.'

He frowned. 'I'm not with you.'

'I mean, I'm glad that you used water and not spit.'

She saw the second the penny dropped. 'That's really *gross*!' But he laughed.

'It's what my mum used to do,' she said with a grin. 'Didn't yours?'

'No.' His tone was short and his smile faded.

What was Dylan's issue with his mum? Emmy wondered. Was he not close to her? Was that why he kept people at a distance?

He switched the subject by tasting the rice. 'I think I know why he's spitting it out.'

'Why?'

'Try it.'

She did. 'It's tasteless. Bland.' She grimaced. 'But I guess it's about getting him used to texture rather than taste.'

'So we'll have to keep going.'

They muddled through the next few days, and finally Emmy cheered. 'Yay! He's actually eating it.'

She put up a hand to high-five Dylan. He paused—but then he surprised her by high-fiving her. 'Result.'

'*The Baby Bible* says we should introduce one new food at a time, leaving three or four days in between, so we can spot any food allergies,' Emmy said later that evening. 'They say it's good to start with carrots—so I'll steam some and purée them for him tomorrow night.'

The carrots went down as badly as the baby rice had the previous week.

'It's a new taste. It took a couple of days with the baby rice, so we'll have to just persevere,' Dylan said. He scooped Tyler out of his high chair. 'And I will clean up this little one while you, um…' His eyes crinkled at the corners. 'While you de-carrot yourself.'

'I am *so* wearing an apron, next time I try and get him to eat solids,' Emmy said. 'Thanks. I need to change.'

But when she came out of the bedroom, she saw Dylan coming out of the bathroom wearing just his jeans and no shirt, with the baby cradled in his arms.

'Did you get splashed?' she asked.

'Just a bit.' He grinned at her.

Oh, help. Her mouth had gone dry. She knew he went to the gym regularly, but she'd had no idea how perfect his musculature was. That he had a six-pack and well-shaped arms.

And she really hadn't expected to feel this surge of attraction to a man who'd always been prickly and standoffish with her, and sometimes downright rude.

Then again, she had a rubbish choice in men. She'd picked loser after loser who'd let her down and made her feel like the most unattractive woman in the universe. OK, Dylan wasn't a loser, and he wasn't the stuffy killjoy she'd also thought him; but he was the last person she could get into a relationship with. Her relationships never lasted, and Tyler would be the one who paid the price when it all went wrong. She couldn't do that to the baby, especially as he'd already lost so much. So instead she made a light, anodyne comment, let Dylan put Tyler to bed, and fled to the safety of her workbench. Working on an intricate piece would take all of her mental energy, and she wouldn't have enough space left to think about Dylan. To dream about something that just couldn't happen.

The next night, Tyler woke an hour after she put him to bed, and started crying.

She groaned. 'I'm rubbish at this parenting business. He's never going to sleep again.'

Dylan followed her up to his room. 'The book said babies cry because they need a nappy change, they're hungry, they're tired, they're bored, or they want a cuddle.'

'I've fed him, and he's had more solids today, so I don't think he's hungry. He's clean and dry, so it's not that. I don't think he's bored. But this isn't the same cry as when he's tired or wants a cuddle.' She bit her lip. 'I think I might need to call Mum.'

'Wait a second. Do you think he's teething?' Dylan asked. 'Didn't the health visitor say something about that?'

Emmy frowned. 'His face is red, so he might be. Give him a cuddle for a second, will you, while I wash my hands? Then I can check his mouth.'

Dylan held the baby until she came back with clean hands. She put her finger into Tyler's mouth and rubbed it gently over his gums. 'I can't feel anything—but, ow, his jaws are strong.'

Tyler was still crying.

'What are we going to do, Dylan?'

He grimaced. 'I was reading something the other day about you have to let them lie there and cry so they get used to falling asleep on their own.'

She shook her head. 'I hate that idea. He's upset about something or he wouldn't be crying.'

'Let me try something.' Dylan rocked the baby and seemed to be talking to him, but his voice was so soft that Emmy couldn't quite catch what Dylan was saying. But the amazing thing was that the baby actually settled and went back to sleep.

Dylan put him down gently in the cot, and Tyler started crying again.

'What did you do before?' Emmy asked.

He flushed. 'I sang to him.'

Emmy was surprised; she hadn't thought Dylan was the type to sing. 'Do it again—but don't pick him up, because maybe it was putting him back down that woke him.'

Dylan shrugged, and sang 'Summertime' in a rich baritone.

And she was mesmerised. OK, so she'd heard him sing in church at the funeral, but she'd been preoccupied then. She'd had no idea he could sing like this. Like melted chocolate, rich and smooth and incredibly...

She stopped herself. Not sexy. It would be a bad move to think of that word in conjunction with Dylan Harper.

The baby yawned, and finally his hands flopped down and his eyes closed.

Dylan stopped singing and leaned over the edge of the cot. 'How can they sleep like that? He looks a bit like a frog—and I'm sure that can't be comfortable.'

'It's probably a lot more comfortable than it looks, or he'd lie in a different position,' she pointed out. 'I think he looks cute.' She shared a glance with Dylan. 'You have a good voice, Dylan.'

He raised an eyebrow. 'Was that grudging or surprised?'

'Surprised,' she admitted. 'I didn't think you'd—well, be a singer. Or know a song like that.'

'My grandmother used to sing it to me when I was little.'

She smiled. 'It's a beautiful song.'

'Yes.' And it was weird how much that compliment from her had warmed him. Nobody had ever commented on his singing before. Then again, he'd never really sung in front of anyone, except in church at a wedding or christening. His throat tightened: *or at a funeral.* 'We'd better leave him to sleep,' he said gruffly, and left the room abruptly before he did anything stupid, like asking Emmy to spend time with him. They were co-guardians, and that was all.

A couple of days later, Dylan came home early to find Emmy in tears. His stomach clenched. What was wrong?

'Is something wrong with Tyler?' he asked.

She shook her head. 'I would've called you if there was a problem.'

'What's the matter?'

'I just—' she gulped '—I just miss Ally. Tyler...She's missing out on all his firsts. He's getting his first tooth—you can actually see a little bit of white on the edge of his gums now.'

'That must be why he was crying the other night.'

She nodded. 'And he said "dada" today.' She dragged in a breath. 'Ally would've called me to talk about all this. And I'm the one seeing it, when it should be her, and I can't even talk to her about it. This is all so *wrong.*'

Tears would normally send Dylan running a mile. He'd hated it when Nadine cried. He'd always found an excuse to back away. But he couldn't just walk away and leave Emmy distressed like this.

'I miss them, too,' he said, and wrapped his arms round her.

Big mistake.

She was warm and soft in his arms. Her hair smelled of spring flowers, and felt like silk against his cheek, smooth and soft and shiny.

Emmy froze. This was bad. Dylan was holding her. And she was holding him right back.

Comfort. This was all this was, she told herself.

But then she pulled back and looked up at him.

His eyes were a dark, stormy blue.

And his mouth—since when had Dylan had such a lush mouth? She wasn't sure whether she wanted to stroke it first, or kiss it, or what. Just that she wanted him.

She glanced back up to his eyes and realised he was staring at her mouth, too.

No. *No.* This was a seriously bad idea.

But her mouth was already parting, her head tipping back slightly in offering.

His mouth was parting, too.

And slowly—oh, so slowly—he lowered his head to hers. His mouth skimmed against hers, the touch as light as a butterfly's wing. It wasn't enough. It wasn't anywhere near enough. She wanted more. Needed more.

Even though her common sense was screaming at her to stop, her libido was doing the equivalent of sticking fingers in ears and saying, 'La, la, la, I can't hear you.' And she found herself reaching up on tiptoe to kiss him back, her lips brushing against his. It was like some kind of exquisite torture; close, yet not close enough.

His arms tightened round her, and then he was really kissing her. His mouth moved against hers, tentative and unsure at first, then more demanding. And she was kissing him all the way back, matching him touch for touch.

She'd never, ever felt like this before. Even the guy she'd once thought she'd end up marrying hadn't made her feel like this when he kissed her. What on earth was going on?

Dylan untucked her shirt from the waistband of her jeans and slid his fingers underneath the cotton, splaying his palms against her back. He moved his fingertips in tiny circles against her skin; his touch aroused her still more, near to fever pitch.

If he asked her, she knew she'd go to bed with him right now and to hell with the consequences. She wanted Dylan more than she'd ever wanted anyone in her entire life.

She made a tiny sound of longing, and he stopped.

He looked utterly shocked. His mouth was reddened and swollen, and she was pretty sure hers was in the same state.

This was bad. Really bad.

'Emmy, we—I—' He looked dazed.

'I know. We shouldn't have done this,' she said quickly, and pulled away from him. She needed to do some serious damage limitation, and fast. 'Let's pretend this didn't happen. I was upset and you were comforting me, and you're missing Ally and Pete as much as I am, and it just got a bit out of hand.'

His face was suddenly inscrutable. 'Yes, you're right. It didn't happen.'

'I—um—I'd better start making dinner. I'm running a bit late. Sorry, I know you hate it when things aren't on time.' Flustered, she rushed out to the kitchen before he could say anything else. She really didn't want to humiliate herself any further.

Dylan watched her go, not stopping her. Oh, help. He really shouldn't have kissed her like that. Now he knew what Emmy tasted like, it was going to haunt his dreams.

But he knew she was right. They couldn't do this. It would make things way too complicated because of Tyler.

They'd just have to be firmer with themselves in future. A lot firmer.

CHAPTER SEVEN

EMMY PUT THE phone down, beaming and hugging herself. She wanted to leap up and cheer and do a mad dance all through the house, but she knew she couldn't or else she'd wake the baby.

This was the best promotional opportunity she'd ever been offered. It could lead to a real expansion of her business; and it could be the making of her name.

Her smile faded as she thought about it. The deadline was tight. She was going to have to work crazy hours to get the pieces made on time. Which meant that she was going to have to ask Dylan to help her out.

And things had been awkward between them since—well, since she'd wept all over him and he'd held her and they'd ended up kissing. He'd kept out of her way as much as possible, and they only stayed in each other's company for as long as it took to update each other about Tyler or to eat dinner. And dinner meant no talking, because Dylan had retreated into reading journals at the table. It was horribly rude and she knew he knew it; but it was an excuse to avoid her, and there was nothing she could do about it.

They'd agreed early on that they'd work as a team and support each other when they needed it. But had their kiss cancelled out that agreement?

Maybe if she made something really special for dinner,

it would knock Dylan off balance and he'd talk to her. And then she could ask him.

She browsed through Ally's cookery books and found a fabulous recipe for monkfish wrapped in parma ham. It seemed pretty simple to cook but it looked really swish. That would have to do the trick, surely? She made a list of what she needed and took Tyler out in his pram to the parade of shops round the corner. After the fishmonger's, she went to the deli, the baker's and the greengrocer's.

She chatted to the baby on the way. 'This could be my big career break. Clap your hands and wish Aunty Emmy good luck, Ty.'

Tyler clapped his hands and giggled. She laughed back at him. 'You're just gorgeous—you know that?'

So was Dylan.

And she wasn't supposed to be thinking about that.

She played with the baby when they got home; both of them thoroughly enjoyed the bubble-blowing. Tyler was grabbing toys now and rattling them. It was amazing how a little one could take over your life like this. Emmy could see entirely why Ally hadn't wanted to go back to the job she'd once loved, not once Tyler was around.

Then her phone beeped. She checked it to find a text message from Dylan. *Sorry, emergency project meeting. Will be late home. Let me know if problem.*

Normally, Emmy would've been a bit cross at the late notice of a rota change; but today she was relieved, as it would mean that Dylan would come home feeling slightly in her debt and he might be more amenable to what she wanted to ask.

And then she felt horrible and manipulative. That really wasn't fair of her. It was an emergency meeting, after all, so he must be up to his eyes.

She fed Tyler some puréed apple—his food repertoire

was expanding beautifully now—then gave him a bath, not minding that he kept banging his toy duck into the foamy water and splashing her. She put him to bed, sang to him and put his light show on, then changed into dry clothes and headed downstairs to the kitchen.

There was another text from Dylan on her phone. *On way now. Sorry.*

Oh, help. He'd be here before dinner was ready, at this rate.

She prepared the monkfish hastily and put it in the oven, then finished laying the table in the dining room.

Dylan walked in holding a bouquet of bright pink gerberas and deep blue irises, the kind of flowers she loved and bought herself as an occasional treat. 'For you,' he said, and handed it to her.

She stared at him, surprised. Why on earth would Dylan buy her flowers? It wasn't her birthday, and they weren't in the kind of relationship where he'd buy her flowers. 'Thank you. They're, um, lovely.'

'But?'

Obviously it was written all over her face. She gave him a rueful smile. 'I was just wondering why you'd bought me flowers.'

'Because I'm feeling guilty about being late,' he said.

Even if he said no to helping her, at least this late meeting had thawed the ice between them. And she was grateful for that.

'I bought them from the supermarket on the way home from the office. Sorry I'm late,' he said again.

'It's not a problem. You gave me as much notice as you could. Come and sit down in the dining room; dinner's almost ready. You've obviously had a tough day.'

'You could say that.' He didn't elaborate, and Emmy wasn't sure enough of herself to push him.

She poured him a glass of wine, then served dinner.

He frowned. 'This is a bit posh. And we normally eat in the kitchen. Is it some sort of special occasion? Your birthday?'

'No-o,' she hedged. 'I just wanted to make a bit of an effort, that was all.'

Except the second she took her first mouthful she realised that something had gone wrong. Really, *really* wrong. Instead of the nice, tender fish she'd expected, it was rubbery and tough, and the potato cakes she'd made were a bit too crisp at the edges.

'Oh, no—I'm sure I followed the recipe to the letter. I must've had the oven up too high or something.'

But Dylan didn't look annoyed, just rueful. 'Well, it *looked* nice.'

'And it tastes vile.' She grimaced. 'I'm so sorry.'

'Don't worry. Tell you what—get rid of this, and I'll order us pizza.' He took his mobile phone out of his pocket and tapped in a number.

She took their plates to the kitchen and scraped the food into the bin. Right then, she wanted to burst into tears. She'd ruined dinner. How could she ask him a favour now?

'Hey, it could easily have happened when I was cooking. Don't worry about it,' he said, coming into the kitchen to join her.

She wasn't worried about the *food*.

When she didn't reply, he rested a hand on her shoulder. 'Emmy, what's wrong?'

She took a deep breath. 'I was going to ask you a favour. I can't now.'

'Why not?'

'Because, instead of giving you a decent dinner, I served you something disgusting.'

He waved a dismissive hand. 'It's not a problem,

Emmy—though maybe in future it might be an idea to stick to stuff you actually know how to cook?'

'I guess so,' she said ruefully.

'So what did you want to ask me?'

She squirmed. 'There isn't an easy way to ask.'

'Straight out will do.'

'I got a call from one of the big glossy magazines. They want to do a feature on up-and-coming British jewellery designers and they want to interview me.'

'That's good, isn't it?' he asked.

'Ye-es.'

'But?'

She sighed. 'But they want me to make some jewellery and their deadline's massively tight. My guess is that someone dropped out at the last minute and I was a second choice, and I think there are another two designers they've asked as well, so there's no guarantee I'll be included anyway.'

'But they still asked you, and that's the main thing. How tight is the deadline?'

This was the deal-breaker, she knew. 'They've asked me to create something totally new for them. So I need to spend the next four days working solidly to get the pieces made on time for their shoot.'

'So you need me to take over Tyler's care for the next four days?'

She nodded. 'But you had an emergency project meeting tonight, so you're clearly up to your eyes and it's not doable.'

'I can delegate.'

'I'll just have to pass and ask if they'd consider me in the future. If I tell them about Ty, maybe then they'll be understanding and won't think I'm too lazy and just making up feeble excuses.'

He placed a finger over her mouth, making her skin tingle. 'Emmy, were you listening? I said I'd do it. I'll delegate.'

Her eyes went huge. 'Really?'

'Really,' he said softly.

Then he dropped his hand, before he did anything stupid—like moving it to cup her cheek and dip his head to kiss her. That kiss was still causing him to wake up at stupid o'clock in the morning and wonder what would happen if he did it again. He needed to keep a lid on his attraction towards Emmy. Now.

'Thank you,' she said. 'I—well, I feel bad about asking. Four days is a lot.'

'This is your big break, Emmy. And we're a team. Of course I'll do it.'

'Thank you.'

He couldn't resist teasing her. 'I will be exacting repayment, of course.'

Then he wished he hadn't said it when she blushed. Because now all sorts of things were running through his head, and none of them were sensible. All of them involved Emmy naked in his bed. Which would be a very, very bad idea for both of them. Hadn't he spent the last week or so trying to get his feelings under control and forcing himself to think of her as just his co-guardian?

'I mean, I want four days off in lieu,' he said.

She dragged in a shaky breath, and he had the feeling that her thoughts had been travelling along very similar lines to his own. 'That's a deal,' she said.

The doorbell rang, and the pizza delivery boy saved him from saying anything else stupid—such as suggesting they sealed the deal with a kiss. He made sure they had the full width of the kitchen table between them when they sat down to eat. Maybe, just maybe, his common sense would come back and do its usual job once he'd eaten. He needed carbs.

Sharing a house with a woman he knew he shouldn't be attracted to was turning out to be much harder than he'd expected. Though he knew that at least work was a safe topic. 'Tell me about the magazine,' he invited.

'It's one of the biggest women's monthly magazines, glossy and aspirational stuff.' She smiled. 'It's not exactly the kind of thing you'd be likely to read.'

No, but he knew the kind of thing that Nadine had flicked through and he had a pretty good idea of what they required.

'And they're featuring your work?'

'*If* they like it. There aren't any guarantees,' she warned. 'As I said, there are a couple of other designers in the running.'

'They'll like your work,' he said. 'What do they want you to make?'

'A pendant, rings, earrings, and a bangle—they want an ultra-modern set and an ultra-girly, almost old-fashioned set.'

'Like that filigree stuff you do.'

She nodded. 'Exactly that.'

A pendant, rings, earrings and a bangle. And his imagination *would* have to supply a vision of Emmy wearing said jewellery, and nothing but said jewellery.

'Are you going to show them your jet animals as well?' he asked, pushing the recalcitrant thoughts away.

She wrinkled her nose. 'No, they're just a bit of fun.'

'But they're different, Emmy. People might forget your name if they want to buy your jewellery, but they'll definitely remember your jet animals, so they'll look them up on the Internet and find you.'

She thought about it. 'Fair point.'

'Go for it,' he said. 'Maybe that little turtle you made for Ty last week. And the dolphin.'

'I could do a seahorse,' she said, seeming to warm to the idea.

'That would definitely do it,' he said. 'A jet seahorse.'

'I owe you,' she said, finishing her pizza. 'Would you mind…?'

'Go. You're off housework, childcare and everything else,' he said. 'Go beat that deadline.'

She went off to work, and he made a phone call to delegate his work for the next four days so he could take over from her. It was a lot to ask, but he also knew that if he'd been the one to ask the favour her reaction would've been the same: total support. And he could give her some help to chase her dream.

Over the next four days, Emmy worked crazy hours to get the pieces done—a solid jet heart with silver filigree radiating out into a larger heart-shaped pendant, matching earrings, and delicate filigree cuffs containing the shape of a heart in solid jet. The other set included a modern pendant of a jet cone with a slice of amber running through it, matching earrings, a jet ring that entwined with an amber one, and a bangle that replicated the same effect, a thin band of amber entwined with a thin band of jet. And to finish the collection she carved the jet seahorse she'd discussed with Dylan.

Outside her work, she didn't have time to do anything other than have a quick shower in the morning, then fall into bed exhausted at night. Dylan brought her coffee and fruit and sandwiches to keep her going during the day, but didn't stay long enough to disturb her. He did insist on her taking a short break in the evening, though, to eat a proper dinner. She gave him a grateful smile. 'Thank you, Dylan. You've been a real star.'

'You'd do the same for me. How's it going?'

'I'm getting there.'

When she'd finished, she showed him the two collections.

'This is beautiful. I know a lot of women who'd love something like this.' He smiled at her. 'You're definitely going to get this.'

'There are no guarantees,' she reminded him.

Emmy delivered the jewellery to the magazine offices by hand, including the jet seahorse. She knew she was being paranoid, but she couldn't trust them to anyone else. She'd put too much of her heart and soul into the project now for things to go wrong.

Then it was a matter of waiting.

Were they going to choose her?

And how long would they keep her waiting before they delivered the verdict?

Every second seemed to drag—even though she knew she was being ridiculous and she probably wouldn't hear for at least a week. But by the time she got back to the house in Islington, she felt flat.

Dylan took one look at her. 'Right. We're going out.'

'Where?' she asked.

'You need some fresh air, and Ty and I are going with you to keep you company—isn't that right, sweetheart?' he added to the baby. 'I've got his bag organised. All I need to do is get a couple of bottles from the fridge, and we're good to go.'

She gave in. 'Thank you, Dylan.'

'I know you like the sea,' he said as he finished packing the baby's bag. 'And I think it's what you need to blow the cobwebs out.'

'But it's nearly five hours from here to Whitby,' she blurted out.

He laughed. 'I know. I'm not taking you there. I thought we could go to Sussex.'

In the end he drove them to Brighton, where they crunched over the pebbles next to the sea. Part of Emmy was wistful for the fine, soft sand of the east coast she was used to, but she was seriously grateful that Dylan had thought of it. 'You're right. The sea's just what I need. Thank you so much.'

'My pleasure.' He smiled at her, and her heart did a flip. Which was totally ridiculous.

They ate fish and chips on the pier. He fed little bits of fish to Tyler, who absolutely loved it and opened his mouth for more.

'I think we've just found the next food for his list,' Dylan said with a grin.

The woman sitting on the bench next to them looked over. 'Oh, your baby's just adorable.'

Emmy froze.

But Dylan simply smiled. 'Thank you. We think so, too.'

For a moment Emmy wondered what it would be like if this were real—if Dylan were her partner and Tyler were their baby. Then she reminded herself that they were co-guardians. They'd agreed that kiss was a mistake. She'd be stupid to want more than she could have.

'You're quiet,' Dylan remarked when they were wandering through the narrow streets of boutique shops, with Tyler fast asleep in his pushchair.

'I'm just a bit tired,' she prevaricated.

'And worrying about whether they're going to like your designs?'

She frowned. 'How did you know?'

'I'm the same whenever I bid for a project. I always

know I've done my best, but I always worry whether the client will like what I've suggested.'

'And I guess you have the added pressure, because you have people relying on you for work.'

He shrugged. 'There is that.'

She grimaced. 'Sorry, that was patronising and a stupid thing to say.'

'It's OK. You've done the equivalent of a week and a half's normal office hours over four days. I'm not surprised your brain is a bit fried. Come on. Let's get an ice cream.'

'Good idea. And it's my shout.'

Emmy fell asleep in the car on the way back. Dylan glanced at her.

Now he understood exactly what Nadine had meant. The idea of having a partner and a child to complete his life. He hadn't understood it at the time. After his own experiences of growing up, he'd sworn never to have a child of his own. Even to the point where he'd split up from the woman he'd loved rather than have a child with her.

And yet here he was in exactly that position: a standin father to Tyler. Something he hadn't wanted to do, but guilt and duty had pushed him into it. He wasn't sure what surprised him more, the fact that he was actually capable of looking after the baby and giving him the love he needed, or the fact that he was actually *enjoying* it. Part of him felt guilty about that, too. He hadn't given Nadine that chance. Maybe if she'd forced his hand, stopped taking the Pill without telling him and just confronted him with the news that he was going to be a dad, he would've got used to the idea. She'd played fair with him by giving him the chance to say no; and he'd been stubborn enough and selfish enough to say exactly that.

On paper, Nadine had been the perfect choice: focused, career-orientated, organised. Just as he was. Except it hadn't worked, because she'd changed. She'd wanted something he'd always believed he hadn't wanted.

On paper, Emmy was just about the worst choice he could make. OK, she was more organised and together than he'd thought she was, but they were still so different. How could it possibly work between them?

Besides, this was meant to be a three-month trial in co-guardianship. Any relationship between them could potentially wreak huge havoc on Tyler's life. She'd said herself that her relationships always failed, and he'd made a mess of his marriage. He just couldn't let himself think of Emmy in any other role than that of co-guardian. No matter how attractive he found her. No matter how much he wanted to kiss those soft, sweet lips until her eyes went all wide and dark with passion.

Not happening, he told himself. Stick to the limits you agreed.

CHAPTER EIGHT

THE FOLLOWING WEEK, Emmy had a phone call that left her shrieking and dancing round the house. She called her mother, and then Dylan.

'Sorry to ring you at work,' she said, 'but I couldn't wait to tell you—the magazine just rang. They loved my designs and they're going to run the feature with me in it. Apparently what swayed them was the seahorse—which was your suggestion, so it's all thanks to you.'

'No worries,' he said, sounding pleased for her. 'But it was just a suggestion. You're the one who did all the hard work.'

'I'm going to stand you a decent meal to say thank you.' She laughed. 'Don't worry, I'm not cooking it myself, so you're in no danger of getting rubbery monkfish again. Mum says she can babysit Ty on Friday or Saturday, which-ever suits you best.'

'Emmy, you don't need to take me out.'

'Yes, I do. You more than earned it, taking over all my duties and giving me the time to work, so don't argue. We'll sort out the time when you get home tonight, and I'll book somewhere.' She paused. 'One last thing. They want to take a few shots of me here, at my workbench. Um, this afternoon. Do you have a problem with that?'

'No, it's fine. Do you need me back early to look after Tyler?'

'Hopefully the photographer will be here while Tyler's taking a nap. Or, if he wakes, it won't matter if he's in the shots. If that's OK with you, that is.'

'It's fine,' he said again. 'I'll see you later.'

The journalist arrived while Tyler was still awake, so Emmy made her a coffee and played with the baby while she answered questions, hoping that she didn't come across as too flaky or too distracted. And Tyler decided to forego his nap, so when the photographer arrived—two hours later than they'd arranged—he ended up being in the shots.

They were halfway through the photo shoot when Dylan arrived.

'Sorry—am I in the way?' he asked, coming in to Emmy's workroom.

'No—we're running late,' Emmy said.

Tyler held out his hands to Dylan, who smiled and scooped him into his arms, then kissed him roundly. 'Hello, trouble. Aren't you supposed to be having a nap right now?' he asked.

The baby gurgled and clapped his hands.

'Come on. Let's give Emmy some peace and quiet.' He glanced over at Emmy, the journalist and the photographer. 'I'm about to put the kettle on. Coffee?'

'Thanks, that'd be great,' Emmy said gratefully. 'Oh, sorry, I haven't introduced you. Dylan, this is Mike and Flo from the magazine. Flo, Mike, this is Dylan Harper.'

'Nice to meet you,' Dylan said. 'Milk or sugar?'

'Just milk for me,' Flo said.

'Black, two sugars,' Mike said.

'Back in a tick,' Dylan said, winked at Emmy, and whisked Tyler out of the workroom.

'Wow, he's gorgeous *and* domesticated. The perfect man,' Flo said wistfully.

Just what Emmy was starting to think, though wild horses wouldn't make her admit it, especially if there was a danger of Dylan overhearing her. 'He has his moments,' she said gruffly.

'You're just so lucky. This house, that cute baby, and that gorgeous man. And you're talented as well. If you weren't so nice, I'd have to hate you,' Flo said.

'Hang on—you've got the wrong end of the stick. Ty's not ours. Well, he *is* ours,' Emmy said, 'but we're not his parents.'

'Adopted? That's lovely.'

'We're his guardians. We were his parents' best friends.' Emmy explained the situation with Ally and Pete as succinctly as she could. 'Dylan and I just share a house and Ty's care.'

Flo raised an eyebrow. 'Just housemates—with the way you two look at each other? Methinks the lady doth protest too much.'

Oh, help. Emmy didn't dare ask Flo to expand on that. Obviously she thought Dylan looked at her as if he were in love with her—which Emmy knew wasn't the case. But she really hoped that she didn't look at him as if she were mooning over him. Because she wasn't. Was she? 'We're just…' Her voice faded.

'Good friends?' Flo asked.

No. They weren't. Though they were on the way to becoming friends. There was a real easiness between them nowadays. 'Something like that,' Emmy said carefully.

'Gotcha.' Flo tapped her nose. 'So what does he do?'

'He's—well, I guess you'd call him a computer super-guru,' Emmy said.

Flo scribbled something on her notepad. 'Clever as well as easy on the eye. Nice.'

'Mmm.' Emmy wriggled uncomfortably, and was relieved when the photographer asked her to pose for some more shots and Flo changed the subject back to her work. Something safe. Whereas Dylan Harper was starting to become dangerous.

On Saturday evening, her planned thank-you meal with Dylan felt more like a date. Which was crazy. Though of course she'd had to dress up a bit for it; she couldn't just go out in her usual black trousers and a zany top.

And it felt even more like a date when the taxi arrived and her mother kissed them both goodbye at the door. 'Don't worry, Tyler's in safe hands—just go out and enjoy yourselves. And don't hurry back.'

Emmy felt almost shy with him, and she didn't manage to make any small talk in the taxi. Neither did he, she noticed. Was it because he was a geek with no social skills, or was it because he felt the same kind of awkwardness that she did? The same kind of awareness?

'Nice choice,' Dylan said approvingly when they reached the small Italian restaurant she'd booked. 'And I'm buying champagne. No arguments from you.'

Even though that was pretty much negating the point of the evening, it also broke the ice, and Emmy grinned. 'When have you known me argue with you, Dylan?' she teased.

He laughed back. 'Not for a few weeks, I admit.'

'I really appreciate your support over the article.'

'You would've done the same for me,' he pointed out.

'Well, yes. But it's still appreciated. You put yourself out.'

The waiter ushered them to their table, and the awkwardness returned. Emmy didn't have a clue what to say to Dylan. This was ridiculously like a first date, where you knew hardly anything about each other. She'd lived with him for weeks now and knew a fair bit about what made him tick—what brightened his day, and what he needed before he could be human first thing in the morning—but at the same time he was still virtually a stranger. He hadn't opened up to her about anything emotional. She knew nothing about his childhood or why his marriage broke up or what he really wanted out of life. He kept himself closed off. They were partners of a sort, stand-in parents to their godchild; and yet at the same time they weren't partners at all.

The champagne arrived and Dylan lifted his glass in a toast. 'To you, and every success in that magazine.'

'Thank you.' She lifted her own glass. 'To you, and thanks for—well, being there for me.'

'Any time.'

Given that Dylan didn't have a clue how to be nice to people for the sake of it, she knew he meant it, and it made her feel warm inside.

'It was good of your mum to babysit. She's really nice,' Dylan said.

Was she imagining things, or did he sound wistful? 'Isn't yours?' she asked, before she could stop herself.

'She travels a lot.'

Which told her precisely nothing. She could see that Dylan was busy putting up metaphorical barbed-wire fences with 'keep out' notices stuck to them, so she stuck with the safer topic. 'You're right, my mum's really nice. I'm lucky because she's always been really supportive.' She sighed. 'I just wish I could find someone for her who deserves her.'

Dylan raised an eyebrow. 'Your mum's single?'

She nodded. 'I nag her into dating sometimes. So does her best friend, but she always turns down a second date with whoever it is, or agrees they'd be better off as just friends. I guess she's never found anyone she really trusts.'

He sat and waited, and eventually Emmy found herself telling him the rest of it. 'My father pretty much broke her heart. While they were married, he had a lot of affairs. Now I'm older, I can see that it chipped away at her confidence every time she found out he was seeing someone.' Just as her own disastrous relationships had chipped away at her confidence, one by one. Every man who'd wanted to change something about her—and it had been a different thing, each time, until in the end the only thing she knew she was good at was her work.

She bit her lip. 'The worst thing is, Mum always wanted more children after me but couldn't have them. He refused to consider adoption or fostering. And then his current woman found out she was pregnant, and he left us for her. Mum felt she'd failed.'

Dylan knew exactly how it felt when your marriage failed and you were pretty sure it was all your fault. First-hand. And it wasn't a good feeling. 'It wasn't your mum's fault,' he said. 'I might be talking out of line, here, but sounds to me as if your dad was incredibly selfish.' Just like his mother. He knew how *that* felt, too, realising that you were way down someone's list of priorities. The amount of times he'd come home from school and let himself into a cold, empty house, and there was a note propped on the kitchen table telling him to go to his grandparents' house because they'd be looking after him for a few days. Days that stretched into weeks.

'My dad was incredibly selfish. He probably still is.'

'Probably?' Dylan was surprised. 'Don't you see him?'

'He didn't stay in touch with us, and for years I thought it was my fault that my parents split up. It was only later, when I'd left university and Mum told me what really went on when I was young, that I realised he was the one with the problem.'

And now Dylan understood why she'd accused him of breaking up his marriage because of an affair. She'd been caught in the fallout from her father's affairs, and it clearly still hurt.

She blew out a breath. 'I think he decided not to see me because whenever he did see me it reminded him of my mum, and that made him start to feel guilty about the way he treated her.'

'So is that why you're single? Because you don't trust men?' And that would certainly explain Spiky Emmy. It was clearly a defence mechanism, and it had definitely worked with him. He'd taken her at face value.

She frowned. 'Not quite. I just have a habit of picking the wrong ones. Men who want to change me—everything from the way I dress, to what I do for a living. Nothing about me is right.'

At one point Dylan would've wanted Emmy to change—but now he knew her better and he understood what made her tick. And he knew that she wasn't the woman he'd thought she was. 'You're fine as you are. There's nothing wrong with what you do for a living. Or how you dress.'

'I wasn't fishing for compliments.' She shrugged. 'I'm tired of dating men who can't see me for who I am or accept me for that. I'm tired of dating men who are all sweetness and light for a couple of weeks, then start making little "helpful" suggestions. All of which mean me changing to fit their expectations, rather than them looking at their expectations and maybe changing them.' She sighed. 'It's not that I think I'm perfect. Of course I'm not. I'm like everyone else, with good points and bad. I just wanted a partner who understands who I am and is OK with that.'

'Maybe,' he said, 'you should've got Ally to vet your dates before you went out with them.'

'I wish I had.' She sighed. 'The last one…' She grimaced and shook her head. 'No, I really don't want to talk about him. But he was definitely my biggest mistake. And he was my last mistake, too. So if you're worrying that I'm going to be flighty and disappear off with the first man who bats his eyelashes at me, leaving you to look after Tyler on your own, then don't. Because I'm not. I've given up looking for Mr Right. I know he isn't out there. My focus now is being there for Tyler while he grows up.'

'So you're not looking for a husband or a family, or what have you?'

'No. But I have Tyler. That's enough for me.'

Before they'd become co-guardians, the Emmy Jacobs Dylan knew was flighty as well as spiky. He'd disliked her because she'd reminded him so much of his mother. Selfish, always apologising for being late but never seeming sincere.

Now, he was seeing a different side of her. The way she looked after Tyler and put the baby's needs first: she was definitely responsible. She was kind; without being intrusive, she'd worked out what he liked to eat and the fact that he loathed lentils, and changed her meal plans to suit. She was thoughtful. And she was fiercely independent; from what she'd just told him about her childhood, he could understand exactly why she wouldn't want to rely on someone. She'd seen her mother's heart broken and had learned from that.

And he didn't want Spiky Emmy back. He liked the woman he'd got to know. More than liked her, if he was honest with himself. 'I'm not worried at all,' he said lightly.

'You didn't need to tell me that. I already know you're not flighty.'

'Oh.' She looked slightly deflated, as if she'd been gearing up to have a fight with him and now she didn't have to. 'So what about you? Are you looking for Ms Right?'

'No, I made enough of a mess of my marriage.' And then he surprised himself by adding, 'And it was my fault.'

'How? You didn't have an affair.'

'Neither did Nadine.'

'So what went wrong?' She put a hand to her mouth. 'Sorry. I know I shouldn't ask you personal stuff.'

Absolutely. He didn't want to talk about his feelings or his past. But he surprised himself even more by saying, 'Given our situation, you probably ought to know. And I know you're not going to gossip about me.'

'Of course I'm not.'

'Nadine and I—we wanted the same things, at first. A satisfying career, knowing we could reach the top of our respective trees. Neither of us wanted kids. Except then she changed her mind.'

'And you didn't?'

He shook his head. 'She gave me an ultimatum: baby or divorce. So I picked the latter.'

She blew out a breath. 'And now you're in exactly that situation with Tyler—a stand-in dad. Though obviously you and I—we're not…'

Her voice faded, and he wondered if she was thinking about that kiss. He most definitely was. He forced himself to focus. 'Yeah.' But his voice sounded slightly rusty to his ears. He hoped she wouldn't guess why.

'So does that mean…I mean, the three months are up in a couple of weeks. And you don't want to…?' She looked worried.

'I'm glad you brought that up,' he said. 'It's working for

me. I think we're a good team. I know we're never going to be as good as Pete and Ally, and I for one still have a lot to learn about babies, but Tyler seems happy with us.'

'Are *you* happy?' she asked.

'Yes. And I feel a bit guilty about it. I said I didn't want to be a parent. But, actually, I'm enjoying it,' he confessed. It was a relief to admit it out loud, at last. 'I like coming home to a baby. I like seeing him change. I like hearing him babble and I like seeing his face when he tries something new.'

'Me, too,' she said softly.

'So we keep going?' he asked.

'What about your ex?'

He grimaced. 'As I said, I feel guilty. Maybe it could've worked, if I hadn't been so stubborn. Or maybe it wouldn't. I don't know.'

'Why didn't you want a child?' she asked.

He blew out a breath. 'I just don't. Didn't.'

'You mean, back off because you don't want to talk about it?' she asked wryly.

He was slightly surprised that she'd read him so well. 'Yes. Tonight's meant to be about toasting your success, not dragging through my failures. So, yes, I'd rather change the subject. I'm not the kind of guy who talks about my feelings and wallows in things,' Dylan said. 'I just get things done. With the social skills of a rhino.'

She gave him a rueful smile. 'You're never going to let me forget that, are you?'

'No. Because, actually, it's true,' he said. 'Anyway. The main thing is that we both know where we stand—we're both single, and we're both planning to stay that way. And we can just get on with looking after Tyler.'

'Yeah.' She raised her glass again. 'To Tyler. I wish things could've been different—but I think we're managing to be the next best option for him. Even if we do have to rely on looking things up in a book or asking my mum, half the time.'

'Absolutely.' He clinked his glass against hers. 'To Tyler, and to being the best stand-in parents he could ever have.'

Somehow the awkwardness between them had vanished, and Emmy was surprised at how easy it was to talk to Dylan. And to discover that they had shared loves in music and places they wanted to visit.

She was beginning to see why Pete and Ally had made that decision, now. She and Dylan had their differences, which would be good for Tyler; but they also had much more overlap than either of them had ever imagined. She actually liked his company.

And she was shocked by how late it was when she finally glanced at her watch. 'We'd better call a taxi. And I'd better ring Mum and let her know we're on our way back.'

'You ring your mum, and I'll call the cab,' Dylan said.

In the taxi, their hands kept brushing against each other, and it felt as if little electric shocks were running through her veins. Which was crazy. Dylan was the last man she could afford to be attracted to. This shouldn't be happening.

But what if it did?

What if Dylan held her hand?

And then she stopped breathing for a second when his fingers curled round hers. Was he thinking the same as she was?

She met his gaze, and the remaining breath whooshed out of her lungs.

Yes. He was.

She wasn't sure which of them moved first, but then his hand was cupping her cheek, hers was curled into his hair, and his mouth was brushing against hers. Slow, soft, gentle kisses. Exploring. Enticing. Promising.

He drew her closer and the kiss deepened. Hot enough to make her toes curl and her skin feel too tight. This was what she wanted. What they both wanted.

And then she was horribly aware of a light going on and someone coughing.

The taxi driver.

Clearly they were home. And they'd been caught in a really embarrassing position.

She looked at Dylan, aghast. Oh, no. This was a bad move. Yes, she wanted him and he wanted her. But what would happen when it all went wrong? Tyler would be the one who paid the price.

So they were going to have to be sensible about this. Stop it before it started.

'Um. That shouldn't have happened,' she muttered, unable to look him in the eye.

'Absolutely,' he agreed, to her mingled relief and regret. 'Blame it on the champagne. And it won't happen again,' he added.

Which ought to make her feel relieved. Instead, it made her feel miserable.

'Go in. I'll pay the driver.'

'Thanks.' She fled before she said or did anything else stupid. And tonight, she thought, tonight she'd have a cold shower and hope that her common sense came back—and stayed there.

CHAPTER NINE

DYLAN PUT THE phone down and leaned back against his chair, his eyes closed.

This was potentially a huge deal.

And it came with an equally huge sticking point: the client was a family man who liked to work with people who had the same outlook on life.

Strictly speaking, Dylan wasn't a family man. He was an almost-divorcee who happened to have co-guardianship of his godson. His marriage breakdown would certainly count against him; and his arrangement with Emmy was hardly conventional.

Could he ask her to help him out?

After all, he'd helped her when she'd needed it. And she *had* offered…

He thought about buying her flowers, but that would be manipulative and tacky. No, he'd just ask her once Tyler was in bed. Talk it over with her. And maybe she'd have a creative way round the situation—because Emmy definitely had a different take on life from his.

It helped a bit that it was his turn to cook that night. And he totally appreciated now why she'd tried to cook the monkfish. Except he played it safe, with pasta. 'Emmy, can I ask you a favour?' he asked over dinner.

'Sure. What?'

'I've put in a tender for a project.'

She looked thoughtful. 'So you're going to be working longer hours and need me to pick up the slack for a bit? That's fine, because you did exactly that for me. Of course I'll do it.'

He grimaced. 'Not exactly. I'm learning to delegate, so I don't need you to pick up the slack. Anyway, I haven't got the deal yet.'

She frowned. 'So if you don't need me to take over from you, what's the favour, then?'

This was the biggie. 'The client. He's a family man. He likes to work with—well, people who have the same outlook.'

She raised an eyebrow. 'Isn't that discrimination?'

'It would be, if he was employing me,' Dylan agreed, 'but this is different. It's a project and my company's put in a bid for it, so the client can choose his contractor however he likes.'

'And you want him to think you're a family man?' She looked wary. 'Dylan, this is a seriously bad idea. You're not a family man.'

'I'm Tyler's co-guardian, so *technically* that makes me a family man.'

'But you and I...' Her voice faded and she looked slightly shocked. 'Oh, no. Please tell me you're not expecting me to lie for you and pretend that you and I are an item?'

'I'm not expecting you to lie. Just...' How could he put this nicely? 'Just fudge the issue a little.'

She shook her head. 'It'll backfire. When he realises you lied—and he *will* realise, if you get the contract and he works with you—then he'll have no faith in you. Professionally as well as personally. Which will be a disaster for your business.'

He folded his arms. 'What happened to looking out for each other?'

She narrowed her eyes at him. 'I *am* looking out for you, Dylan. This isn't the best way forward, and you know I'm right.'

There wasn't much he could say to that, so he remained silent.

'But,' she said, 'I'll help you. Invite him round to dinner. I'll cook.'

He looked at her. 'Thank you for the offer, but I think I'll pass on that one.'

She rolled her eyes. 'You're not going to let me forget that monkfish, are you?'

'It was pretty bad,' he said. 'Not that I could do any better myself. Which is why I think inviting him to dinner's a bad idea. The kitchen isn't my forte or yours.' He frowned. 'Though I suppose I could buy something from the supermarket that I just have to put in the oven and heat through.' His frown deepened. 'But could I ask you to do the table setting, please?'

She gave him a sidelong look. 'Because I'm a girl?'

'No. Because you have an artist's eye and you're good at that sort of thing,' he corrected.

He'd actually paid her a compliment. A genuine one. And Emmy was surprised by how warm it made her feel.

'Of course I'll do the table setting. But this meal needs to be home-cooked if you invite him round. We can't just give him a ready meal from the supermarket.' She thought for a moment. 'OK. If he's a family man, invite his wife and kids. We'll make it a family meal.'

His eyes narrowed. 'So what are you planning? Are you going to talk your mum into cooking for us?'

She shook her head. 'I don't need to. We'll keep it simple. Something like...hmm. A roast dinner.'

He grimaced. 'I remember the student house I shared with Pete. The four of us made our first Christmas dinner and the turkey wasn't properly cooked. We were all ill for three days afterwards.'

'This isn't a student house. And I'll ask my mum about timings so it won't go wrong. How old are his kids?'

'I have no idea.'

'Find out.' She looked thoughtful. 'Actually, if they're little, they won't have the patience for a starter, and if they're teens they probably won't want to come anyway. So we'll skip the starter. We can do a roast dinner for the main, and fresh fruit salad and ice cream for dessert. We're both working and we're looking after Tyler, so it's OK to take the odd short cut.'

'But you'll be there at the table, won't you? You're not just going to be in the kitchen?'

'Why, Dylan, anyone would think you wanted me there,' she teased.

He gave her a speaking look. 'All right. You can have your pound of flesh. I want you there. You have good social skills.'

'Thank you.' She grinned and punched his arm. 'And yours are a bit better than they were. Go and ring him. Find out if there's anything they can't eat—either because of allergies or because they hate it. And we definitely need to know if anyone's vegetarian.'

'Because then we'll have to rethink the menu?'

'Because then dinner will be pasta,' she said. 'We can both cook that. And we'll serve it with garlic bread and salad. Simple and homely.'

Dylan rang his potential client the next morning, and then rang Emmy. 'It'll be just Ted Burroughs and his wife.

You were right about the kids—they're teens, and he says they'll pass on the invite.' He smiled. 'Mind you, he has girls. If I'd said I live with a top jewellery designer…'

'No, they would've been bored with the conversation, so it's better that they don't come,' Emmy said. 'What about the food?'

'No allergies, and he appreciated you asking.' He paused. 'I appreciate you, too. I wouldn't have thought of that.'

'Which is because,' she said, 'you only have one X chromosome.'

'That's *so* sexist.'

She laughed. 'Bite me, Dylan.'

She was adorable in this playful mood.

Then Dylan caught his thoughts and was shocked at the fact he'd used the word 'adorable' about her. What was happening? Emmy Jacobs was his co-guardian, and that was all.

The kisses and the hand-holding in the taxi had been… well, mistakes.

Even if he did want to repeat them.

Even if a little, secret part of him thought that yes, he'd like to be partners with Emmy in more than just sharing Tyler's care.

'See you later,' he said. 'And thanks.'

The day of the dinner arrived, and Dylan made sure that he was home early to help. Emmy had already set the dining room table with candles, fresh flowers, a damask tablecloth and silverware, and the chicken was in the oven.

'Is there anything you need me to do?' he asked.

'Make a start on peeling the potatoes?' she suggested.

He did so, and noticed that there was a list held onto the fridge with a magnet. 'What's this?'

'The timing plan for dinner,' she said. 'And I'm using the oven timer to make sure I don't miss anything.'

She definitely looked strained, he thought. 'Stop worrying. I'm sure it will be fine.'

'That's not what you said when I first suggested cooking a roast dinner.'

He rolled his eyes. 'OK, O Wise One. You were right and you know better than I do.'

'I hope so.' Though she didn't sound convinced.

'So you got the timings from a book?' he asked.

'Better than that—Mum helped. She did offer to come and cook for us, but I thought that'd be cheating.'

Would it? he wondered.

She'd obviously caught the expression on his face just before he masked it, because she sighed. 'You think I should've taken her up on the offer, don't you?'

'No, I'm sure all will be just fine.' He finished peeling the potatoes. 'Do you want me to make the fruit salad?'

'It's already done so the flavours can mingle.' Almost on cue, there was the sound of gurgling and cooing from the baby listener. She smiled. 'It sounds like someone's just woken. Go and play with Tyler—you're getting under my feet and being annoying.' She shooed him out of the kitchen, though he was careful to make sure that she really didn't need any help before he agreed to go.

He spent some time playing with the baby. Again it surprised him just how much he was enjoying this domestic set-up. He'd never thought a family was for him; or maybe Nadine just hadn't been the right person for him to have a family with. He pushed away the thought that maybe Emmy was the right one. He knew she had issues about relationships, and he wasn't sure how it could work between them. They couldn't risk fracturing Tyler's world again.

* * *

Emmy ticked off everything she'd done on her list, checked the list a second time in case she'd missed anything, and then did a final read-through just to be absolutely certain.

Everything was ready, as far as it could be. Barring having to rescue everything from a last-minute catastrophe in the kitchen—and she hoped she'd done enough planning to avoid that—there was nothing else to do.

She changed into a simple black dress and some of her more delicate jewellery, and adopted the 'less is more' principle when it came to her make-up. She stared at herself critically in the mirror. How many of her ex-boyfriends hadn't been happy with the way she looked? The colour of her hair, the fact that it rarely stayed the same colour for more than a couple of months at a time, the way she dressed...

She took a deep breath. Dylan wasn't her boyfriend, and she looked just fine. Professional. Competent.

All the same, when she came back down into the kitchen, she grabbed an apron, just in case she spilled anything over herself while she was cooking.

Dylan was already there, feeding Tyler in his high chair. The baby beamed and banged his hands on his tray when he saw her.

'Hello, Gorgeous. Is Uncle Dylan in charge of dinner tonight?'

'Dih-dih.' Tyler gurgled with pleasure—and bits of carrot sprayed all over Dylan's shirt.

'Oops. Sorry,' she said.

He flapped a dismissive hand, then grinned.

'What?' she asked suspiciously.

'If anyone had ever told me I'd see you wearing an apron, looking all domestic...'

'Oh, ha ha.' She rolled her eyes. 'Ty, make sure you spit more carrot at him.'

Dylan just laughed. 'We're about done here. I'll sort out bath and bed. Is there anything else you need?'

'No—I'm fine. And you'd better change, Dylan— you've got mashed carrot on your shirt.'

'I guess so.'

It wasn't that long ago that Dylan had been so formal and stuffy that even his jeans were ironed and his T-shirts were pristine and white. He'd unbent an awful lot if he wasn't that fussed about mashed carrot on one of his work shirts, Emmy thought, especially as she knew carrot could stain.

She fussed around downstairs while Dylan sorted out Tyler's bath and bedtime, and changed his shirt. And then the doorbell went, and her stomach went into knots. This deal could mean as much for Dylan's business as the magazine thing meant for hers so she really couldn't afford to mess things up tonight. If the veg wasn't cooked enough or, worse, cooked to a mush...

Breathe, she told herself. Everything's going to be just fine. You've used the timer and ticked everything off the list. It's not going to let you down and you're not going to let Dylan down.

Dylan answered the door; she stayed in the kitchen for just a little longer, nerving herself, then came out to meet their guests.

'Emmy, this is Ted and Elaine Burroughs—Ted and Elaine, this is Emmy Jacobs,' Dylan introduced them.

'Delighted to meet you. Thank you for having us,' Ted said, and shook her hand warmly.

Emmy was horribly aware that she was still wearing her apron. So much for being sophisticated. 'Um, sorry,

I hope you'll excuse…' She indicated the apron with an embarrassed grimace.

'Of course,' Ted said.

'So how long have you been together?' Elaine asked.

Emmy and Dylan exchanged a glance.

Be honest, she willed him. Tell them the truth, or it'll come back to bite you.

'We're not actually a couple, as such,' Dylan said. 'We share a house. And we're also co-guardians of Tyler, our best friends' son—they were killed in a car crash three months ago. They'd asked us both to look after Tyler if anything happened to them. So here we are.'

'So you moved out of your own homes and in here together?' Elaine asked.

'It was the best thing for Tyler,' Emmy said. 'He needed to be somewhere familiar.'

'Plus my flat in Docklands wasn't really baby-friendly,' Dylan added.

'And mine in Camden was only big enough for me, not for the three of us,' Emmy explained.

'That must have been hard for you,' Ted said, his face full of sympathy.

'We've been thrown in a bit at the deep end,' Emmy said, 'but we're managing. I should tell you now that dinner's not totally a home-made thing. I'm afraid we cheated and bought the gravy and the ice cream, but I hope you'll forgive us for that.'

'My dear, it's very kind of you to invite us over—especially given your circumstances,' Elaine said.

'We support each other,' Emmy said. 'Sometimes Dylan has a late meeting and needs me to pick up the slack, and sometimes I have a rush on at work and need him to hold the fort for me.' She exchanged a glance with him. 'And he's better than I am at getting Ty to sleep. He sings better.'

'That always worked with our two,' Elaine said with a smile.

'Would you excuse me?' Emmy asked. 'I need to check on the veg. Dylan, can you—'

'—sort the drinks?' he finished. 'Sure. Would you like to come through to the dining room, Elaine and Ted?'

He sorted out the drinks while she did the last-minute things in the kitchen. She was putting the vegetables in serving dishes when she overheard Elaine complimenting the table setting.

'That's all down to Emmy,' Dylan said. 'She has an artist's eye. You should see her jewellery—it's amazing, so delicate and pretty.'

It warmed her to know he was being absolutely serious. Dylan never gushed.

She brought the serving dishes and warmed plates through, and Dylan carved the chicken.

To her relief, the food seemed to go down well. The vegetables were fine—not too hard or too soft—and she'd managed to get the potatoes crispy on the outside and fluffy inside, thanks to her mother's instructions.

'Dylan tells us you're a jeweller,' Elaine said. 'Our eldest daughter is about to turn sixteen, and I know she'd like some jewellery for her birthday. Could you make some for her?'

'Sure,' Emmy said. 'Most of the stuff on my website is either in stock or won't take long to make, or I could design something especially for her.'

'Why don't you show Elaine the pieces you made for the magazine?' Dylan suggested. 'Or is that embargoed?'

'Officially it's embargoed,' Emmy confirmed, 'but I guess it's OK for you to see the photographs I took. Excuse me a second?' She grabbed her phone from her bag, and showed Elaine the photographs.

'That really delicate stuff—that's so Claire. She'd love something like that,' Elaine said.

'Do you want it to be a surprise? If not, you could bring Claire over and I can talk to her about what she'd really like, and design it for her there and then.' Emmy smiled. 'Actually, why don't you do that and we can make it a really girly session? It'll make her feel special to have something designed just for her.' She put a hand on Dylan's arm. 'Sorry, this wasn't meant to be about my business tonight. I didn't mean to take over.'

He smiled. 'You weren't taking over. I just think what you make is really amazing. She does these jet carvings as well, little animals. She made me a fantastic bear.'

'Teddy?' Ted asked with a grin.

Dylan laughed back. 'Ah, no. It's a grizzly. She was making a point,' Dylan said.

'You're lucky I didn't make you a rhino,' she teased.

'A rhino?' Elaine looked mystified.

'Because she says I have the same level of social skills as a rhino,' Dylan explained. 'I guess it goes with being good at maths.'

'You're a total geek,' she said, but her tone was affectionate.

She cleared the table and brought out the fruit salad; she'd bought thin heart-shaped shortbread from the deli and vanilla ice cream to go with it.

'Pineapple, raspberries, kiwi and pomegranate,' Elaine said as she looked at the bowl. 'How lovely. I'd never thought of making a fruit salad like that. You really are good in the kitchen.'

'Not always,' Emmy confessed. 'I tried making monkfish in parma ham a few weeks back, and it was absolutely terrible. That's why we decided to cook a roast dinner tonight, because it's much simpler and less likely to go wrong. And I still had to call my mum for the timings and instructions on the roast potatoes.'

'You did her proud, love,' Ted said.

Emmy found herself relaxing now that the trickiest part of the meal was over. But then Tyler woke, and they could all hear him crying on the baby listener.

'I'll go,' Emmy said.

'No, it's my shift,' Dylan said.

'Not anymore,' she corrected him. 'I put a sticky note on the board so it's my shift. You stay with our guests.' She realised her slip almost immediately, but hoped she hadn't messed it up. It had felt so natural to call the Burroughses 'our' guests rather than 'your'.

'I'd love to see the baby,' Elaine said wistfully. 'But I guess you can't bring him down as it'll put him out of his routine.'

'You can come up to the nursery with me, if you like,' she offered impulsively, and Elaine beamed.

'I'd love to.'

And maybe this would give Dylan and Ted the chance to discuss business, Emmy thought.

Elaine clearly loved having the chance to cuddle a baby. 'How old is he?'

'Seven months, now.'

'You forget how cute they are at this age. He'll be crawling, next.'

'And we'll have baby gates all over the place,' Emmy said with a smile.

She settled the baby down in his cot again, and put his light show on.

'It's very sad about your friends,' Elaine said, 'and it must be difficult for you. How are you both coping?'

'It was pretty tough at first,' Emmy admitted. 'Dylan wasn't a very hands-on godfather when Tyler was really tiny. I guess he was waiting to do all the stuff like kicking a ball round in the park, going to the boating lake, and helping teach him to ride a bike—stuff I wouldn't do as a godmother, because I'd rather take him swimming or to baby music classes. But we've muddled through together for the last three months, and it helps that we take alternate night shifts.' She blew out a breath. 'It means we each manage to get one good night's sleep out of two. I have no idea how my best friend coped the way she did. She always looked fresh as a daisy, even if the baby had been up half a dozen times in the night.'

'You must miss her,' Elaine said.

'I do—and Dylan really misses Pete. They were the nearest we had to a brother and sister.'

'But Dylan helps you now.'

Emmy nodded. 'He's been brilliant. Actually, he's helped right from the start, even though he's never had anything to do with babies before and was obviously scared to death that he'd do something wrong and hurt the baby. He's never just left me to deal with everything; he's always done his fair share, even if it involves dirty nappies or having stuff dribbled all over him. He's stubborn and sometimes he comes across as a bit closed off or he says totally the wrong thing, but his heart's in the right place and he thinks things through properly.' She smiled. 'Don't tell him I said this, but when we do argue he's usually right.'

Elaine smiled back. 'He sounds like my Ted.'

Emmy checked the cot once more; satisfied that Tyler had settled again, she ushered Elaine back downstairs to the dining room. She made coffee and brought in the posh chocolate truffles she'd found in the deli, and helped Dylan make small talk until the Burroughses finally left.

Dylan helped her clear up. 'By the way, do you know

the baby listener was still on when you were upstairs with Elaine?'

Emmy looked at him, horrified. 'You're kidding!'

He shook his head.

'How much did you hear?' she demanded.

'Let me think.' He spread his hands. 'That would be…' He met her gaze. 'All of it.'

She closed her eyes briefly. Obviously she'd wrecked everything, because she just hadn't been able to keep her mouth shut. 'I'm so sorry, Dylan. Ted must've thought…' She bit her lip.

'He was laughing.' Dylan's eyes crinkled at the corners. 'Especially at the bit when you said I'm usually right. And I hope you realise I have every intention of using that one against you in the future.'

She knew that was an attempt to stop her worrying, and ignored it. 'I just hope I haven't screwed up the deal for you.'

'I think,' he said, 'you showed Ted what he wanted to know. That I'm not just this efficient machine.'

'Well, you're that as well.'

Dylan raised an eyebrow. 'Thank you. If that was meant to be a compliment.'

'A backhanded one,' she confirmed.

He smiled at her. 'That's what I like about you. You never sugar-coat stuff.'

'There's no point. I've had it with charm.'

'Ouch.' He looked serious. 'Want to talk about it?'

'We already have. I told you I had rubbish taste in men. That's just another example. I fall for the charm every time—hook, line and sinker.'

He reached over and stroked her cheek, and every nerve-end in her skin zinged. 'Something I should tell you. You're usually right, too, when we argue. You make me think things through in a different way. And that's a good thing.'

'Think outside the regular tetrahedron?' she asked

'There's absolutely nothing regular tetrahedron about you, Emmy.'

'Thank you. If that was meant to be a compliment,' she threw back at him.

His eyes crinkled at the corners again. And how ridiculous that it made her heart skip a beat.

'It was. And thank you for your help. You might just have made the difference.' He looked at her mouth. 'Emmy. You were brilliant, tonight.' His voice deepened, grew huskier. And then he leaned forward and pressed the lightest, sweetest kiss against her lips.

It was anatomically impossible, but he made her feel as if her heart had just turned over. How could she help herself resting her palm against his cheek, feeling the faint prickle of stubble against her fingertips? Especially when his hands slid down her sides, resting lightly against her hips as he drew her closer.

Then she panicked. She couldn't feel like this about Dylan. She just couldn't. She took a step back. 'We...'

'Yeah. I know. Sorry.' He raked a hand through his hair. 'That didn't happen.'

'No. It was just adrenaline, because we were both panicking about dinner.'

'Absolutely,' he said as she took another step back. 'I'll finish up in here. You go and...' He blew out a breath. 'Whatever. I'll see you later.'

She took the hint and made herself scarce. Before she did something really stupid, like kissing him again.

CHAPTER TEN

DYLAN WAS TWITCHY for the next couple of days, though Emmy understood why. She'd been in the same situation herself, not so long ago.

On Saturday morning at breakfast, she said, 'Right, you need to get out of the house.'

'What?' Dylan looked at her as if she were speaking Martian.

'Waiting. It's the pits. And if you stay in and try and concentrate on work, you'll end up brooding. So you're coming out with Ty and me to get some fresh air. Isn't he, Ty?'

The baby gurgled and banged his spoon against the tray of his high chair. 'Dih-dih!'

'It sounds as if you have something in mind,' Dylan said.

Emmy nodded. 'I've been making a list of places to go with him. We can always go to the park with the slide and the swings on sunny days, but it's no good on rainy or cold days. And this is one I've been looking forward to.'

She was mysterious about where they were going, and Dylan didn't have a clue until they were standing outside what looked like an Edwardian greenhouse with a large banner that proclaimed it to be the House of Butterflies.

When they were inside, he discovered that the greenhouse was full of lush vegetation and had a slightly humid, warm atmosphere. He could hear the sound of water falling, so he realised there must be a fountain somewhere. There were butterflies of all sizes and colours, some huge and vivid. He'd never seen so many in one place before.

Ty seemed to love it, watching the butterflies opening and closing their wings as they perched on a flower or fluttered overhead. He reached out to them, waggling his fingers as if copying the movement of their wings.

'Look—those people over there are standing very still, and the butterflies are landing on them,' Emmy exclaimed, looking enchanted.

She tried it herself, and her face was suffused with wonder when a butterfly landed on her. Dylan wished for a second that he had a camera to capture that expression.

They wandered through the different sections of the enormous greenhouse, looking at the butterflies and the flowers; Dylan was surprised by how much it made him relax.

'Thank you for bringing me here. I was getting a bit scratchy. Sorry, I haven't been very nice to live with.'

She patted his arm, and the feel of her skin against his made him tingle. 'That's OK. I was the same when I was waiting. And you did the same for me, when you took me to the sea,' she said. 'I just thought this might be something different.'

'I would never have thought to go to a butterfly house.'

'To be fair, it hasn't been open for that long, so you probably wouldn't have known about it.' She smiled at him. 'Do you mind if I take a few photos?'

'Sure, go ahead. I'll take Ty.'

He took over the pushchair, and she took various photographs with her phone. Including, to his surprise, the roof of the greenhouse. He'd expected her to concentrate on the butterflies. Then again, Emmy seemed to see things in a different way from most people.

In the next section, there was a terrarium full of chrysalises, and they could actually see some of the pupae emerging from their cocoons.

'That's amazing. I never saw anything like that when I was a kid,' Dylan said.

'Did you have a garden?'

He nodded. 'My grandparents had a huge garden, and my gran loved butterflies and bees—she had shrubs to attract them. My grandfather preferred the more practical stuff, growing fruit and vegetables. And I used to have to help weed the garden whenever I was there.'

'Sounds as if you weren't keen.'

'I was a child,' he said. 'But I've never had a garden since.'

And they'd neglected Pete and Ally's garden, just mowing the lawn.

In the section after, there was a waterfall and a pond with huge red and white goldfish. Emmy unbuckled Tyler from his pushchair and held him up so he had a good view of the pond. 'See the red fish, Ty?'

'Fiiih,' said the little boy.

He saw the shock on Emmy's face and the way she suddenly held Tyler that little bit tighter, as if she'd been near to dropping him. 'Did you hear that, Dylan? He said "fish"!'

'I heard.' And it was crazy to feel so proud of him. Then again, Tyler was the nearest he'd ever get to having a son. Something he'd always thought he didn't want, but now he knew he did.

Tyler clapped his hands with delight, and Emmy beamed at him. 'Clever boy.'

* * *

This, Emmy thought, was the perfect day. Tyler learning a new word. Sharing this amazing spectacle with him and with Dylan. And the butterfly house definitely seemed to have taken Dylan's mind off the wait to hear from Ted Burroughs.

In the next section, Dylan found a giant stripy caterpillar and pointed it out to the baby. 'Hey, Tyler, what pillar doesn't need holding up? A caterpillar!'

He chuckled, and the baby laughed back. And Emmy was enchanted. The joke was terrible, but Stuffy Dylan would never have done something like that. He was definitely changing and she really liked the man he was becoming.

'We'll have to take him to the zoo. I've noticed he really likes that tiger story you bought him,' she said.

'Maybe we could go next weekend?' he suggested. 'Though it's your weekend off.'

'No, that'd be good. I'd like that.'

'And maybe we can look at planting things in the garden,' he said, 'flowers that butterflies really like. Then, next summer, when Tyler plays in the garden he might get to see a few butterflies.'

And maybe it would also bring back nice memories of his grandmother, Emmy thought. Dylan had mentioned her before; and she had the strongest feeling that he'd been closer to his grandmother than he was to his mother. He certainly missed her, from what he'd let slip.

'That's a great idea,' she said. 'Though I had a flat so I'm afraid I'm not much of a gardener. I tended to have cut flowers rather than houseplants. Ally bought me a couple and...well, let's just say I don't have green fingers.'

'We'll learn,' he said. 'Looking after a garden can't be

any harder than bringing up a baby, and we're managing fine with Tyler.'

Emmy felt warm inside that not only were they working together as a team, he was also acknowledging that. And this was beginning to feel like being part of a real family. It was taking time, but they were finally bonding.

She was fascinated by the terrarium with the dragonflies in the next section. 'Just look at the colours,' she said, pointing them out to Tyler. 'Blue and green dragonflies.'

'Fiiih,' the baby said again.

She laughed and rubbed the tip of her nose against his. 'Fly, sweetie, not fish. But I guess they both sort of have scales.'

When they stopped in the café, she mashed a banana for Tyler and leaned down to feed him in his pushchair while Dylan went to get the coffee. When Tyler had finished, she scooped him onto her lap and cuddled him with one arm while she made a couple of quick sketches in the notebook she always carried in her handbag.

Dylan put the coffees on the table, out of Tyler's reach. 'What are you doing?' he asked.

'Just noting down a couple of ideas for jewellery.'

He looked intrigued. 'So this sort of thing is where you get your inspiration?'

'Sort of,' she hedged.

'Sorry, is this a creative thing? You don't like to talk about work in progress?'

'No, it's fine.' She felt relaxed enough with him to know that he wasn't like her exes—he was asking because he was interested, not because he wanted her to stop or thought he had better ideas that she ought to go along with. She pushed her notebook across the table to him. 'Have a look through if you want to. Sometimes I take pictures, sometimes I sketch.'

He flicked through the pages. 'That spiderweb reminds me a bit of that necklace you made.'

'With the heart in the middle rather than the spider?' She smiled. 'You're right, that was the inspiration. It was a frosty morning and the cobwebs were really visible. They looked incredibly pretty, delicate yet strong at the same time.'

He reached the page where she'd sketched a couple of pictures of Tyler asleep. 'I had no idea you could draw. I mean, I knew you designed stuff, but that's not the same as a portrait. These are really good.'

'Thank you. I was working while he was napping and I just thought he looked so cute and peaceful. I couldn't resist it.'

He handed the book back to her. 'Very cute. So you carry a notebook all the time?'

'Yes. Because you never know when you're going to see something that sets off an idea,' she explained. 'Though I guess it's not quite like that with your job.'

He smiled. 'No, it's talking to the client that does that.' He indicated the slice of chocolate cake he'd bought. 'Would you like some of this?'

'Thanks, but I'm fine.' Mr Stuffy had changed absolutely, Emmy thought. A couple of months ago, he would barely have spoken to her. Now he was offering to share cake with her, for all the world as if they were partners.

Though she knew better than to kid herself. Yes, Dylan was attractive. Especially when you saw past the superficial eye-candy stuff to the real smile, the one that lit up his eyes. He could tempt her to break every single one of her rules and fall in love with him.

But then what? She couldn't take the risk. If she had an affair with Dylan, she knew it would be amazing at first.

But then it would go the way of all her other relationships and end in tears. Hers.

Dylan flicked through the leaflet he'd picked up at the counter. 'Did you know that a butterfly tastes through its feet?'

She raised an eyebrow. 'You expect me to believe that?'

'Seriously, a butterfly can't bite or chew food. It just sucks everything up with a proboscis, so it has to taste things through sensors in its feet.'

'Did you hear that, Ty?' She traced circles on his palm, making the baby giggle.

'Round and round the garden,' Dylan said.

He knew this? Then again, she'd noticed what he'd been reading. He'd left child development books in the living room. Being Dylan, he took things seriously and did it the geek way. 'Like a teddy bear,' she said.

'One step.' He put a finger on Tyler's wrist.

'Two step.' She put a finger on Tyler's elbow.

'And a tickle under there.' He tickled Tyler under the armpit, and the baby's rich chuckle rang out.

'Come to me so Em can drink her coffee?' Dylan asked, holding his arms out.

Tyler echoed him, holding his arms out to be picked up. 'Dih-dih!'

Dylan scooped him up. 'How did he do with the banana?'

'He ate about three-quarters of it.'

'Good boy. Is the milk in his bag?'

'Sure is.' And how Dylan had come on as a father, she thought. In the early days, he'd been wary, unsure of himself. Now, he was confident, and Tyler responded to that. The baby clearly adored him.

She could easily adore Dylan, too—the man he'd become.

But she needed to keep her burgeoning feelings under control. This was as good as it was going to get, so she was going to enjoy it for what it was and not let herself wish for more. Even though, secretly, she did wish for more.

They really did look cute together, Tyler cuddled on Dylan's lap, holding his own bottle and yet with Dylan's hand held just under it as a safety net. She couldn't resist taking a picture on her phone. 'That's lovely. I'll send it to Ally's and Pete's parents.'

'I was talking to them the other night,' Dylan said. 'They told me you write to them every week with pictures and updates.'

She shrugged. 'Well, they don't really use email. It's nearly the same, just that I print it out rather than send it electronically. It's not a big deal.'

'It's nice of you to bother, though.'

'Just because they've lost their children, it doesn't mean they have to lose their grandson as well,' she said. Then an idea hit her. 'Would you like to send a copy of this photo to your mum? I could send it to your phone, or even directly to her if that's easier for you.'

'No, it's OK.' But it was as if she'd thrown up a brick wall between them, because he went quiet on her.

What had she said?

They'd talked about sending a picture to Tyler's grandparents and she'd suggested sending it to his own mother, too. And it wasn't the first time he'd gone quiet on her after the subject of his parents had cropped up.

Clearly there was some kind of rift there, and she'd just trampled on a really sore spot.

'I'm sorry, Dylan. I didn't mean to…' Help. Given that the intensely private man seemed to be back, how could she phrase this without making it worse? 'I'm sorry,' she said again.

He sighed. 'It's not your fault. Sorry. I'm stressing about the contract. I shouldn't take it out on you.'

She let it go, but still she wondered. She'd noticed that Dylan's mother had never visited or even called the house. He'd said before that his mother was travelling, so maybe she was somewhere with poor phone connections, or maybe she just called him during office hours, when he wasn't in the house. But it was as if almost everything to do with Dylan's family was in a box marked 'extra private, do not touch'.

They still hadn't quite got that easiness and family feeling back by the time they'd finished in the café and went to the gift shop.

Until she spied the butterfly mobile. 'That's lovely. We can put it over his cot. It'd look great with the stars from his nightlight floating over it, and he'll see it first thing in the morning when he wakes.'

'Mmm.' Dylan didn't sound that enthusiastic, but she knew he secretly liked the nightlight.

They continued to browse, and Dylan picked up a board book. 'We need to get this.'

She glanced at it; it was a story about a caterpillar, and there was a finger puppet. So New Dylan was back. Stuffy Dylan might have read a grudging bedtime story, but New Dylan would read it with voices and props so a child would really enjoy it. She grinned. 'You like doing bedtime stories, don't you?'

'Yes. If anyone had told me I'd like doing all the voices, I would've said they were crazy. But I do.' He looked a bit wistful. 'I wish Pete was here to share it. He would've loved this.'

'So would Ally,' she said softly. 'And you know what? I think they're looking down on us right now, hugging each other and saying they made exactly the right choice.'

To her surprise, he reached over to touch her cheek. 'Know what? I agree.'

Emmy felt warm all over. Right now they were definitely in accordance. And nothing felt better than this.

CHAPTER ELEVEN

TWO NIGHTS LATER, Tyler wasn't settling in his cot as he usually did after a bath and a story; he was just grizzling and looking unhappy. It didn't look like teething, because although his cheeks were red he wasn't dribbling. Emmy laid her fingertips against his forehead and bit her lip. He felt a bit too hot for her liking.

Where was the thermometer?

She looked through the top drawer of Tyler's dressing table. Ally had shown it to her when she'd bought it. All she had to do now was put a thin plastic cone over the tip of the digital thermometer, place it in the baby's ear, and press a button.

Except she couldn't get the thermometer to switch on.

Oh, no. And she had a nasty feeling that they didn't have any spare batteries that would fit.

Although it was her night on duty, she wanted a second opinion—especially as the thermometer was out of action.

'Shh, sweetie, we'll do something to make you feel better,' she said, scooping the baby up and holding him close. She carried him down to the living room, where Dylan was working on his laptop.

'Sorry to interrupt you,' she said, 'but I need a second opinion.'

'What's up?' he asked.

'The thermometer battery's run out and we don't have a spare. Does Tyler feel hot to you, or am I just being paranoid?'

He felt the baby's forehead. 'No, he feels hot to me, too. What do we do now? Where's the book?' He grabbed *The Baby Bible* and looked something up in the index. He frowned as he swiftly read the relevant page. 'Do we have any baby paracetamol?'

'It's in the kitchen with the medicine cabinet.'

'Good. We need to give him that to help bring his temperature down, and while that's working we have to strip him down to his vest and sponge him down with tepid water.' He held out his arms for the baby. 'I'll give him a cuddle and sing to him while you go and get the stuff. I'll meet you in the bathroom.'

The baby was still crying softly when Emmy came upstairs with the baby paracetamol and the syringe. Dylan had taken the babygro off and was rocking Tyler and singing to him.

Dylan glanced at the syringe and his eyes widened. 'What, we have to give him an injection?'

'No. The instructions say it's easier to give medicine to babies with an oral syringe than a spoon,' she explained.

'Right.'

Between them, they managed to administer the medicine, then sponged the baby with tepid water.

'Sorry, I interrupted you from your work.' She blew out a breath. 'It's my shift, and I should be able to cope. It's just… This is what keeps me awake at night. I worry about him. I worry that every cough and sneeze will turn into meningitis. That he'll die and it'll be all my fault for not looking after him properly.'

'Emmy, he doesn't have meningitis. He doesn't have a rash.'

'There isn't one at first. We could blink and he'll be covered in purple stuff that won't go away when you press a glass against it.' She'd read all the books. She knew the signs. And she had nightmares about it. Terror that made her breathing go shallow.

'We're both keeping an eye on him, so we won't miss anything between us.' He rested his fingertips against her cheek, his touch calming her. 'Deep breaths, Emmy. He's not going to die and you're doing a great job of looking after him. And don't apologise for interrupting me.' He cradled the baby tenderly. 'He's not well, and he needs to come first. I would've done the same if it was my shift.'

'I'll get him a drink of cooled boiled water. It might help him feel better.'

'Good idea. It must be some sort of bug. There are quite a few people at work with rotten colds.' He looked stricken. 'Oh, no. I probably brought the germs home with me.'

She shook her head. 'It's not your fault, Dylan. He could have caught a virus absolutely anywhere.'

Three hours later, the baby was fast asleep, but Emmy was still worried about him. 'I think I'll sleep in his room tonight.'

'You're not going to get a lot of rest on the floor,' Dylan pointed out.

'I know.' She sighed. 'Or maybe I'll bring him in with me. Except I'm a bit scared of rolling over in the night and squishing him.'

He looked at her. 'If it was my shift tonight, you still wouldn't be able to sleep because you'd be worrying about him, right?'

'I guess so.'

'Don't take this the wrong way,' he warned, 'but maybe we could both look after him, tonight. I do trust you—of *course* I do—but this is the first time he's been ill since we've been looking after him, and it worries me.'

'Me, too,' she admitted.

'We could take two-hour shifts, so one of us stays awake and keeps an eye on him while the other of us has a nap,' he suggested

She nodded. 'But it isn't fair to keep moving him between our rooms—and, as you said, the nursery floor isn't that comfortable.' The sensible course was obvious. But actually saying it… She took a deep breath. 'OK. Your bed or mine?'

Dylan gave her a rueful smile. 'I never thought I'd hear those words from you, Em.'

'Believe you me, I never thought I'd say them to you,' she said dryly. 'And this is only because we both need to look after him. I'm not coming on to you.' Though even as she said it, she felt her face flood with colour. She was horribly aware that, in another life, she *would* be coming on to Dylan—because she liked the man he'd become. And she definitely found him attractive.

Which was why she found her most frumpy pair of pyjamas before she showered, just to make the point that there was nothing sexual about this. She felt amazingly shy as she changed into her nightwear—which was ridiculous, considering that she was covered from head to toe and she knew that Dylan had seen more of her body when she was wearing a dress. Even so, she kept the bedside light on its lowest setting.

There was a knock on the door.

And how stupid that her heart missed a beat.

'Come in,' she called, hoping that her voice didn't sound as husky and nervous to him as it did to her.

He walked in wearing just a pair of pyjama bottoms, carrying the sleeping baby.

'I, um, don't tend to wear a pyjama top because I get too hot at night. Is that a problem for you?'

'No, it's fine.' She really hoped he hadn't heard that little shiver in her voice. *Too hot at night.* Oh-h-h. He looked amazingly hot right now. She could really see that he worked out at the gym regularly because his muscles were beautifully sculpted; he had good abs and strong arms, and he wouldn't have looked out of place in a perfume ad. Especially dressed the way he was, right now.

And that was totally inappropriate. He was here in her bedroom because Tyler was sick and they were sharing his care, that was all.

'Which side of the bed do you prefer to sleep on?' he asked.

'The right side—nearest the door,' she said.

'Fine by me.' He pulled the covers back and gently laid Tyler in the middle of the bed. He touched the baby's forehead and grimaced. 'He still feels hot.'

'We'd better not put a cover over him, then.'

They both climbed into bed, on either side of the baby.

'Poor little mite,' Emmy said softly. 'I wish I could have that high temperature for him.'

'Me, too,' Dylan said. 'It's weird how protective I feel about him. I never thought I'd ever feel this way about a baby.'

It was as if Tyler were their natural child, Emmy thought. She wasn't his birth mother, but she was in the position of his mother, now, and she loved him deeply. Dylan clearly felt the same way, as if he were Tyler's real father.

'We're privileged,' she said softly.

'Yes, we are.' He paused. 'Shall I take the first shift while you try to get some sleep for a couple of hours? I'll wake you when it's your turn.'

'OK. Thanks, Dylan. I appreciate the backup.'

'You'd have done the same if it'd been my turn to look after him,' he said. 'Try to get some sleep.'

She turned over so her back was to him, but she was so aware of him. He was in her bed, barely an arm's reach away. And if Tyler hadn't been there...

No, no and *no*. She was not going to allow herself to think about the possibilities.

Eventually Emmy managed to get to sleep. Then she became aware of someone stroking her arm and shaking her shoulder very gently. 'Emmy? Wake up.'

'Uhh.' It took a second for her to think why Dylan would be shaking her awake; then she remembered and sat up with a jolt. 'Is Tyler OK?'

'He's still a bit warm, but I put a single sheet over him because his legs and arms seemed a bit cold.'

'Good idea. You get some sleep now. I'll stay awake.'

Still feeling groggy, she placed her fingertips on Tyler's forehead. Dylan's assessment was spot on.

She was glad that Dylan turned his back to her to go to sleep, because she really didn't want him to catch her looking lustfully at him. Even his back was beautiful. She itched to sketch him, though it was years since she'd taken her Art A level and sketched a life model. Apart from those brief sketches she'd made of Tyler, she'd stuck mainly to abstracts and the designs for her jewellery. But Dylan was beautiful. He'd be a joy to sketch. She fixed the picture in her mind, intending to indulge herself later, then watched Tyler sleeping. The baby looked angelic with that mop of dark curls; and she was glad to see, even in the low light in the room, that his cheeks didn't look quite so red.

In his sleep, Dylan shifted to face her. In repose, he looked younger. It took Emmy a while to realise what the difference was, and then she worked it out: he didn't have that slight air of wariness she was used to.

Someone had hurt him pretty deeply, Emmy was sure. Nadine was the obvious candidate, but Emmy had a feeling that it went deeper than that. Why had he been so resistant to the idea of having a child of his own? Had he had a rotten childhood?

Not that he'd tell her, she knew. Even if she asked him straight out. He was way too private for that, and it was surprising that he'd already let this much slip to her.

Finally her two-hour watch was over. She checked Tyler's temperature again. Good. It was definitely going down. She reached over to lay a hand on Dylan's arm. His skin felt so good against her fingertips. Soft and smooth. Tempting her to explore further.

Get a grip, Emmy Jacobs, she lambasted herself silently. This isn't about you.

She patted his arm lightly, but it didn't wake him at all. She shook his shoulder, and there was still no response. Dylan was clearly in a really deep sleep. And he had taken the first shift; he must've been exhausted. She decided to leave him sleeping for another hour, then tried to wake him again. This time, she climbed out of bed and went round to his side, so she could shake him harder without waking the baby.

In response, Dylan reached out to her and mumbled something she didn't quite catch. It sounded like 'Mmm, Dee'.

'Dylan,' she said in an urgent whisper.

'Mmm,' he muttered. This time, he actually pulled her into his arms and snuggled closer.

Oh, help.

If it weren't for the baby lying next to him, she could be oh, so tempted. All she had to do was to move her head slightly and her mouth would touch against his. She could kiss him awake. See where it led them.

But he'd said 'Dee', and she had a nasty feeling that he was dreaming about his ex. Mmm, Dee. Nadine. They sounded the same, mumbled in sleep. And how stupid she was to think that Dylan would get over his wife that quickly. He was obviously still in love with his ex. Yes, there was a definite attraction between the two of them, but physical attraction wasn't enough. Her relationships never lasted. If she had a fling with Dylan, it would make everything way too complicated. She really couldn't do this.

She managed to resist the temptation—only just—and wriggled out of his arms.

'Dylan,' she said, more loudly this time.

He woke with a start and looked at her in utter confusion. Then his expression cleared as he obviously remembered where he was and why. 'How's Tyler?'

'Still a little bit warm, but nowhere near as hot as he was. He's asleep.'

'Good. Is it three o'clock?'

'Four.'

He looked shocked. 'You were supposed to wake me at three.'

'Dylan, you sleep like a log. I couldn't wake you.'

He grimaced. 'I'm sorry. OK. I'll take the next three hours and I'll wake you at seven, not six, OK?'

'OK.' She was still feeling slightly lightheaded; but that had to be from lack of sleep. It had absolutely nothing to do with the way Dylan had pulled her into his arms and held her close. Did it?

Emmy looked absolutely shattered, Dylan thought—and no wonder, since her shift had lasted longer than his. He felt guilty about it, and lapsed into silence to let her sleep.

He touched Tyler's forehead, just to check; she was right, the baby felt cooler.

He shifted onto his side to watch the baby. Emmy had turned away from him to sleep, but he could still feel her warmth in his arms. When she'd woken him, for a moment he'd been confused and thought he was back in his old house, the one he'd shared with Nadine before he'd moved into the Docklands flat. It had seemed natural to draw her closer, hold her.

Hopefully she'd forget about that by the morning. He didn't want her to think he was coming on to her, because it could make things so awkward between them. And he didn't want it to go back to the bad old days, when they hadn't got on.

Funny, sharing a house with Emmy hadn't been like sharing with Nadine, even in the early days when he and Nadine had been happy. With Emmy, he didn't feel any pressure. He didn't have anything to live up to, because they'd started from the lowest possible point and thought the worst of each other.

And these past few months had been a revelation. He'd been so sure that he didn't want a family. That he didn't want to risk things going wrong and for his child to grow up as unhappy as he'd been. Even when Nadine had given him an ultimatum, his feelings hadn't changed and he knew he'd made the right decision.

Yet, ever since he'd become a stand-in father, things had been different. Over the months, he'd grown to love his godson. He loved seeing all the little changes every day, hearing the little boy's vocabulary grow from a simple da-da, ba-ba, through to 'Dih-dih' for Dylan and 'Ehhhm,' for Emmy, and sounds that resembled real words—like the time in the butterfly house when Emmy had been convinced that he'd said 'fish'. He enjoyed seeing Tyler's anticipation as they read through a story and were about to reach his favourite bits. He enjoyed the simple clapping games Emmy had taught him to play with the little boy.

And Emmy herself...

There was the rub.

She was Tyler's stand-in mother. Dylan's co-guardian and housemate.

They were well on the way to becoming friends. He enjoyed her company, and he thought she enjoyed his, too. And, although they'd agreed to have alternate weekends off from childcare, in recent weeks they'd ended up spending a fair bit of those weekends together.

It felt like being a family. What he'd always said he didn't want. And what he'd discovered that, actually, yes, he did want. Very much indeed.

She shifted in bed, turning to face him, and he held his breath.

Spiky Emmy, the cynical and brittle woman he'd loathed so much in the past, wasn't here. This was sweet, gentle, soft Emmy. Vulnerable Emmy, who'd had her confidence chipped away by exes who couldn't see her for who she was, only what they wanted her to be. Emmy, who didn't really believe in herself.

Dylan could see her for who she was. And he liked her. More than liked her.

But could he ask her to take a chance with him—to make their unexpected family a real one?

It would be a risk. A huge risk. It had gone wrong with Nadine; he couldn't make any promises that he'd get it right, second time round, with Emmy. And he knew she shared similar fears, given that she'd been let down in the past.

Somehow he'd have to overcome those fears. Teach her

that he wasn't like the men she'd dated before: that he saw her for who she was and he liked her just the way she was. And then maybe, just maybe, they'd stand a chance.

CHAPTER TWELVE

A WEEK LATER, Emmy opened the thick brown envelope that had just been delivered, to discover an early copy of the glossy magazine that had interviewed her.

'Ty, look—it's Aunty Emmy's feature,' she said, waving the magazine at him.

Tyler was much more interested in picking up the bricks they'd been playing with, and dropping them.

She built him another tower to enjoy knocking down, counting the bricks for him as she did so, then flicked through the magazine to the article. There was a nice picture of her with Tyler, and they'd really showcased her jewellery beautifully. But her delight turned to dismay as she skimmed through the text.

She'd explained the situation to the journalist. She'd made it totally clear that she and Dylan were Tyler's co-guardians and they weren't an item. So why did the article make reference to Dylan being her partner?

Oh, no. He wasn't going to be happy about that. At all.

She paced the house all morning. What was the best way to deal with this?

In the end, she decided to tell him straight. Sooner rather than later.

She waited until Tyler took his late morning nap, then called Dylan at work.

He answered immediately. 'Is Tyler all right?'

'Yes, he's fine.'

Her shakiness must've shown in her voice, because he asked, 'What's wrong?'

'There's something you need to know. It's pretty bad.' She took a deep breath. 'The magazine's coming out next week. They sent me an early copy today.'

'And they didn't use your jewellery in the end?' He sounded sympathetic. 'More fool them.'

'It's not that. They did use my pieces.' She swallowed hard. 'But they've used a picture of me with Tyler—and they've said in the piece that you're my partner. They actually named you as computer superguru Dylan Harper. And it—well, basically it implied that Tyler's our child. I told the journalist why we were sharing a house and sharing Tyler's care. I can't believe they got it wrong like this! I'm so sorry. If this causes you any problems...' Her voice faded. If it caused him problems, she had no idea what she could do to fix it. Would it make his divorce more difficult?

'They got the wrong end of the stick. So what? It doesn't matter. Stop worrying,' he said, surprising her. She'd been so sure he'd be annoyed about it. 'The main thing is that they showcased your jewellery.'

'They did. And the jet animals.'

'Good. Now breathe, Emmy.'

'Thank you,' she said in a small voice. 'I thought you'd be livid.'

'It could be a lot worse. Most people know the press exaggerate, so don't worry about it. Just wait for people to start contacting you with commissions—and then you'll be so busy you won't have time to worry about it anymore.'

It was another week until the magazine was in the shops. Although Dylan had told her not to worry about it, Emmy still couldn't help fretting. If anyone who knew him read the piece, they'd get completely the wrong idea.

The day before the magazine came out Dylan distracted her when he called her from work.

'Don't tell me—an emergency project meeting and you're going to be late?' she asked.

'No—and I'm bringing champagne home. I got some good news this afternoon.'

'You got the Burroughs contract?'

'I certainly did.'

'Fantastic.' Emmy was genuinely pleased for him. 'Well done.'

'It was partly thanks to you,' Dylan pointed out.

'No, it's because he recognises your skill. Actually, I have some news for you. Elaine Burroughs rang. She's bringing her daughter over to see me next week.'

'For a commission? That's great. Well done. Got to go but I'll see you later. Oh—and please don't cook monk-fish.'

She just laughed. 'For that, I'm ordering a takeaway. See you later.' She replaced the phone and cuddled Tyler. 'You know what? This is all starting to work out. It's not quite how Dylan and I wanted things—we'd both do anything to have your mum and dad back with us. But, as second-best goes, this is pretty good.'

Over champagne, that evening, Dylan said, 'I want to take you out to dinner to say thanks—being here with us really made a difference to Ted's decision to give us the project. Do you think your mum would babysit Ty for us?'

'Probably. I'll ask her,' Emmy said.

'Do you mind if I ask her?' Dylan asked.

She smiled. 'You know her number.' Dylan might not be that close to his own mother, she thought, but he definitely got on well with hers.

The following evening was Dylan's turn to cook. Over pasta, he told her, 'I spoke to your mum this morning. It's all arranged; we're going tomorrow.'

'Going where?' she asked.

'Out to lunch,' he said. 'Except we need to leave really early tomorrow morning, and you'll need your passport.'

She frowned. 'Why do I need my passport?'

'Don't be difficult,' he said. 'I was going to take you out to dinner, but I thought lunch might be more fun.'

'Lunch is fine, but what does that have to do with my passport?'

'Surprise.'

She sighed. 'You do know I hate surprises, don't you?'

'I think you'll like this one.' Annoyingly, he refused to be drawn on any further details.

'Are you at least going to tell me the dress code?' she asked in exasperation.

He thought about it for a moment. 'Smart casual—probably a little bit more on the smart side. You definitely need shoes you can walk in.'

'So we're walking somewhere?'

'End of information bulletin. No more answers,' he said, and gave her the most infuriating grin. Worse still, he refused to be drawn for the rest of the evening.

'I swear I'm never playing poker with you,' she said. 'You're inscrutable.'

He just laughed. 'I've been called worse.'

The next morning, Dylan knocked on Emmy's bedroom door at what felt like just before the crack of dawn. 'We're leaving in half an hour.'

Which gave her just enough time to shower, wash her hair, dress, and check in on Tyler. Her mother was already in the kitchen when Emmy came downstairs, and the kettle was on. 'Hi, Mum. Thanks for babysitting. Tyler's still asleep, given it's the crack of dawn.' She greeted her mother with a hug and kiss. 'Coffee and toast?'

'We don't have time,' Dylan said.

She gave him a sceptical look. 'You know I'm horrible if I haven't eaten. And why do we have to leave so early if we're going out to lunch, which won't be for hours?'

He answered her question with one of his own. 'You've definitely got your passport in your bag?'

She gave him a withering look. 'I'm not *that* flaky, Dylan.'

'Sorry. Old habits die hard.' He ruffled her hair. 'Let's go. We have a train to catch.'

So wherever they were going, it was by Tube. She still had no idea why he wanted her to bring her passport; though, knowing Dylan, that could be a red herring. She kissed her mum goodbye; to her surprise, so did he. Together, they headed for the Tube station, a ten-minute walk away.

Emmy noticed that although Dylan was wearing one of his work suits, teamed with a white shirt and highly polished shoes, at least for once he wasn't wearing a tie. She'd opted for a simple black shift dress teamed with black tights and flat shoes; a silver and turquoise choker; and a turquoise pashmina.

'You look lovely,' he said.

She inclined her head. 'Thank you, kind sir. Actually, you don't look so bad yourself.'

He smiled back at her. 'Why, thank you.'

Ten minutes later, they arrived at King's Cross. The second he directed her through the exit to St Pancras, she realised where they were going. 'We're going to *Paris* for lunch, Dylan? That's incredibly decadent!'

'Not really. It's as quick to take the train from London to

Paris as it is to drive from London to Brighton,' he pointed out. 'Anyway, I love Paris. It's a beautiful city.'

To her delight, he'd booked them in business class so they could have breakfast on the train.

'So this is why you wouldn't let me have even a piece of toast at home,' she said, surveying the feast in front of her. Champagne with fresh orange juice, smoked salmon and scrambled egg, fresh strawberries, and good coffee. 'This has to be the most perfect breakfast ever. I feel totally spoiled.'

He smiled. 'Good.'

'I've never been in business class before.' Because she could only really afford standard class. And only then if she booked the seat early enough to get the supercheap rate.

He shrugged. 'The seats are more comfortable.'

'Thank you, Dylan. This is a real treat.'

Dylan watched her selecting what to have next; he loved the fact that she was enjoying her food rather than picking at it, the way Nadine always had.

She caught him watching her. 'Sorry. Am I being greedy?'

He laughed. 'No, I was just thinking how nice it is that you enjoy your food instead of nibbling on a lettuce leaf.'

'This is a lot better than you or I can cook,' she said with a smile. 'And if we're going to Paris, I take it we're walking, so I'm going to burn all this off anyway.'

The journey to the Gare du Nord was quick and uneventful; a short trip on the Métro took them to the Champs Elysées.

'It's too long since I've been to Paris. I'd almost forgotten how lovely it is—all that space in the streets, all the windows and the balconies.' She gestured across to a terrace on the other side of the street. 'I love that wrought ironwork.'

He smiled at her; he recognised that light in her eyes. The same as it had been at the butterfly house, and he'd seen drafts of designs that reminded him of the metalwork in the old Edwardian conservatory. 'Are you going to get your notebook out and start sketching?'

She smiled back. 'Not in the middle of the street. But would you mind if I took some photographs to remind me later?'

''Course not. Enjoy.'

They wandered down the street and stopped in a small café. Macaroons were arranged in a cone shape on the counter, showcasing all the different colours available, from deep pink through to browns, yellows and pistachio green.

'I guess we have to try them, as we're in Paris,' he said, and ordered macaroons with their coffee.

'This is just *lovely*. The perfect day.' Her eyes were all huge and shiny with pleasure—and that in turn made Dylan feel happy, too.

This was definitely as good as it got.

And taking her to Paris was the best idea he'd ever had. Romantic and sweet—and this might be the place where he could ask her to change their relationship. Be more than just his co-guardian. If he could find the right words.

'What would you like to do before lunch?' he asked.

'Are you planning to go somewhere in particular for lunch?'

'Yes. We need to be in the fourth arrondissement at one o'clock, but before then we can go wherever you like. I assume you'd like to go to an art gallery?'

'That's a tough one,' she said. 'Even at this time of day, I think there will be too much of a queue at the Louvre.'

She looked at him. 'You said the fourth arrondissement, so that means the old quarter. Could we go to Notre Dame and see the grotesques?'

'Sure,' he said. 'I've never been. It'd be interesting to see them.' He'd visited most of the art galleries and museums, as well as the Sacré-Coeur and Montmartre, but he'd never actually been to Notre Dame.

'It's a bit of a trek up the tower,' she warned.

'I don't mind. I know you said you wanted to walk, but how do you feel about going by river?'

She nodded. 'That works for me. I love boat trips.'

He made a mental note; it might be nice to take Tyler to Kew on the river, in the spring.

When they'd finished their coffee, they took the Batobus along the Seine to the Île de la Cité, with Emmy exclaiming over several famous buildings on the way. They walked up the steps from the bridge, then across the square with the famous vista of Notre Dame and its square double tower and rose window. The stone of the cathedral looked brilliant white against the blue sky.

'I love the shape of the rose window, the way it fans out—almost like the petals of a gerbera crossed with a spiderweb,' she said.

'Are you thinking a pendant?' he asked.

She nodded. 'Do you mind if I take some pictures?'

He laughed. 'You really don't have to ask me every time, Emmy. Just do it. Today's for you to enjoy.'

'Thank you.' She took several photos on her phone, and then they queued at the side of the cathedral to walk up the tower to the galleries.

'I always think of poor Quasimodo, here,' Emmy said. 'So deeply in love with Esmeralda, yet afraid she'll despise him like everyone else does.'

'So you cried over the film?'

'No, over the book,' she said, surprising him.

'You read Victor Hugo?' He hadn't expected that.

She looked at him. 'It was one of my set texts for A level.'

'English?'

'French,' she corrected.

He blinked. 'You let everyone think you're this ditzy designer, but you're really bright, aren't you?'

'Don't sound so surprised. It kind of spoils the compliment.' She rolled her eyes. 'I'm really going to have to make you that jet rhino, aren't I?'

'Hey.' He gave her a brief hug. 'I didn't mean it like that. But you do keep your light under a bushel.'

'Maybe.'

They walked up the hundreds of spiral steps; the stone was worn at the edges where thousands of people had walked up those steps before them. At the first stage, they had amazing views of the square and the Seine, with the Eiffel Tower looming in the background. They carried on up to the next stage and saw the famous chimera grotesques in the Grande Galerie. Dylan was fascinated by the pelican. 'And that elephant would look great carved in jet,' he said.

'For Ty's Noah's Ark? Good idea,' she said.

'So why are the gargoyles here?' he asked.

'Strictly speaking, gargoyles carry rainwater away from the building. These ones don't act as conduits; they're just carvings, so they're called grotesques. These are Victorian ones, done at the same time as the restoration. And there's a fabulous legend—see the one sitting over there, looking over the Seine?'

'Yes.'

'Apparently it watches out for people who are drowning, then swoops down and rescues them.'

He raised an eyebrow. 'Is that something else you learned for your A level?'

'No. Actually, I can't even remember where I heard it, but I think it's a lovely story.'

Emmy liked the brighter side of life, he noticed. Trust her to know about that sort of legend.

They walked across to the other tower to see the bell, then back down all the steps.

'Did you want to go inside the cathedral?' he asked.

'Yes, please. I love the stained glass,' she said.

As he'd half expected, she took several photographs of the rose window with its beautiful blue and red glass.

'Is this a Victorian renovation, too?' he asked.

'Most of this one's original thirteenth-century glass. If I were you, I'd tell me to shut up, now,' she said with a grin, 'because stained glass was one of the modules in my degree, and Ally says I get really boring about it, always dragging her off to tiny churches to see rare specimens.' Her smile faded. 'Said,' she corrected herself.

He took her hand and squeezed it. 'You really miss her, don't you?'

'Yes. But I'm glad we have Tyler. We'll see her and Pete in him as he grows up.'

And then he forgot to release her hand. She didn't make a protest; it was only as they strolled through the streets of the old quarter that he realised he was still holding her hand. And that he was actually *happy*. Happier than he could remember being for a long, long time.

Maybe he didn't need to struggle with words, after all. Maybe all he had to do was *be*.

She insisted on stopping at one of the stalls and buying a baby-sized beret for Tyler. She gave him a sidelong look. 'I'm tempted to get you one as well.'

'You expect me to wear a beret?' he scoffed.

'Mmm, and you could have a Dali moustache to go with it.'

He shuddered. 'What next, a stripy jumper and a red scarf?'

She laughed. 'OK, so a beret is a bit too avant-garde for you—but men can look good in a beret, you know.'

'I think I'll pass,' he said. 'Though I admit Tyler will look cute.'

As they crossed the bridge she asked, 'Where are we going?'

'Time for lunch,' he said.

They stopped outside a restaurant in the old quarter right next to the Seine with view of Notre Dame. She looked at him, wide-eyed. 'I know of this place. Zola, Dumas and de Maupassant all used to come here—it's hideously expensive, Dylan. It's Michelin starred.'

And it had a great reputation, which was why he'd booked it. He simply shrugged. 'They might have monk-fish.'

She let the teasing comment pass. 'I've never eaten in a restaurant with a Michelin star.'

'Good. That means you'll enjoy this,' he said.

Enjoy?

This was way, way out of her experience. Dylan, despite the fact that he wasn't keen on cooking, clearly liked good food and was used to eating at seriously swish restaurants like this one.

Enjoy.

OK. She'd give it a go. Even if she did feel a bit intimidated.

The maître d' showed them to a table in a private salon. She'd never been to such an amazing place before; the décor was all gilded wood and hand-painted wallpaper.

There was a white damask cloth on the table along with lit white candles and silverware, and gilded Louis XIV chairs. The windows were covered with dark voile curtains, making the room seem even more intimate. And the maître d' told them that the waiter would be along whenever they rang the bell.

Emmy's eyes met Dylan's as they were seated. For a moment, she allowed herself to think what it would be like if this were a proper romantic date. A total sweep-you-off-your-feet date.

He'd held her hand as they'd wandered through the city together; so was this Dylan's way of taking her on a date without having to ask her? He didn't like emotional stuff, so she knew he'd shy away from the words; but this definitely felt like more than a thank you. More like the fact that he wanted to be with her. Some time for just the two of them. Together.

Unless she was projecting her own wants on him and seeing what she wanted to see...

When she looked at her menu, she noticed that there were no prices. In her experience, this meant the food was seriously expensive. And it made her antsy.

She coughed. 'Dylan, there aren't any prices on my menu.'

He spread his hands. 'And?'

She bit her lip. 'I'm used to paying my way.'

'Not on this occasion. I'm taking you out to lunch to say thank you.'

So not a date, then. She tried not to feel disappointed.

'Just as you took me out to dinner,' he reminded her.

'But when I took you out, it wasn't somewhere as swish as this.'

He sighed. 'Emmy, if you're worrying about the bill, then please don't. I can afford this. My business is doing just fine—and, thanks to this new contract, it's going to be doing even better. I couldn't have got this contract without your help, so please let me say thank you.'

'Can I at least buy the wine?' she asked.

'No. This one is all on me. And, I don't know about you, but I've got to the stage where I fall asleep if I drink at lunchtime, so I was going to suggest champagne by the glass.' His eyes crinkled at the corners. 'But I might let you buy me a crêpe later.'

A crêpe. Which would only cost a couple of Euros, whereas she was pretty sure the bill here was going to be nearer half a month's mortgage payment for her. 'I feel really guilty about this.'

'Don't. I'm doing it because I want to treat you. So enjoy it. What would you like for lunch?'

Protesting any more would be churlish. Emmy scanned the menu. 'It's all so fantastic, I don't know what to choose. I'm torn between lobster and asparagus.'

'We could,' he said, 'order both—and share them.'

Now it was starting to feel like a date again. And that made her all quivery inside. 'Sounds good,' she said.

She actually enjoyed sharing forkfuls of starter with him. Especially as it gave her an excuse to look at his mouth as much as she liked. And she noticed he was looking at her mouth, too. As if he wanted to kiss away a stray crumb and make her forget the rest of the meal.

Oh, help. She really had to keep a lid on this.

After that, she had crayfish with satay and lime, and he chose lamb.

'Look at this. It's beautifully cooked and beautifully presented,' she said. 'I can see exactly why they have a Michelin star. This is *sublime*.'

He chuckled, and she narrowed her eyes at him. 'What's so funny?'

'That you're such a foodie—and, um, in the kitchen...'

She rolled her eyes. 'Yeah, yeah. I'm never going to live that monkfish down. You'll still tease me about it when we're ninety.'

Oh, help. Had she really said that? Implied that they were going to be together forever and ever?

'Yes. I will,' he said softly, and it suddenly made it hard for her to breathe.

She fell back on teasing. Just to defuse the intensity before she said something really, really clueless. 'I could point out that this is a bit of a pots and kettles conversation, given that you're clearly a foodie and you're about the same as I am in the kitchen.'

He laughed. 'I admit my monkfish would've been just as terrible. But you're right. This is sublime. Try it.' He offered her a forkful of lamb.

'Mmm. And try this.' She offered him some crayfish.

'So are you going to tell me that lunch in Paris was the best idea ever?' he prompted.

'That,' she said, 'depends on the dessert.'

They scanned the menu when they'd finished. 'How can you not order madeleines in France?' she asked with a smile.

'When there's chocolate soufflé on the menu,' he retorted, and she laughed.

Again they shared tastes of each other's pudding, and she enjoyed making him lean over to reach the spoon—especially when he retaliated and did likewise.

'That was fantastic,' she said when the meal was over. 'A real treat. I admit, yes, it's the best idea ever. Thank you so much.'

'My pleasure. I enjoyed it, too.'

And his smile reached his eyes; he wasn't just being polite.

They spent the rest of the afternoon browsing in little boutiques. Again, he held her hand; and again, neither of them commented on it.

Emmy bought a box of shiny macaroons for her mother. 'And I think we should go to a toy shop, so we can bring something more than just a beret back for Ty.'

Dylan smiled. 'He probably hasn't even noticed we're gone. Unless that's just a flimsy excuse for toy shopping, Ms Jacobs.'

'It's a really flimsy excuse,' she said with a grin. 'I love toy shops.'

'I'd already noticed that,' he said, 'given how much Tyler's toy box seems to have grown recently.' He checked on his phone to find the nearest toy shop, and when they looked along the shelves Emmy was thrilled to discover a soft plush teddy bear with a beret and stripy shirt. 'This is perfect,' she said, and gave Dylan an arch look. 'Beret and stripy shirt. Hmm.'

He laughed. 'Don't you dare call it Dylan.'

'Spoilsport,' she teased.

'You know, we'll have to bring Ty to Paris when he's a little older. He'll love seeing the Eiffel Tower sparkle at night,' Dylan said.

Making plans for the future, she thought. Neither of them had said it. This was too new, too fragile. But she was beginning to think that there was a future…

When they'd finished shopping, Dylan allowed Emmy to buy him a coffee before they headed back to the Gare du Nord to catch the train to London.

Back in London, Emmy shivered when they came out of the Tube station and pulled her pashmina closer round her. 'I wish I'd brought a proper coat with me, now. It's colder than I expected.'

'Have my jacket,' he offered, starting to shrug it off.

'No, because then you'll be cold. And it's only a few minutes until we get home.'

'I'll call a taxi.'

'By the time it gets here, we could've walked home,' she pointed out.

'OK. Then let's do it this way.' He put his arm round her shoulders, drawing her close to him.

Oh, help. Her skin actually tingled where he touched her. And the whole thing sent her brain into such a flutter that she couldn't utter a word until he opened the front door and ushered her inside.

Her mum greeted them warmly. 'Did you have a good time?'

'The best,' Emmy said. 'Oh, and these are for you.' She handed her mother the bag from the patisserie. 'How's Tyler?'

'Asleep, and he's been absolutely fine all day.' She hugged them both. 'I'll call you tomorrow.'

'Thanks for babysitting for us.' Dylan hugged her back. 'I only had one glass of champagne at lunchtime, so I'm OK to drive. I'll run you home.'

'That's sweet of you.'

Emmy checked on Tyler while Dylan drove her mother home.

Today had been magical. The way Dylan had fed her morsels from his plate at lunchtime, and walked through Paris hand in hand with her; the way he'd automatically offered her his jacket and then, when she'd refused, put his arm round her to keep her warm... Was she adding two and two and making five, or was it the same for him? Had they become something more than co-guardians? Was this a real relationship—one for keeps?

Dylan was back by the time she came downstairs.

'Everything OK?' he asked.

'Tyler's fine. Thank you for today. It really was special.' She stood up, intending to kiss his cheek. But somehow she ended up brushing her mouth against his instead.

She pulled back and looked up at him.

His eyes were intense, darkened from their normal cornflower-blue to an almost stormy navy. She shivered, and couldn't help looking at his mouth again.

He leaned forward and touched his mouth to hers in the lightest, sweetest kiss. Automatically, she parted her lips and tipped her head back in offering. He drew her closer and she could feel the lean, hard strength of his body. So much for Dylan being a geek; he felt more like the athlete she'd once dated, all muscular. And she couldn't help remembering the way he'd looked in her bed, half-naked and asleep.

Her hands were tangled in his hair and his arms were wrapped tightly round her as he deepened the kiss. Her head was spinning, and it felt as if the room were lit by a hundred stars.

He shuddered as he broke the kiss. 'Emmy.'

'I know.' She reached up to trace his lower lip with the tip of her forefinger.

'Are we going to regret this in the morning?' he asked, his voice huskier this time.

'I don't know. Maybe not.' She shivered as he drew the tip of her forefinger into his mouth and sucked; she closed her eyes and tipped her head back, inviting another kiss.

He released her hand. 'Emmy. My common sense is deserting me. If you don't tell me to stop…' he warned.

Then she knew what was going to happen.

And every nerve in her body longed for it.

She opened her eyes and looked at him. 'Yes.'

Still holding her gaze, he scooped her up and carried her up the stairs.

CHAPTER THIRTEEN

EMMY LAY IN the dark, curled against Dylan.

Are we going to regret this in the morning? His words from earlier echoed in her head.

Would they?

Part of her regretted it already. Because she was scared that now everything could go *really* wrong. When had she ever managed to make a relationship last? When had she ever picked the right man? What if Dylan changed his mind about her?

'I can almost hear you thinking,' he said softly, stroking her hair.

'Panicking,' she admitted. 'Dylan—I'm not good at this stuff. I've messed up every relationship I've ever had.'

'You're good at picking Mr Wrong,' he said. 'And you think I might be another.' He shifted so he could brush his mouth against hers. 'Maybe I'm not.'

She swallowed hard. 'I swore I'd never risk anything like this again, not after the last time.'

'What happened? He was another one who wanted you to change?'

'No,' she said miserably. 'Far worse. I should've told you before. He was married.' She grimaced. 'Finding out that I was the other woman…I hated myself for that.'

'You didn't know?'

'No. Especially after what happened to my mum, no way would I ever have tried to break up a family like that. I found out when I called his mobile phone and his wife answered.' Her breath hitched. 'I wasn't the first. Far from it. But I felt so horrible that I'd done that to someone. My mum was devastated when my father had affairs; and I felt like the lowest of the low for making someone else feel like that.'

'It's not your fault if he lied to you,' Dylan pointed out. He sighed. 'Though I don't have room to talk, do I? Technically, I'm married.'

'You've been separated for months, and you're just waiting for that last bit of paper to come through. That's totally different. You've been honest with me. He wasn't. Though I should've worked it out for myself,' Emmy said. 'Afterwards, when I thought about it, it was really obvious. We always went to my place rather than his, and he never stayed overnight. If we did go out, we only ever went to obscure places, and half the time we'd have to call it off—he said it was because of work, but it was obviously because he was doing family things. I should've seen it.'

'It wasn't your fault,' Dylan said again. 'You wouldn't have had anything to do with him if you'd known he was married. He was the cheat, not you.' He sighed. 'And his wife…maybe she loved him very much, but it's still a shame that she'd let herself be treated like that. It sounds to me as if she deserved better. And so do you.'

'I don't know, Dylan. Sometimes my judgement is atrocious.'

'Mine, too,' he said. 'But it's late, we've had a long day, and now maybe isn't the best time to talk. Go to sleep, Em.' He drew her closer.

Well, at least he hadn't walked away, she thought.

Yet.

* * *

The next morning, Emmy was dimly aware of crying. *Loud* crying, which was turning into screams.

She sat up, suddenly wide awake. Tyler. She hadn't put the baby listener on last night. Because she'd…

Oh, no.

She looked at the other side of her bed.

Where Dylan was also sitting up. Completely naked. And looking shocked, embarrassed and awkward.

That made two of them. They'd complicated things hugely, last night. How were they ever going to fix this?

She glanced at the clock: half past nine. A good two and a half hours later than they were usually up. No wonder Tyler was crying. She'd missed her Pilates class. And Dylan would be lucky to get to the office on time for a meeting she knew he had this morning.

'Oh, my God. We're really late,' she said. 'And Tyler's screaming.'

Dylan looked at her. 'Emmy, we need to talk about this, but—'

'You have a meeting, and I need to feed Tyler.'

'I feel bad about leaving without…' He grimaced.

'We'll talk about it later,' she said. 'Can you close your eyes for a moment?' It was ridiculous, she knew, considering they'd both explored each other's bodies in considerable detail the night before; but she felt shy and exposed.

He mumbled something, clearly feeling as embarrassed as she did, and closed his eyes; she fled to the door, grabbed her bathrobe, and put it on as she raced to the baby's room.

And hopefully by the time she and Dylan talked, she would've rediscovered her common sense and worked out how they could deal with this with the minimum fallout for Tyler.

She scooped Tyler out of his cot and held him close. 'OK, babe, Aunty Emmy and Uncle Dylan messed up. But we'll fix things.' And they would fix things, because they didn't have any other option. 'Come on, let's get you some breakfast.'

The crying subsided, and Tyler was back to being all smiles and gurgled after she'd fed him his usual baby porridge and some puréed apple, and given him some milk.

Dylan was clearly as glad as she was of the respite, because she didn't see him at all before he left the house.

She put Tyler back in his cot with some toys to keep him amused, while she had a shower and dressed. Then she scooped him back out of his cot, changed him, and took him downstairs to play.

'I might've just made the biggest mistake of my life, Ty,' she said. 'Or it might've been the best idea ever. Right now, I just don't know.' And it terrified her. She'd already made too many mistakes. 'I don't know how Dylan really feels about me. But we both love you.' She was sure about that. 'And, whatever happens between us, we'll make sure that your world stays safe and secure and happy.'

She still didn't have any solutions by the time that Tyler had his morning nap.

And then a mobile phone shrilled. It wasn't her ringtone, so the phone must be Dylan's. He'd obviously left it behind and was probably ringing to find out where he'd left it.

She found the phone and picked it up, intending to answer and tell him yes, he'd left it here, and yes, she could drop it in to the office if he needed it. It wasn't his name on the screen; but she recognised it immediately. *Nadine*.

What should she do?

This might be important. She ought to answer it. On the other hand, if she answered the phone and Nadine demanded to know who she was, or got the wrong idea, it could make everything much more complicated.

She grabbed the landline and rang Dylan. 'You left your mobile behind.'

He groaned. 'Sorry. Well, don't think you have to bring it out to me or anything. I'll manage without it for today.'

'You might not be able to. Um, Nadine just rang.'

'Why?' He sounded shocked. 'What did she say?'

'I don't know. When I saw her name, I was too much of a coward to answer. Sorry.'

'It's fine. Probably just as well.' He sighed. 'Did she leave a message?'

She glanced at the screen of his phone. 'It looks like it.'

'What does it say?'

'How would I know? I don't listen in to your messages, Dylan.'

'It's probably something to do with paperwork for the divorce,' he said, and sighed. 'I'll sort it out. And I'll see you later. Em…'

'Yes?'

'Never mind. We'll talk when I get home.'

Emmy spent the morning playing with Tyler. But when the baby had a nap, she looked a few things up on the Internet. And then she really wished that she'd let it go. Now she'd seen a picture of Nadine, she could see that Dylan's ex was perfect for him. Poised, sleekly groomed, very together—everything that Emmy wasn't.

And the divorce was taking a very long time to come through. Assuming that they'd split up before Tyler was born…why hadn't it been settled yet? Did Nadine want him back? Had she heard from a colleague that Dylan was guardian to the baby she'd wanted, and did she think that Dylan might be prepared to give their marriage another chance?

She blew out a breath. OK. Dylan wasn't a liar and a cheat. He wouldn't have slept with her if he'd still been in love with his ex. She knew that.

But…

Her relationships always went wrong. What was to say that this would be any different? And there had been that night where he'd pulled her close and murmured Nadine's name…

The doubts flooded through her, and she just couldn't shift them. What if Dylan had changed his mind about her? What if, when he came home tonight, he wanted them to go back to their old relationship—at arm's length and only sharing the baby's care? What if they got together and, once the first flush of desire had worn off, he started realising how many flaws she had, just as her exes always had? What if he started wanting her to change, and she couldn't be who he wanted her to be?

Tyler woke; feeding him distracted her for a little bit, but still the thoughts whizzed round her head. And the doubts grew and grew and grew until she felt suffocated by them.

'I need to think about this,' she told the baby. 'I need to work out what I want. Find out what Dylan wants. And I think we need to be apart while we work it out.'

She knew exactly where she could go. Where she'd be welcomed, where the baby would be fussed over, where she'd be able to walk for miles next to the sea. Where she could talk to someone clear-sighted who'd listen and let her work it out.

She rang her great-aunt to check that it was convenient for her to visit, then packed swiftly. 'We're going to the sea,' she told the baby, who cooed at her and clapped his hands. 'Where I used to go when I was tiny. You'll like it.'

Then she picked up the phone again. It was only fair to tell Dylan what she planned. Except he was unavailable, in a meeting with a client. This wasn't the kind of thing she wanted to leave in a message, and she could hardly text him because his mobile phone was still here.

But she could leave him a voicemail.

She dialled his mobile number swiftly and waited for the phone to click through to his voicemail. 'Dylan, I need some space to think about things,' she said. 'To get my head straight. I'm staying at Great-Aunt Syb's. I'll text you when I get there so you know we've arrived safely.' Given what had happened to Ally and Pete, she would've wanted him to text her if he'd been the one travelling. It was only fair.

Honestly, Dylan thought, if you were going to leave a message on someone's voicemail, you could at least make sure you were around to accept the return call.

On the third attempt, he finally got through to Nadine. 'You wanted to talk to me,' he said.

'Yes. I saw that article in the magazine.'

'Uh-huh.'

'And Jenny at the office said you were looking after Pete's son since the accident.'

Where was she going with this? He had a nasty feeling about it. 'My godson. Yes.'

She dragged in a breath. 'So you're a dad.'

Uh-oh. This was exactly what he'd thought she wanted to talk to him about. 'A stand-in one.'

'So we could—'

'No,' he cut in gently before she could finish her suggestion. 'Nadine, you're seeing someone else.'

'On the rebound from you. I still love you, Dylan. We can stop the divorce going through. All you have to do is say yes. We can make a family together.'

'It's not quite the same thing, Nadine. You wanted a baby of your own,' he reminded her.

'And we still can. We can have a brother or sister for Tyler.'

'No. Nadine, it's over,' he said, as gently as he could. 'I'm sorry.'

'So you're really—' she took a deep breath '—with that jeweller?'

'I am,' he confirmed. And it shocked him how good that made him feel. Tonight, he'd leave the office and go home to Emmy and Tyler. His partner and his child. His unexpected family.

Her voice wobbled. 'What does she have that I don't?'

'That isn't a fair conversation,' he said. 'You're very different. Opposites, even. But she complements me. And it works.' He paused. 'Be happy, Nadine. And try to be happy for me. We've both got a chance to make a new life now, to get what we wanted.'

'I wanted it with you.'

'I'm sorry,' he said, guilt flooding through him. 'But there's no going back for us. I know that now. We wouldn't make each other happy.'

'We could try.' Hope flared in her voice.

'I'm sorry,' he said again. 'Goodbye, Nadine. And good luck.' He cut the connection.

And now he could go home. See Emmy. Tell her that everything was going to be just fine.

Except, when he opened the front door, he realised that the house was empty.

Maybe she'd taken Tyler to the park or something. He tried calling her mobile phone from the house landline, but there was no answer. Maybe she was somewhere really noisy and hadn't heard the phone, or maybe she was in the middle of a nappy change. 'It's me. I'm home,' he said when the line clicked through to voicemail. 'See you later.'

He went in search of his mobile phone. Emmy had left it in the middle of the kitchen table. He flicked into the first screen, intending to check his text messages, and noticed that he had two voicemail messages. The first was Nadine's from earlier, asking him to call. He sighed and deleted it.

The second was probably work. He'd sneak some in until Emmy got home, and then—well. Then he could kiss her stupid, for starters.

He smiled at the thought, and listened to the message.

And then his smile faded.

I need some space.

Uh-oh. That wasn't good. Did that mean she'd changed her mind about what had happened between them? That she didn't want to be with him?

Or had he been right about her all along and she was like his mother, unable to stick to any decisions and dropping everything at a moment's notice to go off and 'find herself'?

Feeling sick, he listened to the rest of the message.

So she was going up north. To the sea. That figured. And she'd left the message two hours ago, so right now she was probably in the car. Of course she wouldn't answer while she was driving. She'd never put Tyler at risk like that.

OK. He'd talk to her when she got there. And in the meantime he'd get on with some work.

Though it was almost impossible to concentrate. The house just didn't feel right without her and Tyler. Going for a run didn't take his mind off things, either, and nor did his shower afterwards. And he was even crosser with himself when he saw the text from Emmy when he got out of the shower. *Here safely. E.*

Just his luck that she'd texted when he wouldn't hear it. He called her back immediately, but a recorded voice informed him that the phone was unavailable. Switched off? Or was she in an area with a poor signal?

'Leave a message, or send a text,' the recorded voice told him.

Right.

'Emmy, call me. Please. We need to talk.' They really had to sort this out. Did she want him, or didn't she?

Except she didn't call him.

And Dylan was shocked to find out how much he missed them both. How much he wanted them home safely with him.

Maybe she wanted space because she wasn't sure of him. Maybe he hadn't made her realise exactly how he felt about her. Maybe she needed something from him that he wasn't good at—emotional stuff. The right words.

Maybe his mother went to find herself because she had nobody to find her. But Emmy had someone to find *her*. She had him. And he needed to tell her that.

It was too late to drive to Whitby now. It'd be stupid o'clock in the morning before he got there. But he could go and find her tomorrow. Tell her how he felt. And hope that she'd agree to come back with him.

First, though, where did Syb live? He had a feeling that if he did manage to get through to Emmy's phone to ask for the address, she'd come up with an excuse. And this was too important to put off. He needed to see her *now*.

Knowing Emmy, all her contacts would be on her phone rather than written down somewhere. But he knew she was savvy enough to keep a backup. If she had a password on her computer at all, he reasoned, it would be an easy one to crack. He switched on the machine, waited for the programs to load, and typed in Tyler's birthdate when the computer prompted him for a password.

Bingo.

It was a matter of seconds to find Syb's address in Emmy's contacts file. He made a note of the address for his GPS system and shut down the computer.

Tomorrow—he just hoped that tomorrow would see his life getting back on track. Back where he belonged.

CHAPTER FOURTEEN

AT FIVE O'CLOCK the next morning, Dylan gave up trying to get back to sleep. He had a shower, chugged down some coffee, and headed for Whitby.

He'd connected his phone to the car and switched it into hands-free mode, so he was able to call his second in command on his way up north to brief him on the most urgent stuff he had scheduled for the day. And, with that worry off his mind, it let him concentrate on Emmy.

As he drove over the Yorkshire moors the heather looked resplendently purple, and there was a huge rainbow in the sky. When he was small, his grandmother used to tell him there was a pot of gold at the end of a rainbow. Well, he didn't want gold. He wanted something much more precious: he wanted Emmy and Tyler.

At last he could see the sea and the spooky gothic ruin of Whitby Abbey that loomed over the town. Almost there. He didn't want to turn up empty-handed, so he stopped at a petrol station to refuel and buy flowers for both Emmy and her great-aunt. He managed to find a parking space near the house; when he rang the doorbell and waited, his heart was beating so hard that he was sure any passersby could hear it. Finally, the door was opened by an elderly lady. 'Yes?'

'Would you be Emmy's great-aunt Syb?' he asked.

She looked wary. 'Who wants to know?'

'My name's Dylan Harper,' he said.

'Ah. So *you're* Dylan.'

Emmy had obviously talked to her great-aunt about him. And probably not in glowing terms, either. He took a deep breath. 'Please, may I see her?'

'I'm afraid she's not here.'

His heart stopped for a moment. OK, so she'd probably guess that he'd lose patience with the situation and come to see her, but surely she hadn't disappeared already? 'Where is she?' he asked.

'Walking by the sea. I told her to leave Tyler with me— she needed some fresh air and time to think. It's hard to think when you're looking after a baby.'

'Is he OK?'

'He's absolutely fine and he's having a nap, so don't worry. Just go and find her. She'll be on the east foreshore.' He must've looked as mystified as he felt, because Syb added, 'Head for the Abbey, then instead of going up the steps just keep going forward until you get to the beach, then hug the cliffs and keep heading to the right. You'll see her.'

'Thank you.' He thrust the flowers at her. 'These are for you—well, one bunch is. The other's for Emmy.'

'Thank you, Dylan,' Syb said gently.

A cheap bunch of flowers. How pathetic was he? And the only other thing he had to give Emmy was his heart. Which was incredibly scary. What if she rejected him? What if she was here because she was trying to work out how to tell him that it was a huge mistake and she didn't want to be with him in that way? 'I, um…'

'Go and find her,' Syb said. 'Talk to her. Sort it out between you. I'm here for Tyler, so don't rush. Take your time.'

As Dylan walked through the town he felt sick. What if she wouldn't talk to him, wouldn't listen to what he had to say? What if she didn't want him?

There were a few families on the beach, and his stomach clenched as he saw them. That was exactly what he wanted—to be able to do simple things like building a sandcastle on the beach with Tyler, and playing with him and Emmy at the edge of the sea. Family things. A *forever* family.

Please let her listen to him.

There were a few people beachcombing on the foreshore; some had hammers and chisels, and Dylan assumed they were collecting fossils. Then he rounded a corner and saw her. She bent down to pick up something from the sand; probably some jet, he thought. Syb had sent Emmy out to do something to soothe her soul, and he already knew how much she loved the sea.

He quickened his pace and nearly slipped on the treacherous surface; he blew out a breath and picked his way more steadily over towards her.

She looked up as he reached her side. 'What are you doing here?'

'I've come to see you. Talk to you.' He took a deep breath. 'Emmy, I'm good at business words and computer code and geek. I'm rubbish at the emotional stuff. I know I'm going to make a mess of this, but…' His voice faded.

She nodded. 'What did Nadine want? Was it about the paperwork?'

'No. She'd seen the article.'

'You said she wanted a baby. You have a baby, now.' Her voice wobbled. 'Is that what she wants?'

He knew with blinding clarity what she was really asking. Was that what he wanted, too? 'I'm not going to lie to you, Emmy,' he said softly. 'She did suggest it. But I said no. Because that's not what I want.'

She bit her lip. 'You don't want a child.'

He squirmed. There was no way out of this. He was going to have to bare his heart to her, even though he hated making himself that vulnerable. 'Not with her. We're not right for each other.' He dragged in a breath. 'I guess that's something else you need to know. I didn't want a child,' he said slowly, 'because of the way I grew up.'

She waited. And eventually the words flooded in to fill the silence.

'I never knew who my dad was. My mum used to go off to "find herself" every time she broke up with whoever she was dating, and she always dumped me on the nearest relative. Usually my grandparents.' He looked away. 'My grandmother loved me and had time for me but my grand-father always made me feel I was a nuisance and a burden.'

She reached out and linked her fingers through his; it gave him the strength to go on, and he looked back at her.

'I hated it. I hated feeling that I was always in the way. Then, as I grew older, I was scared that maybe I wouldn't be able to bond with a child because my parental role models were—well, not what I would've chosen myself. I was scared that I wouldn't be any good as a parent, and I never wanted a child to feel the way I did when I grew up, so I decided that I was never going to have children.' He blew out a breath. 'I suppose I married Nadine because I thought she was safe. Because I thought she wanted the same thing that I did, that her job was enough for her. But then she changed her mind about what she wanted and I just couldn't change with her. I couldn't give her what she wanted, because I was too selfish. Because I was a cow-ard. Because I was scared I'd fail at it, and I walked away rather than trying to make it work.'

'And yet you stepped up to the mark when Ty needed you,' Emmy said softly.

'I didn't have a clue what I was doing. I still don't,' he confessed wryly.

'Me, neither—but we're muddling through, and Ty definitely feels loved and settled.' She paused. 'Is that why you didn't like me? Because you thought I was flaky and selfish and just thought of myself, like your mum? Because my relationships never lasted and Ally always had to pick up the pieces?'

He bit his lip. 'I was wrong about that. But—yes, I admit, I did.'

She sighed. 'I don't blame you. I probably would've thought the same, in your shoes.' She paused. 'Is that why you think I went away? To find myself?'

'You said you needed space. Time to think.' He paused. 'I think my mum went away to find herself, because there wasn't anyone to find her.' He looked her straight in the eye. 'But I came to find you, Emmy.'

She dragged in a breath. 'I'd never dump Ty on anyone. The only reason he's with Syb is because he's asleep—and I have my mobile phone with me. She promised to call me the second he woke up, if I wasn't already back by then.'

'I know,' he said softly. 'She told me to take our time. To talk. She's wise, your great-aunt.'

She nodded.

'So why did you leave?'

'Because I was scared,' she admitted. 'I had doubts.'

'Doubts about me, or doubts about being with me?'

'I was scared that things would change. Scared that you'd compare me to Nadine and find me wanting.' She looked anguished. 'I always pick the wrong guy. It starts off well, I think it's going to work—and then I find out that there are things he doesn't like about me. Things he expects me to change. And you used to loathe me.'

Hope flooded through him. She didn't have doubts about being with him; what she doubted was herself. Which meant she needed total honesty from him. 'Yes, I used to loathe you. But that was before I knew you properly. I don't loathe you now. And I don't want to change you, Emmy. I don't want to change a single thing.' He drew her hand to his mouth and kissed it. 'I'm sorry. I should've cancelled my meeting yesterday morning and talked to you, instead.'

'You couldn't. You were late, and it was important.'

'I never thought I'd ever say this to anyone, but I don't care if it was important. You're more important to me than work,' he said.

She stared at him, as if not quite daring to believe that he meant it.

'I should've stayed with you. Better still, instead of telling you to go to sleep, the night before, I should've talked to you about what happened between us. Listened to you. Soothed your worries, and asked you to soothe mine. But I'm rubbish at the emotional stuff, so I bailed out on you. I thought it'd give me time to work out what to say.'

'Did it?'

'No,' he admitted. 'I still don't know what to say. Or how to say it without it coming out all wrong. But...' He took a deep breath. 'My world doesn't feel right without you in it.' His heart was racing. Had he got this wrong? This could all implode, become so messy. But he owed it to their future to take that risk. 'I love you, Emmy.'

Hope blossomed in her expression. 'You love me?'

'I don't know when it happened. Or how. Or why. I just know I do. And Paris clinched it for me. I finally got why they call it the City of Light. Because you were there with me, and I was so happy.' He took a deep breath. 'It isn't the same thing I felt with Nadine. You're not safe, like I thought she was. I'm not entirely sure what makes you tick. I think we're always going to have fights—you're going to think I'm stuffy and I'm going to think you're flaky. But that's OK. We can agree to disagree. What I do know is that I love you. I want to be with you. And I want you, me and Tyler to be a proper family. Maybe we could have a little brother or sister for him. If you…' He broke off. 'Sorry. That's too much pressure. I never expected to feel like this. I've made a mess of one marriage. I can't guarantee I'll get it right with you. But I'll try. Believe me, I'll try.'

She reached up and stroked his face. 'Dylan. I'm rubbish at relationships, too. It scares me that everything's going to go wrong.'

'But maybe it won't. Not if you want me the way I want you.'

'I do.'

'Are you sure?' She'd already walked away from him.

'I've worked you out, now. You're a goalpost shifter,' Emmy said. 'You never think you're good enough—and that's not your fault, it's because your mum's as selfish as my dad and she made you feel you weren't good enough. Except you are good enough. You *are*. You've got the biggest heart. And I…' She swallowed hard. 'I love you too, Dylan. So the answer's yes. Yes, I want to make you, me and Dylan a forever family. Yes, if we're blessed and when Ty's a little bit older, it might be nice to have another baby.' She smiled. 'We might even have more of a clue what we're doing as parents, the second time round.'

The trickle of hope became a flood. He dropped to one knee, not caring that the foreshore was rocky and slippery and wet. 'Emmy Jacobs, I know I ought to wait for that piece of paper to come through before I ask you, but

I can't. I want the rest of my life to start right now. Will you marry me?'

She leaned down to kiss him. 'Yes. We'll still make mistakes, Dylan. Neither of us is perfect. But we'll be in it together. We'll talk it through and we'll make it work.'

He got to his feet and kissed her lingeringly. 'You're right. And we don't have to be perfect. We just have to be ourselves. Together. I love you, Emmy.'

'I love you, too.' Her phone rang, and she smiled at him. 'I think that might be Syb. Our cue to go home.'

Home, Dylan thought. He was home at last. Because home was wherever Emmy was. 'To our baby. Because he is ours, Emmy. Just as you're mine.'

'And you're mine.'

He nodded. 'For now and forever'.

* * * * *

A sneaky peek at next month…

Cherish™

ROMANCE TO MELT THE HEART EVERY TIME

My wish list for next month's titles…

In stores from 17th January 2014:

☐ Daring to Trust the Boss — Susan Meier

& Heiress on the Run — Sophie Pembroke

☐ A Sweetheart for Jude Fortune — Cindy Kirk

& Celebration's Bride — Nancy Robards Thompson

In stores from 7th February 2014:

☐ Rescued by the Millionaire — Cara Colter

& Moonlight in Paris — Pamela Hearon

☐ The Summer They Never Forgot — Kandy Shepherd

& His Forever Girl — Liz Talley

Available at WHSmith, Tesco, Asda, Eason, Amazon and Apple

Just can't wait?

Visit us Online

You can buy our books online a month before they hit the shops! **www.millsandboon.co.uk**

0114/23

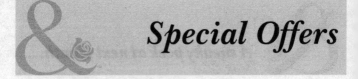

The World of Mills & Boon®

There's a Mills & Boon® series that's perfect for you. We publish ten series and, with new titles every month, you never have to wait long for your favourite to come along.

Blaze®
Scorching hot, sexy reads
4 new stories every month

By Request
Relive the romance with the best of the best
9 new stories every month

Cherish™
Romance to melt the heart every time
12 new stories every month

Desire™
Passionate and dramatic love stories
8 new stories every month